Blood of Escape

D.M. Wyatt

Maggie Valley Publishing

ISBN: 978-1-7351339-2-8 (Paperback)

First printing edition 2022

Maggie Valley Publishing
Rolla, Missouri

For Glennda
Family by marriage
Sisters by choice

She just wanted to come up for air

Blood of Escape

D.M. Wyatt

- September 1995 -

Chapter One

What the hell was she doing? Alexa had gone from crawling into the trunk of a car to now standing across the street from a liquor store in an unknown town! Five nights of couch surfing in different strangers' homes seemed equally uncertain. She stood staring at the liquor store and the hive of activity in and out its doors, shaking her head at herself. This was definitely fucked up.

She knew exactly how she had landed here – it was all part of the plan. Brie and Tess with their mothers figured out that Alexa could slide out of town by hitching a ride with Tess' dad for his weekly visit with his mother. She couldn't just lie down in the backseat. No, she had to hide in the trunk of his car in case any of her father's guards happened to pull the car over. Thank goodness he didn't drive like a maniac. Sure it was annoying as hell as a teenager when riding in the backseat with Tess. Alexa recalled how they groaned as he obeyed the speed limits and he ever so slowly rounded each corner. She finally appreciated his cautious driving while traveling like a piece of luggage.

When Mr. Nichols arrived at his mom's house, he pulled the car into the garage so none of the neighbors saw Alexa. She hid in the garage until after nightfall when Grandma Nichols rang the bell for her cat to come to the backdoor – the signal for Alexa to go inside and make the phone call to Tess' former college roommate, Abbey.

Alexa enjoyed talking to Abbey and quickly understood why Tess suggested her assistance. Abbey latched onto the idea and in a matter of hours, she had a network of people lined up to help. At 2am, Alexa ran through neighbors' yards and hopped fences like she did as a kid when visiting with Tess. She knew the fastest route to Benny's Corner Market by heart. However, this time, she wasn't bolting over fences to spend the dollar Grandma Nichols handed to each Tess and her friends for ice cream, rather Alexa was meeting up with the first of several people to transport her across the country. What she hoped to accomplish by running to Minnesota hadn't really come together in any tangible plan.

This was stupid.

Sighing, Alexa now leaned against the brick wall. Here she was in a strange town, states away from home, somehow further away from Minnesota. She didn't know a single person here and as she looked down the street where the powder blue Buick had driven after dropping her off – it was nowhere in sight.

Abandoned.

In a bout of self-pity, tears began to well. She contemplated marching across the street and dropping a couple of quarters into the pay phone to ask mom and dad to pick her up.

No. That was even more stupid. Alexa held back the tears and stared down the street again where the Buick had disappeared. The bare minimum that cow could have done was wait to make sure the next host even showed up!

Cow? Alexa admonished herself. Where was the gratitude? The woman *did* open her home to a hybrid after all. She put her own safety at risk just so a scared little girl could run away from home!

An echoing boom startled Alexa, jolting her out of her thoughts. Across the street, a metal ramp of a delivery truck hit the ground at the liquor store. With her heart resuming normal function she watched the driver emerge from the back of the truck pushing a dolly loaded with cardboard boxes down the ramp. He disappeared inside the store as new customers arrived and others left, several stopping to look at the contents inside the truck.

The brick wall of the furniture store radiated unnecessary warmth while shade of an aluminum awning helped protect her eyes from the bright afternoon sun. Did she even thank the woman for hosting her and then driving across the state to drop her off? Yes. Yes, Alexa clearly remembered thanking her multiple times.

Movement caught the corner of Alexa's eye. In watching the humdrum details of the liquor store Alexa failed to notice the sporty yellow car pulling into the furniture lot. A petite blonde emerged with a big welcoming smile.

"Are you Alexa?"

"Yeah. Are you Sarah?"

"Yep." Sarah stepped forward and extended a hand.

Alexa approached Sarah on the parking lot and shook hands with her.

"I'll help you with your bags," Sarah said.

Alexa smiled and shook her head. "It's not much. I can handle them." She turned back to the building where she had been waiting and picked up a backpack and a zipped tote provided by friends days earlier for this escape.

"How on Earth do you plan to travel like *that*?" Sarah asked.

"It's not exactly like going on vacation," Alexa said as she rounded Sarah's car. "I'm only carrying the bare necessities as I coast from one couch to the next."

Sarah met her at the rear of the car and popped the trunk. "I can't imagine being on the run like that."

Dropping her bags in the empty trunk, Alexa shrugged. "Eh, I really haven't had much time to think about it. Just get up and arrange the next ride and go."

"Well, I hope you can find peace soon. This pace can't be healthy."

"It won't be like this forever."

Chapter Two

Passing a sign for "Windemere," they pulled into a condominium community where the street twisted in soft curves. The afternoon sun danced between young trees lining the road casting shadows onto tiny blocks of perfectly manicured green lawns. When at last they pulled into a driveway Alexa looked up to see a two-story brick building with a simple peak roof giving the illusion of being a singular entity while connected to four other units of identical shape.

Sarah held the front door open as Alexa made her way inside bumping Sarah with the backpack.

"Crap, I'm sorry," Alexa said.

Sarah smiled and ushered Alexa further into the home. Shades of coral, ivory, and honeydew splashed on plush pillows and throws. Softness and elegance defined the space. Pleasant scents wafted up to Alexa's nose – a meal brewing in an unseen kitchen and a candle burning nearby.

A clash of pots and pans echoed from the kitchen and then a brunette appeared.

"Alexa!" she said, with a broad smile. "I am Valerie. Welcome to our home."

"Thank you for hosting me."

"Here have a seat," Valerie said waving toward the couch as she backed toward a chair. "Supper needs to simmer for a bit."

Alexa sat where indicated. "It smells delicious."

"We were told you are a hybrid but your scent doesn't reveal it one bit," Valerie said.

"Actually, there is a faint hint of it but I don't think most vampires can detect it either," Alexa said.

"But some can?" Valerie asked.

"Evidently."

Sarah leaned forward. "We were told you were raised as a human."

"Yes," Alexa said with a nod. "I didn't find out until my teeth came in a couple months ago."

"Your teeth came in?" Sarah asked with raised eyebrows.

Alexa smiled remembering Brie and Tess having the same

expressions upon hearing she had vampire teeth. "It was traumatic for me," she said. "I didn't even know how to retract my fangs."

"Huh," said Valerie, tilting her head. "How *do* you retract them?"

"The same way to drop them, by opening my mouth really super wide."

Valerie nodded her head slowly. "Interesting. But, you also did not know you are a witch?"

"No, not at all." Alexa grinned feeling foolish for having been oblivious her entire life. "When my mother told me I was part witch, it actually made sense. I have visions. I also could make things, um wiggle? The day my teeth came in I discovered that ability is actually manipulating air and I can do a lot more than make stuff in my room wiggle on the shelf."

"You are also a pyromancer," Valerie said, without question.

"I don't know," Alexa said with a shrug. "If I have it I wouldn't know how to summon that power."

"How do you not know?" Sarah asked.

"Raised as a human," Alexa said with another shrug.

"But when you found out you're a witch didn't your mom tell you about your powers?" Sarah asked.

"She couldn't. Where I live there are restrictions about teaching hybrids and I guess it's just easier to not let us know what we're capable of."

"That's such a ridiculous rule," Valerie said. "Fortunately, hybrids are allowed to practice here." She stood up and looked over her shoulder toward the kitchen. "I think supper is ready."

"Can I help?" Alexa asked.

"Not tonight," said Valerie. "Please be a true guest and take a seat at our table."

Alexa followed Sarah to the dining table while Valerie tended to the meal. Sarah pointed to the end of the table for Alexa's seat and then lit five tapers lined down the middle of the table where miniature apples and pumpkins wrapped around the candleholders with bits of glitter glistening in the light.

A formal setting of china sat before Alexa and for the first time in her life, she appreciated her father's strict guidance in proper etiquette. She sat erect, not that she often slouched, and folded her hands in her lap as Sarah bustled around the table filling water glasses and then wine goblets.

Valerie emerged from the kitchen with two plates that she handed off to Sarah before retrieving her own plate and a basket of bread. After she and Sarah took their seats they bowed their heads and murmured a quiet prayer. "Blessed be," they said in unison.

Valerie lifted her glass of wine. "Alexa, thank you for joining us tonight. We pray your journey is smooth and you find the answers you seek."

Alexa lifted her glass and said, "Thank you. I certainly hope peace is on the horizon." All three took a sip and returned the glasses to the table. "Seriously," she said. "Thank you for opening your home and thank you for this meal. It looks divine and if you tell me that bread is homemade I'm going to faint."

A broad grin spread across Valerie's face. "Please don't faint, it was baked earlier today."

Sarah passed the basket to Alexa.

"Alexa, will you tell us why you are traveling in secret?" Valerie asked.

She sighed, thinking of the questions from each of her hosts, and how she tried to protect her identity while remaining sincere to the truth. "It's tough to explain without revealing too much," she said.

"Let's start with your cover story."

"An old boyfriend is stalking me."

"A vampire?" Valerie asked.

"Yes. I say he raped and tagged me and claims I'm his."

"And what is the truth of the story?"

"I did have a former boyfriend who stalked me, but he was no threat." She shook her head and chuckled. "He was a human. But I did date a vampire." She stopped short, the heartache still too raw.

"You loved him? The vampire?" Sarah asked.

She nodded and closed her eyes to maintain her composure. After a few deep breaths, Alexa took a sip of wine. "I really haven't had a chance to process everything that's happened." After a deep breath, she whispered, "But yeah, I love him." She tore off a piece of bread and smeared butter across the rough edge, focusing on the sponginess against the knife. Alexa held the buttered bread in one hand and the knife in the other as she looked across the table. "There's a lot more to it, but…" She placed the bread onto her plate to take a sip of wine. "This vampire thing is too much for me. It all happened so fast, without explanation. Eric, the vampire boyfriend, was the only person to explain anything to me, so I just need time. I don't know, to come up for air? To process what has happened. I just need some peace. And even though for the past week I've been running from place to place constantly looking over my shoulder, it's been a welcome distraction from the chaos of that last couple of months."

"You just need sanctuary," Valerie said.

They locked eyes as Alexa allowed the words to sink in. She liked the idea of sanctuary, a place allowing for contemplation and release. She nodded her head slowly. "Yeah."

Alexa put her focus on the plate - thick chicken breast stuffed with cheese and ham covered in sauce and a side of roasted squash, broccoli, cauliflower, and tomatoes. She took a bite of her buttered bread as she contemplated whether to cut into the chicken or sample the vegetables. She paused to appreciate the homemade bread in her mouth.

"This bread is divine," she said.

"Thank you," Valerie said. "A bread machine does most of the work."

"So how long have you lived here?" Alexa asked.

"Almost four years," Sarah said.

"The complex looks like it was just built."

"We are the original owners of this unit," Valerie said. "This and the building across the street were the first ones built."

"Are they done with construction?"

"No," Valerie said. "The ground has been cleared on the other side of the lake behind us for three more buildings."

Alexa looked between the two women and asked, "So, um… are you two a couple?"

They both smiled. "Ten years," Valerie said. "Is that a problem for you?"

Alexa shook her head. "Not at all. It didn't even cross my mind until you said you both owned the place. How did you meet?"

"Valerie is a bibliophile and I work at a bookstore. It was kismet," Sarah said with an impish grin.

"That's wonderful! Are your families accepting of your relationship?"

"Mine, yes," Sarah said. "Hers not so much."

"And yet they adore Sarah," Valerie said. "My father is proud of my legal career but he still believes I need a man in my life."

Alexa rolled her eyes. "Yeah, fathers and their wonky ideas about what's best for their daughters."

Valerie smiled in sympathy.

"It took a bit for my family to accept my choices, " Sarah said. "They also imagined me having the big wedding and adoring husband. It was my dad, though, who stood up for me and convinced my mom that I was genuinely happy – and wasn't that what they ultimately wanted for me?"

"So did you have the big wedding?"

"That's a lot of expense and hassle for a celebration of something that's not recognized by the state," Valerie said. "We opted for an intimate gathering of friends and family."

"With expensive food and a lot of wine," Sarah said lifting her goblet.

Alexa lifted hers. "May the years ahead be filled with joy and abundance!"

"Spoken like a true witch," Valerie said with a nod.

Valerie leaned over to Sarah and said quietly, "Are you good?"

Sarah said, "I thought so from the beginning." They nodded in agreement.

"Alexa," Valerie said. "Let's talk about your travel arrangements. I've had a couple conversations with your friend Abbey. You might not know, but she has been dispatching several decoys because evidently there is a high likelihood you are being tracked by a very determined vampire. I assume, not your boyfriend."

Alexa nodded.

"I took it upon myself to have you investigated a bit. I have a coworker with some connections, one of whom determined your father is the vampire in question."

Alexa averted her eyes and quietly cleared her throat. When she returned her gaze to Valerie they locked eyes.

Crap. She again nodded.

"Would your father harm you?"

"No, never. Like I said, I just need time to come up for air."

Valerie nodded. "Your father is using an alias."

"I know," Alexa whispered. Panic jutted through her. She was enjoying this meal and now she worried it was time to go home.

"Do you know his real identity?"

"I found out before I left. It's part of why I left."

Valerie softened her expression. "I'm not asking you to reveal anything. My connection didn't tell me any more than her concern about your father, that maybe he was your threat. I don't know his name, either real or alias. I also don't know where you're from, but I have my guesses based on your restrictions with witchcraft."

"Thank you," Alexa said trying to hold back tears. "My dad would never hurt me or anyone helping me, but I suspect if people knew I'm connected to him… well I become bait."

"Therefore we must be vigilant in guarding your location. Abbey suggested maybe you extend your stay a few days while the decoys do their work."

Alexa scrunched her face. "Who are these decoys? This is the first I've heard of them."

Valerie chuckled. "As it turns out, there is already a network established to help women fleeing difficult situations, usually violent situations – abuse and stalkers. Abbey and I had a long conversation about her discovery of this network. To be honest, I didn't know it existed either. Anyway, some of the decoys are women just needing to flee but don't have a destination so they're bouncing from spot to spot until something permanent can be arranged. Others are people who just love going on road trips."

"But I have a destination," Alexa said.

"Abbey made it sound as though the people at your final destination don't know to expect you, so if you're a few days late they won't be worried."

In slow motion, Alexa leaned her head to the side as she processed the breadth of what Valerie was saying. "And if they do know to expect me then other people know as well."

Valerie nodded.

"How long should I wait?"

"At least two or three days, but if we are all amenable to the idea you could just make this your home for a while until you're ready to move on."

Alexa stared at Valerie, speechless.

Valerie smiled in sympathy. "It could be an opportunity for you to learn more about the craft."

"It's very generous of you. It's definitely an attractive offer."

"You don't have to decide immediately," Valerie said. "But the offer stands. We already have the decoy transfer ready for tomorrow. Think on it, sleep on it."

Alexa ate as she pondered the offer to stay with these two witches. She recalled Abbey's nearly obsessed fascination with trying to construct an underground-railroad style of helping someone escape. Suggesting Alexa actually stay at one of her stops instead of continuing to her destination sounded like something Abbey would contrive.

Sarah sliced and served cheesecake for dessert. Accepting her plate, Alexa considered what problems her presence would cause for her hosts. "As far as your offer," she said, "you should know I've killed two men."

"Vampires?" Valerie asked.

Alexa nodded.

"In self-defense?"

Again, she nodded.

"Did you, um, use your... teeth?" Sarah asked.

"Yeah, I did."

The room fell quiet.

"It's my understanding most hybrids don't have the, uh, dental strength to manage that type of defense," Valerie said.

"I don't know how to explain it, but it's not like I'm three parts witch and one part vampire," Alexa said. "It's more like I'm two full people in one. And evidently, both come from really strong lines."

"Well, yes, your witch side is evident and definitely strong. Had you been trained properly you would be a force to be reckoned with," Valerie said. "I am surprised you have any vampire traits at all."

"Yeahhhh," Alexa said, drawn out and slow. "That is what I have been told by every single person I encounter. No one expected me to be anything but a witch... and it's been a lethal mistake to assume."

"How does that work for you? Being both at the same time?" Sarah asked.

Alexa shrugged. "I don't know. I mean it's only been a few months so like a newborn I'm still wobbly and flopping around. Let's hope I don't have any more major surprises, but I *think* I've learned the extent of all of my abilities. Now I just need to learn how to develop them."

"I just dropped a new one on you with pyromancer," Valerie said.

"But it's not a super big surprise. Powers with fire? Would that explain why I've never burned my fingers on the stove?"

"Yes." Valerie tipped her head with a smile. "We are the witches they couldn't burn."

Alexa looked at Valerie and Sarah as she contemplated what that meant. She thought of the witches in 1600s and of her mother, and friends, and even her wretched grandmother... A slow smile spread. Yes indeed, the witches they could not burn.

Chapter Three

The sun nearly blinded her but she had to keep running. The man behind her broke through the tree line and she screamed for help. She kept screaming and ran harder but the uneven ground slowed her escape. With a deep breath, she screamed again, fear consuming her body. She kept running but he advanced shortening the distance between them. He grabbed her arm and pulled her backward.

As she landed on the ground her teeth dropped but she knew she had to retract them. The man landed on top of her, yet breaking his fall so as not to drop all of his weight onto her.

Alexa opened her eyes gasping for air but the darkness startled her.

Ugh, the nightmares had returned.

She managed to stop panting and stretched her mouth open to retract her teeth. Sitting up on the daybed in a small room not much larger than the bed, Alexa took in the tiny space and yet felt like she sat in a mansion. Expecting to sleep on yet another couch, the daybed in a room with a door felt exquisite.

Sarah had fussed over her when showing Alexa the room, ensuring plenty of blankets and pillows were on the bed while worrying the room was too small. Alexa smiled at the memory while looking at the closed door. No, this was perfect.

She did wonder about the original intent for the space – nursery? Office? Maybe a closet? But who puts a window in a closet? And what closet has another closet? No, this weird little space was meant to be. Whatever the intended purpose Alexa found the room quaint.

Staring at the window where a beam from a streetlight illuminated the room, she considered pulling the blind shut yet she found comfort in the light. The previous week played in her head – - transfers and drop-offs by strangers, different houses and apartments, the couches serving as beds, and always a dark room filled with weird sounds. The darkness disturbed her most. She didn't let fear take over her emotions but still, she remained on guard, always watching. This space, however, felt calm and safe... its noises identifiable, almost predictable.

The nightmare, one of many horrible, awful nightmares that defined her normal sleep was the first since she left Brentwood. She grinned realizing she had actually fallen asleep without worry. Evidently, a sense of security was necessary for her to have nightmares. Alexa rolled her eyes at the revelation.

She didn't know what to expect or even hope for in accepting Sarah and Valerie's offer to stay with them, but this sense of calm assured her.

With a calming sense of peace, she snuggled into the pillow and closed her eyes.

Chapter Four

The delicious aroma of coffee filled her nose as Alexa wrapped her hands around the mug. She typically opted for creamer and while a bottle sat on the counter, oh so far away, retrieving the bottle would involve too much effort. Besides, straight, black coffee felt like the only solution for such a dreary morning.

Sarah sighed as she reached the bottom of the stairs. "There's something beautiful about a day like this," she said gazing toward the sliding patio doors.

"It's gray and windy," Alexa said without removing her focus from her still too-hot-to-sip coffee. The heat radiated to her hands and up her arms. "The only thing glorious about this morning is the heat of this cup and the scent of its coffee."

"Not a morning person! Duly noted," Sarah said.

"Eh I'll be functional soon," Alexa said. "I don't find much pleasure in drab and dreary days, though. I need sunshine to thrive."

"What about the moon?" Valerie asked as she came around the corner from the living room.

"Oh I love the moon," Alexa said with a much perkier voice. "What?" she asked looking at the smirks on Sarah's and Valerie's faces.

"Witches honor the moon," Sarah said. "It is energy and magic. Some address it as 'goddess.'"

"I have a lot I could learn from you."

Sarah nodded. "Yes, and we would like to teach you."

Alexa looked at the pair now standing side by side. She released the mug and said, "I realized last night was the first time since my teeth came in that I truly felt safe. I've been thinking about accepting your offer and I would love the opportunity to learn more about being a witch. My concern, though, is that I don't put either of you in danger."

"Well let's sit down and talk about this," Valerie said as she moved to the chair across from Alexa. Sarah followed and took the seat next to Valerie.

"We made the offer because neither of us feels any form of malevolence from you," Valerie said.

"Thanks. It's never been my intention to hurt anyone like I've never initiated an attack on anyone." Alexa paused and looked at the ceiling. "Well, there was a tussle with my dad… and, well that wasn't *self-defense* but I was protecting someone else. And even at that, I didn't really injure him, just tossed him against the wall."

Valerie chuckled. "I think that validates our read on you."

Alexa looked down at her coffee, barely cool enough to sample. She took a small sip – yes, just a tad too hot. "You should know I have horrible nightmares that evidently cause me to growl and for my teeth to drop."

"Do you walk in your sleep?" Sarah asked.

Alexa shook her head as she took another sip. "Nah. I just wake up in a sweat, sometimes crying. I'm always disoriented, but no, I don't leave the bed until after I wake up."

"How often do you have these nightmares?" Sarah asked.

"Several times a night."

"*Every* night?"

Alexa nodded.

Sarah wrinkled her forehead in concern. "How do you get any rest?"

"I have no clue. I don't remember hardly any of my dreams and usually don't remember waking up, but they're a constant stream. It's what has kept me with my parents until now. I…" Alexa gulped as the urge to cry bubbled up out of nowhere. "I'm afraid to live by myself." She took a deep breath. "My nightmares are terrifying and my mom and dad have always been able to comfort me. It's hard to deal with these on my own. Not too long ago I moved in with a friend, she's a witch. She's always known about my bad dreams but she said while I was living there I scared the shit out of her so she locked her bedroom door when she heard me growling in the other room. A couple times I've had to retract my teeth when I woke up. In fact, it happened last night. So, um…"

"We can lock our door," Valerie said matter-of-factly.

"Last night?" Sarah asked.

Alexa nodded. "I think the last week has been so much stress that I didn't have any nightmares. I actually didn't sleep very much. So to finally have a nightmare, I think, means I've relaxed and evidently feel safe. It's why I'd like to accept your offer."

"That's fantastic," Valerie said.

"But like I said, I want to make sure I'm not bringing you any harm."

Sarah grinned in sympathy and leaned forward. "I'm really good at reading people's vibes. You are a dangerous person, I got that immediately and it's more than being a dark witch, but I also read that you are a protector with a kind heart. There is no harm that is going to come to us because of you." She reached across the table and took Alexa's hand. "I feel like your presence is going to be a shield for us."

Alexa squeezed her hand. "Thank you. So if you guys are sure…"

"We are," Valerie said.

"Well okay. Coming up for air would be nice," Alexa said.

"However long you need," Valerie said with a reassuring smile.

Alexa winced. She saw Valerie's death in a hospital bed. The lights and beeping equipment faded as the image of Sarah floated through the wall and welcomed her to the other side.

"What was that?" Valerie demanded.

Alexa cleared her throat and cast a nervous look across the table. "I see death," she said looking between the two women.

At Sarah's death Valerie sobs uncontrollably, stroking her head, murmuring words of comfort. Alexa could feel the love between these two women.

"It's not enough I dream about death and destruction all night long," she said, "but when I'm awake I see and hear the last moments of everyone around me. So I winced when you looked at me because your last moments played out again – I've seen it several times already, but it struck me stronger for some reason."

"So it's really bad?" Valerie asked.

Alexa shook her head. "No, not all. It's actually very sweet. The two of you love each other so much." Alexa grinned. "You both manage to comfort the other when it's time to go. The first welcomes the other over the threshold when it's time."

Sarah and Valerie looked at each other and then back at Alexa.

"You won't tell us which will go first," Sarah said.

"Does it matter?" Alexa asked. "You both will be equally devastated to let the other go."

Sarah raised an eyebrow and said, "true." She shifted her position and leaned forward again. "This is why you're a dark witch."

Alexa grinned and nodded. "It's not enough that as a vampire I'm a harbinger of death, but as a witch, I walk with death day and night, everywhere I go."

Sarah scowled. "That's pretty grim."

"It is. But on the upside, I also see birth."

Sarah tilted her head and asked, "How so?"

"People have orbs around them, baby orbs. They dance around their future parents. I've actually seen when a couple first meet and the orbs bounce with joy like 'mom and dad just met!' So sometime after the baby is conceived the orb disappears."

"Does everyone have orbs around them?" Valerie asked.

"No. I mean I'm not ruining anything by telling you that neither of you have orbs because neither of you is ever going to get pregnant… I mean, not that it couldn't happen… oh crap… are you guys wanting a baby?"

Valerie burst out laughing. "Oh God no. We are blissfully child-free. It's actually reassuring to hear no one is getting pregnant."

Sarah stared at Alexa. "If you have all of this clairvoyant ability, how did you never suspect you're a witch?"

"I've always known I was psychic, I just thought it was an ability like that chick on TV."

"And you never said anything to people around you?"

"Oh, I talked about it a lot. My grandpa managed to get me to stay quiet, emphasizing how people freak out over hearing the future. He actually showed me a lot of movies to drive home his point. Do you know I saw the Exorcist as a little girl?"

Valerie and Sarah's eyebrows shot up in surprise.

"Yeah, it didn't scare me which says how gross my dreams are, but it also drove home the lengths people go to when dealing with unseen forces. That movie shut me the hell up."

Chapter Five

Leaning against the sliding glass door Alexa watched a goose waddle across the common ground to the lake. Or was that a pond? She wondered how they differed.

"It will take decades for the trees to fill in," Sarah said.

Alexa jolted. She knew Sarah came down the stairs sometime earlier but didn't realize she was so close.

"Sorry, didn't mean to scare you."

"It's okay. You know an open field has its charms," Alexa said, noting the scrawny line of trees evenly placed between the shore and a paved path. On the opposite side of the lake lay leveled ground awaiting construction and a hillside filled with mature trees, the last vestige of a once thick forest.

Sarah came closer to the door. "There is nothing charming about that view."

"I was attacked by some vampires while jogging on a gorgeous path where the tree canopy created a perfect cover for them to hide."

Sarah appeared shocked. "You were attacked?"

Alexa nodded her head. "It's when my teeth came in. I was out for an early morning jog to clear my head after a really horrible nightmare. A group of men popped out of the tree line and instinct must have taken over — I blasted them with air to keep them away, except one. When that guy plowed into me I ripped him apart, like literally, with teeth I didn't know I had." She looked out over the water as a flock of geese paddled to the middle. "I've only jogged once since then and it really wasn't jogging so much as standing on a path in my jogging clothes."

She pressed a hand to her mouth as she recalled standing on the path surrounding the ball fields where Eric and his friends played. That morning she had decided she needed to leave and all she wanted was to tell him goodbye. Regret swept over her for causing so much chaos.

"Maybe a good jog would help you deal with your pain."

Alexa looked at Sarah. "Maybe," she said, tilting her head.

"Do you have something to jog in?" Sarah asked.

"Yeah."

"Well get changed and meet me out back."

When Alexa returned Sarah was already on the back porch stretching.

"Ready?" Sarah asked.

"Yep."

They trotted toward the path, making a detour around several goose droppings. "This path was one of the selling points of the condo," Sarah said.

"Does Valerie run?"

"She does, but lately she has been using the track at the gym. Maybe we can coax her into joining us sometime. Fresh air heals."

Alexa took in the common grounds surrounding the lake and she fell into a slow, gentle rhythm next to Sarah. "I know it's all orderly and planned, but it's nice."

"It is, mostly because it's so open, but my heart craves the woods with tiny creeks and hidden caverns. I want to smell dead leaves in the air," Sarah said.

"That does sound wonderful."

"If you're up for a little detour, there's a creek beyond that building over there." Sarah pointed in the distance beyond the third complex of condominiums. They jogged on the path until they were even with the building then crossed the grass toward the line of trees.

Brambles, vines, and branches intertwined. While the area reminded Alexa of the portion of the park from her home where she had been attacked, her curiosity led her forward.

"I'm too much of a green witch to avoid this area," Sarah said. "I picked blackberries over the summer and then found reeds just a couple weeks ago. I tried my hand at making a basket. Oh, and there's an awesome tree just before the bridge." She pointed in the distance.

Alexa looked beyond the copse where Sarah pointed yet saw nothing but a jumbled mass of trees and overgrowth yellowing and losing leaves. She heard the buzz of cars in the distance and assumed the bridge to be part of that roadway. She followed Sarah around the edge of the brush revealing a small opening. Sarah stooped under a vine to enter but as Alexa tried to follow, her hair tangled on a twig.

"Hang on," Alexa said as she stepped back onto the lawn. She pulled out the ponytail, rearranged her hair, and replaced the band.

With her hair pulled out of her face, she bent lower on her second attempt to enter the overgrowth. The space beyond the vines provided ample room to stand upright. The opening narrowed to a path where twigs and vines brushed against Alexa's legs and arms.

The two walked in silence allowing Alexa to appreciate the delicate hum of bugs, birds, and what she assumed to be frogs. She enjoyed the woodsy scents of leaves on the ground and as they came closer to the creek, the musty smell of water.

All of the sounds stopped and Alexa grabbed the back of Sarah's shirt. In a soft whisper, she said, "Don't move, don't say anything." Alexa could smell Sarah's fear jolt through her. A panicked expression filled Sarah's face when she turned to look at Alexa.

Animals falling silent at the same time could only mean a predator was nearby. She had noted this in the past when vampires were near, yet at the moment she detected nothing.

"We need to leave, now." Alexa pulled on Sarah's arm to lead her back to the lawn.

They hurried up the path brushing against branches and vines. Alexa stopped short as four vampires approached. They all wore bicycle shorts and shirts.

"How many men are down there?" asked one man.

Alexa shook her head. "Dunno. We turned around when we sensed danger."

"Wise move," he said. "Andy and I will escort you out of here." He waved his hand and two men moved forward, squeezing past as best as possible to not touch either Alexa or Sarah.

"Uh, we're fine, really. But, thanks," Alexa said. She looked after the two men who continued down the path. She caught Sarah's frightened expression and grabbed her hand. The man and Andy stepped off the path, pushing the brush back so Alexa and Sarah could pass.

Alexa continued to scan the area and knew when Andy left the man's side to follow the other two men. She never detected other vampires and wondered how they evaded her senses. She had no idea how many were involved or even what was going on. And while she itched to know, she kept moving forward.

Manicured lawn peeked through the branches as they neared the opening. At last, Alexa dared to look behind them. She couldn't see the man but knew he hadn't moved from where they met on the path. She turned back to the opening and peeked out to avoid any other surprises. Four bicycles lay on the ground.

Alexa followed Sarah down the jogging path to the condo and in through the sliding glass door. Valerie met them with a broad smile, but the grin dropped and turned to concern. "What happened," she asked.

"Vampires were down by the creek," Sarah said.

"I think there was a dead body down there," Alexa said.

"WHAT?" Valerie asked. She pulled Sarah to her but Sarah turned to Alexa.

"We didn't see a body," Sarah said.

"No, but I smelled one," Alexa said. "It's why I pulled you back and said we needed to leave."

"There was a dead body?" Sarah repeated.

"Yeah, and it was a recent kill."

"Did those guys kill him? Or was it a woman?"

"Yeah it was male, but no the guys that ran into us were looking for him, not that they killed him. I didn't catch his scent on any of them."

"Did they watch you come home?" Valerie asked.

Alexa caught the scent of Sarah's fear jolt through her. Sarah glared at Alexa, then glanced out the glass door.

"I'm pretty sure they're not interested in us at all," Alexa said. "They gave us wide berth to exit and as soon as we hit the lawn the guy who escorted us out turned around to join the others. I didn't sense any other vampires nearby." She softened her expression. "They were on a mission and we were just in the way. They were probably relieved we weren't nosy humans."

"What if they have more questions to ask us?" Sarah asked.

"We never got near the body and we didn't see anyone."

"How do they know that?"

"Because our scents were the only ones on that path and we didn't go much further from where we ran into those guys."

Valerie wrinkled her forehead. "How powerful is a vampire's nose?"

"I don't know how strong a bloodhound's nose is, but that sounds like a fair comparison. There is a scent in the living room that is remarkably similar to Sarah's and is female so within the last month I'd guess either her mother or sister, maybe a grandmother has visited. She sat on the couch."

Sarah and Valerie both raised their eyebrows at the same time.

"My mom was here a couple weeks ago," Sarah said.

"That's amazing," Valerie said. "I guess it's not very hard for a vampire to find a witch?"

"Not really. I heard some like to hunt for sport, but that it was outlawed in my hometown."

"And yet you've been attacked as a witch?" Valerie asked.

"Your job exists because people break laws."

Sarah snickered.

"I'm not a criminal lawyer," Valerie said.

"A law is a law, and people break them all of the time."

"Wait," Sarah said glancing at the glass door. She looked back to Alexa. "That means the vampires in the creek don't need to follow us. They can just sniff their way here and know this is where we live?"

Alexa nodded her head.

Sarah turned to Valerie. "We need to get a dog!"

"I don't think a dog is much deterrent to a determined vampire," Alexa said. She received blank stares. "What?"

"Aren't you scared of dogs?" Sarah asked.

"No. Why would I be?"

"Is your dad scared of dogs?" Valerie asked.

Alexa wrinkled her forehead. "I don't think so. I mean he's not into having pets. But are you saying vampires avoid dogs?"

They both nodded their heads.

"Why?" Concern filled Alexa as she saw the confused looks on their faces. What didn't she know?

Sara said, "Werewolves?"

Was she joking? What the hell? Alexa looked to Valerie whose expression changed as she prepared to explain something complicated. "Hold on," Alexa said. "You're not pulling my leg?"

"You don't know about werewolves?" Sara asked.

Scanning back and forth between Sarah and Valerie, Alexa

checked for any hint of humor and found none. "Only what I've seen in movies... fictional creatures like... vampires." Her shoulders drooped, feeling like she had been hit. "So you're telling me they're real? I mean, what the fuck? Are zombies and mummies real too?"

Valerie cleared her throat. "Why don't we sit down?"

"No. Nah uh," Alexa said waving her hands in the air. "I'm still wrapping my head around vampires. I don't know where or how to categorize werewolves."

Valerie said, "Werewolves were real, but they're now extinct. Nobody turns into wolves or howls at the moon anymore."

Alexa turned to the table to find a chair. Werewolves were real? They weren't made up, imaginary monsters? She wanted to scream, but was that an angry scream or a terrified scream? She had no idea.

"Extinct?" she asked.

"Yep. They bred mostly with humans diluting their bloodlines to the point they eliminated themselves. Their descendants don't have any wolf traits other than possibly a faint scent of dog. Most don't even know their lineage."

Alexa dropped into a chair, stunned. "Wow."

"They are the biggest reason there's such disdain for hybrids today. Half-blood witches have weaker powers than their parents and as they breed with other hybrids the powers become less and less effective with each generation. I've heard hybrid vampires also weaken through the generations. Evidently, they have deformed or stunted fangs to the point they don't have them at all. I realize you're strong, evidently both as vampire and witch, but that's really abnormal."

Recalling her interaction with a hybrid in Brentwood who said her teeth were super short, Alexa nodded understanding. But werewolves were real? She couldn't process that.

Valerie cleared her throat. "But since you asked, zombies and mummies are real too."

Alexa raised her eyebrows.

"Zombies are an act of dark witchcraft which is banned everywhere around the world. Now like vampires not being allowed to hunt witches, there are some witches who... *practice*...

things they ought not. And there are... ramifications for those acts. The problem is bringing a body back to life does not also resurrect the soul that was once tied to the body, so you just have a physical being whose only drive is to sustain itself. They just want to eat and fornicate."

Glad she was seated Alexa leaned back with her mouth open.

Valerie offered a faint grin. "Think about who would want to bring back the deceased – usually a former lover. It never ends well. The zombie goes for anyone in the room, including the witch who brought it to life, trying to wrestle them into sex but also wanting to sink their teeth into flesh. Nobody turns into a zombie from the bite; they just die and are usually consumed before anyone can stop the mess. As for mummies, they're just well-preserved dead bodies and were good candidates to become zombies – with the same results."

"What about unicorns, dragons, fairies, elves, gnomes, um... the headless horseman, sasquatch..."

"I've never seen any of those in person, but I believe they do, or at some point did exist."

Alexa nodded slowly, contemplating a whole world of creatures she thought all to be make-believe. "Why don't vampires like dogs?"

"Werewolves hunted vampires."

A silent "oh" fell from Alexa's mouth. She thought for a moment. "So werewolves hunt vampires, vampires hunt witches... what do witches hunt?"

"Energy. We seek energy." Valerie smiled.

"We get energy from the moon," Sarah said. "And from crystals, and the four elements. I even hear that some witches absorb energy from other people."

"Evidently vampires have a lot of excess energy," Valerie said.

"Huh." Alexa thought about her energy but considered that maybe hers was altered by being a hybrid. "Wait. Why did the werewolves mate with humans? Was that reciprocal? Are humans drawn to werewolves?"

"Humans are drawn to dogs – makes them feel safe," Valerie said. "In a world with vampires and witches lurking around every corner I can see how befriending a werewolf would be reassuring to a human."

Chapter Six

"What would you think about doing a little temp work?" Valerie asked as she poured wine.

"Doesn't that sort of blow away my attempts at hiding?" Alexa asked.

"How so?"

"Application, references check, um, basically using my name."

"Just use a fake name and bogus info; no one will know the difference. I'll speak to the partners and the head of HR – they will be the only people who know your identity. Just keep with the story about the stalker boyfriend, they're very sympathetic for those situations."

"A lawyer telling me to lie," Alexa said chuckling.

Valerie took her seat at the table. "The people who need to know will protect you."

"What name do I use?"

"What about Lexie?" Sarah suggested.

"Is that enough of a difference from Alexa?"

Valerie shrugged, then joined hands with Sarah. They bowed their heads and together they said, "Blessed be the Earth for giving birth to this food. Blessed be the Sun for nourishing it. Blessed be the Wind for carrying its seed. Blessed be the Rain for quenching its thirst. Blessed be the hands that helped grow this food. To bring it to our table, to nourish our minds, bodies, and spirits. Blessed be our friends, our families, and our loved ones. Blessed Be."

As they lifted their heads, Valerie smiled at Alexa. "If you wish to participate, and there is no pressure to do so, you can say 'Blessed Be.'"

Alexa smiled in return. "Blessed Be."

"You'll need a different last name," Valerie said.

"My mom's maiden name is Meyers."

"Lexie Meyers sounds convincing," Sarah said.

"I guess so."

Valerie said, "But Lexie is a nickname. How about Alexandria?"

"Hmmm no, Alexa is a tribute to my father's mother, Alexandra. Hell, the way things are going Alexandra could be my real name. No. Also can't use Alexis, that's too similar.

"I knew a girl in college named Lexann," Valerie said.

Alexa raised her eyebrows. "Lexann! I like that. Lexann Meyers... now that has possibility. It sounds professional, too." She pictured a name plaque on a desk, imagining herself as an office manager; not that temping would bring her any closer to becoming management. She paused as she mentally ran through the contents of her bags. "I'll have to go shopping first. I don't have anything appropriate for work."

"What size are you?" Sarah asked.

"Ten, medium."

Valerie said, "I think we can hobble something together out of our closets – we both have an obscene amount of clothing."

"I might enjoy shopping a bit too much," Sarah said with a grin.

Valerie shook her head. "She shops for both of us and I swear I have tons of things with the tags still on them."

"But I couldn't pass them up, they were perfect for you!"

"I have a friend like that!" Alexa said, thinking of her friend Chloe. "I can't tell you how many times she's shoved a bag in my face saying 'this had you written all over it!'"

With wide eyes, Sarah said, "That's exactly it!"

"Well, there's ample clothing to dig through," Valerie said. "Even if it's not quite your style, it will hold you over until you're able to hit the stores for yourself."

"That's very generous, thank you."

"It's really no problem. Are you going to use Lexann as your name?" Valerie asked.

"Yeah, I think so. Calling me Lexie is okay. I'm totally used to it; I get called that plenty of times." Alexa stopped to savor the bite of pork in her mouth. "This food is amazing. Do you cook like this all of the time?"

"On the weekends I do," Valerie said. "We package up the leftovers like TV dinners and freeze them so we have plenty to eat through the week."

"Don't you get tired of the same meal several days in a row?"

Sarah shook her head. "We have a chest freezer loaded with prepared meals from previous weeks, so if I feel like having tetrazzini tomorrow, it's right there."

"That's amazing."

"She's a wonderful cook," Sarah said with pride.

"I completely agree," Alexa said. "Where did you learn to cook?"

"My grandfather was a French chef and his father was a sommelier," Valerie said. "I was brought up around fine dining and the importance of pairing the right wine with your meal."

"Pinot noir does go well with this pork," Alexa said, nodding her head with approval.

"Mostly because of the sweetness of the braise and the honey on the carrots," Valerie said pointing to the last carrots on her plate.

"There's honey on them?"

Valerie grinned. "Yes, with butter and lemon juice. It makes it wonderfully rich."

Alexa took another bite, slowly assessing. "Okay," she said, "I now taste it. It's very delicate."

"Do you enjoy cooking?" Valerie asked.

"I'm comfortable in the kitchen and make a *fine* grilled cheese and tomato soup, but none of it is from scratch."

Valerie laughed. "There's no shame in that. My mother was not the skilled chef my father had grown up with. She would remind me as I struggled to master cooking basics that it's okay to open a can of soup instead of constantly making your own broth. She also taught me how to roll with my mistakes. Some you can fix and other times, like the night she burned pineapple chicken, you just need to throw it all away and order pizza."

"Well, that's not necessary if you have a freezer full of luscious leftovers!" Alexa said, knowing the stench of burnt rice.

"I have to admit having that stash has brought a sense of security. It allows me to experiment knowing there's still food in the house," Valerie said. "That's not to say we don't order pizza or some Chinese take-out every so often."

"I programmed them into the speed dial on our phone," Sarah said.

"My friend, Brie, had Angelo's Pizza on her speed dial," Alexa said. "Although I think mostly because she had a crush on one of the delivery drivers." She wrinkled her forehead as she remembered the man carrying a red bag. "No, I guess not. He was human." Alexa saw the confused looks on their faces. "I'm sorry, I'm still learning to register people's scents and as I think back about that guy, he was really good-looking, but now I remember he smelled like an old tin can. It still amuses me that humans smell like metal."

"You never knew the difference?" Sarah asked.

"No clue," Alexa said. "My sense of smell got stronger just before my teeth came in. I seriously thought I was suffering a sinus infection all summer long except that my ability to smell increased. Before that, I sort of noticed people had different scents but I always chalked that up to perfumes, dryer sheets, or poor hygiene."

"And this was all part of the plot to hide vampires and witches from you?" Valerie asked.

Alexa nodded her head.

"I can't imagine how difficult this discovery has been for you," Valerie said. "The reason I asked if you like to cook is that it is a good way to teach you spells and potions. It's not the only way to teach you, but if you know your way around the kitchen then you have a base of knowledge to build from."

Alexa perked up. "That would be great!"

"Spells and potions can be learned even by humans, some practice without even knowing it," Valerie said. "That's not saying it's all easy, but it's a good way to learn fundamentals."

"So humans practicing witchcraft is actually a thing?"

Valerie nodded. "It is. I'm not sure who let them in the circle or how long ago it happened, but their existence helps the rest of us hide."

"Do they know about real witches?"

Valerie raised an eyebrow. "Be careful using the word 'real'. Some humans are quite accomplished in their witchcraft and I think it's fair to acknowledge them as real as much as you and I are real."

Alexa nodded understanding. "And they're accepted among the larger witch community?"

Valerie sighed. "It's a mixed bag and here's where the problem comes in because we don't have a term to designate those of us born as witches as opposed to..." she lifted her fingers in quotation marks, "humans who practice witchcraft." She shook her head in frustration. "Some born witches accept them, others don't. Oh hey, I found a phrase to use! 'Born Witch'! Anyway, some support the humans; others mock them. Some *born witches* go as far as pretending to be human and act offended that anyone would try to practice witchcraft at all." Valerie leaned in and said, "I'm pretty sure those types of witches were active in the witch trials and condemned some very innocent humans."

Alexa tipped her head thinking of her grandmother. "Yeah, I'm pretty sure I've crossed one of those already. She wasn't very pleased that I was a hybrid."

With a nod, Valerie said, "Oh of course! Only pure blood is good enough and even then they get pretentious about how the rest of us practice our craft. They're the ones who insist on fresh herbs in the winter and would travel across the country to find a live newt. You know what? Dried herbs sold in the grocery store work just fine and I'll be damned if I'm touching a newt, dead or alive."

"Ugh," Sarah said with snorted disgust. "I hate spells that use animals as a sacrifice."

"Wait, newts are real?"

"Of course they are," Sarah said. "They're a tiny lizard."

"Salamander," Valerie corrected.

"And people really do use 'eye of newt'?" Alexa asked with raised eyebrows.

Sarah grinned. "Actually it's code for mustard seed, but there are witches who use small animals like newts for sacrifices."

"And there are witches who go out of their way to use something exotic sounding like newts or elephant hide when they could easily capture a slug in their own garden to accomplish the same thing," Valerie said.

Questions filled Alexa's head as she thought about a wiggly little salamander. "Where on earth would you get something like that? I mean are there special stores or do you have to hunt your own?"

"Newts aren't exotic," Valerie said. "You could probably find one in that creek with the dead body." She pointed her thumb over her shoulder in the direction of the creek.

Sarah shivered. "But yes, there are apothecaries where you can buy them or other sorts of gruesome ingredients." She wrinkled her nose. "You can get critters live or in various states of dead like frozen, dried, powdered. The bigger the critter the more likely you're just shopping for parts like organs or toes. But if they're already dead then they're not a sacrifice, but just an ingredient. I try not to think about the type of people who collect innocent little creatures to sell to these shops."

"Back up. Sacrifice?" Alexa asked.

Sarah leaned forward. "Well, all things come with a price, even the good stuff. We each have an allotment of energy and capacity. When we ask for more than our allotment we must offer up something in its place. You can either willingly offer honor, gratitude, service, physical sacrifices, or have them taken from you. The bigger the request, the larger the offer must be. Sometimes a small cut on your hand offering a few drops of blood is necessary – it's an easy but significant offering. Something like using the blood of a salamander is a little more work and sometimes its blood isn't as useful. It just depends on the spell and exactly how dark you want to go."

Alexa opened her mouth to ask, shook her head, then found the words and asked, "Maybe I'm missing something obvious, but who is receiving these offers?"

"That's a hard question to answer," Sarah said. "It depends on your belief system. Whether you call the energy 'god', 'goddess', 'spirit', whatever, there is a.... um... presence that seeks balance."

"A metaphysical presence," Valerie offered.

"Yes, exactly!" Sarah said. "A yin for the yang, light for the dark. The bigger the request, the larger the offer, but whatever you do, balance and equilibrium will be sought. And even for good acts, there is a price."

"Something bad for wanting good?" Alexa asked.

"No," Sarah said. She turned to Valerie and asked, "How do you explain that?"

"There is a saying that whatever you manifest comes back to you threefold," Valerie said and Sarah nodded her head.

"But you have to watch your intention," Sarah said. "If you give a homeless person a dollar hoping to find three dollars, later on, your intention is greed and at some point, your greed will come back to haunt you threefold."

"You look overwhelmed," Valerie said.

Alexa shook her head. "Not at all. Just absorbing. It all makes sense."

"Sorry about that, I did jump in kind of deep," Sarah said. "I'm just so excited to have someone to teach."

Chapter Seven

Alexa rode to work with Valerie as agreed. She wore a navy blue skirt borrowed from Sarah and a short-sleeve ivory blouse plucked from Valerie's closet as well as a pair of new blue shoes matching the skirt. That she and Valerie both wore size eight shoes seemed like a miracle.

Valerie asked, "What does your father do for a living?"

"He works for a holdings firm," Alexa said. "Why are you smiling?"

"Let me guess," Valerie said. "His company is based in some major metropolitan area in a very tall building?"

"That's not a difficult guess to make."

"No, it's not," Valerie said. "It's even easier to guess knowing your father is a vampire."

"What does that mean?"

"Pay attention to the upper floors the next time you drive past a tall building. You'll notice at night there are usually one or two floors with several, if not all of the lights on. Typically the top couple of floors, penthouses and such... those are vampire floors."

"What?"

"Vampire Floors. They're not just offices, they're also residences. They have secret entrances and separate elevators. The important part is that witches try to avoid those buildings if at all possible, but those floors specifically."

"But I know vampires who live in regular houses," Alexa said. "I mean I grew up in a subdivision and so did my boyfriend... the vampire one."

"It's impossible for all of the vampires to be tucked away in those buildings."

Alexa recalled seeing buildings lit up in such a way. "Have you been on one of these floors?"

"No, but I have been in those buildings several times, very unnerving to say the least." Valerie said with raised eyebrows.

Valerie drove through a maze of streets from one office park to another, all lined with abnormally green lawns for early October. The office buildings sat squat behind young trees and tiny shrubs molded into orbs. If not for the vehicle traffic she would have assumed the buildings to be vacant.

They parked behind one such building with several cars in the lot. Following Valerie into the office, Alexa noticed the chatter of songbirds silenced when the doors closed behind her with a whoosh of quiet. The soft tinkling of a piano drifting in from a sound system oddly contributed to the essence of quiet. Dimmed lights and tufted chairs gave the room a soothing feel and Alexa felt inclined to whisper. The receptionist looked up from her tall wood desk and smiled.

Alexa saw the receptionist's death in a hospital bed with a good-looking man beginning to gray holding her hand, tears in his eyes. She felt the receptionist's remorse for causing such heartache for the man. Alexa held the vision longer than usual and nearly broke into tears herself. She sorely missed Eric.

Valerie paused at the desk. "Heather," she said, "This is Lexie. I'm going to see if she can temp with us for a bit."

"Glad to meet you, Lexie," Heather said, her voice soft and smooth.

Alexa offered a weak grin as she tried to recompose herself. She forgot about the agreement to use the name, Lexie.

Yes, she answered to the name frequently, typically by strangers or people who barely knew her and forgot her name, but never had she been introduced as Lexie. She much preferred Lex, but that was reserved for her closest friends. She shook off her confusion and accepted the new moniker with a smile.

She sat in the reception area while Valerie spoke to the powers-that-be beyond a set of tall doors. Heather fielded a steady stream of morning phone calls while Alexa scanned each surface for distraction. She felt every bit like a child waiting outside of the principal's office ready to be scolded.

People entered the vestibule to either drop off or pick up large envelopes at Heather's palatial desk. An occasional person would sit in the chair next to Alexa until the tall doors opened and someone emerged to escort the visitor inside. Alexa tried to see what lay beyond the doors, but the green carpet and beige walls revealed nothing.

After an insufferable wait, nearly an hour, Valerie appeared from behind the tall doors with a broad smile on her face. Alexa nearly jumped out of her seat to join Valerie.

"You're going to meet with Ms. Swanson our HR director," Valerie said as they headed down the green carpet hallway. Once the doors closed Valerie turned and said in hushed tones, "she's a hybrid."

"I've only met one other hybrid," Alexa said.

Valerie stopped and faced Alexa. "Really?"

"Well as far as I know."

"Huh. Well, there are plenty here in town so I'm sure you'll meet more. Anyway, the partners here are human as are the rest of the employees."

They walked past a set of double glass doors revealing a small cluster of cubicles. Alexa craned her head to take in the space. All she could assess were the cubicle units appeared more modern than the drab grayish walls of her former workspace. The next set of double doors stood open to an empty meeting room with a massive conference table in the middle. She and Valerie turned the corner where a series of closed single doors lined the hall that Alexa assumed to be offices of managers and executives. At last, they stopped in front of a door with a bronze plaque, "Human Resources".

Valerie tapped three times and opened the door slowly as if ensuring she wasn't intruding. Alexa lingered a few steps behind as she followed Valerie inside. The combined scents of vampire and witch hit Alexa's nose - the peppery scent of a hunter, a mid-range vampire reminding her of Eric; and something very herby, a witch's scent.

"Lexie, this is Donella Swanson, our HR manager."

Alexa stepped forward feeling off-guard between the hunter scent in the room and Valerie introducing her as Lexie again. She forced a smile and a slight nod. "Glad to meet you."

Donella looked over to Valerie and said with almost a hiss, "You said she was hybrid."

"I am," Alexa whispered. She used the silent whisper of vampires - inaudible to anyone but the person she chose to hear the message.

Donella's eyes widened. "That's witchcraft!"

Alexa relaxed her abdomen and stirred the internal sensation that brought her vampire scent forward. Valerie stepped backward and closed the office door.

"How are you able to mock a hybrid?" Donella asked.

"I'm not mocking. My teeth came in two months ago."

"Are you using a masking spell?"

Alexa shook her head. "No. I've always presented as a witch. I discovered this scent after a kiss. It took me a bit to figure out how to make it show up intentionally."

Donella nodded. "I imagine passion could override a spell like that."

Alexa glared at Donella. A spell? Who would have cast a spell on her? Anger simmered as she contemplated the swath of lies she had been told throughout her life. Her parents said they were protecting her. Her friends acted as unwilling accomplices in the cover-up. Only when her teeth came in did the truth come crashing through. And here she stood in front of a stranger revealing yet another secret – someone had cast a spell on her.

"Lexie?" Valerie said stroking Alexa's arm.

Alexa turned to Valerie. "This is a spell?"

Valerie shrugged. "I've never heard of anyone being able to change their scent. That you can override it says it's a spell."

With a deep sigh, Alexa shook her head. "There's just so much I don't know."

"What do you mean?" Donella asked.

"I'm untrained," Alexa said. "Where I lived, hybrids aren't allowed to practice so I've never been taught anything other than the bits and pieces I've figured out on my own."

"But you present as a full-blooded witch," Donella said. "No one but your family would know otherwise."

"Yeah... there's someone in my family that is probably the core of the problem. She could very well have been the one to put a spell on me so as not to embarrass her in public. Who knows?"

"So there are problems in your family?" Donella asked.

"Yeah, that would be an understatement."

Donella nodded and offered a weak grin. "Well sit down and let's get you processed."

Valerie and Alexa sat in the beige chairs in front of the desk as Donella lowered herself into a large black leather chair, then rolled forward to the desk. She pulled several pieces of paper from a drawer and handed them to Alexa.

Extending a pen, Donella said, "Let's start with your work experience. Tell me a little about what you did at your last job and how long you were there."

"I reconciled accounts receivable, making sure all of the sales and returns balanced. I was also backup to the person monitoring inventory adjustments. I worked there for two years – it was the first job I landed out of college. I have a degree in business administration. Before that, it was a part-time job at a local ice cream store. I did that since my senior year in high school and all through college."

Donella nodded her head as she listened. "What are your career goals?"

Alexa shrugged. "I really enjoyed my marketing classes when I was in college. Now that I've worked with numbers, I think I'm interested in a higher-level management position, like in operations, that looks at trends and finding solutions." She thought of conversations with her father, who always encouraged her to seek management opportunities.

"That is quite ambitious," Donella said with a more fervent nod. "Did you do any internships while in college?"

"No," Alexa said shaking her head. "I did some job shadowing, with different people but no official internships."

"That's odd," Donella said.

"Yeah, it was frustrating."

"Well, what we have available isn't a management position, however, we have a gentleman leaving in a few days in our accounting department who happens to do our accounts receivable. So far you're the best candidate to hit my desk and since you don't need to give notice, we can start training you immediately."

Alexa looked at Valerie for clarification and back at Donella. "I'm only here to temp. I... I really have no idea how long I'll be in town."

"I understand," Donella said. "Whatever work we can get out of you would be appreciated and of course, we will pay you for that time. Today we can start you off in the copy room assisting in compiling client files – Lisa is begging for help. Now if you return tomorrow, I would really appreciate if you spent the day shadowing

Greg, the gentleman who is resigning. He's never had a chance to document his procedures so whatever you can extract out of him would be greatly appreciated."

"So there's no commitment?" Alexa asked.

Donella shook her head. "None."

"Well… okay, I can do that."

Chapter Eight

Alexa's mind wandered as she stood in the copier room with five boxes of legal briefs to be copied, packaged into folders, and arranged alphabetically. In some ways, the monotonous work brought relief in its simplicity, but her thoughts drifted back to Eric time and time again.

She recalled Eric in his repairman uniform dismantling a copier with toner casting a gray sheen over his tools and work mat. Only a few weeks ago he popped his head over the cubicle wall to arrange another date. She felt like years had passed since that day.

Did Eric resent the mixed messages of having sex and then breaking up? She told him she needed time to sort things out between the recent discovery of being a hybrid and the speed at which their relationship progressed. At that point, she planned to find her own apartment and hunker down in as much isolation as possible. She just wanted to come up for air. Leaving her family, hell leaving the state hadn't even crossed her mind!

But then mayhem broke loose that night when her father barged into Eric's parent's house and tried to rip Eric to shreds for having sex with Alexa. Forget the fact that Alexa fully consented and very much wanted to be with Eric. Actually, she may have forced herself on him.

Crap.

Did Eric even *want* to have sex with her? Of course, silly, he made that clear early on.

Taking a deep breath Alexa stared at the machine in front of her. On the verge of tears and swimming in her thoughts, she quickly regained her composure. She opened another folder and shoved the pile of papers into the slot on the copier. The groan of the tumbler receiving the papers filled the room. A soft flitting sound joined the chorus as the new copies floated into the receiving tray.

Did he blame her?

She gathered the copies and the originals, turning the piles in opposite directions so they remained separate, shoved them into the original folder, and dropped them on the table. She grabbed the next folder out of the box and repeated the process.

Her mother said Eric was conscripted into the Queen's army after her father tried to kill him. The Queen, her great-grandmother. Alexa couldn't wrap her mind around being related to royalty, even if it was vampire royalty. Her father and grandfather were princes but she didn't know what that made her. She didn't know if being a hybrid affected her standing in the family or if she held a title. Ugh, of all the times as a little girl she played princess with her friends in pretend castles and here she was a daughter of a real-life prince! She left town before the big formal family meeting where details were to be revealed. A small part of her wanted to know what they would tell her, but only a very small part. Mostly she wanted silence. Of course, she had questions, lots of questions, but those could wait. The big reveal, whatever her father's family had in mind, would be them talking and her listening. Nope. Leaving was the right decision.

But she missed Eric. Staying in Brentwood wouldn't have eased her sorrow any. He was likely in Austria already, probably enduring a tortuous boot camp. What the hell do vampires do to new recruits in their army? Did he regret ever meeting her? She didn't doubt he loved her, but did he love her enough to forgive her for turning his life upside down? Could Eric forgive her for leaving him?

Did he miss her?

Alexa sighed at herself and shoved another stack of papers into the copier.

He could never forgive her, she was sure.

Eric said he didn't remember Austria. His family left when he was just a baby. Did he speak the language? His parents had an accent, but he was American as anyone else she knew in Brentwood.

Was he safe?

She dropped the folder in the pile and grabbed the next.

Would he look for her when he returned?

She grabbed another folder.

The rhythmic flow came to an abrupt stop, jarring Alexa from her thoughts. She checked the receiving tray to find only two sheets of paper. She looked at the other end of the copier and over twelve pieces of paper had run through the imager. Alexa pulled the front door of the copier open and stared at the drums and levers.

"What are you doing?"

Alexa spun around to see a woman standing in the doorway: Human, smelled like hot iron and olives, died gasping for air with a horrible headache. Olives? She wrinkled her forehead as she tried to decipher whether the woman questioned if Alexa belonged in the room or why the copier was hanging open. Moreover, why would a human smell like olives? Was she a human-witch hybrid?

Clearing her thoughts, Alexa said, "I'm copying files."

"Why is the copier door open?"

"Oh. The paper jammed up."

"Then we need to call a repairman right away."

"It's just a paper jam. They're usually easy to clear out."

The woman dropped her chin a notch and scanned Alexa from foot to head. "You know how to repair copy machines?" Her disbelief exuded from every pore.

Alexa looked from the woman to the machine. "There are directions printed in the door," she said pointing to the extended door. "It's, uh, usually just a lever release and pull out a drum. Then you just take out the paper and close it all up."

"Just that easy?" the woman asked with a smirk.

Alexa shrugged. "Usually. It's a lot faster and cheaper than calling a repairman."

The woman rolled her eyes. "Our service calls are free."

"Well, um, do you want to watch me pull this lever and, uh, make sure I don't break anything? If it doesn't work, then we can get some help?" Alexa turned to the machine without waiting for a reply. She pulled a red lever and returned it to its original position. She skimmed the directions on the door and found a corresponding lever, pulled it, and the first one. A drum released with a click revealing the jammed paper that she easily extracted. Alexa waved the wrinkled paper to show her success, dropping it on top of the copier. Then she gently pushed the drum back into its original station and returned the two levers to the upright position. She closed the door and pushed the green button, hoping to hear the churn of gears resume their noisy thrum.

Turning to the woman who had stepped closer to observe her destruction of the expensive machine, Alexa beamed a triumphant smile. "Like I said, it's usually a quick and easy fix."

Unimpressed, the woman flattened her lips. "Very well," she said. "If this continues to happen let Heather at the front desk know so we can get a repairman here."

"Considering the amount of dust I see in there it wouldn't be a bad idea to have someone come out and clean it."

"Let Heather know."

Chapter Nine

A swoosh of hot air flowed out of the car as Alexa opened the door. She sank into the passenger seat absorbing the warmth.

Valerie slid into the driver's seat and looked at her. "Tough day?"

"Work-wise? No. Emotionally..."

"Are you okay?"

"Not really," Alexa said, latching the seatbelt. "But that's why I left home – to figure out how to move on with my life." She saw Valerie's concern. "Spending all day in the copier room reminded me of the guy I left behind. He was a copier repairman that came into my office a lot."

"Oh."

Tilting her head in dismissal she said, "Yeah today was rough. I'll just have to cry it out until some point..."

Silence hung between them.

"Until you forgive yourself?" Valerie asked.

Forgiveness? How the hell was Alexa supposed to forgive herself for ruining a man's life? For ripping his heart out and leaving the scene? For derailing his dreams? For being the reason he had to join an army in a country he hadn't visited in over twenty years? Alexa wanted to crumble into a ball of tears there in the car.

Valerie offered a sympathetic smile. "Yes," she said softly, "at some point, you have to forgive yourself or this will haunt you forever."

"I deserve to be haunted forever," Alexa said with a grumble.

Valerie shifted the car into gear and drove out of the parking lot. "On the upside, I think you won't be stranded in the copy room much longer. Donella said she received positive reports about you... well, from everyone except Brenda."

"I guess that was the woman who thought I was going to destroy the big, expensive, scary machine in the copy room?"

Valerie chuckled. "Yes, that was her. She is vying to be a partner and is extremely cost-conscious. I find her tedious and not in a good way."

"When is tedious good?"

"Oh, you want your lawyer to be tedious and tenacious, but

Brenda carries those traits right into happy hour."

"A killjoy."

"Yes, exactly. I can't imagine living with someone so... rigid."

"So how do you balance tedium and your private life?" Alexa asked.

"I have Sarah," she said with a broad grin. "She tosses the right amount of chaos into my world reminding me that wine stains don't matter and dishes can soak overnight. When I'm wound up her favorite thing to remind me is how the clouds never make that formation ever again."

"She reminds me a lot of my friend, Brie."

"Is Brie a witch?"

"Yeah." Alexa grinned thinking of her. "We've been friends since we were little girls. Somehow our parents joined forces and convinced her and our other friend, Tess, to not talk to me about witchcraft. They were the shield that kept me in the dark for so long, but they were also the ones who helped me run away."

"They sound like good friends."

"They really are."

"I can't imagine hiding witchcraft from a witch, especially someone like you who just oozes witchy energy."

"Witchy energy?" Alexa asked with a laugh. "That sounds like something Brie would say. Does Sarah say that?"

"She does."

"Speaking of witchy energy, I was surprised by Brenda's olive scent," Alexa said.

"What do you mean?" Valerie asked.

"She smells like hot iron and olives."

Valerie wrinkled her forehead. "Yeah, she has that human/metal smell, but I've never noticed olives before."

"Oh it's definitely there," Alexa said. "I assume she's a human-witch hybrid. But I think maybe one of her parents is the hybrid because the olive is pretty weak."

Valerie shook her head. "That has to be your vampire sense of smell because I can't even distinguish what type of metal she smells like."

"Cast iron skillet on a hot stove."

"That's very specific," Valerie said, again shaking her head.

"I have to say, I don't catch any of that. I do think it's interesting that she could be a hybrid. I wonder if she knows?"

"Or if she has any powers?"

"Ha! I can only imagine her grimoire arranged alphabetically and free of smudges," Valerie said with a roll of her eyes.

"What's that?"

"A grimoire?" Valerie took her attention off the road to look at Alexa. "Oh wow, you really don't know?" She returned her attention to driving and said, "You have so much to learn." Her voice teetered between pity and dismay. "A grimoire is almost like a diary – it's personal for each witch. Sarah has one, I have one. A proper grimoire is where you record spells, recipes, meditations... whatever helps you grow with your power. Some are passed down through families, like a Bible. In fact, some are bibles."

"Wow, that must piss off some people."

"There's some mystic stuff in those pages," Valerie said. "However, you're correct, it does piss off people, humans. It's one reason why a grimoire is kept private. The other, she said with a manicured finger raised in warning, "if your enemies know where to find your grimoire and what spells and talismans you use, they can undo your work as well as use them against you."

"So it's a messy journal?" Alexa asked.

"Not intentionally, of course. Sarah's is filled with a lot of pressed flowers so that's messy by nature. Mine, as you can imagine, has a lot of recipes. And like my grandmother said - you can tell if a cookbook is any good if it has smudges of food on the pages. A well-used grimoire will have smudges of charcoal, bits of herbs... sometimes blood. It's all part of spell-work. The best way to start is a pretty new journal – I guess we should go shopping soon."

"I'd like that!" Alexa realized she had relaxed at some point in the conversation and no longer felt the urge to cry about being away from Eric.

When they arrived home four people stood around a nearby mailbox.

Valerie sighed. "The town gossips have gathered," she said. "I wonder what has their tongues wagging today?"

"What's their opinion of you and Sarah?"

"We've always kept our relationship private. As far as any of them know we're just roommates."

"And now that I've arrived?"

"Ooh! I should introduce our new roomie, nip that rumor in the bud."

Alexa smiled. "And give you a chance to find out what has them buzzing today!"

Valerie faced Alexa. "I'm not a gossip."

"Of course, you're not. You're curious. And so am I!"

After parking the car Alexa followed Valerie to the mailbox two units down from the driveway.

Valerie waved to them as she approached. "Hey, guys! I want to introduce you to our new tenet!"

The man and three women turned with broad smiles to face Valerie and Alexa. "Lexie, this is Barry. He lives in this unit here," Valerie said pointing. "And this is his neighbor on the other side, Bonnie. Tina lives down there with the red geraniums on the porch. And this is Leigh – she lives over here, across the street. Everyone, this is Lexie, she just moved in with us and we got her set up with a job at my office today."

"We didn't know you were looking for a roommate," Bonnie said.

"We have a friend in common who knew Sarah and I had room to spare. Lexie just left a rather dangerous boyfriend situation."

Heads nodded in understanding and each person offered warm greetings to Alexa.

"Well, I hope nobody is following you," Tina said. "It would be dreadful if they were connected to the body they found in the ravine over the weekend."

"Body?" Valerie asked.

"You didn't hear all of the sirens up on Hillview?" Tina asked.

Barry craned his head toward Tina. "I've told you we do not hear the goings on up on Hillview over here on this side of the street. Your units block all that noise."

"We heard nothing," Valerie said. "Do you know anything about the person? How long they were there?"

"I was watching the news at lunchtime," Leigh said. "They

aren't releasing the identity or cause of death until family has been contacted. It was quite the stir well after nightfall last night. News teams from all of the stations were up there, a helicopter, and all of the flashing lights. I had to pull the blinds."

"Did you hear helicopters last night?" Valerie asked Alexa. Alexa shook her head.

"It's bad enough the high school kids play in that ravine," Tina said. "All of that graffiti. It's just a perfect spot for a crime to happen."

"Well if someone would remove all of those weeds and overgrowth we wouldn't have this problem," Bonnie said. The gossips all nodded in unison.

"Sarah has to be wondering what's taking us so long. Please keep us updated," Valerie said. "We'll make sure to double-check our locks at night."

Barry nodded his head. "That's a good idea."

"Nice meeting everybody," Alexa said with a smile before she turned away.

Chapter Ten

Sitting at an awkward angle not too close to touch Greg, yet able to see his computer screen, Alexa strained her back and neck. She had another seven and a half hours to go. Greg, a human in his late thirties, possibly early forties, seemed equally strained to have someone so close watching his every movement.

Although Alexa found men attractive in dress shirts and ties, Greg made the ensemble drab and boring. She even found his death drab and boring – lying in bed in a dark room coughing and sputtering. He coughed a lot, unconsciously, so much so she couldn't discern if the sound came from her vision or from the seat next to her.

She dutifully jotted down his directions for booting the computer, logging in, and the various applications available. He guarded his password entry like a hawk over a fresh kill. Alexa politely turned away whenever a login screen appeared, although she thought the whole ordeal pointless with his departure only a few days away. But still, she extended the courtesy.

"It's time for lunch," Greg announced as he pulled a brown sack from under the desk.

"I'll be back in a half hour," Alexa said.

"Actually," he said. "We get an hour."

"See ya then." Alexa spun on her heel and left the cubicle.

She arrived in the break room to find each of the six café-tables occupied. Her previous office used an old conference table, making the seating sometimes cramped, but also resolved her current problem of asking to join someone. She approached a table with two women chatting. As soon as they looked up Alexa doubted her decision, feeling like the dorky new kid at school.

The redhead smiled and said, "You're the new girl training for Greg's job."

Alexa nodded. "Yeah, I'm uh... Lexie." She flushed as she stumbled over her name.

"Hi Lexie," the redhead said. "I'm Velma and this is Daphne."

Alexa snapped her head looking between the two. But Daphne had short black hair and Velma had shoulder-length red hair? This Daphne and Velma were the exact opposite of the characters in

Scooby-Doo. "Wait. Are you shitting me?" She snapped her mouth closed, realizing she had just cussed at work.

Velma roared with laughter.

Daphne grinned and nodded. "Oh, you're definitely one of us. You should sit here."

Velma gasped for air a few times. "You are the first person here to understand the Velma and Daphne reference. *EVER*! My real name is Laura and this is Rena."

Alexa slid into a chair relieved to find fun people.

"How's training going?" Rena asked.

Alexa shrugged. "Slow." She removed a sandwich and can of soda from the bag Sarah packed for her that morning. "We're covering basics right now."

Laura rolled her eyes. "Let me tell you what. He's going to be covering basics the entire time. He's full of shit and spins his wheels doing a whole lot of nothing. I'm glad to see his ass go."

Alexa grinned sweetly. She had no idea who to trust or what to believe. "Well, he seems nice."

"Where did you work before?" Rena asked.

"A management company. I worked with mostly billing reconciliation."

Laura tilted her head with a doubting look on her face. "Are you not going to say the name of the company?"

Alexa shook her head. "I've had a situation where I had to pack up and leave everything behind me. So, um, no, I'm not giving too many details."

Laura raised her eyebrows. "Well, now, that's much more intriguing!"

Rena leaned forward. "We promise not to pry, but I need to know – is this about a guy?"

With a chuckle, Alexa nodded her head. "Yeah."

"I guess you're not ready to get back up in the saddle, are you?" Rena asked.

"No. Not at all."

The hour passed quickly as Laura and Rena talked about people Alexa didn't know. Grateful for their chatter as if she were a long-time friend, but more importantly she appreciated they never asked for any information about her past.

Returning to Greg's desk Alexa felt lighter and ready to receive the next round of training. Greg, however, still had nearly a whole meal spread in front of him. She cleared her throat as she approached.

"I guess the clock in the break room is off," she said with perky surprise. Alexa smiled as she dropped her lunch bag next to her chair. "Don't rush on my account. I'm pretty sure there is some paperwork in HR I still need to fill out." Without waiting for Greg's response Alexa turned and left his cubicle. She knew perfectly well that she had spent exactly an hour away at lunch. She had no idea why Greg would still have his food laid out. Maybe he was a slow eater or possibly screwing off and wasting time? Whatever his reason she felt returning to the break room seemed like a bad idea.

She walked past Donella's closed door. Relief swept over Alexa because didn't wish to bother Donella or explain why she was up and walking around. She thought saying something about Greg dawdling might be a bad idea. She simply did not know the dynamics in this office. Instead, Alexa found herself standing in the copy room offering to help Lisa with more boxes of files.

Lisa said she welcomed the opportunity to leave the room and get caught up on filing. The copier groaned on with the pile of papers Alexa fed through. This time she kept her mind off of Eric as she continued to glance at the hallway expecting Greg to show up.

Nearly forty-five minutes later Greg stood in the doorway looking upset and slightly frazzled. "Why didn't you go back to the break room?" he asked.

"Because I was done eating," Alexa said. "I figured I could be of assistance in here."

"Well, you should have said where you were going. I've been looking all over for you."

Alexa resisted the urge to grin and instead feigned innocence. "I'm sorry. The thought didn't occur to me."

She turned to the adjacent room. "Hey, Lisa, I'm heading back to Greg's desk."

"Okay." Lisa's voice echoed from the far end of the room.

Alexa straightened the folders she completed and followed Greg down the hall. Donella's door stood open as they passed. Donella sat at her desk watching the doorway with an unenthused expression. Alexa didn't know if the dour look was intended for her or Greg or something unrelated.

Resuming her seat Alexa politely listened to Greg discuss file structure.

"Greg," she said, "I don't mean to interrupt you, but I've been using computers for the past couple of years. I understand file structure, saving, startup sequences... I even know a little bit of DOS. Can we fast-forward into actually how you do receivables for this company? Otherwise, my time is better spent helping Lisa with her file conversion."

"Not all computer systems are the same," he said.

"I understand that, but we've covered the basics. It's time to move into the application."

He shifted in his seat with his lips thinned in displeasure. "If you're such an expert, then why am I training you?"

"You haven't shown me anything to do with A.R., just computer basics."

"The computer is *essential* to this job," he said angrily. "It's not like you can just flip a switch and expect the numbers to fall into place."

"Of course not. I need to see where you get the numbers."

"In the computer."

They sat staring at each other. Surely he thought she was an idiot.

"It's clear I don't understand the complexities of this job," she said. "Why don't I go back and help Lisa for the rest of the afternoon so you can actually get something done today and we'll start tomorrow off brand new where I just take notes as you go through a typical day"

"No two days are alike."

"Ok. I feel like I've upset you so can we just start fresh tomorrow?" Without waiting for a response Alexa left Greg's desk and returned to the copy room for the rest of the day.

Chapter Eleven

"Good morning!" Alexa said to Heather as she entered the office.

"Donella wants you to see her first thing," Heather said.

"Crap, that can't be good," Alexa said, exchanging glances with Valerie.

Heather offered a sympathetic grin as she picked up the ringing telephone.

With a deep sigh, Alexa pushed through the big doors into the office. She resigned herself to the fact she would be dismissed for her confrontation with Greg the previous day.

"Ms. Swanson, you wanted to see me?" Alexa asked from the doorway.

"Donella. Please call me Donella," she said. "Come in and sit down." As Alexa sat in one of the beige chairs a man entered the office and closed the door. "Lexie, this is Jeff Larson, our finance manager."

Alexa thought his presence odd for a simple termination of a temporary worker.

Jeff stood next to the chair beside Alexa and extended his hand. She clumsily shook his hand from her seat.

"How do you do," he said with a pleasant smile. He pulled a chair toward the side of the desk so that he could face both Alexa and Donella at the same time. He crossed an ankle over the opposite knee and folded his hands in his lap giving an air of casualness.

Why did he need to be so casual?

"Lexie," he said, "will you recount everything that transpired yesterday? What was covered while you were shadowing Greg and then what led you to work in the copy room?"

What the hell did Greg say to these people? Wait, wasn't Jeff supposed to be on vacation?

"Um, well," Alexa said, "we spent the morning reviewing computer basics – booting up, login, password security, and then we broke for lunch. And when I came back..."

Jeff held up a hand with a confused look on his face. He glanced over to Donella. "Didn't you say she had previous data experience?"

"I do," Alexa said. "It was all redundant information."

"But it took all morning?" Jeff asked.

Alexa nodded. She pulled her purse to her lap and dug out the green notebook Valerie had given her the previous morning. "I took a lot of notes," she said as she fanned six pages of handwriting.

"Oh. So you asked a lot of questions. Just being thorough," Jeff said.

"No, I didn't say anything at all. He just kept talking."

His eyebrows raised then lowered and his face held a strained expression. Alexa couldn't decide if it was anger or humor, or a combination of the two.

"May I look at your notebook?" He asked. He quickly held up a hand. "Don't feel obliged if you have anythi..."

"No, there's nothing in here but rudimentary directions on booting computers," Alexa said as she extended the notebook to Jeff.

He flipped through the pages and looked up at her. "Where's the rest?"

"That's everything."

His face filled with confusion. "When did he train you, give you your passwords, guide you through our software?"

"That never happened."

Jeff handed the book back to her. "Okay, you said you went to lunch and then I interrupted you. What happened when you returned?"

Alexa took a second to consider if she should say Greg hadn't completed his break. She looked to Donella realizing maybe this conversation had nothing to do with her. "Um, Greg hadn't finished his lunch so I left to help Lisa like I had done on Monday. And, uh, a little while later Greg found me, was upset that I didn't tell him where I was going, and I followed him back to the desk."

"Go on," Jeff said.

"Well, he said he was going to cover file structure and I... well I said I already understood that and asked to jump ahead on his daily tasks and show me how to do receivables here. I was, um, out of line and kind of upset him so I returned to the copy room."

Jeff's raised his eyebrows again. "You weren't training with him in the afternoon?"

"No."

Jeff and Donella exchanged looks. "Donella, will you verify this?"

Donella picked up the telephone and dialed a number. Alexa wondered what the hell was going on. She suspected Greg was in trouble, but maybe she was too. Her already racing heart felt like it lodged into her throat. She smelled her fear rising. Alexa focused on lowering her fear and slowing her heart as she listened to Donella talk on the phone. The call ended and Donella looked to Jeff with a simple nod.

"Well then," Jeff said, running his hand through his hair. "Luke Avery's bill is incorrect and something in the back of my head says we need to review all of Greg's work. It's not how I wanted to spend the rest of my vacation, but it looks like I'll have to get the last three weeks of data loaded onto an independent drive and run a cross-check..."

"Is that an automated process or does it have to be done by hand?" Alexa asked.

"The system will flag all files with modification," he said.

"So everything still needs to be physically reviewed? That's basically what I did at my last job."

"Really?"

Alexa nodded. "Compare and contrast, look for irregularities and outliers. It will take me at least a day to get my bearings and compile the paper copies – fortunately, I know where to find those."

A look of relief swept over Jeff. "That would be great. So let's get you started on pulling copies of the last four weeks of billing and receivables and I will get the data retrieval set up on Dan's old computer." He looked over to Donella and said, "We will have to isolate Greg's terminal and get Lexie a new login and appropriate access."

"Okay, I'll get that set up immediately," Donella said.

"No, you need to talk to the partners first thing. I have to get started on this data crap. If they have any questions they'll need to come back to the server room."

"Well, Erin can get her set up while I deal with the partners," Donella said as she stood up.

Alexa scrambled to her feet as Jeff stood.

"Okay," he said. "I'll isolate his computer and get rolling on the data retrieval." He stopped in the doorway and turned to face Alexa. "I realize you're here on a temporary basis, but thank you for stepping up." He spun away before Alexa could respond.

Donella whisked past Alexa and motioned for her to follow. They walked into the cubicle area closest to Donella's door, stopping at the first desk on the right. The woman looked up appearing annoyed.

"Erin, this is Lexann. I gave you her paperwork yesterday to process. Would you get her set up with computer access and figure out a place for her to work? Greg's space is unavailable for a while. By the way, he is no longer with the firm so once you have Lexie set up let's get his termination paperwork rolling."

Erin's eyebrows peaked but she didn't seem otherwise surprised. "Okay. Lexie, take a seat while I get this started." She waved to the empty chair, then started writing a list.

By the time Alexa sat down, Donella had walked away. Erin began typing so Alexa sat quiet, taking in Erin's workspace – a sea of exact neatness and one houseplant. Alexa wondered if she used a ruler to get everything so evenly spaced on her desk.

"What's your middle name?" Erin asked.

Alexa snapped her head to look at Erin. "Marie."

"Okay." Erin resumed typing.

Worried she should have given a different middle name Alexa sighed and hoped this wouldn't bite her in the ass later. Three sheets of paper churned out of a desktop printer. Erin pulled the first sheet off, placing it in a blue folder. She handed the second to Alexa and asked her for a signature. Alexa accepted the offered pen and paused, curious where she could find a flat surface. She didn't want to disturb Erin's desk, but a small corner remained empty so Alexa awkwardly placed the bottom of the paper there long enough to scribble her new name.

With a nod, Erin accepted Alexa's form – Alexa didn't even bother to read what she had just signed, worried she would use the wrong name.

"Follow me," Erin said.

Alexa scrambled to her feet, grabbing her purse off the floor.

Erin looked down at Alexa's purse and back up at Alexa. "You know it's bad luck to put your purse on the floor?" Erin turned without waiting for Alexa's response and walked out of the cubicle into the maze of cubicle walls.

Flaring her nose Alexa didn't detect anything more than the faint scent of tin on Erin. She expected at least a hint of witch between the dry reception and the wives' tale comment.

"Our layout here is for the paralegals to be positioned close to their lawyers and the rest of the staff to be on this side of the office," Erin said gesturing toward her desk.

"That's fine," Alexa said. "I'm pretty sure being close to the records room will be useful as I work through Greg's recent billings."

Erin turned to face Alexa. "Oh, that makes sense. Okay, let's head over here instead." She walked into a bare cubicle with only a chair and computer. "If you need a desktop printer you'll have to work that out with Donella and Jeff, but the workhorse of the office is just over on that wall," Erin said pointing beyond the cubicle. "It's a dot matrix that's slow and constantly running. Hopefully, you can appreciate it as background noise, but this does place you closest to the records room."

Chapter Twelve

Piles of client folders surrounded Alexa in the cubicle. She separated each pile according to the week of their most recent billing and instructed Lisa to place any new files on the floor. The whole space looked chaotic, but Alexa knew where to find everything.

Valerie leaned on the edge of the cubicle wall. "Hungry?"

Alexa finished entering the September bill for Samuelson and looked at Valerie. Hungry? What time was it? She looked at the computer screen – six p.m. She looked back at Valerie. "Not really, but I guess I should stop for the night."

"Probably. Are you at a point where you can wrap up?"

Alexa placed a post-it note on the September bill to flag where she left off. "Yep. I think this is as good of a place to stop as any."

"You're putting in a lot of hours on this project. Does this mean you're sticking around?" Valerie asked.

"If that's okay with you."

"Of course it is! We were earnest in our offer and you may stay as long as you like." Valerie tilted her head. "Sarah is going to be so excited!"

Alexa smiled. "Thank you."

"Do you need to come in tomorrow?"

"Yeah, it would be helpful."

"Well so do I," Valerie said. "Sarah is going to hate we're both working on a Saturday. We're going to have to bribe her with a shopping trip or something."

"Shopping would be a nice diversion," Alexa said. She logged out of the computer, grabbed her purse, and followed Valerie out of the office.

"Are you finding anything in those files?"

"I think so, but I need a little more time to collect the information. If my hunch is correct we will be going back to the beginning of Greg's employment to get a grasp of the size of the problem."

"This sounds criminal," Valerie said with a raised eyebrow.

Alexa puckered her mouth as she scowled. "I would hate to make that speculation when it could really be just a matter of incompetence."

"But it's a possibility."

"Well yeah, but that's not for me to decide. My job is to pull the records and show the patterns of inconsistency and I think I found a pattern, but there may be other patterns too."

With a nod of approval, Valerie said, "In an office filled with lawyers that is the absolute smartest approach. The partners will value what you're doing." She sighed. "I should have binded him earlier."

"What?"

"Binding? Or earlier?" Valerie asked as she locked the building doors.

"Uh, both."

"I've never had a good feeling about Greg," Valerie said. "I always know when someone is lying, even you." She winked. "But, wow, Greg? Almost everything he ever said was veiled in half-truths. So I should have binded him as soon as I had the chance instead of waiting until last week."

Alexa got in the car and pulled the door closed. "So what is binding?"

"It is a spell to prevent harm. It can be to prevent harm to you or others, harm to an event, or harming oneself. I chose to bind him from doing harm to the law office."

"How do you know it will work?"

Valerie flashed a smile. "It already has. I did the spell last Friday after lunch. He left early with a stomach ache. Then on Monday, his computer dropped off the network at least three times that I heard of. On Tuesday all of his passwords had to be reset – I know this only because I could hear him down the hall complaining to one of the partners that he wasn't able to run some report. On Wednesday he was working with you and then he quit. Binding blocked him each and every time his intent was to commit malice."

"Is it hard to do? To bind someone?"

"No, not at all. It's one of the easier spells to learn." Valerie drove out of the parking lot and Alexa noticed movement on top of a building across the street. Long shadows from the setting sun hid most of the building, but as she strained to watch, Alexa spotted someone jump to the ground. The jump didn't concern her – a single-story building was simple, she had been jumping out of trees and off her family's roof since grade school. The three-story art building at her college took a bit more skill, which of course she had mastered. No, the concern was, as she had recently discovered, that people who jump off of buildings were usually vampires. In Brentwood the queen's guard had routine patrols that included rooftops. Was this the practice here in Radcliff or was someone following her?

"Huh?" Alexa said, snapping her head to Valerie.

"I said a vampire owns that company. It's a heating and air conditioning service, they've done work at our office and seem pretty professional, but there's always someone guarding the building."

"Oh."

"Anyway like family recipes, spells vary from person to person and according to what's available. The way I was taught to bind was to have something connected to the person like hair or a possession – I tore an old page out of his desk calendar where he had written deadlines that had already passed. The piece of paper wasn't really personal, but the handwriting was. Hair would have been even better, but..." Valerie made a face. "I made sure to use a page from a previous month so as not to impact his future plans, but also something he wouldn't notice missing. I didn't want to cause too much chaos, just bind him from hurting the company. Now Sarah just writes the person's name on paper and it seems equally effective, so maybe any calendar page would have been good. I just prefer to have something as personal as possible. The next step is to wrap twine or black thread around the item, and speak your intention like, 'I bind Greg Jorgenson from doing harm to Emerson, Murray, McNeil Law Offices and its employees.' Then just stash it away in a safe place until you are satisfied your mission was accomplished."

"Does that create a large stash of things?"

"That depends on how many people you bind. It does explain why so many weird things are found inside of walls during remodeling," Valerie said. "If you use Sarah's method then it's easier to just tuck in the back of your grimoire, which is what I did with

Greg's calendar page."

"So you hold onto it forever?"

"Until you are sure the situation has passed. While Greg is no longer associated with the firm he could still cause malice. I'll probably hold onto that calendar page for a very long time."

Alexa tilted her head and shrugged. "In about ten years you can get rid of it. He'll be dead."

Valerie snapped her head to glare at Alexa then returned her attention to the road. "What happens to him?"

"Does he have asthma? At his death, he keeps squeezing an inhaler and not getting relief so he panics which makes his breathing even more strained until everything goes dark. It's dark for a long time so I assume he passes out."

Valerie glares at her, looks back to the road, and then again at Alexa. "That sounds horrible!"

"The panic portion is pretty scary. I caught my breath several times sitting next to him it bothered me so much, but once the vision goes dark it's peaceful."

"How often do these visions hit you?"

"I'm never without them," Alexa said. "If I'm alone then mine is there, just looping over and over. It's quick and short. At this point in my life it's just white noise so to watch it would a take conscious effort, or like now that I'm talking about it then that sort of mutes yours which has been looping since you approached my desk. Which by the way, yours is a lot more soothing than mine. In fact, Greg's was even more soothing than yours with over ten minutes of peaceful quiet until it looped back to the beginning and I have to listen to him gasp for air, click the inhaler thingy, and feel his sense of panic. It takes a lot of mental gymnastics to push those sounds and feelings to the side."

"You see your own death? What does that look like?"

"Something hits my neck and a pain shutters back toward my spine. I gasp for air then everything goes dark. It's like just a couple of nanoseconds – pain, gasp, black-out."

"What hits you?"

"I don't know," Alexa said. She saw Valerie's expression and anticipated a string of questions. "You have to understand," she said. "I see people's death only from their perspective, not like from a TV camera hovering overhead. And I see it only from the point the death has been activated. So I don't see what happens beforehand, meaning I don't usually know what caused it. So, for me, I don't know what hits me. Oddly enough though, I recently met someone who will be there when I die, evidently being killed at the same time."

Valerie swerved the car as she whipped her head to look at Alexa. She straightened the vehicle back into the lane and glanced several times at the passenger seat. Alexa cleared her throat, amused by the expression on Valerie's face.

"The person says my name, it's the last thing I hear before the blackness hits. Well, I could never place this person's voice until a certain conversation when everything started to make sense. Their death is a searing pain in the middle back. Again, I don't know for certain, but like a knife or something. Their pain is sharp but they're more focused on a woman whose head is lying on the ground in a huge puddle of blood. It's disgusting."

The car slowed down and came to a stop on the side of the road. Valerie twisted to face Alexa. "Are you telling me you're decapitated?"

Alexa nodded.

"Who the hell gets decapitated these days? I mean that is a brutal attack! Especially with someone watching!"

"Well, that person is also being killed at the same time."

"But why decapitation?"

"I try not to think about it too much, but I suspect it's somebody who knows what I'm capable of and is smart enough not to fight me."

A flash of shock crossed Valerie's face and she quickly erased all expression. Alexa watched the lawyer kick in. "Exactly what are you capable of?" Valerie asked.

"Well, so far killing two vampires and then the tussle with my father who is pretty damn strong. Then *his* father stepped in, who is even stronger. Granted he took it easy on me, but it was clear I gave him a run for his money. And then, of course, there's my witchcraft. Dunno. I may be inexperienced in both areas right now, but I imagine by the time that fateful day rolls around I will have mastered a few things and likely pissed off the wrong people. Yay me."

"I don't understand. Why were you fighting with your dad and grandfather?"

Alexa shook her head. "It was about my boyfriend and they were just trying to get me out of there, but I fought back. That's when I realized my dad might have higher connections than just being a run-of-the-mill vampire."

Valerie nodded understanding. She opened her mouth to say something then shook her head. "Well, back to knowing about how you die, at least now you know how to fend it off."

"Right, but I'm pretty sure I'm defending the person watching me die. So someone knows to use that person as a distraction."

"That means you're murdered by someone you know?"

Alexa pondered that possibility. "Not necessarily, but the killer knows of me, of my abilities, and my ties to the person I'm protecting."

"Wow."

Valerie stared at Alexa. Alexa nodded and diverted her eyes to her hands. She looked up to find Valerie still staring at her. "I hope I can trust you telling you this."

Valerie nodded.

"The guy I'm trying to get over, my boyfriend, he is the one who calls my name." Alexa watched Valerie's eyes widen. "I told him what I saw. Of course, it freaked him out." She recalled the night she layed in his arms, realizing how much she loved him even though she had to walk away. Tears filled her eyes. "But like I told him, it gives me hope. I know one day we will reunite. But like all of my visions, the why, when, how, and where are all unknown to me."

Alexa sniffled and looked away. "I'm always frustrated that my visions and nightmares don't give me more information. I mean why do I have them if I can't prevent what's going to happen? It just seems cruel to know these random details."

"I doubt they're random details," Valerie said. "It seems to me you're either still developing your skills or the time has not yet arrived for you to use the information you're being given."

"I can't imagine what more skills are necessary to develop with visions," Alexa said.

"Maybe you can spend more time with the visions paying

attention to the way things sound or smell or non-physical sensations. I mean you've been viewing them through the lens of someone who didn't know about witches and vampires. Watch these visions with a new eye."

Alexa watched Valerie as she pulled the car back into traffic. Valerie's death scene played out with Sarah's ghost floating into the room. Alexa took a moment to listen and heard the distant sounds of beeps and carts of a busy hospital. She focused on scents and noted the antiseptic smell... and urine.

"You piss yourself when you die."

Valerie laughed. "I think most people do, but why are you focusing on my death and not your own? You're murdered!"

"When I'm a very old woman. Chances are the person won't be born for several more decades. Besides, my scene is super short. Yours takes time and isn't traumatic so it's easier to pluck out scents and sounds."

"And sensations?"

Alexa leaned her head back as Valerie's scene played again. She shook her head. "There's no sensation, at least not physically. As for the sounds and scents those are super faint, not necessarily because they're far away but probably because you're drifting away from the physical realm. The only sensation you have is peace. It's a very nice death."

"As disturbing as it is to learn details of my death, finding out it's peaceful is, well... it's a blessing. It's a wonderful gift you've given me. Thank you."

"It's one of the reasons I like being around you," Alexa said giggling. "You're quiet."

Valerie laughed.

"But I should be thanking you. Challenging me to dig into these visions could help me find out what I'm supposed to do with them. I'm glad I met you, other than your quiet death."

Chapter Thirteen

"Lexie, we didn't bother to ask - do you enjoy shopping?" Sarah asked from the front seat.

"Yeah!"

Sarah turned to face Alexa. "Really? I mean I have a long list and there are so many cute shops so if I go overboard you have to speak up."

"Pretty sure I can keep up."

"If not, you can join me," Valerie said looking in the rearview mirror. "I tend to bail after two hours. There's a restaurant with a great patio and good wine."

"Sounds like I have options!"

Exiting the highway they followed signs for Charlestown Historic District and turned at McDonald's where the modern world faded into a 1740 French settlement... well except for the presence of cars, and shoppers in modern clothing. Alexa craned her head to look at the different shops: tobacco, quilt, Christmas, board games, jewelry, and candy.

"Ooh, hand-dipped ice cream!" Alexa said.

Valerie chuckled. "There's also kettle corn in one of the parking lots."

Watching a woman struggling to hold a door open as a little girl attempted to exit while grasping a towering ice cream cone, Alexa twisted in her seat to watch the pair uneventfully make their way to the sidewalk. She chastised herself for hoping for any other outcome.

"All of the time?" Alexa returned her focus towards the front of the car, just in time to see Valerie turn off Main Street.

"At least on Saturdays," Valerie said.

"This is like an amusement park without the rides," Alexa said.

"Carnival rides are here for Settler Fest," Sarah said.

"When is that?"

"Uh, I think in early summer. I'm not exactly sure."

They turned onto Third Street and Alexa noticed the contrast from the previous streets - rundown houses with chipped paint, cracked front walks, and rusty iron fences. One house boasted a hair salon and another yoga classes. Valerie parked in front of a two-story duplex where the ground-level unit appeared to be a residence with toys cluttering the doorway. When Alexa stepped out of the car she noticed a mangy yellow mum in a faded planter near the gate.

A sign for "Charlotte's Candle Shoppe" hung above the porch on the far left of the building. Valerie opened the door revealing a stairwell to the second floor. Alexa mused the residence and the business were backward – wouldn't it make more sense to have the store at street level?

Scents of different candles filled the air, becoming stronger as Alexa followed Sarah upstairs. Alexa stood on the top step taking in the open space. She assumed at some point the area had been cleared of all vestiges of being an apartment except the exterior walls to maximize retail space. Shelving and tables of matching dark wood leaned against ancient brick walls. Pendant lamps hung overhead compensating for insufficient light from the front windows. The soft music of flutes and chimes floated through the air and a stick of incense burned somewhere out of sight.

Choosing not to follow Sarah or Valerie, Alexa strolled around the perimeter of the shop perusing the various packs of incense, chimes, stones, jewels, charms, and other baubles. At the top of one shelf sat nondescript narrow boxes. At first, Alexa thought they were extra inventory but the faint handwriting caught her attention. One box was marked "Vampire Stake" and the other "Nickel Chain."

Nickel? Not silver?

Alexa startled when she felt a hand on her shoulder. "Come on," Valerie said.

She resisted and darted a look back to the box with nickel chains. "Why nickel?"

With an uneasy look, Valerie ran a finger over her necklace. "It burns vampire flesh."

Alexa stared at the thin chain resting on Valerie's chest. Told she was allergic to nickel, and that her jewelry had to be all silver or gold, Alexa's eyes flicked back to Valerie's face. "Sarah wears one too?"

Slowly Valerie nodded and Alexa raised an eyebrow.

"It's pretty. Probably need another twenty to be of any protection, though," Alexa said.

"You're not offended?" Valerie whispered.

"Of course not," Alexa said softly. "That you don't lace all of my meals with sage to temper my 'evil side' is actually quite surprising."

Valerie laughed. "Come on, help me pick out some candles." She led Alexa to the set of shelves closest to the cash register.

"I'd say you're looking for clarity." Valerie pulled a white pillar off the shelf and placed it in Alexa's hands. Alexa took a deep breath to redirect her attention away from the death scenes in her head and focus on the weight of the candle.

"Brown is for grounding. That would be good too." Valerie fished a brown candle from the back of the shelf. "The colors are fairly obvious in their purpose. Red is for love and passion, blue for tranquility, green for finance and luck." She grabbed two blue candles and another white.

"What about the scents?" Alexa asked.

"To make your house smell good," Sarah said.

Alexa turned to find Sarah behind her, grinning. "Don't dismiss the power of aroma therapy, though. Do you have a favorite scent?"

"Pine, it always makes me think of Christmas. For the rest of the year, I like rose and most the fruit scents. Not a big fan of the spicy ones."

"Bit old to be learning the basics," the old lady said. Alexa had felt her constant gaze since she left the stairwell. A squat woman wrapped in a shawl, perched on a stool behind the counter - she looked every bit like a grandmother except for her brown hair and lack of wrinkles. Alexa saw her death of lying on the floor, gasping for air with something lodged in her throat. With the vision so crisp, she knew the woman would die within the year.

"I wasn't raised in a home that practiced and there were, um, other difficulties," Alexa said.

"Sleeping with vampires sure ain't a path to truth."

Alexa gasped as she realized the penetration of the woman's statement. She looked at the woman with a near-desperate plea to take it back. She couldn't explain to the woman that she had only slept with one man, a man she dearly loved. The two other vampire scents on her were the ones she killed, deaths that played frequently in her mind, filling her with worry and guilt. Could she have dealt with those situations differently? Anger replaced guilt - no one trained her, always telling her to just be human.

Valerie slipped an arm around Alexa's shoulder. "She's in our care now and so it's up to us to show her the way."

The woman's face rested just a bit, satisfied with Valerie's attempt to save Alexa's poor misguided soul. As they deposited the candles on the counter, Alexa caught the scent of an animal lurking at the feet of the woman on the stool but she couldn't see past the cash register.

Valerie leaned in and tipped her head to a door at the back of the store. "May we enter?"

The woman hopped off her stool and opened a plain brown door marked "employees only". She stepped to the side, allowing Valerie to enter, but then moved further away as Alexa followed Sarah. The space felt raw showing the true age of the building. And while the room wasn't especially large it definitely captured more sunlight than the rest of the store. Windows decorated with strands of cut crystals and pendulums casting prisms in different directions. A simple shelf housing chalices and cloths ran the length of the back wall with a small cauldron at one end next to a cage of mice.

A dry aquarium with a desert scape caught Alexa's attention. A cricket jumped and a black tendril stretched out from behind a rock. Alexa assumed a tarantula resided in the aquarium so she moved to the opposite end of the room toward a skull sitting in the far corner.

Under the watchful eye of the shop owner, Valerie and Sarah hovered around the chalices passing one back and forth. Alexa stared at the skull; she could smell it - a human. She saw the person's death, a woman in full skirts, struck by a horse. She gazed into the eyes and felt an essence, an energy, in there and not of the dead woman – a different entity. Alexa drew closer and hovered her hands around the skull. In what felt like a flash, she jolted and jumped back.

Alexa turned around to see the shocked looks of the shop owner, Valerie, and Sarah. "What the hell is in there?" she asked surprised.

"Something that does not like you," the woman said with a sneer. A cat appeared in the doorway and glared at Alexa. When she took notice the cat arched its back and hissed.

She turned to Sarah and Valerie. "Take as long as you need. I think it's time for me to get some fresh air." Alexa quickly exited the shop, the cat following her down the stairs to the door as if to escort her out. Before Alexa closed the door she turned to the cat and growled like a vampire. The cat jumped and scampered back upstairs.

Alexa chuckled as she walked to Valerie's car. She thought a silver Audi looked horribly out of place on this street. Her friend Megan had a beat-up Toyota that would have fit in better.

Ugh, the friends she left behind in Brentwood! She had been away from them for only a few weeks and already missed them. What would they think of Alexa's little adventure on the road? Brie and Tess who helped her escape Brentwood were witches; they understood what was going on. They would adore Sarah and Valerie. They would adore Ms. Charlotte's shop. But the other four friends? They were human. They were supportive and loving and playful, but could they deal with knowing the truth about witches and vampires? Would they change how they interacted with Brie and Tess knowing they were witches? What would they think about Alexa having vampire fangs?

Slumped against the shiny Audi Alexa gazed down the street. She thought maybe after the initial shock of learning about vampires and witches her friends would accept Brie, Tess, and herself and even willingly help serve as buffers around vampires. Was it fair to ask them to do that?

What she did know is if Chloe was on this shopping trip she would be in hog heaven with all of the cool stores in this town while Lindsey and Jess joked around about spooky old buildings and Megan made friends with the cat.

Sarah and Valerie joined Alexa at the car. "Are you okay?" Sarah asked as she rubbed Alexa's arm.

"I'm fine. She knew what I was as soon as I walked in."

"Ms. Charlotte has no idea you're part vampire," Valerie said. "She said you're a powerful dark witch and warned us to be wary of you."

"I don't know," Sarah said. "Her cat seemed to sense something else. What happened when you left? He nearly leaped into her arms and started howling."

Alexa grinned. "I might have growled at it."

Sarah giggled. "Growl?"

Alexa replicated the sound. Sarah's eyes widened and her fear filled the air. She stared at Alexa for a bit and finally cleared her throat. "That's terrifying."

"And effective," Alexa said.

"But what happened with the skull?" Valerie asked.

"Somebody is trying to contact her," Sarah said.

"What do you mean?" Alexa and Valerie asked at the same time. They looked at each other and back at Sarah.

"There was a force in there trying to reach Alexa, but didn't know how to communicate with her."

"Friendly or evil?" Alexa asked.

"Um… strong." Sarah looked skyward as she searched for words. "I didn't sense menace but uncertainty. Maybe testing you?"

"But Ms. Charlotte said it didn't like me."

"I think Charlotte was imposing her feelings onto the situation," Valerie said. She turned to Sarah. "What do you mean strong?"

"Lots of energy but it came in so fast and then disappeared that I couldn't read it. It seemed like feminine energy but I really don't know."

"The skull was female," Alexa said.

"How the hell can you tell *that*?" Valerie asked.

"The death vision hit me. I could see her death as a horse struck her. It was like in the old west with like, stagecoaches and dirt roads and old-timey buildings where you would see a saloon."

"And that is who was trying to reach you?" Valerie asked.

Alexa shook her head. "No, the vision hit me but I sensed something else inside of the skull. Sarah's word 'energy' describes it perfectly. I put my hands near the skull and it was just, I don't know, pulsing. But it was distinct from the person who the skull belonged to."

"And then it just zapped you?"

"Eh, I wasn't electrocuted or anything but I definitely felt it whiz past me." Alexa turned to Sarah. "Now you have me wondering who or what is trying to contact me. And why?"

Chapter Fourteen

Alexa exited The Tipped Cup carrying a bag with three different teas. She found Valerie leaning against the aged brick wall with her arms crossed and eyes closed, absorbing the afternoon sun.

"You're done shopping," Alexa said.

"mmhmm."

"And Sarah is getting more energized by each store."

"Yep."

"How long can she last?"

Valerie took a deep breath. "Hours."

"Time to retreat to that patio you were talking about?"

Valerie pushed off the wall and faced Alexa. "Yes, I'm done for the day. But, please, keep shopping. When Sarah comes out I'll head down the street." She pointed southward, but Alexa didn't see the destination.

"Well, my wallet can't handle any more impulse purchases," Alexa said. "I think I'll join you."

Sarah exited the store with a wide grin and a large bag.

"Restocked?" Valerie asked.

"Yes, but I'll need to return. I spotted several things for my Christmas shopping."

"Of course," Valerie said with a conciliatory grin.

Sarah turned to Alexa. "Are you bailing or do you want to hit a few more stores?"

"I'm ready for wine," Alexa said.

"I think I am too," Sarah said.

Valerie leaned around Alexa to stare with raised eyebrows at Sarah. "You have at least two more hours of shopping left in your veins."

"We hit my favorite stores and that's good enough for now," Sarah said. "It's such a beautiful day, why waste it inside? Let's go eat and have a couple of glasses of wine then plan to come back when the streets are all decked out for Christmas." She turned to Alexa. "It is so gorgeous here with the lights and garland and they have Victorian carolers. The shops have mead and mulled wine. It's just the best."

Valerie glared at Sarah.

"I'm hungry," Sarah said in a subdued confession.

Valerie laughed and turned toward the restaurant. As they walked Alexa took note of the various buildings, admiring the architecture. She easily pictured the neighborhood adorned in pine wreaths and red bows.

The Sunflower Bistro stood mid-block with a bold, yellow sunflower on its placard dangling above the sidewalk. Two skinny doors stood open, welcoming hungry patrons. Alexa twisted to look at the size of the doors as she passed through trying to assess their height – she decided they towered close to ten feet tall.

Sarah tugged on her arm breaking Alexa from her door survey to follow Valerie. The hostess led them to a table at the back edge of the patio. Mid-afternoon sunlight sparkled between yellowing leaves of the trees and tall bushes surrounding the terrace. Beckoned by a wired chair enshrined by the dancing sunlight, Alexa sat down and absorbed the warmth.

"This place is exquisite!" Alexa said, craning her head back.

"Wait until you try their food," Valerie said with a knowing smile.

"I love their white bean chili," Sarah said. "But honestly, everything is good."

"I can imagine sitting here in the evening with the fire crackling," Alexa said nodding to the firepit behind Sarah.

"You know, we never stay late enough for a fireside dinner," Sara said.

"Well nothing is preventing us from sticking around," said Valerie.

Alexa flipped the laminated menu a few times. She looked at Valerie and said, "I know you come here for wine but Sarah's mention of chili has me wanting a bowl and a good beer."

Valerie nodded. "I agree. There's something in the air that begs for a hearty stout."

Alexa laughed. "Funny you mention stout. I come from a family that has strong opinions about beer. I don't know how many times my grandfather has mentioned some Swiss weissbier and how it's superior to any bottle of piss found here in the states and then goes on with a long tirade about the superiority of stout over lager. Evidently, a good American stout doesn't exist so he just drinks wine while he visits us."

"Well he's wrong," Valerie said. "Mass-produced beer like you find at the store is crap, but places like this have suppliers connected to smaller breweries. It's the same thing with their wine and using local wineries, which I absolutely love. When we leave here I will buy at least a case, usually, two if Sarah's hands aren't too full from her shopping."

"They have flights of beer here, so you can sample different ones," Sarah suggested.

The waitress arrived at the table ready to take drink orders.

"We aren't very beer literate," Valerie said. "Our friend here would like to try a variety of lagers and stouts… actually Sarah and I would too. Can you make some suggestions?"

The waitress pointed to different selections in Valerie's menu. Alexa watched her with curiosity. Her death wasn't overly interesting as she faded into darkness sitting in a recliner with a book in her lap. The woman's scent however carried heavy notes of wet copper with the lightest touch of clover - another witch/human hybrid.

Alexa snapped her attention back to the conversation. The server stared at her waiting for a response. "I'm sorry," Alexa said, "my mind wandered off thinking about my grandfather and his beer comparisons. It's been a while since I last saw him." Alexa offered a weak grin in the wake of her lie – only weeks had passed since she had seen, and fought, her vampire grandfather.

The waitress said, "I heard you mention a Swiss beer. Possibly Edelweiss? We carry something very similar, would you like to try that as well?"

Alexa nodded. "Yes, that would be great!"

"Would you ladies like an appetizer? Hot pretzel?"

Valerie took a quick glance at Sarah and Alexa then nodded. "Yes we would like some pretzels, but we would also like your white chili."

The waitress grinned as she wrote out the order. "I'll be back with your drinks."

After the waitress walked away, Alexa said as quietly as possible, "she's part witch." Met with raised eyebrows of disbelief Alexa nodded her head. "I doubt she knows it. It's super weak." She looked around the patio to ensure no one else heard her comment.

Valerie raised an eyebrow. "Like Brenda at work?"

"Weaker, much weaker."

"It's so interesting you can pick up all these subtle nuances," Valerie said.

Alexa nodded. "I'm surprised when I can detect anything at all. It's such a new skill."

"What do you mean new?" Sarah asked.

Alexa said as she tapped her lip. "Since my, uh, dentistry has changed I'm more sensitive to smells."

"Does it work for everything?" Sarah asked, "Like with food?"

Alexa nodded. "I could probably detect all of the ingredients of the chili before tasting it."

Valerie's face lit up. "Oh, we're going to need proof of that. I'll write down what you say and then tomorrow I will recreate this chili based on your notes."

Alexa laughed. "Challenge accepted! This sounds fun!"

She adjusted her chair to better watch people walking in and out of shops lining the street. Humans and witches accounted for most of the crowd but an occasional pair of vampires strolled down the sidewalk. Witches and vampires walking past each other without any acknowledgment still surprised Alexa. She watched the humans drift between the groups completely unaware of their purpose as buffers, the safety cloak each group used to avoid confrontation with the other.

Two vampire men exited a plain brown door between shops and walked down the street beyond Alexa's view. A second pair of men exited, followed by another man. They also casually walked down the street in the same direction.

"What's behind that door between the jewelry store and the tobacco shop?" Alexa asked.

Sarah twisted in her seat to look at the row of buildings. "Maybe it's an apartment up for rent?" Another man exited as she spoke.

"That's not the type of traffic coming out of there," Valerie said.

A pair of vampire women walking toward the door made an abrupt turn toward the Sunflower Bistro. Three more men exited the door and followed the path of the previous men.

"Maybe it's a lodge meeting or something," Sarah said.

In the window above the tobacco shop, the curtains opened and a woman surveyed the street below. She scanned across the Sunflower patio and then to her left in the direction where the men all headed. She stared in that direction for a short time before she turned as if someone spoke to her and then she disappeared.

The two vampire women from the street arrived at the patio, following the hostess to a nearby table. Valerie and Sarah turned back to face Alexa, almost in unison, behaving as if humans had just arrived. Valerie smiled sweetly and tilted her head. "I still can't believe you spooked that cat."

Alexa had to think for a second about what cat she was talking about – oh the candle store! "That old woman did not like me."

"Well not after you terrified her poor kitty!" Sarah said.

"That damn thing had his back arched and every hair on his body standing straight up the moment I walked into that back room," Alexa said.

"If Ms. Charlotte had a broom she would have swept us out. She couldn't get us out of there fast enough!" Sarah said.

"And then the cat came scampering up the stairs," Valerie said. "Usually Ms. Charlotte chats up a storm, but she could barely tally up our candles, she was in such a rush."

"Did you decide on a chalice?" Alexa asked.

Valerie and Sarah looked at each other with blank expressions. "Well crap," Valerie said. "With all of the commotion we left them sitting in the back room."

"I guess you'll have to go back," Alexa said.

"We can find those at other stores closer to home," Valerie said.

"Ms. Charlotte's inventory really wasn't up to par," Sara said.

"It really wasn't," Valerie said. "She also didn't seem on top of her game."

"I'm sure my presence didn't help," Alexa said.

"No, she's going downhill." Valerie paused and glared at Alexa. "What do you know?"

"What?"

"Your expression changed. It was momentary, very quick, but I saw it."

Alexa had seen the woman's death, something she felt would happen in the near future – a collapse behind the counter with the cat howling as he circled her body. Alexa assumed a stroke as no pain resonated in her body other than what hit the floor. She debated what she could say with so many people in the vicinity. "Um, it's probably a good thing you have other stores for your supplies."

Raised eyebrows from both Valerie and Sarah greeted her.

"What did you do?" Sarah whispered.

"Nothing! I told you I can see... well, you know. Oh here comes the waitress."

Three flights of beer samples with a basket of pretzel nubs and dipping sauces were placed on the table. Sarah grabbed a pretzel and said, "Ooh, these are nice and warm!"

Alexa sipped the lightest of the beers noting tastes similar to the popular American beers she normally drank.

Valerie tipped her head toward the beers. "Try the dark one."

Alexa complied running the flavors around her mouth. "If coffee, oatmeal, and a beer had a child..."

Valerie laughed. "But is it good?"

"It's not bad, but it's not something I would seek out."

Sarah took a sip of hers and contorted her face. "No, that's nasty. Where did you get oatmeal out of that?"

"Eat a pretzel to clear your palate," Valerie said to Sarah.

Alexa picked up the tiny glass of weissbier. "Mm, this is good."

"Better than American piss?" Valerie asked.

"Uh, different. I wouldn't mind if either were set in front of me. I can only imagine the arguments my grandfather and I will have over this."

Sarah timidly sipped her glass of weissbier. "This is much better than that coffee stuff."

"Do you see reuniting with your family?" Valerie asked.

"I know for sure I'll reunite with my mom, so I assume my dad too."

"How are you so certain about reuniting with your mom?" Sarah asked.

Aware of eavesdroppers Alexa couldn't say how she saw her

mother's death scene with Alexa bending over her, crying. "Just a strong feeling," she said. "I mean, I already miss her. I'm sure at some point I'll break down and call her."

"What about your dad?"

"I don't know. I really miss the relationship we used to have, but I don't see how that will ever return. I feel betrayed."

"You need to forgive him at some point," Sarah said.

"I will, " Alexa said. "I just need time to work through it all."

"Why aren't you mad at your mom?" Sarah asked.

Alexa stared at her. "I… I honestly don't know." She ran the past months through her head and saw her mother's role in perpetuating the secrets and hiding Alexa's identity from her. She had an equal hand in raising Alexa as a human, keeping her ignorant of her witch and vampire lineages. Alexa questioned if the story about teaching witchcraft to hybrids was also a lie. And yet, Alexa held no animosity towards her mother. She shrugged her shoulders. "Dunno. Maybe I sense somehow she's as much of a victim in this as I am."

"Is she in danger?" Valerie asked.

Alexa shook her head. "No. She said something about my father's presence being a shield. There are issues with her mother. In fact, there was recently a confrontation with my grandmother that solidified I will never have anything to do with her ever again in my life. I don't want to call her my grandmother anymore – that sounds too loving. Maybe 'wretched bitch who birthed my mother.'"

"That's a bit harsh," Valerie said. Sarah nodded.

"I'm pretty sure the woman would kill me if she had the chance. Dunno, maybe she tried and I was oblivious. Who knows."

"Hmm, well, we've had our own struggles with family. Setting boundaries is a good start, but sometimes completely cutting them out of your life is the only option," Valerie said.

Alexa sipped a different beer from the flight board finding it okay, but still liking the weissbier better.

"Do you see your father being restricted or limited from your life?" Valerie asked.

"Probably not. He says he has done all of this to protect me. So maybe his methodology was wrong but his intent was right. I don't think he's tried to cause me harm."

Sarah smiled.

"What?" Alexa demanded.

"You're forgiving him," Sarah said.

As the waitress passed their table Alexa asked for a pint of the weissbier. She leaned back in her chair, soaking in the warm afternoon, listening to the gentle breeze rustle through the trees. In the distance, a motorcycle engine revved – far enough away not to detract from the calm washing over Alexa.

She leaned her head to the side and smiled at Sarah. "This is exactly what I needed."

"I'm glad you like it. We really enjoy coming here."

"This is the calm souls beg for."

"Totally agree," Sarah said. She nodded toward the doors. "It looks like our chili is arriving."

Alexa sat up, taking in a deep breath of the earthy scents surrounding the patio. She smiled again as a cozy chill ran down her body. The waitress placed three bowls of chili on their table and Alexa's fresh glass of beer while Valerie fished a notepad and pen from her purse.

Alexa shook her head. "That's a genuine notepad! Nothing like the tiny green one I carry."

"I'm a lawyer. You never know when something needs to be recorded."

"She has another in her car," Sarah said.

Valerie cast a stern look at Sarah then jerked her attention back to Alexa. "I'm ready."

Alexa pulled her bowl of chili toward her and closed her eyes as she inhaled the steam. "Okay, the obvious things are beans and turkey. There's a tinny scent to the beans so I'd say they came from a can. Now the turkey was roasted with rosemary and thyme. I'm sure other things like onion and garlic but I can't separate that from what was added while cooking the chili."

"You can tell it was roasted here?" Valerie asked.

"Not specifically where, but it was roasted recently and while the bird had been frozen at some point – there's a smell to that – none of this meat was frozen after it came out of the oven." Alexa sniffed the chili again. "Cumin, pepper... I guess white pepper, not that I can smell the difference but I don't see any telltale signs of black pepper. Oh and I smell fire." She paused to focus on the scents. "I think the green chilis were charred. I don't smell the can scent on anything other than the beans. I already said onion and garlic. Um, I swear I smell greasy chicken, so that has to be broth. I think that's freshly prepared too - again rosemary, onion, garlic, butter, wine, and parsley. Those last three are really subtle. Oh and sea salt."

She pointed at the bowl piled with chives, melting parmesan cheese, and bacon crumbles. "There's more bacon in there. I'd almost say the onion was sautéed in it. There are other herbs in there, um, something Italian. Oh oregano and basil, but there's another one, it's pungent."

Valerie tipped her spoon into her bowl and ran it under her nose. She shook her head. "I can't detect it."

"That's a lot of work for a pot of chili, " Sarah said.

"It makes sense they use their own chicken broth," Valerie said. "Their chicken salad is absolutely divine. It's certainly made with chicken roasted here. That flavor is infused deep in the meat."

"It is good," Sarah agreed.

"Fortunately I have homemade stock in the freezer, but I'll need to roast a turkey. I guess a trip to the grocery store will be in order tomorrow morning."

"Are you really going to make this?" Sarah asked.

"Absolutely! Lexie did the hard part. Now we have to see if I can get the portions right. Fire-roasted chilis are not something I would have thought to add."

Alexa remained aware of the two vampires at the next table despite her attempts to appear oblivious. She could tell from their scents they were civilian vampires, weaker than most except for scavengers. Alexa recalled her confrontation with a scavenger before leaving Brentwood - the man clearly wanted to take her back to his elderly grandmother as a meal; The old woman had just given Alexa a tour of a horribly small apartment. The vampires' stench of fish and rotten meat rose from Alexa's memory and she took a deep breath of the more pleasant scents currently surrounding her.

The two women at the neighboring table smelt like cooked ground beef, not at all unpleasant, and definitely better than the memory Alexa was trying to suppress. She knew the stronger the scent the weaker the vampire and that these two posed very little threat to her. In a casual glance, she looked over to the pair as they received their own bowls of white chili. She turned back to her table and grabbed a pretzel nugget off the tray to swirl in her bowl.

"Marjoram," said one of the vampires.

Alexa turned back to look at them again. They were staring at her.

"Marjoram," the woman repeated. "You missed marjoram in your recipe. I'm sorry but we were captivated by your breakdown."

Alexa looked back down at her nearly empty bowl. Lifting a spoon to her nose she sniffed. "Whoa, that's really subtle."

"It has to be part of the broth," the woman said. "I typically use marjoram when I roast chicken."

"I do too," Valerie said.

"You have an impeccable sense of smell," the woman said. The other nodded.

"Well, a basic understanding of cooking and spice shelves helps a lot," Alexa said.

The woman raised her eyebrows.

Alexa shrugged. "There have been a few rumors about someone in my father's family but we never talk about that."

The woman nodded understanding. She looked around as if to check if anyone was listening then leaned forward. "I hope you ladies parked nearby. Something suspicious has been going on across the street." She cautiously glanced to the upper floor. "I've never seen so much activity on a Saturday. I don't think we'll be returning for a while until things settle down."

"Then why did you come over here?" Valerie asked.

"To just turn around to go back to our car might have caught their attention. We were hoping they would clear out soon."

Alexa looked over to the mystery door. A man stood inside holding the door open as another man came out with a casual scan up and down the street then stepped to the side as a man and woman exited.

Alexa assumed the woman to be the same as the one who had been looking out the window earlier. Her attention darted up to the window as if to see if anyone was peeking out. Followed by the doorman and lookout, the couple headed in the opposite direction than the previous vampires.

Something about the doorman caught Alexa's attention – the shrug to readjust a recently donned jacket and the jerk of his head to tame his perfectly coifed hair. Or maybe his gait teetering on a strut? He looked like an asshole.

Realizing she was being watched by the two women warning her about vampire activity, Alexa returned her attention to the patio and the conversation at hand.

"But you're not in any danger are you?" Sarah asked.

"Lots of weird stuff has been happening for a while now so we just prefer to avoid any large gatherings of men."

"And who are the men from across the street?" Valerie asked.

Alexa's gaze returned to the group from the apartment as they made their way down the sidewalk.

"Hard call," the first woman said. "It could be a business meeting or nothing at all. Like she said, we're just trying not to attract attention."

A motorcycle revved its engine and then another. Alexa wrinkled her forehead. "Bikers?"

"Oh, those are the good guys," the second woman said pointing toward the revving engines.

"What?"

"They're the royal guard," the first woman said.

As the waitress came through the doorway their conversation stopped. Then the hostess brought a human couple to the patio, seating them near the vampires.

"Well," Alexa said, "thank you for the heads up."

The women nodded and turned back to their chili.

Chapter Fifteen

Motorcycles rumbled in the distance. Alexa couldn't see anything but heard commotion nearby and shouting in the distance. She moved to see what was going on only to discover she was restrained from moving her arms or legs and rolled up in a blanket or maybe a rug. Panic rippled through Alexa and she smelled her own fear.

She rocked to get loose without any success and someone kicked Alexa's feet, telling her to stay still. She didn't know where she was, what was restraining her, or who was on the outside. An awful stench from her coverings filled her nose as she rocked side to side. The roar of motorcycles neared and the noise increased with people screaming and yelling.

Her rocking intensified – Alexa refused to be left behind in the middle of who-knows-where, bound by who-knows-what. Normally able to control her fear, slow-building panic escalated to hysteria. Alexa thrashed against her restraints; panting and crying. She rolled back and forth, breathless. The noise in the distance dulled and Alexa bawled, terrified she had been left behind to suffocate in wretched darkness.

The restraints released and Alexa came up for air. She sat up gasping for air, blinded by a beam of bright light. Alexa shook her head and looked around. The air had changed from frigid and breezy to warm and still.

Another goddamned nightmare. Alexa looked around the tiny room illuminated by a streetlight. Placing her feet on the floor she leaned forward and shook the remnants of the constrained feeling from the dream.

In reviewing the nightmare she recalled the sounds of people moving around, she assumed fighting. Screams and shouting floated in the background and she remembered the scents of fear and death. But motorcycles? Oh... The bikers from Charlestown, the royal guard.

Relieved she discovered the source of her dream Alexa took a deep breath and wiped her tears. But what did it mean? Who would tie her up like that? Was the royal guard looking for her? Was she hiding and got stuck? Oh, that would be grand, hiding where no one knew to find her and get left behind to die all alone?

No, she reasoned with herself, that was not how she died. Alexa had seen her death like everyone else's and for however gruesome and awful she understood it to be, she was not stranded alone. So maybe she didn't die at this event, but someone tied her up. How did they accomplish that without her putting up a fight? Maybe she put up a fight but was outnumbered?

Anger bubbled up. Her father never taught her how to fight. Girls aren't supposed to fight. Only Eric took the time to teach her anything. She learned one maneuver for hand-to-hand combat, a way to kick her foot behind the enemy causing them to fall. The two men Alexa managed to kill died only because of her strength, intuition, and dumb luck. She knew better than to rely on that trio of ineptitude forever. She needed skill; she wanted training.

Training from Eric only lasted mere minutes and he nearly got himself killed. Quick thinking on his part redirected Alexa's focus from his neck to the hand he ran up her thigh. No longer did she want to sink her teeth into him but have him inside her.

Alexa pictured his face as if he stood in front of her. She wanted to reach out and touch him. She wanted him to touch her.

Chapter Sixteen

Alexa watched Valerie march toward her desk. She entered the cubicle and squatted next to Alexa. "I really need your help," she whispered. "Melissa called in sick this morning and I need you to come into my client meeting as a paralegal."

"Why are you whispering?"

"I don't need a paralegal, I need another person in the room with me." Valerie raised her eyebrows trying to convey something to Alexa.

Alexa mouthed "vampire" and received a nod. "Sure. What do you need me to do?"

"Bring a notepad and just take notes. Basically, transcribe everything we say."

"But don't you have a recorder for that?"

Valerie shook her head. "It's not a deposition, just a first contact. So having a secretary or paralegal present is a bit of overkill but not unheard of. Just take notes as if it's something you do every day."

"Um, okay." Alexa ripped the top page off the notepad she had been using, logged out of the computer, and grabbed three ink pens. She followed Valerie to the conference room where two men sat with their own notepads. Two vampires. They stood as Valerie and Alexa entered.

Valerie cleared her throat as she moved toward the chair opposite the men. "Gentlemen, this is one of our paralegals, Lexie."

Alexa forced a grin and nodded as she pulled out a chair. The man on the left was the guy she saw over the weekend in Charlestown, the strutting doorman.

"I am Diederich Coburg and this is my associate, Elmar Planer." Both men nodded formally and took their seats.

Alexa noticed Diederich, the younger of the two, staring at her. She recognized him as well, but couldn't figure out where… oh the man in the clearing when she and Sarah were exploring the creek near the apartment. They made eye contact, as he appeared to make the same realization. She quickly averted her gaze to the paper in front of her and scribbled the date and time.

Their scents caught Alexa's attention – Elmar was a ranger and

Diederich a noble. Their working relationship seemed very similar to the one her father had with his guard, Sebastian. She assumed Elmar was a guard, especially after seeing him hold doors. She wondered who the man and woman were. Did Diederich know them? Crap, did her dad know any of these people?

Dutifully transcribing the conversation, Alexa tried not to let her mind wander, but she had questions. She wondered if Charlestown vampires were part of the same group as Radcliff? Group? No, colony, like her hometown, Brentwood. Eric once explained that they were Carinthian vampires from a kingdom in Austria. She doubted the men in front of her were Carinthian or that either Radcliff or Charlestown were part of the Carinthian colonies. Diederich had a soft accent, possibly Germanic. Dutch? She wasn't sure, but he was not Austrian like her father.

For the next twenty-three minutes, Alexa transcribed the conversation between Valerie and Diederich with the occasional input from Elmar. He didn't have an accent.

To Alexa the case seemed superfluous, a visitor to their office claimed a crumbled rug caused her to fall although video showed no rug existed.

"As I told Diederich, getting a second opinion on this situation was warranted but I firmly believe we should make a nominal offer and avoid going to court," Elmar said.

Alexa stared at the man. His arrogance seethed with each word. And that hair – every strand seemingly placed just so. She pictured him spending hours preening each morning, but there was more to her disdain than this man's self-indulgence and arrogance. She didn't trust him.

Flipping her attention to Diederich, Alexa found him polite and possibly sincere. She trusted him in the brambles by the creek and she trusted him here at the conference table. Alexa understood a good businessman wouldn't reveal everything, so she assumed he had his own vault of secrets and ulterior motives, but he didn't seem quite as nefarious as the man next to him.

Elmar's death came forward. Alexa had been ignoring the screams and the searing pain in his neck, but this time she allowed the scene to play out fully in her head. Diederich's scent floated nearby - if he didn't kill Elmar, he also didn't act to stop the attack. She shuddered as the scene closed to darkness and she turned to face Valerie before the scene started again. Alexa sought the calming light of Sarah's ghost welcoming Valerie to the other side. The scene drowned out Elmar's screams and Alexa brought her focus back to the current events at the table.

"Ladies, thank you for your time. I hope you have a chance to enjoy this beautiful weather today," Diederich said.

"Actually, I was hoping to hit some trails after work but my bicycle keeps tossing the chain." She turned to Valerie and asked, "You don't know of a good repair shop nearby, do you?"

Valerie looked at her like she grew a second head. "No..." she said confused.

"Tucker's on Ninth Street is the only place worth taking your bike," Diederich said. "I know popping the chain back on is simple enough but if it keeps coming off then you need to have the gears inspected."

Alexa looked at him intently, nodding her head. "Yeah, that's kind of what I suspected."

"Mark Tucker is a great guy. Just a regular human and he loves to help people plus his prices are reasonable. Now if you go to buy a bike from him, he's going to get some money out of you."

"Really? That's good to know."

"Ahem, I have a lunch appointment," Elmar said. "So if everyone will excuse me, I'll just show myself to the door."

Alexa watched the two men shake hands before he left.

"I'm surprised you haven't heard of Tucker's," Diederich said.

"Well, I'm new to the area," Alexa said as she watched the doorway with Elmar's scent fading down the hallway. Convinced Elmar walked far enough away she snapped her attention back to Diederich. "Honestly I don't ride bikes, I just have a bad vibe about that guy and he didn't seem like the type who enjoyed discussing bicycles."

Diederich's eyebrows raised as he glanced at the door and back at Alexa.

"You're present when he dies. I'm not sure that you are the one killing him, but you're not making any attempts to stop the act from happening."

His eyebrows remained perched as his eyes darted between Alexa and Valerie. He appeared as though he wanted to ask a question, but the words never formed. Alexa noticed he seemed a little freaked out.

"Also, this case feels weird," she said. "Not related to your partner in any way, but there are a lot of weird vibes hitting me." She watched as he almost nodded while he listened. "I mean why do you need a second opinion on such a trivial claim unless there's more at stake? It reminds me of a story if you've got a quick second. I would just feel remiss if I didn't share it with you."

He nodded with a bewildered look on his face.

"Understand, I have no legal experience. I'm in here just because Valerie needed another person in here, you know, because..."

He nodded.

"So, this isn't legal advice, just a story a business professor told us one time," Alexa said. "So he had a client who owned a large company with a solid name and made ridiculous amounts of money, but he finally sold it at a rock bottom price. He said it wasn't until years later that he realized what happened. There had been a series of legal battles: trademark infringements, workmen's comp, land battles, severance disputes, product liabilities... just a huge financial toll. Some he won, others he lost. On top of that were internal failures with broken machines, lost records, power outages, accounting errors... And this wasn't all at one time or in a single department. It was over several years but he said it felt excessive, more than routine failures. Departments were restructured, and new managers hired, some within, others from outside. He brought in an endless stream of consultants." Alexa saw his expression change from confusion to concern.

"Anyway," she said, "after the sale, most of his longtime employees were fired. The new ones that had come in during various departmental restructuring quickly rose to upper management and executive positions. When he dug into the buyer's background he found ties to one of his competitors."

Diederich looked at the door and then back at Alexa. "Do you think Elmar is trying to steal my company?"

"I have no idea who he is or what his goals are, but something is screaming in my head to tell you to hold your cards close."

He stared at Alexa for a few moments before nodding his head. "Okay. Why am I present when Elmar dies?"

"No clue. I see a snippet of everyone's death, but not the whole picture." Alexa tried to run the scene through her mind but the details evaporated. She shook her head. "There's a lot of commotion, it's hard to tell. I assume it's a big fight."

He nodded. "Do you see my death?"

"I do. It's peaceful."

"A man in my position ought to die a warrior's death."

Alexa looked sideways at Diederich. "I have no idea what that means."

"To die in battle."

She looked him in the eye. Anger at her father bubbled again. These men believed dying in battle was honorable yet no one bothered to teach their daughters how to fight. She snorted. "Well, your path is what it is. Maybe you will find some consolation that a beautiful woman tends to you in your last moments. I assume she's your wife – you feel affection for her."

His shoulders relaxed and his expression softened. "She is an exquisite woman." He looked at Valerie and then to the empty hallway. He sighed when he returned his attention to Alexa. "You're an intriguing creature. You're not scared of me."

Alexa assumed he had detected her noble scent as soon as she arrived in the conference room. "Should I be?"

"No." He picked up his notebook and slid it into a leather portfolio. He looked at her again. "Your story was heard; it was interesting. And thank you for sharing your concerns. I'll be mindful of what you said." He looked over to Valerie. "Thank you for meeting with us. Your input was valuable."

Chapter Seventeen

Relief and panic raged at the same time when Alexa realized the dull ache in her lower back was period cramps. Despite *knowing* she wasn't pregnant, she had worried about her skipped period and unprotected sex with Eric. She could sense when people were pregnant, even knowing the sex of the baby, but that didn't stop fretting maybe she couldn't detect the same in herself.

Rummaging through the bathroom she shared with Sarah, she grabbed a handful of tampons and two pads with the intention of stopping at a grocery store either before or after work to get the brand she preferred as well as replace what she had taken from Sarah's stash.

At the office, Alexa stopped briefly at her desk to deposit her purse and lunch and proceeded to Donella's office. Grateful she didn't sense anyone with Donella, Alexa still made a timid peek in the doorway.

"Lexie! Good morning!"

"Do you have a minute?"

"Actually, my morning is quite open. Come in."

Alexa closed the door behind her and sat in the chair that seemed to be her assigned seat. "I have a really stupid question to ask you. Um. How do vampires deal with periods? More specifically, what do *we* do to protect ourselves?"

Realization flashed across Donella's face. Her expression exposed amusement quickly replaced by professional concern. "You haven't started bleeding yet, but are about to."

Alexa nodded.

"Did your mother give you any guidance?"

"Just the same talk my friends had with their mothers – where to find supplies and dealing with PMS. Well and of course don't have sex because babies never keep boyfriends around." Alexa stared at the edge of Donella's desk as she remembered her teen years. "You know, thinking back, some of my friends thought it was weird I took supplements in high school. I always said it was because my mom was this free-spirit hippie that we always had to go all-natural but I have no idea what the supplements were." She shrugged. "So…

what do you suggest? And is there a spell or do we hide or does it matter?"

Donella shook her head slowly. She pulled out her purse and extracted a bottle, handing it to Alexa. "Take three of these every day."

"Garlic pills? Won't they dull my senses?"

Donella tilted her head a bit. "Some but it also masks the scent. The added benefit is that it helps reduce the pain and your periods will be shorter."

"Huh. I've always had short periods. I guess garlic was in those supplements my mom kept giving me."

"I'm sure. It's standard, not that it will slow down a determined vampire. Fortunately, most are coming for fresh blood."

Alexa leveled a look at Donella. "Are you saying some are attracted to period blood?"

With a slow, thoughtful nod Donella cast an apologetic grin. "There's a class of vampire that prefers rotting flesh and blood that hasn't circulated in a while."

"Oh. Scavengers. Yeah, I've had an encounter with a couple of them. Some punk thought he would serve me to his grandmother for dinner." Alexa shivered. "I've never smelled a person so vile."

"I'll take your word for it. You should know, however, that some people consider, um.... What comes out to be a, uh, *romantic* delicacy."

"Blood wings?"

"I've never heard of that term."

Alexa cleared her throat and shifted in her seat. "When a guy, uh, face-plants in her lap during that time."

Donella raised her eyebrows. "I didn't know there was a term for that, but yes. Exactly. And um, I've heard that some women will also eat what comes out."

Alexa dropped her mouth open in horror. "That's awful."

Donella nodded.

"I've never once looked down at that mess and thought about popping it in my mouth." Alexa shuddered and contorted her face hoping to erase the thought of having a bloody, chunky piece of menses in her mouth. She shuddered again. "That's disgusting."

Donella laughed. "I think you'll be fine. Keep the garlic – I have several more bottles at home. My mother taught me changing napkins regularly through the day was really the best defense and on heavy days to just stay home, which really that's all we want to do anyway."

"True. Thank you. I'll get out of your hair, but I do appreciate the honesty."

Donella grinned. "It's no problem. If you have any questions at all, please stop by any time."

Chapter Eighteen

Rena tapped on the cubicle wall as if a door were present. Alexa grinned and said, "Come in, the door's unlocked"

"Got lunch plans? Laura and I are walking up to Donna's Diner. You should join us."

"Oh my gosh, yes. I need to get away from this mess and clear my mind. Can you give me a minute so I can log out of everything?"

"Sure. Meet us up front."

Before securing her computer, Alexa pulled the bottle of garlic pills from her purse and popped a tablet in her mouth. She screwed up her face while swallowing the pill. The bottle touted odorless and flavorless, but nonetheless, her vampire nose caught the scent. On the upside, as she walked to the front reception area she didn't smell the metallic odors of her coworkers.

"I'm so glad you're joining us," Laura said. "I got Heather's order and Tina said she's meeting up with her sister."

Rena pushed the door open and Alexa raised a hand to shield her eyes from the sun.

"That office is like a vapor lock or something," Alexa said. "No sunlight, no sounds, perfect temperature control."

"Yeah, it's a bit of a crapshoot walking out the door," Rena said.

"Just wait," Laura said. "The days are getting shorter and soon we will be leaving work in complete darkness. I hate not having windows at work. The weather changes and we have no idea. I can't tell you how many times we've come out here to see our cars buried in snow."

"You said we're walking to the diner. How far away is it?"

Rena pointed across the street. "It's just behind those trees over there. There's a cute little path with a bridge that crosses a creek."

Fear jutted through Alexa's body thinking about going across the street. She tamed her emotion as she scanned the gray building, the one where she had seen a vampire patrolling the roof. Remembering humans serve as shields, she stayed close to Rena and Laura as they crossed the street. She continued to scan the building, but with her ability to smell blocked by the garlic pills, she couldn't tell if there was any recent vampire activity.

"Oh my gosh!" Alexa exclaimed as they neared the bridge. "This is adorable. Do people come here for their wedding photos?"

"I told you it was cute," Rena said.

"This really would be a great place for pictures," Laura said.

Alexa stood on the bridge looking over the side and Rena stepped next to her. "The water is low now," Rena said, "but when it rains this thing gets FULL."

"Wow." Alexa continued looking over the rail searching for any traces of vampires. She didn't see anything but she was amazed at how much she relied on her nose. She turned and caught up to Laura and Rena.

Reaching the diner involved crossing another street, a busy street. Instead of walking to the end of the block and using the crosswalk, Laura waited for a break between cars and dashed to the center lane. Surprised by the jaywalking but not daunted, Alexa followed Rena across the road.

They stood in front of a 1950's building with an oddly angled roof and a bank of windows stretching across the front. The white exterior had big block letters "Donna's Diner" in red. Alexa wondered if Donna was still alive.

Inside Alexa caught a hint of vampires in the air. She looked around the crowded restaurant trying to decipher which were the vampires. The only open booth sat next to two men in yellow vests with hard hats sitting on their table and they were watching her. She assumed they were the vampires. She hoped she could encourage Laura and Rena to sit at the lunch counter, but before she could make the suggestion Laura headed toward the empty table. Alexa debated whether to sit facing the men or with her back to them - she opted to face them, hoping for no eye contact.

The waitress approached from the counter wearing a white blouse and black skirt. As she distributed menus to the table she forced a weary smile. "Welcome to Donna's. I'm Judi, what would you ladies like to drink?"

"I'll take an iced tea," Laura said.

Alexa nodded. "Me too."

"I think I'll just have a water," Rena said.

"Okay, I'll give you time to look over the menu and I'll have your drinks out as soon as I take care of these gentlemen over here."

When Alexa looked in the direction the waitress nodded, she made eye contact with a man – yes, definitely a vampire. He quickly averted his gaze back to the waitress.

Alexa flipped the menu over twice and looked between Laura and Rena. "What do you guys like to get here?"

"I don't recommend the chili mac unless you like bland," Laura said. "But the sandwiches are worth the hike over here. The BLT is basically a package of bacon with a side of toast." She squinted her eyes at Alexa. "Do you never slouch?"

Alexa chuckled as she shook her head. "My dad was a stickler for proper etiquette, particularly at meals and that included sitting up straight, napkin in the lap, and no playing with the cocktail fork and sorbet spoon. Of course, I have never been to a meal where cocktail forks and sorbet spoons were an option, but dammit I know better than to coo over how cute they are."

"I don't think I would know what either of those look like," Rena said.

"My mom laughs that we live in a basic three-bedroom house but his parents made sure she had all of the pieces necessary for a proper dinner party of eighteen people. Our dining room table only seats six!"

"I thought my grandma's china set for twelve was excessive," Laura said.

"Do people even have dinner parties anymore?" Rena asked.

"Dunno, but I know how to set that table and what each piece is used for and when each of those courses is supposed to come out."

Judi delivered styrofoam to-go cups to the vampires and then turned to Alexa's table for their orders. Rena handed her menu to the waitress and said, "I'll take a pastrami on rye with an extra pickle."

"Do you want chips or fries?"

Rena thought for a moment. "Chips."

Laura tilted her head with a smile. "BLT and chips."

"What about you, kiddo?"

Alexa handed Judi the menu. "Turkey, bacon, swiss on white and I'll go for chips as well."

After the waitress left Alexa leaned on the table. "How bland is the chili?"

Rena cackled. "Hamburger, ketchup, beans! Maybe some dried onion flakes."

"Just a dusting, though," Laura said. "They wouldn't want to go overboard."

"But the sandwiches are okay?"

"Yeah, I don't get it," Laura said.

The vampires stood up to leave but one turned toward Alexa. "It was Donna's recipe when she opened the place. She swore by it and no one is allowed to change it and oddly people around here love it." He shrugged.

"But when you ask for onions and cheese, they heap it on. That changes everything," the other vampire said. He flipped a five-dollar bill on the table. "Ya oughta try it sometime." He flashed a sincere smile before heading to the counter to pay. The first vampire raised his eyebrows as he considered the added ingredients and tipped a nod to the women as he followed his friend.

"Well, cheese and onion do tend to improve most meals," Laura said.

Rena said, "If not cheese and onions, then whipped cream."

"So true!" Laura nodded in agreement. "Pancakes – horrible with cheese and onions, splendid with whipped cream."

"Cantaloupe would be good with whipped cream," Rena said.

"Mashed potatoes, cheese, and onions," Laura said.

"Fish?" Alexa asked.

"Yuck, I hate fish," Rena said. "There is not enough cheese and onion to fix that nastiness."

"Sauteed onions would be great on a lot of fish dishes!" Laura said.

"Why ruin onions that way?" Rena looked at Alexa. "Do you like fish?"

She shrugged. "I don't really know. I've only had the fried stuff you get at fast food places and honestly you could feed me shoe leather if it were batter-dipped and deep-fried."

"Didn't your school have fish every so often?" Rena asked.

Laura wrinkled her forehead. "Whose likes and dislikes are based on what was served in a school cafeteria? That stuff was crap. Chili was beans added to leftover spaghetti sauce from the day before, and that spaghetti was tomato sauce added to crumbled-up hamburgers from the day before that."

Alexa laughed and took a sip of her iced tea. She fluttered her eyes at the lack of sugar and reached for the sweetener packets at the end of the table.

"Hey, how are things going with finding Greg's mistakes?" Laura asked.

Alexa sighed. "Tedious."

"So you're finding something?" Laura asked with raised eyebrows.

"I'm pretty sure I can't talk about what I'm coming across, but what you think I'm finding is probably spot on."

Rena sighed. "Ugh, that is the drawback to working with a bunch of legal eagles. Everything is hush, hush, client confidentiality and all that."

"I could write a tell-all book about the shit that's come across my desk," Laura said. "And this isn't the juicy stuff my friend sees, the one who works over at the courthouse in family division."

"I can only imagine," Alexa said.

Rena turned to Laura and scowled. "Speaking of tell-all, what's the update on the dead body they found by your house?"

"Nothing," Laura said shaking her head. "Of course, no one comes and tells the neighbors anything but you would think someone would know who the guy was or why he was there or something. They just scooped up his body and all traces of him ever being there."

"Dead body?" Alexa asked.

"Some kids found a body in a field behind my subdivision. Nobody can figure out whose kids saw it or what they saw. Then the guy down the street walked through the field and said there's a barren six-foot patch where everything was just... removed. It's just a patch of dirt where all of the plants and rocks were removed and smoothed over."

Alexa raised her eyebrows thinking how it sounded like somebody didn't want any trace left behind. But were they investigators collecting evidence or were they actually vampires disposing of all traces of a kill? She never received exact details as to what vampires do with their deceased victims – her mother mentioned something about a connection to a crematorium. Did vampires universally have such connections? Or was that just an arrangement back in Brentwood? What did vampires in Radcliff do with their kills?

"Yeah. Evidently, there was another dead body found a few weeks ago over by where you and Valerie live," Laura said.

Alexa snapped her attention back to Laura. "Do you think they're related?"

"Hard to say. I don't know if there are any similarities between the two other than someone died."

"Is there a blank piece of dirt at that site?" Rena asked.

Alexa pulled her head back with a horrified expression. "I'm not going back there to look around!"

"Do you know where they found him?"

"Not exactly. It was down in a ravine and I just saw several people going down in that direction. I was headed back to the condo so I really didn't pay attention."

Rena gasped. "You were there?"

Alexa shrugged. "I guess. Sarah and I were out for a walk on our way back to the condo when we saw a lot of commotion. She got a bad vibe about it, so we didn't stick around to watch. Then the next day the neighbors were talking about a dead body. Somebody said something about ambulances and police cars but I didn't see any of that while we were out, they must have arrived after we went inside and I certainly didn't hear any sirens later on."

"So how is it living with Valerie?" Rena asked.

"Great," Alexa said. "She and Sarah are both super sweet and their condo is really cozy. Did you know Valerie is like a professional-level chef? Everything she cooks is absolutely delicious."

"Really?" Laura said in disbelief.

"Yeah, I'm pretty sure I've gained ten pounds already."

"So... are the two of them a couple or just roommates?" Laura asked.

Alexa wasn't ready for the question. "Oh, they're just roommates," Alexa lied.

"I guess that explains why we've never met Sarah," Laura said. "Valerie has only mentioned her in passing a few times."

Chapter Nineteen

Alexa pulled a container of leftover chicken from the refrigerator when she heard Sarah come in the front door. With the container still in her hand, she left the kitchen to find Valerie giving Sarah a hug.

"I'm sorry I don't have a warm dinner planned for tonight," Valerie said.

"It's okay." Sarah dropped her purse and bag on the couch so she could remove her jacket. "Oh hey, Lexie. How was your day?"

"Fine, but you look frazzled."

"There was a huge accident at the Lowry Bridge and no way for me to turn around and find a different way home. The heater isn't working in my car, I sliced my thumb at work and bled all over a book. When I sliced my thumb it also nicked my thumbnail so bad I need to trim it off. The zipper on my coat is all mucked up. It's just been a miserable day."

"Oh crap, I'm so sorry. You need some wine!" Alexa said.

Patting Sarah's back, Valerie said, "She's right. I'll get the wine while you get ready for dinner." She looked up at Alexa and asked, "Is it almost ready?"

"I just need to chop up this chicken and pull the bread out of the oven." Alexa returned to the kitchen to complete the dinner prep she had volunteered for the night before. She balanced the three plates on her arm like a professional waitress as she backed through the door into the dining room. Valerie turned just in time to miss colliding with Alexa. They stared at each other wide-eyed.

Alexa exhaled heavily. "Can you take this top plate?"

Valerie relieved Alexa of the plate, placing it in front of Sarah while Alexa set the other two on the table. Once settled the three women laid their hands on the table, not quite touching each other, bowed their heads, and recited their gratitude. "Blessed be," they said in unison.

"How bad is your thumb?" Alexa asked.

"Sore, but not horrible," Sarah said. "I don't need stitches but it did take a while to get the bleeding to stop."

"Did you keep the book?" Valerie asked.

"Of course I did."

"Of course?" Alexa asked.

"She spilled her blood on the book. Remember? Blood is very useful in spell work," Valerie said.

"It's just important that nobody else has my blood, that I maintain the distribution. So yeah, I paid for the book and have it in my backpack."

"So your boss isn't upset over it?" Alexa asked.

"Not at all, especially once I insisted on paying for it. I mean Glennda is really cool about accidents in general – she's a total klutz herself. Any damaged books can be returned to the distributor, but this was totally my fault and I certainly don't want my blood to fall into the wrong hands."

"Because someone could cast a spell on you?"

Sarah nodded as she poured dressing over her salad.

"It's ridiculous how often I order salads when I'm out, but never think to make one as a meal at home," Valerie said. "This is really good."

"You're too busy making complicated recipes," Sarah said.

"Well yes, I do like to challenge myself, but I also need to remember there's beauty in simplicity."

"Or you can just do the complicated stuff and when you need a night off I will step up with grilled cheese sandwiches or salads," Alexa said.

"I am grateful you offered to make dinner," Valerie said. "I have so much to get done tonight, but hopefully I won't need to go into work early." She looked at Alexa. "Do you need to go in early?"

"No. I have plenty of time to review my report before meeting with the partners."

"Are you scared?" Sarah asked.

"Absolutely terrified, but I just keep reminding myself that none of this is about me. I'm just reporting what I've found."

"That's a smart way to approach it," Valerie said. "It's hard not to ask about what you've found. I know better, but I'm dying to find out."

Sarah tilted her head. "It's not about a client, so why is confidentiality an issue?"

"It's an employee issue which we're never allowed to discuss.

But, I'm sure this will involve our clients as well."

Alexa cocked a half grin with a raised eyebrow.

Valerie laughed. "That expression tells me everything. The partners are not going to be pleased."

"I hate that I'm the one who has to tell them."

"Don't worry about it. You will have Donella and Jeff at your side and they will take the heat."

"But tomorrow's Friday the thirteenth! It's just…" Alexa sighed. "I mean of all days to schedule this meeting."

"Or any meeting," Sarah said.

"Friday the thirteenth holds only as much luck or misfortune as you assign it," Valerie said.

"So we just pick and choose how things affect us?" Alexa asked.

"I'd say that's fairly accurate. Intention is everything. Have you heard of numerology?" Valerie asked.

"Like astrology but with numbers?"

"At an elementary level, yes. But, dear god, do not say that to anyone who practices either of those!"

Alexa laughed. "So I guess you don't practice them?"

"I'm not hardcore. I definitely pay attention to planetary phases and enjoy seeing how much people fit their signs. That's not to say I think numerology is crap, I just haven't really studied it," Valerie said.

"I don't know anything about numerology, I believe Friday the 13th is cursed, and my horoscope in the newspaper is accurate about every nine days or so," Sarah said. She received a disappointed glare from Valerie. Sarah shrugged her shoulder. "What can I say, I'm a lazy witch."

"What do you mean?" Alexa asked. "You're constantly teaching me about witchcraft."

"That doesn't mean I'm good at it."

"You're much more powerful than you give yourself credit," Valerie said. "I could shoot your aunt for making you so insecure about your powers."

"But she was right. I never put enough intention into my spells and my mediation is sloppy."

Valerie raised a hand. "Stop right there. Your ability to manifest chaos is spectacular."

"But I can't do it on command..."

"And yet your timing is always so perfect. I think sometimes just your mere presence brings it. You always think it's a complete catastrophe, but something good or... hmmm... purposeful comes as a result. Like cutting your thumb at work is somehow going to bring a benefit, much more than just having your blood for spell work."

Sarah cast a doubting look toward Valerie, who responded with raised eyebrows of encouragement.

Alexa grinned at their silent conversation of facial expressions. "Is generating chaos a magical element?"

"It is. Like I said, intention is at the core of everything." Valerie said. "Some people bring chaos for malevolent reasons, but Sarah brings the type of chaos that disburses tension. It's like an ill-timed laugh that changes the mood of the room. She just hasn't figured out how to harness it. And maybe harnessing would remove the purity of the magic."

"So we just wait to see what comes from it?" Alexa asked.

Valerie tilted her head.

Sarah raised her hands in exasperation. "See? It really is lazy!"

"I don't think so," Valerie said, grabbing Sarah's hand. "You are so adept at seeing the good in nearly every situation that you bring more good. Just last week you told me how you're feeling weak with your spell work lately and here you've created a powerful tool to help. You didn't hurt anyone else in the process *and* the author of the book is going to receive a royalty. How is that bad?"

They exchanged glances again. Valerie looked to Alexa with an expression she was ready to change the topic. "Lexie, we were planning on having some friends over for Samhain. Would you like to participate?"

"Saw win?" Alexa repeated.

"Yes. It's a day of observance on the Wiccan calendar. Halloween.   On paper, it looks like Sam Hane, but the pronunciation is 'sow win.'"

"Um sure. I'm always up for learning more. What do I need to do?"

"We like to do a sit-down dinner after the trick-or-treaters have thinned out. There's a little bit of a ceremony to honor our ancestors and basically, we just eat and drink. We might try out a few spells or help someone with manifesting a job promotion. It's positive camaraderie."

Alexa grinned. "When I found out my friends Brie and Tess were witches I asked if the parties their parents always hosted were coven gatherings. And they were. When I think of their homes it always involves food and drink – it's impossible to picture their moms without a glass of wine in their hands. I don't know what I expected to happen in a coven or a gathering of witches, but I would never have guessed sitting around eating and drinking."

Valerie laughed. "I can't speak for everyone but you can't deny how a gathering is enhanced by food - it builds a sense of community. When we dine together people relax and share and that builds trust, which sets the stage for combining energies. I mean humans even manage to manifest group energy. You see it at concerts all of the time and it's also what happens when we get mobs and riots. Communing and shared energy are incredibly powerful forms of witchcraft."

Alexa stirred her fork through the salad and then looked up. "Do we tell them that I'm a hybrid?"

"That's completely up to you. I don't think any of them would have an issue."

"How many people do you expect to be here?" Alexa asked.

"We invited seven and two have declined since it's a school night."

"Lisa bowed out too," Sarah said. "So that just leaves four."

"And three of us makes seven. Perfect. Seven is a good number."

"Numerology again?" Alexa asked.

Valerie nodded. "Precisely."

D.M. Wyatt

Chapter Twenty

File boxes filled with folders sat at the end of the table, the sum of Alexa's work over the two weeks since she joined the firm. She stared at the boxes, exhausted and hungry.

Jeff forced a smile through his dismay. "That was impressive work, Lexie."

"Thank you."

He shook his head. "No, thank you. You handled yourself well when speaking to the partners without muddling the information or speaking down to anyone, which is difficult when dealing with minutia. And this report." He covered his mouth as he shook his head again, looking at the folder in front of him. "I wasn't expecting a summary, let alone each folder annotated with your findings." He looked around the table littered with folders. "It's just amazing. Someone taught you very well."

Alexa grinned. "Yeah, I had the same professor for a couple of classes and he drove home the need for documenting everything, and when working with large projects to summarize activities or findings in a short report if for no other reason than to plan out speaking points."

"It served you well. I've lost those men multiple times when running through quarterly reports. No one enjoys hearing long lists of numbers or mathematic equations, but you managed to explain your processes in a methodical way that appealed to the lawyer brain. I've definitely learned something new today." He looked from one end of the table to the other. "How many files did you go through before you hit Burns?"

"Um, about a dozen."

"How long did that take you?"

"It was the second day, sometime after lunch. By the time the office closed, I figured out how to attack the problem but still hadn't put my finger on the issue."

"Again I say it's all very impressive." He shook his head in disbelief. "I've had people review these files for other reasons and not find anything out of order. I fully expected you to find data entry errors from a guy itching to leave and not double-checking his own work. Embezzlement was the furthest thing from my mind."

"Sorry, it was bad news."

"I can't believe how often I defended him, the times people complained about his laziness or how unsocial he was."

Donella pressed a smile and laid a hand on his shoulder. "He conned all of us."

"Had he not left so quickly... I mean I felt betrayed he put in his notice as I was leaving for vacation. And yet... I... I was ready to offer to write a letter of recommendation." He dropped his head into his hands and sighed.

Motioning for Alexa to leave the room, Donella grabbed a box and headed toward the door. Alexa ran her arm across the table, scooping several file folders into a box next to her chair, and followed Donella down the hall to her office.

Donella's office carried an evergreen scent that Alexa suspected was potpourri. The evergreen complimented Donella's natural scent of basil and Alexa found the combination pleasing. She set the box on top of the one Donella placed in the corner.

"Have a seat," Donella said. "That's a lot of hard work you've put in. I was hoping to speak to the partners about that, to see if they were amenable to hiring you permanently. However, after today's meeting, Martin pulled me to the side and suggested I make the offer. You really impressed all three of them."

Alexa sat quiet, unsure what to say.

Donella cocked her head. "If you want time to think about it, you can just let me know next week."

"Uh, thank you. I don't need time; I'm just a little speechless. I'm just concerned about my longevity here. I mean things are working out well. It's only been a few weeks, but I just have this feeling that it's not going to be, um... long term."

"As in you see yourself leaving Radcliff in the near future?"

"I don't know," Alexa said with a shrug. "This was supposed to be an overnight stop. Of course, I didn't have any plans for what would happen once I ended my hopscotch journey across the country. And I don't know what it will take for me to return home. It's just a lot of uncertainty."

"I have found over and over again that answers reveal themselves when the time is right, and not a moment sooner."

Alexa looked at Donella, seeing her death scene of lying in

the grass at night with smoke swirling around her. Where was the answer to that? Does her house burn down? Alexa knew not to warn her – she had learned years earlier that preventing a death only intensified the experience, that the person would still die but more horribly and painfully than the original death.

She said, "I don't make it known that I have premonitions – one because it's never fruitful to tell people what I see and it always comes with questions, but also there's so little context that it's frustrating to receive them, like what am I supposed to do with this information? And hearing you say answers arrive in due time, just works into my overall sense of sit back and watch."

"Does that make you feel useless?"

"Yes." Alexa nodded. "There are things I wish I could prevent, people I could protect. Instead, something happens and I'm like 'oh that's why I saw myself walking down a dark hallway!' It's always after the fact that I piece things together. Yes, useless is the right description."

"I imagine the answer to that will also present itself in due time." Donella offered a sympathetic grin. "As for the job offer or really any major decision, you have to decide what is right for now. Most people cannot see into the future. So when they are juggling the possible variables of what can be, it still comes down to what is the right move for now. With your ability to see the future, you're impacted by the same variables. If you select a different course, does it change the future? I'd say you're just as tied as anyone else in making that determination and then I go back to my standard advice – do what is best for now." She leveled a look at Alexa and raised an eyebrow. "It seems your trepidation is out of concern for the firm if you had to leave suddenly. To that, I remind you we face this dilemma with every single person we hire. Illnesses, death, family responsibilities, finances, and other job offers routinely pluck very content employees out of offices across the country. It is the gamble we make as employers."

Wobbling her head to concede, Alexa said, "Well then, the best move for me right now and my immediate future is to accept your offer. Thank you."

"Fantastic! I want to take you out for lunch to celebrate, but I have an appointment I need to leave for shortly. So let's celebrate early next week."

Chapter Twenty-One

A car door slammed on another level, the boom echoing through the parking garage. Poor lighting did little to dispel the darkness as her heels clicked along the concrete. The night air carried a chill causing Alexa to pull her coat tighter. Unfortunately, the air didn't carry sweet scents of trees or flowers but instead old oil, tires, and soured refuse, likely an overflowing trashcan hiding in a dark corner.

For as much as she wanted the momentary relief from the cold by riding the elevator, Alexa listened to her intuition and headed down the stairs. She appreciated the better lighting so as not to stumble in her heels.

On the first landing, she heard the elevator stop at an upper floor and several men poured out into the garage. Their laughs carried but their conversation was muted by distance. A car squealed turning off a ramp, the engine revved, and tires skidded on the next turn. The men who exited the elevator sounded closer and then Alexa heard their footsteps above her. She scurried down the next flight only to stop short. In front of her sat a black sedan waiting, the rear door open.

The footsteps moved faster as the men descended to the floor above her. The car racing down the ramps sounded nearer. Alexa's heart beat like crazy and she gasped for air. She made eye contact with the driver of the black car and knew his face. He spoke but she couldn't hear him above her panting and the footsteps and the squealing.

Alexa did not want to get in the car but her alternatives seemed to disappear. The footsteps got louder and the racing car came closer. Alexa whipped her head to see who was coming down the stairs and the lights went out. She screamed and turned to run toward the black car but she ran into the wall.

"Alexa!" the driver yelled.

"No!" Alexa yelled and pushed away from the wall. She fell backward and hit the cold disgusting cement floor that reeked of forgotten trash.

A light blinded her as someone held a flashlight above. She froze, panting...

"Lexie?" a woman's voice called. "Are you okay?"

Alexa blinked trying to look past the flashlight. Bedroom light. That was the light in the ceiling. Where was the parking garage? And the cars?

To her side, she didn't see cement but beige carpet. She had fallen out of bed. She looked to the foot of the bed and Sarah stood in the doorway with her hand on the light switch. "Are you okay?" Sarah asked again.

Alexa realized she was still panting and took a deep breath. "Uh. I don't know."

"Your fangs are *huge*."

Alexa touched her hand to her mouth and quickly retracted her teeth. "I was being chased," she said. She looked around and only found the vestiges of a bedroom. All traces of the garage and men running down the stairs had disappeared.

Valerie stood behind Sarah looking equally concerned.

"It was just a nightmare," Alexa said, her voice shaky and weak.

Staggering down the stairs Alexa spotted Valerie and Sarah at the table with coffee and bowls of fruit. She winced at the sun beaming through the sliding glass doors and made her way into the kitchen to find coffee, not saying a word as she passed the table. With coffee and a package of Pop-Tarts in hand, she returned to the table, taking her normal seat across from Valerie and Sarah.

"Do you want me to put those in the toaster?" Sarah asked.

Alexa looked down at the silver packet as she processed the question. She shook her head. "Hmm, no. Raw is fine."

"Raw?"

She shrugged a shoulder. "Uncooked."

Valerie laughed. "Those nightmares really suck the energy out of you, don't they? It's no wonder you're not a morning person."

Alexa looked at Valerie and thought for a moment. "Did I scream or something?"

"You screamed and fell out of the bed," Valerie said.

"What?"

"We turned on your bedroom light and you were laying on the floor. With your fangs out," Sarah said.

Alexa jerked back. They saw her fangs? Her bedroom light was on?

"You don't remember anything?" Valerie asked.

Alexa stared at Valerie and then looked over to Sarah. Neither one was joking. How often had this scene played out at home? She fell out of bed? How could she not remember *that*?

"I was on the floor?"

Sarah nodded. "You were crying."

"Sad or scared?"

"Scared. You were very scared," Sarah said. "You said you were being chased."

Alexa leaned her head in exasperation. "That sounds normal."

"Are you always chased in your dreams?" Valerie asked with raised eyebrows.

In a less groggy state, Alexa would have laughed out loud at Valerie's very therapist-like question and pose. "Yeah, I'm chased a lot in my dreams. I guess I'm always running from something." Alexa's glib response rang a little too true. She slumped back in her chair and stared at Valerie. "Fuck."

Recalling as many dreams as possible, she noticed most involved running away. She had always worried about the monsters chasing her but maybe these nightmares served as a message? Alexa knew how to stand up for herself and she had proven at least twice she could fight. Was she running away from something more philosophical? Were monsters metaphors for something else? But what about the nightmare that turned into a premonition – the one where she was able to stop the attack on Brie's mom? She didn't run away from that.

Startled, Alexa realized Sarah stood next to her and was rubbing her back. With blurry vision, Alexa rubbed her eyes. When did she start crying? "I think I need to go back to bed."

Chapter Twenty-Two

Sitting in the backseat of Donella's car Alexa felt like a child with mom and dad in the front. Jeff talked about a system update he installed on the office computers over the weekend and how he spent Monday fielding complaints and questions from nearly every employee. Alexa recalled the day of chaos as she tried to assist her co-workers to no avail. Even Donella's assistant, Erin, couldn't offer much help.

"Tell me when you want me to run an ad for some assistance," Donella said.

Jeff ran his hand over his head. "I don't have time to train anyone. It's hard enough to set up a new employee with login credentials. Lexie and Erin were of some help, but..."

"Because you don't have them set up with any administrative privileges," Donella snapped back. "I've been your backup admin for a very long time, which is exactly the type of work an assistant can do."

"Once they're properly trained."

At the stoplight, Donella turned to face him. "Set them up with user administration. You're not releasing the keys to the kingdom by doing that. They can help train your new assistant in the basics and general flow of the office. We will make sure to hire someone with actual experience who will quickly relieve Lexie and Erin from these responsibilities, but they will have a working relationship with each other so when the next update or release comes out you have a whole team. I honestly feel like hiring two people is needed, but we will cross that bridge later. Let's get the ball rolling and place an ad."

Jeff grumbled consent.

Walking into Stanson's Restaurant Alexa recognized the undertones of garlic and worried with the garlic supplements already in her system her defenses could be even weaker. Sure enough, a few seconds passed before she registered witches among humans in the dining room.

A middle-aged woman guided them through a maze of tables to one away from the other people. Alexa thought the placement weird, wondering if a witch directed the human hostess to seat their group away from the other patrons. Donella, like most hybrids, could not mask her scent the way Alexa did. She also noted the lack of vampires in the establishment, likely due to the excessive garlic in the air.

Glancing over the menu Alexa felt disoriented, the words mere pictures to be admired. She had been drunk plenty of times to know how to maneuver in this state and lifted her focus to something larger – Jeff sitting across from her. Taking a deep breath and lifting her chin, she asked, "So, whose choice was this?"

"Mine," Jeff said. "I really like the sandwich selection. They're like genuine entrees transformed into lunch."

"That's quite an endorsement," Alexa said with a grin and forced focus as she looked at Jeff. "How did you find it?"

"My wife dragged me here."

"And evidently won," Alexa said with a laugh.

Jeff laughed as he shook his head. "She still gloats – it's been an ongoing battle. You have to understand what a creature of habit I am. If left to my own resources I'd be eating at Donna's Diner three times a week and ordering the same turkey on rye sandwich every single time."

"I guess you don't get something different every time you visit?" Alexa asked, proud of keeping up with all that he had said.

Jeff laughed. "It's a stretch to visit different restaurants. You want me to sample the entire menu too? There are about four different things I order here for lunch. The menu is..." He shook his head. "...Astounding. Very hard to decide."

Jeff snapped his head toward the window. Two men stood on the sidewalk talking, no... arguing. The man in the business suit turned to walk away, but the other one in a t-shirt and jeans put a hand on his shoulder. The businessman turned around and Alexa saw a flash of yellow in his eyes. She felt sobriety take hold as she recognized the man – the one she had met in the conference room with Valerie, the vampire she did not trust. Fear jutted through her system and she looked back to Jeff watching the encounter.

Alexa cleared her throat trying to think of a way to distract Jeff from witnessing a vampire lose composure. "That's kinda weird," she said. "I wonder if we are going to watch a fight?"

Jeff chuckled and returned his gaze to the window. "They don't look evenly matched. I'd put my money on the guy in the t-shirt."

Alexa extended her arm, knocking over her glass of water. "Aw crap!" She stood up quickly, knocking her chair over. Grabbing her napkin she dabbed at the water spilled across the table. "Dammit."

Jeff and Donella both pushed away from the table as the water flowed toward them. The waitress rushed to their table. She grabbed napkins from neighboring tables and helped mop up the water. Donella and Jeff also pulled napkins to assist in the cleanup. Alexa darted a look toward the window and was relieved to find the men had moved on.

With order restored to the table, they returned to their seats and the waitress carried away the evidence of the tiny flood Alexa caused. When she looked at the window again, two men in gray suits ran past the window. They reminded her of the royal guard that continuously followed her when she lived in Brentwood. Alexa stiffened with her attention glued to the window.

"Lexie? Are you okay?" Donella asked.

Rattled, Alexa stared at Donella, unsure what to say. She looked to the window and back at Donella. "The guys fighting... and the ones running... I... I ... um..."

"Do you want to leave?"

Alexa looked from the window and stared again at Donella. "And what? Go outside? No." She looked back to the window. No men in suits, only people casually strolling in and out of shops and restaurants. No one appeared alarmed or behaved as though a fight was taking place.

Realizing she oozed with fear, Alexa took a deep, calming breath. She closed her eyes and repeated the calming breaths.

Jeff stared at the window as if searching for what triggered the change in Alexa. "What did you see?"

"Um, just reminded me of something."

"When we spoke about your position with the firm, I promised that we will accommodate you however necessary. Your safety and your peace of mind are important to me, Donella, and the partners."

"Thank you," she whispered, finally getting herself calm.

"Do you want to leave?" he asked.

She shook her head. "I'd like whatever was happening out

there to just run its course. We should just order our meals and, hopefully, I can distract myself enough to be functional."

The waitress returned with a fresh glass of water. "Are you ready to place your order?"

"I think we need a minute," Jeff said.

"Not because of me," Alexa said.

"Really?" He asked.

"I saw an apple brie sandwich. Might as well try that."

"The Santa Monica? With turkey?" The waitress asked.

"Yeah, that sounds interesting," Alexa said. She looked across the table and caught Jeff's look of disgust.

"I'll take the prime rib sandwich," Donella said.

"Okay, the Victoria's Rib. And you?" the waitress asked as she turned to Jeff.

"The Geneva."

"Did anyone want something besides water?"

"I'd like some iced tea," Donella said.

When the waitress walked away Jeff looked at Alexa. "You looked like you regretted your selection when Donella said prime rib."

Exhaling, Alexa felt some of her stress melt away. Chatter about food seemed like a good distraction. "It's been a long time since I've had prime rib," she said with a weak smile. Turning to Donella she asked, "What's on it?"

"Excellent prime rib seasoned to perfection. It's sliced thin but still holds the juices..."

"Blood," Jeff said.

"It's where the flavor's at," Donella said. "It has a liberal smear of horseradish and that's balanced with creamed spinach."

Alexa wrinkled her nose.

"Trust me, the spinach works. I'll cut off a piece for you to try."

Weary of the offer, Alexa grinned and then turned to Jeff. "What's on yours?"

"It's a cordon bleu sandwich with cognac sauce and grilled asparagus."

"Wow, that sounds amazing. I wish I'd spent more time reading the menu."

Jeff nodded. "The menu is a work of art. The names are fun to read and each item has a bit of history under them."

"There's one with pâté on it," Donella said. Again Alexa scrunched her face. "I know it sounds gross..."

"No, I've had pâté. I can't imagine making a whole sandwich of it, but I guess here it would be the smear with something more substantial."

"Well, I think that's the case. When did you have pâté?" Donella asked.

"My grandparents would come to town and insist on dining at a fancy hotel downtown. They felt it necessary to expand my palate beyond hamburgers and french fries."

A motorcycle engine revved and Alexa stiffened again. She quickly redirected her attention to Jeff talking about another sandwich with scallops and lemon orzo.

When they returned to the office, Donella pulled Alexa to her office as Jeff wandered off in the direction of the restroom. "What was that? I saw you knock the water over."

"The two men fighting were vampires. The one in the suit, his eyes changed colors. I figured Jeff shouldn't watch whatever was about to go down."

"But something changed."

Alexa cleared her throat. "The two guys in suits running reminded me of something I witnessed at home. I wasn't prepared for the rush of memories." She sat down. "I told you I was raised human. My mom wasn't allowed to teach me any witchcraft and I present like this," she said waving her hand toward her face. "So no one was prepared for my teeth coming in. I've been totally freaked out by it and the sudden appearance of vampires, well recognition of them, hell I don't know... I've just been oblivious for so long. And there was this set of vampires all in business suits, I don't know are they called a flock? A pack? Whatever. They're just always around, lurking. Are the guys in grey suits just like the ones in black suits back at home? I mean they could have just been humans, but they seemed really determined to get somewhere right on the heels of what I assume were two vampires about ready to fight."

Taking a deep breath she closed her eyes and shook her head. "I came here to get away from vampires. I mean I'm not so stupid as to think none are here, but I just... I wasn't prepared."

"How much do you know?"

"Uh, day one, figure out how to retract my teeth. I swear my mom was going to faint with me standing there in all of my vampire glory. But after that, not much. I had to be told about people's scents. I mean, I had no clue. I was told about not revealing, the rest I'm just figuring out on my own."

"What about witchcraft?"

Alexa shook her head. "I know nothing. Valerie is actually teaching me basics. I didn't even know what a grimoire was. I now have a pretty little notebook but I haven't put anything in it. I'm like really green behind the ears."

"Do you know what type of witch you are?"

"Oh, I'm a psychic. I knew that before I knew witchcraft was real. I see little glimpses of things, but nothing useful to know the full... um... cause and effect? It feels very useless."

Donella nodded. "I get it." She paused and cocked her head. "Someone has had to tell you that you're a dark witch?"

Alexa nodded.

"That means you're powerful and probably capable of more than just snippets of visions."

She sighed and shrugged her shoulders. "The snippets I get are usually pretty gruesome. Between being part vampire and the macabre visions, I'm pretty sure that explains the volume of dark I carry around."

Donella wrinkled her forehead. "How macabre are we talking about?"

"Horrible. It's fights and death and what I'm pretty sure is torture. Lots of screaming and just so much blood. It's rare I don't have a nightmare that isn't filled with puddles of blood or people dripping with blood being chased." After a heavy exhale she said, "It's a lot. I don't know if I'm relieved or terrified to find out they're premonitions."

"You know for certain they're premonitions?"

Alexa nodded. "At least one was."

"With all of that blood, it sounds like you're around a lot of vampires."

Alexa tilted her head. "That makes sense, although I've seen witches do some pretty awful stuff."

Donella nodded her head. "Yeah, witches can unleash their own brand of gruesome. But so can humans."

"I guess."

"You see vampires as monsters, don't you?"

Alexa sat quiet for a moment then slowly nodded. She evened her breathing as she felt tears come to the surface.

"Lexie, you're not a monster. You emit a lot of energy so there's more to you than just premonitions. But all of that, your vampire side, your witch side can all be wielded for good, to protect others." Donella cast a sympathetic look at Alexa. "You know, you were protecting Jeff at lunch today."

"Well, I..." Alexa sniffled and thought for a moment. "I guess. Maybe."

Chapter Twenty-Three

Driving Valerie's car through the winding streets toward the condo, Alexa passed a few families bringing their small children around the neighborhood for trick-or-treating. She smiled at a man in the crosswalk pulling a wagon loaded with a toddler wearing fuzzy dog ears flapping in the wind. The man nodded as he waved, a silent gesture of gratitude for not mowing him over in the middle of the street.

When Alexa arrived at the condo four witches stood in the dining room with Sarah and Valerie. All wore long black dresses and tall pointed hats and Alexa knew her costume waited for her upstairs. Valerie argued days earlier that overcoming old stereotypes had to be subtle, not all at once. She refused to adorn her face with warts or to cackle, but she saw nothing wrong with wearing what was considered a traditional witch's hat. Alexa suspected Valerie enjoyed wearing costumes and hated being told she was too old to do so.

Valerie pulled Alexa to the table. "Ladies," she announced. "This is our new roommate, Lexie."

Four death scenes flooded Alexa's head, submerging her own, Valerie's, and Sarah's.

"Lexie, this is Patricia and this here is Tracy. I've known them both forever," Valerie said with a beaming smile. She slung an arm around a third woman. "And this is our beloved Heidi, who can do no wrong."

"We love her anyway," Patricia said.

"And this is Linda," Sarah said. "She hired me at the bookstore where Valerie and I met. If you ever need a book recommendation, this is who you need to talk to."

"Glad to meet all of you!" Alexa said. "I'll probably need you to remind me of your names later on."

"No problem," Linda said.

"I never remember names," Heidi said with a grin.

"What's your name?" Patricia asked Heidi. The two burst out laughing.

"I need to change, I'll be back in a minute," Alexa said.

Alexa dashed to her room to wiggle into her black dress and

pop a pointy hat on her head. When she returned to the main floor, Sarah was pouring apple cider into a plastic cauldron and Patricia held a bottle of rum to add to it. The doorbell rang and Alexa diverted her journey toward the table to answer the door, grabbing a different plastic cauldron along the way to distribute candy.

After dropping miniature candy bars in the bags of a princess, transformer, and cowardly lion, Alexa joined the witches at the dining table. They lit candles and placed them strategically around the condo and turned off the lights. Alexa enjoyed the ambiance and wondered why her mother didn't burn more candles – if not as a witch, but maybe for decoration? Heidi excused herself to attend to the firepit on the back porch.

The rest of the women took turns answering the front door to greet children and distribute candy. Tracy slammed the door, muttering that she wasn't going to deal with any damn vampires.

"Are they coming up the walk?" Alexa asked.

"Yes, but you shouldn't face them on your own," Tracy said.

"They're children," Alexa said, "I'll be fine."

She opened the door to find another princess, this one dressed in blue. Cinderella? She wasn't sure. A little boy dressed as a gray fuzzy creature of some sort stood next to a taller boy, scowling with arms crossed and not wearing a costume. Although their parents lingered on the sidewalk, the young teen appeared to be an escort. Alexa smiled as she dropped candy in the bags of the costumed children and extended a handful to the teen.

The teen grabbed her wrist and murmured, "It would be nothing for me to kidnap you."

Alexa broke his grip and dropped the candy, grabbing his shirt. She pulled him close as she tossed a quick look to his parents. She murmured in his ear, "it would be nothing for me to kill you right now," and pushed him away. He stumbled back two steps as fear shuttered through his body. The boy turned and scampered behind his younger siblings, his scent of fear finally reaching his parents. They turned in unison to see him scoop up the little girl and rush to their safety.

"Why are you running away?" Alexa yelled behind him. "The cauldron is waiting for you. Teenaged boys are so delicious!"

The younger boy turned and stared at her in horror. His father grabbed him under the arms and made eye contact with Alexa.

"Your son is making idle threats. This is the wrong place to do that."

The father paused for a moment as concern crossed his face. His eyes darted back and forth as if he was assessing who else was in the vicinity – mostly humans with a few witches and even fewer vampires. Alexa maintained her focus on the family and when the man's attention returned to her he seemed unnerved she hadn't moved from the doorway but continued to glare at him. With his small son dangling in his arms he looked back to the older boy and again at Alexa.

"If he continues to be a little shit, just bring him by and we'll take him off your hands. Forever."

The father stiffened and backed away. His wife scooped up the girl and they rushed their family down the sidewalk missing several stops of free candy.

Alexa adjusted her hat and returned to the condo, slamming the door behind her.

"That was ballsy," Tracy said.

"From what I've seen, most vampires are terrified of witches," Alexa said.

"I've heard that too," Heidi said. "They believe the wives tales like how witches eat little children and we ride brooms."

"What if that father comes back later tonight?" Linda asked.

Shaking her head Alexa said, "Nah, he was as terrified as his son. They're going to spend the evening trying to fish our candy out from the rest of the bag."

"It would be smarter to throw away what they have now and start fresh down the street," Patricia said.

"But what about other witches handing out candy?" Sarah asked.

"They're going to become religious converts who never observe Halloween ever again!" Heidi said giggling.

Everyone burst out laughing and the doorbell rang again. Alexa turned and grabbed a handful of candy. She opened the door to find a pre-teen girl dressed in a denim shirt and holding a jack-o-lantern with a steak knife jabbed in it. Her friend wore a cartoonish costume for a character Alexa didn't recognize. Another group of kids approached the walkway so she waited for them. The witches behind her returned to the table completing the Samhain preparations.

At nine p.m. Valerie turned off the front porch light and locked the door indicating no more candy to the people outside. She asked the women inside to join her on the back porch. Much to Alexa's surprise, there were two fire pits burning and she wondered when the second one arrived.

Valerie turned to face her guests. "As you know, there is a multitude of ways to honor Samhain. The way my mother taught me was to build two fires and walk your livestock between them. Having no livestock, we just walked or danced between the fires." With her stemmed goblet of cider and rum raised in the air, Valerie kicked off her shoes and then twirled in circles as she moved between the fires. The flames became more intense and as she finally passed through a small pop burst in the air. Each woman walked between the pits with varying effects from the fires, but they all ended with a pop.

Alexa slipped out of her shoes and stepped forward, instantly feeling the energy. There was more than heat; it was raw energy. She paused and looked at the fire to her left, pulsing and throbbing. She looked to the fire on her right also pulsing but pulling as well. Alexa closed her eyes and extended her arms. Slowly she turned in circles, feeling the energies dancing with her. Passion and lust built; their intensity burning. She felt the power, so much energy swirling around her. As she left the fires behind, a roar emerged from both pits, and sparks arced between the two. She turned in time to see twinkling embers rain to the ground.

She looked between the two fires as the remaining smoke formed an arch. "Huh!" Questions poured out behind her:

"What was that?"

"How did you do that?"

"Did you do that?"

"I've never seen fires join!"

Alexa turned around to the other witches, eyes wide with surprise. "I have no idea," she said.

Valerie stepped forward. "Did you feel anything?"

Alexa's eyebrows shot up. "Oh yeah. There was definitely a sexual energy between the two."

"Really?" Valerie looked at Alexa as if she were trying to read something more. With a baffled look on her face, she shook her head. "I've never heard of anything like that."

"They were pulsing... like... like they were trying to mate," she said.

Patricia looked up where the fires had joined and said, "I think they reached orgasm."

The women erupted in laughter. Linda pondered aloud how Alexa stirred sexual energy from a fire pit and again more laughter. Alexa felt comfort in the night air. An easy camaraderie fell into place as light conversation and a little banter bounced about. With the fires still burning, Valerie guided the chatty group back into the condo, offering to refill everyone's goblets.

They gathered around the table set for eight. Sarah took her regular seat with Tracy next to her and Patricia across the table where Alexa normally sat. Valerie however opted for the opposite end with Alexa and Heidi on either side of her and Tracy next to Alexa.

They passed a platter of smoked pork loin with orange-herb sauce. Sarah served herself as well as the plate at the empty head of the table. They passed another platter with slices of roasted beets, a bowl with spiced apples, and a basket of homemade bread.

Valerie stood holding her goblet. "To round out tonight's observations we share a meal, including a plate for the deceased." She extended a hand toward the empty seat and tipped a nod. Alexa and the other women raised their goblets for the toast.

Valerie sat down. "Ladies, please bow your heads." Everyone joined hands around the table with Sarah and Patricia resting their hands on the arms of the empty chair. Valerie bowed her head. "We thank the Goddess for the bounty of the previous year and ask for continued blessings for the coming year. We invite a friend from the deceased realm to join our meal in a peaceful gathering."

Everyone dropped hands, but Sarah and Patricia continued to hold the empty chair.

Patricia nervously cleared her throat. "Someone is here," she whispered.

Everyone froze and all eyes rested on the empty chair. Slowly they rejoined their hands.

Valerie gulped and repeated her invitation. "We invite a friend from the deceased realm to join our meal in a peaceful gathering."

A wind swirled around the table as the deaths of two women filled Alexa's head. She smelled them, full-blooded witches carrying the scents of roses and fresh grass, nearly identical scents as if the two were related. The candle flames leaned to and fro with the air current swirling around the table. The swirling stopped but the scents remained, one at each end of the table. The one who died coughing, gasping for each breath lingered near the empty chair. The other died at the bottom of a staircase, sharp pains in her left leg and lower back and a dull ache on the back of her head as she looked toward the upper floor of a beautiful home – she hovered behind Valerie.

The scent of roses became stronger near the empty chair and Alexa watched as a form appeared seated in the chair. The weak image revealed an old woman with hair swept into a loose bun. She nodded in gratitude and extended her hands above the table with her palms upward.

Sarah, seated next to the apparition looked around the table as if to check that others also saw the form. Alexa darted her attention between the apparition and Sarah, nodding that she saw it as well.

Next to Sarah, Linda's fork fell from the table to the ground. The second scent had moved into her seat with Linda still there. Linda jolted and her eyes fluttered. She lifted her head and looked directly at Alexa.

"You. Blood of Nadia," Linda said in French.

Alexa asked who was Nadia. "Qui est Nadia?"

"Our sister," Linda said, extending her hand in front of Sarah toward the apparition. Alexa looked at the form in the empty chair who tipped her head in acknowledgment.

"You are her blood," Linda said.

"Who are you?" Alexa asked in French.

"Natasha," Linda said pressing her hand to her chest then extending her hand to her sister, "Nicolina."

Alexa nodded at the introduction and caught Sarah's expression of panic being caught between the apparition and her possessed friend.

"Where is Nadia?" Alexa asked.

"Trapped... a garden. Release her."

"How?"

"Cord... must cut... her granddaughter... holds... gold charm," Linda heaved for air as she spoke.

Alexa looked at Linda and then at the apparition as she ran through her memory of family members with gardens. Her mom? Her mom's mom? She worried the granddaughter in question was her wretched grandmother, the one who hated hybrids and convinced her mother not to let Alexa know about her own powers. "Is the granddaughter Beverly?"

"Agatha."

Alexa wrinkled her forehead. "Who is Agatha?"

"Edward... mother."

Alexa leaned back in her chair as if she had been struck, her eyes wide. Edward, her grandfather, a vampire, a very strong vampire, was related to these witches? Her grandfather was a hybrid? Then she remembered Eric talking about the queen, something about her being called a witch.

"Agatha... Time is soon," Linda said. "Must help... cross. Release... Nadia."

Alexa stared at Linda unsure what to say. Did she have any other option but to agree? How the hell was she supposed to help anyone "cross" or know how to release Nadia?

"Why me?" she whispered.

"'Tis your path."

Alexa shook her head in protest. "How do I help someone cross?"

"By... tooth."

Alexa gasped, horrified she should kill again. Panting she stared at Linda.

"Release... Nadia," Linda repeated.

Linda pressed back in her chair and took a gasping breath. Alexa turned to look at the apparition at the end of the table just in time to see her raise her head from a nod and disappear. Air swirled around the table brushing each person and then the candles extinguished. The women's scents and death scenes evaporated. Only heavy breathing and strong scents of fear and smoke remained in the dark room.

"Linda, are you okay?" Heidi asked.

"We need to get her to the couch," Sarah cried.

Alexa watched as everyone grappled in the darkness. She sat in stunned silence staring at Linda slumped in her chair.

The lights came on, disorienting everyone in the room. Tracy, already out of her seat, moved toward Linda to help her to the living room.

Patricia looked at Alexa. "What the hell was that?"

Alexa shook her head.

Standing at the light switch Valerie asked, "Patricia, would you mind helping them with Linda? Lexie and I need to talk." She looked at Alexa. "Are you okay?"

Alexa shook her head.

"Come on, let's go outside."

Not realizing she stood up, Alexa looked back to her chair and then to Valerie.

Valerie guided her to the porch where she pulled a metal patio chair from the grass onto the cement and directed Alexa to sit down. Alexa watched her pull up another chair thinking they needed to be returned to the patio anyway.

"So you speak French?" Valerie asked.

Alexa nodded. "My Grandmere is from Lorraine."

"You're damn near fluent."

Alexa offered a faint grin.

"I understood every word that was said. I also have French roots. Who is Edward?"

"My grandfather, Grandmere's husband. Do you think the electrocution thing with the skull at the candle shop was one of these women?"

"I don't know. You probably should have asked them."

Alexa nodded.

"If Edward is your grandfather, then Agatha is your great-grandmother?"

"I guess so. I don't know that I've ever met her. I can't think of a time my father has even mentioned her."

Valerie tapped her forefingers together. "And this Nadia they want you to release is Agatha's grandmother, making her your great-great-great-grandmother."

Alexa raised an eyebrow and tried to follow the number of greats and got lost. "I guess so."

"This really is new information to you."

Alexa nodded.

"By the tooth?" Valerie asked. "You are supposed to *kill* your great-grandmother?"

Alexa's mouth dropped open as she stared at Valerie.

"I hope not! And 'soon'? When is that?"

Valerie grinned in sympathy.

"That's so weird." Alexa cocked her head. "Am I in a dream? No, there's not enough blood or dying, but I can't piece it together. None of this makes sense." She wiped tears off her cheeks and sniffled. "I don't even know what to do with this information. It's so... lacking."

"When the time is right you'll know what needs to be done."

"Evidently kill an old woman with my fucking teeth," Alexa sobbed.

Valerie sat quiet as Alexa sniffled.

"She didn't seem overly concerned about how Agatha would die," Valerie said. "They were asking you to help Nadia."

"Something about a charm and a garden," Alexa said with a sniffle and a shrug.

"It sounded like the cord that bound the curse is inside a charm."

"It's a curse?"

"Absolutely. Someone's soul is stranded in one place for eternity? She can't ever reincarnate? That is one hell of a curse!"

"Wow. And the granddaughter, Agatha, has the charm." Alexa tilted her head. "Do you think Agatha knows she's carrying around the curse for her grandmother's soul?"

"I bet she doesn't. What sort of vile person would do that?" Valerie shook her head in disgust. "This is a lot of very dark magic – powerful, dark magic. And they hid the cord in what sounds like jewelry? If the granddaughter doesn't know she's carrying the curse then I bet it was given to her as a gift. That's just over-the-top evil."

"You think it's jewelry?"

"The word 'charm' seems to indicate that – something like a necklace, bracelet, or a watch fob. Maybe even a ring."

"So destroy the item and release a soul?"

Valerie shook her head. "No, you have to literally cut the cord to dissipate the spell." Valerie pressed a hand to her mouth and shook her head again. "Lexie, be *very* careful handling that cord. You should summon Nadia's sisters and have as many witches available to bring protection, like physically surrounding you, as you cut the cord. I guarantee there is a protection spell on the charm holding that cord."

Chapter Twenty-Four

Smoke swirled through the trees, casting the eerie moonlight in ominous waves. Death twined with the smoke smelling both delicious and frightful. Alexa ran forward, propelled by anger.

When she lifted her head to get her bearings clean air filled her lungs. A light cut through the darkness. Alexa turned her head and saw her bedroom window. She sighed recognizing she had just experienced a nightmare. She couldn't remember what happened before the smoke in the dream, only the sense of anger. Alexa caught a strong smell of smoke and realized the fire pits earlier in the evening infused the scent into her hair, likely inspiring her nightmare.

Alexa stared at the wall, wondering when she had rolled over. A dull light cast a hint of blue on the wall. She scowled at the light and turned to look at the window – daylight. When did she sleep? Was that rain?

With a groan Alexa rolled out of bed, stretching her feet on the sponginess of the carpet. At the stairs she heard the clink of a spoon hitting the side of a porcelain cup, the scent of coffee filling the air. She found Valerie seated at the end of the couch with a coffee cup and saucer on the side table. She held the newspaper folded into one hand as she absently stirred coffee with the other while she read.

Valerie looked up as Alexa came down the stairs. She nodded her head to the other end of the couch inviting Alexa to sit down. Alexa held up a hand and went to the kitchen for her own cup of coffee. As she sat on the couch Valerie dropped her feet to the floor and laid the newspaper on the coffee table.

"Sleep well?" Valerie asked.

Alexa shook her head. "No. I woke up several times."

"I figured. I smelled a vampire in the condo." Valerie chuckled. "It's still off-putting even though I know it's you and you're sound asleep."

"It's still off-putting to me too."

"You need a crash course on how to use your magic," Valerie said. "I thought you'd have time to ease into things, but we have no idea how long until you meet up with Agatha."

"If Agatha is who we think she is that means I will have returned to my family. Well, my father's family."

"And to life as a vampire?"

Alexa nodded.

"But your witchcraft is going to be tested. I don't know how to help you with the vampire side of things but we can work on the witch stuff."

"Ok." Alexa said with a shoulder shrug.

"So we should see what you know how to do at this point."

"Well," Alexa said as she set her cup on the coffee table, "we should go to the back porch for that."

Sarah ran down the stairs. "I don't want to miss this!" She rushed to the sliding door, pulling it open.

Alexa approached rubbing her arms. "How the fuck is it so cold already?"

Sarah offered a sympathetic smile.

"We don't need to go outside," Alexa said standing in the doorway. "I can do this from here." She looked over the debris from the previous night, the two fire pits where the flames had danced above her in a lovers' tango. The rain increased from a gentle drizzle, causing a rhythmic ping from the aluminum downspout next to the patio. She snapped her attention back to Valerie's request – showing her powers. Alexa assessed the common ground, deciding what she should use.

"Okay," Alexa said. "Pay attention to the trees across the pond." She made sure to scan beyond the fire pits, not wanting to spread any live embers. She rested her attention on a scattering of leaves on the distant lawn. She exhaled slowly putting her internal focus on a spot behind her stomach. A slow pulse of energy filled her midsection and she directed the power toward the leaves.

The leaves flipped and twitched. Alexa exerted more energy raising three off the ground. With a deep inhale she generated more power and as she released a slow exhale the leaves skittered across the lawn toward the pond. She felt the power increase and switched her focus to the trees. A wind carried the leaves over the water, fluttering into the tree line. As the trees swished another gust of air swept across the pond. The boughs bent as the air whistled through.

Alexa watched with satisfaction as the wind dissipated and the treetops bobbed to and fro, shaking yellow leaves to the ground. The movement slowed and the trees returned to their sentinel stance, guarding the grounds below.

"I wasn't expecting that," Valerie said. "You're so much stronger than I thought."

"I thought you were going to set the leaves on fire," Sarah said.

Alexa turned to face her. "I don't know how to control fire."

"Then let's teach you," Valerie said as she stepped onto the patio. She turned to Sarah. "You need to close the door and not watch. We can't afford to have your magic interfere with hers and burn the condo down."

Sarah looked between Valerie and Alexa. Without a word, she shut the door and pulled the curtains closed.

Valerie watched the patio doors for a moment then nodded. "You evidently found your solar plexus - where your power comes from." Valerie placed her hands below her rib cage. "Stir that energy, but now think of heat and flames instead of wind. Envision fire, not air." Valerie turned her focus to the fire pit. A puff of smoke swirled up and then another. An ember glowed and more smoke billowed.

Alexa watched as a spark came from the ember and a small flame danced among the debris. She turned to the other pit and sensed warmth, not physically, but in a knowing manner that the wet coals still had fire within them. She stared at one coal while focusing her internal energy. Solar plexus? It had a name? She took a deep breath, feeling the energy in her gut, her solar plexus. A memory arose of her nightmare come to life, the time she walked through her best friend's dark home and encountered intruders. The resulting fight drew in vampires protecting her house down the street and witches from the home next door. She had passed out as her mother used Alexa's energy with another pyromancer to create a flamethrower to destroy the intruders.

If her energy could create flames through another witch then shouldn't she be able to do that on her own? And if she could blast a windstorm across a pond, couldn't she do more than generate a tiny puff of smoke attached to a mere spark? In a measured crescendo, Alexa directed her energy toward the dark coal. She didn't want to create a firestorm, just to fill the pit with flames. The coal pulsed a hint of red. Alexa looked to a neighboring coal. Could she manage two at the same time? Yes, the second coal pulsed. She looked to a third and then a fourth. She felt like an orchestra conductor keeping all of the coals subdued but still churning warmth. Alexa spread her hands out, stretching her fingers as far apart as possible. She could feel the heat and the black coals turned red.

Alexa grinned, nearly losing her focus. Several coals waned to black as she returned her attention to her internal energy and then the coals. Once the coals rebounded to glowing red, she directed a small increase of energy to the pit. One by one the coals popped tiny flames, quickly looking like birthday cake for somebody who needed a lot of candles.

"Stay steady," Valerie whispered. "Don't let this get out of control."

Wanting to look up at the sliding doors to see if Sarah was watching, Alexa instead kept her eyes on the field of tiny flames. With her breathing measured and slow Alexa moved her hands together as if to build a mound. The flames followed her command as they pointed toward the center, extending and building. Alexa pulled her hands upward and closer together, creating a peak. The flames stood taller, creating a central flame nearly two feet tall. Alexa swayed her head and hands to the left and the flames swayed with her. They followed as she leaned right and back to the left. She returned them to the center.

"Now extinguish it," Valerie said.

"How?"

"Reduce your energy and lower the flames."

Alexa exhaled while she lowered her hands, amazed the flames diminished back to the individual birthday candles. She continued to lower her hands and her internal energy. The flames melted into the coals and the coals faded to black.

"Fully extinguish them," Valerie said.

"They're back to where we started."

"No, they could still spark on their own. Make them cold. Suck the heat out of them."

Alexa stared at the coals, tilting her head from one side and then to the other. How was she supposed to suck the heat out? Literally, suck? She inhaled and felt the heat move toward her so she inhaled harder, picturing the heat soaking into her core. A few coals sparked but she could sense cooling in the coals furthest away. She maintained the sensation of soaking the heat into herself and coals went from ashy gray to black. She tried another round of soaking in the heat and weak waves radiated into her even though the coals were all black.

Valerie pressed a hand on the coals and looked up at Alexa. "It took me years to learn that."

Returning inside Alexa and Valerie found Sarah sitting at the table with a cup of coffee in front of her. Valerie kissed her head and said, "I'm sorry I asked you to leave."

"I wanted to watch."

"I know, but we couldn't risk any interference. The good news, though, is that Lexie seems to be able to control her powers so you can watch her next time."

"But that won't be her first time."

"It was really cool. She made a flame bigger than I've ever made and she was able to cool the coals. She's a very strong witch."

Sarah's forced smile made Alexa want to pull her to the patio and replicate the fire she had just made.

Sarah sighed. "You were right to send me away, especially with her working with fire for the first time."

"I think your powers are getting stronger too," Valerie said.

Sarah nodded. "Yeah, last night…"

"Wait," Alexa said waving her hands. "The whole séance thing was *you*?"

Sarah shrugged a shoulder. "It's not normal," she said shaking her head. "We've held these gatherings for several years and *never* had a visitor. I've been to a few séances in my life and the most activity we had was the candles flickering and getting chills. Well, I get chills a lot but…"

"So, the skull at the candle shop was you?"

Valerie cleared her throat. "It's not Sarah trying to stir up anything, but her presence offers a, uh…" Valerie waved her hand as she tried to think of the word. "She's not a conduit but… hmmm… brings an amplification… to energies in her vicinity. What's interesting is that it's always been subtle until recently."

"Like since I showed up?" Alexa asked.

Valerie nodded. "Yes. You carry a lot of energy and I think it makes all of us stronger. I don't know if that's something you can control any more than Sarah controlling her energy. What I do know is the two of you together around other witches spark some very interesting results."

"So we have to avoid each other?" Alexa asked.

Valerie grinned. "Of course not! Your combined powers aren't a bad thing, just interesting how they play off each other."

"And yet we can't control any of it?" Alexa asked.

"I honestly don't know," Valerie said. "Lexie, my guess is with how quickly you've learned to manipulate the elements, which is extremely difficult magic to master, you are more likely able to control who receives your energy. It's not something I can teach, but now that you're aware of it, chances are you'll figure it out. Sarah's abilities, however, probably aren't meant to be controlled - that's the chaos of it. Quite honestly, to be able to harness her energy would require knowing the future as well as the full capacity of people's witchcraft." She turned to face Sarah. "I think your magic is incredible. It's not usually bad, it just brings things to... fruition. Like last night, it was amazing."

"Last night was horrible," Sarah said.

"No, it wasn't," Valerie said shaking her head. "It was frightening. It was a lot to take in. Lexie needed to hear this message, but without the energy you brought to the table, very literally brought to the table, she might not have received that message so succinctly. Instead, it would have come in small blasts, probably through whispers in those phases of half-sleep, but the messages would have been lost in the noise of her nightmares. Maybe she's been receiving them for a long time and didn't understand any of it. " She grabbed Sarah's hand. "Your presence, your energy makes things happen. Last night was scary because we weren't expecting it."

"Val, it was bad news!" Sarah said.

"Was it? She was told how to release someone's soul from a horrific spell."

"She has to kill someone!"

"Let's think about this logically," Valerie said looking between Alexa and Sarah. "Her great-grandmother is likely very old, probably suffering a good deal of pain. Why this is on Lexie's shoulders is a bit of a curiosity, but she doesn't have a close tie to the woman. Maybe others in the family can't bring themselves to do it?"

"Why can't she just die naturally?" Sarah asked.

"That's a very good question, one Lexie won't find the answer to until the time is right. Another question we should ask, is why was this revealed in front of us?"

"Because Linda is a medium," Sarah said.

Valerie shook her head. "No. Mediums and other psychics abound. Why was this revealed here within this gathering?"

Alexa said, "We needed three specific people – one to receive the message, me; one to deliver the message, Linda; and one to explain the magical elements, you. Moreover, two of us needed to be fluent in French." Alexa looked at the row of extinguished candles lined down the middle of the table and snorted. "So it wasn't an accident that I met you two. I'm supposed to be here."

"But you have to kill someone!" Sarah said.

"Well, it's not like I haven't already done that."

"And you're struggling with those deaths," Valerie said. "How do you feel about the news you're supposed to do it again?"

"Dunno."

With wide eyes, Sarah looked between Alexa and Valerie. "How soon do you think this is going to happen?"

Alexa said, "I've been wrestling with that all night. I have this *feeling*, it's not a vision, nothing I can say specifically is giving me information, but just a feeling that it's not in my immediate future like this week, next month, or even several months away, but maybe by summer."

"Next summer?" Valerie asked. "You have a lot to learn by then." She turned to Sarah and smiled. "You can stay but keep control of your mind and intentions."

Valerie grabbed a small pinecone sitting on a side table. She placed the pinecone on an empty plate, balancing it on its tip. As she let go it remained in place, slowly beginning to spin.

Alexa looked up to find Valerie watching her. "I'm a much stronger witch than I let on," Valerie said. "It would be wise for you to learn how to read a witch's strength." The pinecone continued to spin faster and faster, bursting into flames, and fell to pieces on the plate. "You were right. There was sexual energy in the fires last night. Most people never recognize that."

The room filled with the scent of burnt pine. Valerie pinched one of the extinguished pieces and rubbed the ash between her finger and thumb. "The real key, no matter your strength, is to respect your powers. If you dabble in parlor tricks to amuse and entertain your friends, like I'm doing with this pinecone, or to shock and awe audiences, you will never progress beyond being a simple magician. Respect your powers. Learn about them and how to use them. Be humble with your powers and show gratitude every chance you get. Your powers are a gift from the goddess, Mother Earth, and should always be honored as such. Revere yourself as a vessel for these powers, a means to share them for a greater good. As long as you don't come to think you actually own them, you'll be fine."

"Do they own me?" Alexa asked.

Valerie laughed. "No. They exist. You exist. You both exist in the same shell."

"Does the shell own us?"

"Why are you so concerned about ownership?"

Alexa stared at Valerie. Was she concerned about ownership? Was ownership important? "Huh. I don't know. So, this power exists, and I guess it's been in this shell the whole time? And we just met? Now we have to figure out how to coexist?"

"And how to work together," Sarah said.

Valerie smiled. "Exactly. You know there's another entity in that shell?"

"Yeah, I know." Alexa shook her head. "The vampire. I don't know that I can make peace with that."

"You have a lot to learn with your witchcraft, but at some point, hopefully soon, you need to come to terms with being a vampire," Valerie said.

"Well, part of wanting to live here with the two of you was to ease into being a witch."

"Was finding out you're a witch scary?" Sarah asked.

"A little. I mean it wasn't a huge surprise with my psychic

abilities, but yes knowing all of this exists is a little scary. That the myths and spooky stories and wives tales are true is really terrifying. This stuff scares me. Now, learning about my physical powers is very surprising, but I find them amazing. Like when I made the trees wave I got a little thrill, like oh my god, I did that! And now to find out I can do fire... whoa! That's so cool!"

Valerie smiled. "Stop right there. That feeling you have, that awe, that appreciation – THAT is something you should never let fade. It will be the core of your strength as a witch."

"What do you mean?"

"Remember we told you witchcraft comes with a price? Well, gratitude is a form of payment. Since awe is appreciation, a form of gratitude, your amazement of how well a spell or energy works is usually satisfactory in that end. The only catch is that it has to be genuine."

Alexa nodded.

"Ultimately your thoughts and actions convey your true gratitude," Valerie said. "I was taught to take a moment every day to express that. My mother believed in meditation. She said it was important to center yourself by touching the earth in whatever way possible – it could be standing barefoot in the grass, or when I stay in a hotel I'll hold a clump of dirt from a potted plant – and focus inward while expressing gratitude for all that has entered your life. Don't forget, be grateful for your losses, they bring blessings as well."

Alexa contemplated how loss could be a blessing. She wasn't so sure that was possible.

Valerie took a deep breath and pressed her hands together, tapping her fingers against each other. "I feel compelled to tell you... warn you... of the mistake many witches make. In learning to harness... master? their arts, they often slip to try to own the energy. Remember I just said you don't own it, it does not own you, right?"

Again, Alexa nodded her head.

"You can point the energy in a certain direction. You can ask it to do your will. The moment, however, you attempt to own it, contain it, manipulate it... alter it? It will destroy you. You are not a goddess and you never will be. You're a witch and nothing more. You may be a very powerful witch, possibly from a long line of priestesses, but that will never make you a goddess. These powers flow through you, but they are not yours." Valerie locked eyes with Alexa and said, "Exude gratitude."

Chapter Twenty-Five

A week had passed since the Samhain gathering. Shaken by a ghost's near-flippant comment that she was supposed to kill her great-grandmother, Alexa couldn't clear her mind. When was all of this supposed to happen?

Why her?

Alexa stared at the calendar, a large desk calendar where she often doodled along the edges. November. She had been in Radcliff for over a month. How would she know when it was time to move on? What on earth would take her to be near her great-grandmother? Did the woman know about her? Yes, of course, she did – Alexa's dad had said something about waiting for approval from the council to tell her about being a vampire - the council, the one that answered to his grandmother, the queen.

What did the woman think about Alexa? Why was Alexa sent away?

Valerie's paralegal, Melissa, stood waiting for an answer.

Alexa broke from her reverie and cleared her throat. "I'm sorry, what?"

"Are you training to be a paralegal?"

Confused, Alexa wrinkled her forehead and stared at Melissa. "No. Why would you think that?"

"Valerie has an emergency meeting with a client and asked that I *fetch* you."

"Why..." Alexa quickly realized Valerie was with a vampire and stood up. "Yeah, I think I know what this is about."

"Well, I hope your notes are as detailed as last time."

Alexa noted the jealousy in Melissa's snide tone. "Listen," she said patiently. "I'm no threat to your job, but this is sort of unique. I know something about this guy and... it's just better if I'm there. And the more time we stand here and bullshit about it the more uncomfortable Valerie is going to be."

Melissa pulled back with a confused look. "That doesn't make any sense."

Leaning in, Alexa said, "It really is a special situation, if you know what I mean. But... if I tell you anything more I'd have to kill you... *if you know what I mean.*" She raised an eyebrow and turned away resisting the desire to laugh out loud.

The expression on Melissa's face was sheer horror. Valerie's face, on the other hand, was a relief when Alexa came down the hall.

"You need to do damage control with Melissa," Alexa said. "I made it sound like this was a mafia consultation."

"It sort of is," Valerie said. "He specifically asked for you to be present."

A shot of panic shuttered through Alexa. What if the vampire wasn't one of the men she met with before, but her father? No, that was silly - she would have recognized his scent the moment he stepped into the building. Taking a deep cleansing breath, Alexa followed Valerie into the conference room. To Alexa's relief, Diederich Coburg was in the room.

"I apologize for this unannounced visit," he said. "Lexie, I need to ask you about our meeting in the ravine near Hillview Bridge."

Alexa extended her upturned hands. "There's nothing to tell you. I smelled a dead body – a fresh kill... you know I can smell death."

Diederich grinned and nodded, confirming he knew she was part vampire. "Yes, which is I am asking for more information."

"There's not much to say. I made Sarah stop as soon as I sensed it and we were on our way back out of there when we ran into you and your men. She didn't know there was a body down there until we got back to the condo."

"Did you sense any other people down there?"

"No."

Diederich sighed and shook his head. "I've had two more men die the same way and I cannot connect them."

Alexa thought of the dead body near Laura's house. "One of our coworkers said some kids came across a body in a field near behind her subdivision. A neighbor checked out the area and a six-foot plot was completely cleared of vegetation and everything."

With a smirk, Diederich cocked his head. "I am aware of that incident and it is not tied to the men I am inquiring about."

"Oh. But it does confirm my suspicions."

He nodded and then leveled a look at Alexa. "Who are you?"

"I am saying this quite honestly - I don't know. I was raised as a human and was oblivious to all of this until my teeth came in a couple months ago. My family refused to tell me anything, even about witchcraft. I met a guy, the one who tagged me, and he was the only one who taught me anything at all. So with the help of people like Valerie and Sarah, I'm learning about my witch side."

"Your teeth came in?"

Alexa nodded.

He ran a hand through his hair in frustration. "You need to be with your family."

"My family is ashamed of me."

"Your family was hiding you."

Alexa shrugged. "They had plenty of opportunities to clear the air. I've found my community now and I'm happy here."

Pressing two fingers to his forehead, Diederich sighed. "For the moment I must table this topic, but we will continue this conversation in the future. Thank you for the information and what I hope is honesty. If you encounter any more dead bodies please call my direct number and speak only to me." He extended a business card to Alexa and tipped his head as he left the room.

Valerie watched him walk toward the reception area. She turned to face Alexa. "What do I tell Melissa?"

"He was looking for information about a dead co-worker and I was a possible witness."

Valerie nodded her head in agreement and looked back down the hall.

Chapter Twenty-Six

Sensing Laura's approach Alexa busied herself with three boxes of files sitting next to her desk. Alexa learned many years earlier to act surprised when people approached her from behind.

"Want to head over to Donna's?" Laura asked.

Faking a startle, Alexa spun around. "Um, no. I brought a salad today."

"Can I bring back a milkshake for you?"

Alexa spent far too much time contemplating the lure of a really good chocolate shake. She sighed. "I should behave."

Laura shrugged. "Your loss, but I do respect your restraint."

Alexa laughed and shook her head. As she watched Laura walk away Alexa decided to grab her lunch from the fridge. Walking to the break room Donella stopped her in the hallway. "Headed to lunch?"

"Yeah."

"You should join me on the back deck so we can talk."

"It's a little cold outside," Alexa said.

"The sun is out, we'll be fine."

The "back deck", a picnic table on a slab of concrete behind the law office, offered a great view of a pond surrounded by a recently mowed lawn. "It's not the most hygienic of places," Alexa said, observing the goose droppings on and around the table.

"Sorry about that," Donella said. "I'll have to remind our cleaning crew to address this area. I don't think we have smokers in the office anymore so not many people use the space."

"It is kinda peaceful."

"And private. Here, I grabbed these on my way out of the kitchen." Donella pulled a roll of paper towels from under her arm and used several sheets to knock the goose droppings off the table. She laid out a couple more sheets as placemats for her and Alexa.

Alexa grabbed more sheets to line the patio chair before she sat down. "It's really not that bad out here with my jacket on."

Donella followed Alexa's lead for lining her chair. "It's easy to forget the temperatures warm up during the day when you're trapped inside from dawn to dusk." Donella pulled a bowl and spoon from her lunch bag. "I want you to know I generally avoid fraternizing with coworkers. I've seen too many people fall to office gossip so I don't let anyone in my world and I take no part in theirs."

"Are you making me an exception?"

"You need guidance."

"Valerie has been working with me." Alexa placed her dish on the makeshift placemat revealing the salad she assembled the previous night.

"Valerie is a full-blooded witch. She can't possibly help you maneuver the difficulties of being a hybrid." Donella opened a bottle of water and held the cap in her hand. "I realize you can breeze through life as a full-blooded witch, but your vampire side can't hide forever."

"Yeah, I'm aware."

Donella raised an eyebrow.

"Just too many encounters."

Shaking her head Donella said, "It sounds like you need to learn how to maneuver around full-blood vampires."

"I'd rather learn how to avoid them altogether."

"Don't we all."

"So what can you teach me?"

"Not so much what I can teach you, but who I can introduce you to," Donella said with a smile.

"Oh really?"

"I have a circle of friends that I think you would like. They would enjoy meeting you and could be helpful in your journey."

"My only concern is that it really hasn't been to my advantage to reveal myself as a hybrid. It just seems the fewer people who know it the better."

"We're all hybrids and in this group, no one has anything to gain by hurting the others," Donella said. "So if you're curious you should come out with us one night. We're talking about hitting a nightclub that welcomes hybrids."

"That sounds interesting."

Donella hesitated before she spoke. "I've been seeing a guy, which I really don't want to be discussed in front of anyone here if you don't mind?"

"Not a problem," Alexa said. "You're holding my secret, I'm

pretty sure I can hold yours. Even with Valerie."

Donella nodded. "Good. Thank you. His name is Maurice and we've been seeing each other for a while. He's a good guy, quiet for the most part. A big teddy bear." A broad smile spread.

"Aw, you're smitten!"

"A little. It's been a while since I've had feelings like this for anyone. Unfortunately last time it wasn't reciprocated. So I'm taking my time to savor every second."

Donella's death scene replayed yet again – loud and bold like one who would die in the very near future. Alexa forced a smile. "Yes, it is important to savor those wonderful moments."

"It's hard. There are so many challenges out there, but I have to remind myself we are all struggling to capture those fleeting instances of peace and happiness."

"I think some people manage that better than others."

"That's true," Donella said. "I've met plenty of people lacking joy in their lives. I think that's why I like you. You're not dour, full of doom and gloom. Let's be clear, competence counts for a lot, but you manage to bring an air of happiness wherever you go."

Blushing, Alexa didn't know what to say.

"Even when you're rattled, like at the restaurant, you rose above your fears and returned us back to course – not just yourself, but brought the waitress, Jeff, and myself back to focusing on the meal. And yet you didn't dismiss your own feelings but you understood there was nothing to do about them at that time. That's an amazing skill – you're destined to do great things."

"Uh, thank you. That's a beautiful compliment. It's kind of hard to contemplate anything in my future beyond ducking and running."

Donella shook her head. "I doubt it. Running like that means someone else has power over you. You're already taking ownership of your life. What you're feeling right now is the turbulence of transition and not knowing the future. But trust me, your next phase will be you having your feet solidly on the ground and knowing where you're at consciously deciding where you're going."

"I hope so. I really feel lost... adrift. It's like everyone has their act together and knows what they're doing and I'm back here at square one."

A hearty laugh erupted from Donella. "You're in the early

stages of adulthood, virtually no one has their act together. Everything you thought and believed at twenty will be shattered to dust by the time you turn thirty."

"Yeah, I'd say my life exploding would qualify." Alexa looked toward the pond as two geese skidded to a landing on the water. "Before, at least I knew the rules of how to be a human. Now, I don't know anything. I'm just so inexperienced."

"Well I can help with that," Donella said. "It's why I want to introduce you to my friends. I don't know how good of a teacher I am, but some of them are actual educators so I thought maybe they would be helpful. Of course, continue taking in what Valerie and her roommate have to teach you. Just in general I believe we should always be learning to help the evolution of our souls."

Alexa grinned. "That almost sounds like religion."

Donella tilted her head. "Do you believe in reincarnation?"

Alexa chuckled. "Yes."

"But not a higher power?"

"I've never really thought about it."

Donella scowled. "Never?"

"I don't know. The idea of a grey-bearded guy sitting on a cloud controlling our lives seems far-fetched."

"What about a higher energy? Not a single entity dictating but something collective that is part of all of us?"

Alexa averted her eyes to stare at the pond again. "I'll have to think about that." She took a deep breath and looked back at Donella. "What do you know about fate?"

"Well... I'd like to believe in self-determination, that we are the masters of our destiny. If not, why are we working so hard? Where is the payoff for all of that effort? What do you believe?"

"I see things, little glimpses, premonitions. I don't see the path, only the endpoint. So I do wonder exactly that - why exert any effort if the result is already determined?"

Donella grinned. "Maybe you don't see the path because the path was never determined? Maybe our self-determination allows us to choose our paths and alter them along the way?"

Alexa leaned back in her chair and considered the idea of having control over her path. Was leaving Brentwood pre-determined or did she truly hold the reigns on that decision? Was she in control of her life?   "I'd like to believe we have that type of power over our lives."

"Then live it like you do."

Chapter Twenty-Seven

Alexa followed Donella into the nightclub brushing past the bouncer, a large vampire who looked menacing. Loud music, loud patrons, clinking glass, and the stench of sweating bodies attacked Alexa's senses as hundreds of death scenes flooded into her head. With barely a pinhole of focus, she spotted Donella walking in front of her. Dutifully, Alexa kept her sights on Donella's form as she forced one foot in front of the other. She knew this fog would clear in due time but she couldn't lose Donella.

Donella turned and said something but Alexa couldn't hear between her internal noise and the loud music. She shook her head pointing to her ear so Donella motioned for her to follow.

A woman pulled on Donella's arm. She turned and greeted the woman and then tried to introduce Alexa. Alexa grinned - she had finally melded the death scenes into white noise but the thumping music continued to make conversation impossible. The woman smiled in sympathy, grabbed Alexa's hand, and pulled her toward the back of the nightclub. Poor lighting nearly hid a metal staircase along the back wall.

Once at the top of the stairs the woman turned to face Alexa. "You're too young to wince at all of that noise down there. C'mon, we have a table over there."

While not nearly as crowded as the dance floor, the second floor still held a lot of people, bringing new death scenes into her head. Music played overhead, different from the first floor, which was still somewhat distinguishable, but definitely felt as if the bass reverberated throughout the whole building.

They arrived at a table with four people, all hybrids. One man stood waiting for their arrival and greeted Donella with a kiss.

"Lexie, this is Maurice."

"Glad to meet you."

Donella pointed to the woman they met downstairs. "That's Crystal and over there is Dennis and Alicia and Stephanie."

Alicia stepped away from the table toward Alexa. "Wow, that's amazing. I've never met anyone who could mask as a witch!"

"Yeah, I'm a little freak of nature. Gotta say I'm surprised how many vampires and witches are here."

Alicia grinned. "Aw, that's just them playing with fire, pretending we're all the same. The only upside is that it gives us hybrids a place to socialize." She tilted her head, indicating Alexa follow her to the table. "I assume Donella told you about the deal here – no hunting, no tagging, no rape, no murder, no spellwork, no playing with elements. Just singing, dancing, and consensual contact only."

"Yeah, she did," Alexa said with a nod. She sat down as Donella and Maurice approached the table.

Stephanie stared at Alexa. "My God you're young!"

Alexa laughed and shrugged. "I'm over twenty-one."

"Talk to me when you're over forty!"

Surprised, Alexa tried to assess Stephanie's age and scowled. "You're not over forty."

"I celebrated my fortieth with this same group of fools back in June!"

"Well happy belated birthday! You look stunning. I hope I age half as well on my fortieth."

Crystal waved a hand. "The answer to that is usually with our mothers. How has your mother carried her age?"

"Well, my mom is not old."

Stephanie's grin dropped as horror swept across her face. "Is your mother in her forties?"

With a timid nod, Alexa tried to offer a sympathetic grin. "She's forty-four."

Stephanie slumped backward in her chair, Maurice stood up and walked away from the group, Donella stared at Alexa, Crystal laid her head on the table, Alicia shook her head, and Dennis roared with laughter.

Alexa waved her hands in the air. "Friends, I'm so sorry. Let me reintroduce myself. My name is Janice, I'm forty-four. I like to pretend I'm my punk-ass daughter who is twenty-five – she looks just like me and carries my scent." Alexa ran her fingers through her hair. "Now I haven't had my hair long like this for quite some time, but if you remember back in the sixties, this and a headband were all you needed. Clothing optional!" And then she winked. Laughter broke out and Maurice returned to his seat.

"It's been a long time since I've been to a clothing-optional event," Alicia said.

"So, Janice, you were a hippie?" Maurice asked.

"Mom calls me a hippie, but I prefer *flower child*," Alexa said with a broad grin as she mocked her mother

Maurice pointed a finger at her and laughed. "You're damn good at this."

Alexa chuckled. "Oh, it's a whole production any time my grandmother is around because Janice and her mother do not get along. Mom will immediately plop down on the lawn, weave flowers into necklaces and crowns, humming anything from Peter Paul and Mary – her favorite is 'Puff, The Magic Dragon.' She'll say 'groovy' and 'far out' a lot, toss the peace sign, and always reminds grandma we should make love, not war. I mean I've got it all down."

"That's truly impressive," Stephanie said nodding.

"We need to get this girl a drink!" Dennis made his proclamation and strode toward the bar.

"This is a pretty cool place," Alexa said.

"It's changed since we were here last," Donella said.

"How long ago was that?"

Donella leaned back, looking at Alicia. "Has it been a year?"

"Not quite," Alicia said. "It was after Christmas. Oh, it was in January for CeCe's birthday."

"Hmm, yeah I remember that," Donella said.

"So what changed?" Alexa asked.

"The full-bloods found out we were having too much fun and wanted a cut," Crystal said.

"Of the fun or the profits?" Alexa asked.

"Oh shit," Stephanie said. "Girl, you just cut *right* to the chase!"

Alexa grinned. "Tell me when money isn't involved?"

Stephanie tilted her head in consolation.

Dennis returned to the table with two buckets of beer bottles. A waitress followed behind with a tray of shot glasses. With drinks distributed around the table, Dennis lifted a shot glass in the air. "To friends! To those who have always been and to those new to our fold!" He nodded to Alexa with a broad grin.

Donella and her friends raised their glasses and said in unison, "Blessed be!" and drank their shots.

Alexa repeated, "Blessed be" and swallowed her shot. The

whiskey warmed her gullet and she shook her head. "Damn." The group roared with laughter.

With the first bucket of beers empty, two men approached the table. One slapped Dennis' back. "Hey, man!" Dennis jumped up, joined hands with the guy, and the two slapped each other's backs in a casual hug. He extended a hand to Maurice as they said hello.

"Everyone," the man said, "This is my friend Calvin."

Calvin tipped his head in greeting.

The man placed his hand on Dennis' shoulder again. "This is my buddy, Dennis, I've been telling you about. And that there is his wife, Alicia, and her friends – Crystal, Donella, Stephanie, and oh, and a new arrival," he said pointing around the table. "And this old man is Maurice."

Dennis said, "The new arrival is Donella's friend, Lexie."

The man shot a wink at Alexa and leaned close to Dennis and whispered something. Dennis smiled, nodded, and pulled out a chair indicating the men should join their table.

Crystal leaned toward Alexa. "That's Dwight. He used to work with Dennis."

Maurice waved down the waitress. Alexa bounced her attention between the two new men at the table and watched the waitress finish talking to another table of customers. The array of scents and death scenes in the room blurred together, but she finally zeroed in on Dwight and Calvin's deaths. Like others in the group, they would die at night with fire burning nearby. Dwight's death was the most horrific as he tried to scramble out of a burning building, succumbing to smoke as he hacked and gasped for air laying in a doorway. She couldn't discern whether it was a crazy coincidence or if this group of friends would attend the same event where most of them die. As Alexa tried to pluck through the individual scenes she realized someone was speaking to her. She snapped her head to the side to find Crystal and Stephanie staring at her. Alexa took a deep breath relieved to inhale the relatively clean air of a bar and not the vision of Dwight's room filled with smoke. "What?"

"Are you having an anxiety attack?" Stephanie asked.

Alexa shook her head. "No, but I probably need to get some

fresh air."

Stephanie stood up. "Come on. There's a deck out that door."

Crystal also stood up.

"Where are you going?" Alicia asked.

"To the deck," Crystal said.

Donella stood up as the waitress arrived. Donella bent down to Maurice, pointed to the deck door, shook her head, said something to the waitress, and walked toward Alexa.

Alicia bolted out of her seat. "Hey wait for me. I'm not going to be left with this hen party."

Maurice and Dennis shouted their protests as Alexa and the women walked away.

"Did you say 'hen party'?" Alexa asked.

"I swear to God they gossip more than any group of women," Alicia said.

"Oh… female chickens, instead of calling them roosters!" Alexa laughed. "I get it!"

Alexa followed the group past a different flight of stairs she hadn't noticed until Stephanie pointed to the deck enterance. Two vampires stood guard at the base of the stairs watching the women walk by. Alexa looked past the guards toward the top of the steps and a closed door. "What the hell is up there?" she asked Stephanie.

The guard on the left said, "We'll take you up and show you around."

Alexa whipped her head around and stared at the man. She looked at the other man who kept his attention forward, ignoring his partner. Without comment, she turned away.

Crystal pushed through the door bringing a gust of icy air into the steamy bar. Alexa rushed past Crystal toward the edge of the deck, a brick ledge overlooking an alley. The women gathered around her. "Are you okay?"

Alexa turned to the concerned women. "I'm fine. I just prefer to keep my distance from vampires."

"I can tell you've had enough encounters to justify that," Alicia said.

Alexa nodded knowing they could smell three men on her – Eric and the two men she had killed. The scents didn't differ whether she drank blood or had semen deposited in her, so no one would ever suspect she had killed anyone. The only question people would have was whether any of the contact was consensual.

"Well, you're lucky you're able to mask being a hybrid," Crystal said.

"It's not something I do intentionally."

"Really! Did your mom put a spell on you or something?"

"I have no idea," Alexa said. She turned to Donella. "You said something about this possibly being a spell."

Donella nodded. "Oh, it's definitely a spell. Change your scent."

Alexa hesitated – she didn't want more people to catch her noble scent. She relented and took a deep breath to relax and bring her vampire side forward.

Alicia's eyes widened. "Wow, that's some shit!"

Donella extended a hand toward Alexa. "Someone put a spell on her, but she can break through it."

"That's incredible," Crystal said.

"More so because she's just learned how to use her powers."

"What do you mean?" Crystal asked.

"I told you she was raised as a human and doesn't know anything."

Stephanie glared at Alexa. "You were raised as a human?"

Alexa nodded.

"But? Did your parents die? I mean who raised you? And how did..."

"Um my parents raised me, they just kinda kept a big secret from me."

Stephanie wrinkled her eyebrows. "So did they just pretend to be human too?"

Alexa nodded. "Basically. I don't really know all of the details. I got tired of asking and getting no answers, so I just left town." She rolled her eyes. "I mean there was other drama going on, but the lack of information was really the icing on the cake."

"Who's the witch and who is the vampire?"

"Mom is a full-blooded witch – it's her scent I carry. And my dad, well, he's at least part vampire."

"Holy shit," Crystal said. "A witch and a hybrid - that's a rare combo. Are you sure he's your real dad?"

Alexa knew for certain mom and dad were her biological parents. She carried both of their scents, even though her father's scent was barely detectable unless she revealed her vampire side. She shrugged and lifted her hands in despair. "I have no clue. There are so many secrets, lies on top of lies."

Stephanie nodded. "Yeah, that would require a whole web of lies. So were you attacked? I mean did you find out about vampires when you were tagged?"

"Yeah, that's when my teeth came in."

"Your teeth came in when you were being attacked?" Stephanie yelled in disbelief.

Alexa nodded and shrugged. "Yeah, it's all part of a horrible, grotesque nightmare that I'm waiting to wake up from."

"I'll bet," Stephanie said.

"You're losing your focus," Alicia said.

"What?"

Alicia grinned. "Your scent returned to all witch."

"I find it more amazing you're a hybrid at all," Crystal said. "You're such a strong witch."

Alexa looked at Crystal. "How can you tell I'm strong?"

Crystal's eyebrows arched. "You can't tell?"

Alexa shook her head.

"Wow. I've never met anyone with this much energy. I can only imagine what you'll be like when you hit your prime," Crystal said.

"When will that be?" Alexa asked

"Well," Crystal said. "If your mom is forty-four then she's probably just now coming into it."

"You mean, menopause?" Alexa asked.

"Exactly," Crystal said. "You would have come into a good deal of your witchcraft during puberty."

Alexa shrugged. "I don't really know. I was just a human kid trying to get through my day like everyone else." She thought back to her junior high years. She remembered her friend, Brie, becoming agitated in the school hallways as large groups of people passed by. She often burst into tears or would hyperventilate. Brie's abilities, Alexa recently learned, included reading people's emotions. Alexa didn't know the extent of Tess's abilities other than being really good at finding lost items, but she recalled Tess often swinging her head to one side or the other as if something invisible caught her attention. And yes, in that same timeframe Alexa's nightmares intensified. But did anything else stand out? She couldn't think of other phenomena – all of her discoveries had happened in the last few months.

Alexa scowled. "How can I tell *your* strength?"

"Do you know to identify auras?" Crystal asked.

Alexa shook her head.

"If you squint you should see a misty color around a person," Crystal said.

"But I haven't seen you squint at me," Alexa said.

Crystal grinned. "Once you can identify what it looks like, eventually squinting isn't necessary. You'll soon realize you've been looking at our auras all along."

"Some people can hear auras as well," Stephanie said.

"And smell them," Alicia said. "Your aura is dark as midnight. It's invisible out here, but I know you have a smoke ring with yours. You smell like you stepped fresh from a campfire."

Alexa squinted at Crystal and then snapped her head back toward Alicia. "I *smell* like a campfire?"

"Not smell through your nose, but in your, uh, essence," Alicia said.

"Oh." She didn't know what that meant. Alexa returned her attention to squinting at Crystal. "I don't see anything."

Crystal smiled. "Keep working on it. You'll master it in no time."

"So once I see an aura, how do I measure people's strength?" Alexa asked.

"You will be able to tell. It will be in vibrance. The robustness shows energy. You'll also notice when someone is sick because their colors dim," Crystal said. "Now here's a thing that will surprise you – even humans and vampires have auras."

"What's a vampire aura like?" Alexa asked. "Black?"

"Funny you should say that, because yes. But even odder is you," Crystal said.

Alexa jerked back and wondered if she heard right.

"You present completely like a witch," Crystal said. "And there are witches with dark auras, but not as *black* as yours. Usually, there's some color that goes with it, but yours is just straight-up black. Without knowing you're a hybrid you likely scare the shit out of other witches. You present as a *very* powerful dark witch, and I'm sure you are. But knowing you're part vampire? That explains so much. I mean all of us have shades of gray in our auras from our vampire blood, but like I said, yours is *black*. You're a powerful dark witch with powerful vampire blood. You, m'dear are a force to be reckoned with."

"I've had people tell me that being a dark witch isn't a bad thing," Alexa said.

"It's not bad at all. It just is," Crystal said.

Stephanie asked, "Do you understand that dark witches tend to have powers related to destruction and death?"

Alexa shook her head.

"It's not bad. Like Crystal said, it just is. I've seen white witches do some heinous things and dark witches be some of the most compassionate people on the planet. It's all about how you wield your power. Destruction is necessary for rebuilding and death is simply a stage on the wheel of life. Sometimes the most giving thing you can do is help someone make that transition."

Alexa stared at Stephanie as she thought of the spirits at the Samhain dinner. "Help them cross the bridge," she said.

"Exactly."

Crystal looked at Alicia. "Are you cold?"

"She just needs something to drink," Stephanie said.

Alicia looked at Alexa. "Are you okay now that you've had some fresh air?"

Alexa smiled. "Yeah, I'm doing a lot better. The air helped." She glanced around the patio, one corner filled with stacked tables and chairs. "I guess it gets pretty crowded out here during the summer."

Alicia turned toward the corner of patio furniture. "Where's the bar?"

The other women looked at the barren wall.

"They must have taken it down," Crystal said.

"Was it portable?" Donella asked.

Alexa wandered away from the women as they debated the structure and now, absence of the bar. She envisioned a warm summer night here with people dancing, a band or maybe a DJ, and small tables scattered along the perimeter. Alexa looked over the edge as she walked along the walls. An office building stood on one side and an old factory on the other. She hoped the factory hadn't been converted into apartments. Living next to a loud, thumping nightclub would suck.

The back portion overlooked the parking lot. Cars pulled in, others left. People walked to and from vehicles as chatter filled the air with a random laugh or loud voice rising above the others. Alexa smiled when she spotted Donella's automobile in the sea of vehicles, a small victory in her private game of seek and find. She turned in time to see one of the vampire guards come through the doors.

"Ladies," he said, "we have a group arriving that may make you feel uncomfortable… and… uh… this patio is quite… isolated."

"Thank you," Donella said. She turned to Alexa and motioned for her to join the others.

Alexa scurried to follow the women through the door the guard held open.

At the table, Stephanie glared at Dwight. "Where's your friend?"

"Eh, some dude walked by and he bugged out. I'll have to find a ride now."

"I got ya, man," Maurice said. "The taxis double their rates for the people they pick up here. I'll get ya home, safe and sound."

Donella looked at Crystal. "Are you guys leaving?"

"Yeah, we got here when they opened. It's not like it used to be. The music's different, the crowd's different. Hell, I tried to dance. Dunno. It's just not the same."

"Prices went up, too," Dennis said and finished his drink.

"We ought to find a different place," Alicia said.

"It's time to start hosting our own gatherings again," Crystal said.

Stephanie picked up her coat off the back of her chair. "Maybe we need to just start having dinner parties like old people?"

Maurice stood up. "Oh fuck that."

The group turned in unison as five vampires came up the stairs and marched toward the guards. Alicia pulled her coat on.

"Yeah, it's time to go."

Without further discussion they vacated the table and headed downstairs passing three vampires going up the stairs, none of them dressed for a nightclub but in business attire.

The noise didn't hit Alexa as hard as when she first arrived, but she longed to reach the sidewalk if only the crowd cooperated in allowing her to pass. She smelled the night air, but the door stood so far away. Thumping music, people dancing, loud voices, and so many death scenes – Alexa kept her sights on the door. Body by body, she got closer. At last, she and Donella reached the bouncer, a different man than had been there earlier.

Alexa nearly stumbled through the doorway to the sweet release of fresh air filled with cigarette smoke and car exhaust. And while various groups lingered on the sidewalk barraging her with their scents and deaths, Alexa found relief to be away from the dancing crowd inside.

Donella's friends bade farewell and parted in different directions. Donella and Alexa turned down the alley toward the parking lot behind the nightclub. The alley wasn't a desolate canyon, but a busy thoroughfare. A steady stream of people arriving and leaving the club passed, some lingering to chat with friends or smoke.

As Alexa pushed new death scenes to the back of her mind, people's scents swirled around her. One scent in the distance caught her attention. He approached from the parking lot and his scent, along with four other vampires, grew stronger as they neared. Alexa felt uneasy. She knew his scent from her office but the only vampires that had visited were the two she met with Valerie. He had to be the guy who seemed suspicious. The sidekick, coworker, bodyguard, or whatever – the one she didn't trust. The one she saw at the window while at lunch with Donella and Jeff.

Nearly halfway down the alley, their eyes met. Her heart sank with recognition, as indeed, he was the same vampire who pressed a man against the glass at the restaurant. She grinned and scooted to the side to pass. He continued to stare at her but no one in his group moved for her and Donella to walk by.

"Surprised to find you here," he said.

Alexa forced another grin. "Just meeting up with a coworker

and friends for drinks."

"You're going the wrong direction."

"It's a bit loud for my tastes, but hope you guys have a good time."

"I think we can have a good time out here," another vampire said as he stepped forward.

She wiped the grin off her face and lifted her chin. "It wasn't an invitation."

"An invitation would be nice, but not necessary," he said with a smirk.

She assessed the man, likely sentinel or ranger – stronger than a hunter but weaker than a noble. While Alexa had strength to her advantage, the brute had size, training, and backup. She didn't want to reveal herself as a hybrid since these men would identify her noble scent bringing more trouble to her than what currently stood in front of her.

Alexa huffed, grabbed Donella's wrist, and began walking toward the small opening beside another vampire and the wall of the old factory, but the vampire slid to the side blocking their passage. The brute chuckled and the men closed their circle, backing Alexa and Donella to the wall. She sensed more vampires approaching from the parking lot.

With intentions of using wind to blast the men across the alley, Alexa ignored their salacious chatter and kept her sites on the brute's shoulder as she focused on swirling the air between them.

Several vampires jumped back, including the first man who spoke – was his name Elmar?

"Whoa!" One vampire shouted.

"No witchcraft!" Another hollered.

Alexa looked down to see what she had created – a small tornado, only a few feet tall, but enough to cause the vampires to back away. Other people in the alley turned to see the commotion and the newly arrived vampires looked over the shoulders of the ones backing away.

The brute glared at Alexa as if he were contemplating a way to get around her tiny swirl of wind. A hand landed on his shoulder pulling him backward and a new vampire joined the group.

"Witchcraft will have you banned from this club," the new vampire said. Alexa recognized his scent, nearly identical to Diederich, meaning they were related, possibly brothers. She wondered if he had already assessed her faint vampire scent.

As they held each other's attention, Alexa allowed the tornado to dissipate. "That's fine," she said. "The club didn't impress me."

"Shame," he said. "I'm quite proud of the mix of people who come here."

"It's a cool concept, seems to be working at least until we get to the alley here."

He raised an eyebrow with an expression that demanded further explanation.

"Your friends here," she said, "blocked us from getting to our car."

"It's a wide alley."

"Dude. I don't know how much closer to this wall I can get to pass by your little friends here. Not like they're gonna let us go the other side of the alley."

"These men blocked you? And that's why there was a…" he looked to the ground to where the tornado once spun as he searched for a word.

"Yes," Alexa said. "And that baby tornado was about to get a lot bigger."

"Aw now wait a minute," the brute said. "You offered a good time."

Alexa wanted nothing more than to growl as she stared the jackass down. "I said I hoped you guys had a good time, referring to going inside the bar. It was not an invitation to trap me and my friend against this damn wall. And it sure as hell was not an invitation to fuck either one of us."

"Seems to be an invitation you make often," the brute said suggestively raising his eyebrow.

Alexa hated that the men she had killed left their scents on her. If she were a man the lingering scents would be badges of honor for successful kills; however, on a woman, she simply presented as a whore. Why didn't female vampires fight? Why couldn't they be good little soldiers too?

She set her jaw, restraining every urge to lunge forward and rip him apart. "They didn't make it out alive and I guarantee you won't either."

He raised his eyebrows. "I like a good challenge."

"Stand down, Silas," the noble said. "She will kill you and I won't stop her."

Silas curled his lip as if he was going to snarl, but he stopped short and stepped away as told.

"I apologize for the behavior of my men. I understand your use of witchcraft was for self-defense?"

Alexa nodded.

"Very well. You and your friend are not banned from the club. May I have someone escort you to your car?"

"No."

The noble nodded and motioned for the vampires to step back. Alexa scanned the line of men, her sight landing on Elmar. He stood meek, doing as told, but she saw the resentment in the change of power when the noble arrived. She returned her attention to the noble. She didn't know enough about the structure of nobles as to who was a prince or otherwise, but the men all bent to this man's will. Did her father have this type of power?

Alexa dipped a quick nod in gratitude and pulled Donella away from the wall. She looked over her shoulder a few times as they walked away. The vampires with several onlookers watched their departure.

Chapter Twenty-Eight

The locks clicked and Donella heaved a deep exhale as she pulled the seatbelt across her.

"Are you okay to drive?" Alexa asked.

"Yes." She nodded her head and put the key in the ignition. "How did you stay so calm through all of that?"

"Calm?" Alexa cast a sideways glance at Donella. "I was rattling in my shoes! I was sure we were going to die until that one guy showed up!"

"No, you looked like you were ready to go into battle."

"Well, maybe I do have a little fighting spirit. I was contemplating ways to rip him apart."

"With what?"

Alexa forgot that most hybrids had malformed fangs. She tilted her head with a weak grin. "Um, I have fully formed fangs."

"Really? You said something about the guys who attacked you didn't survive. Did you kill them?"

Alexa nodded her head.

"You've tasted blood?"

Again, Alexa nodded.

"Huh! So your story about being stalked is crap?"

"No. I'm being followed, it's only a matter of time before they find me."

Donella raised her eyebrows. "So you can face justice?"

"No." Alexa wondered how much more to say - Donella wouldn't be satisfied with half-truths. "I pissed off a prince."

Frozen for a moment, Donella stared at Alexa. "Oh."

Alexa watched Donella process the gravity of pissing off a vampire prince and worse yet, how that could impact Donella if she knew any of the details.

Donella cleared her throat. "How would you fare against a guy like that back there?"

"Not well. We were outnumbered and I'm sure they're skilled fighters. I might puncture one or two, but that one guy definitely had size to his advantage. I've discovered the hard way that, um, long arms are kinda hard to battle. I've been pinned against a wall leaving me swatting at thin air."

Donella laughed. "Were your feet off the ground too?"

"How did you know?" Alexa said with a chuckle.

"Just a side note for you," Donella said. "Wolves have fangs, vampires have teeth."

"Huh. So I guess commenting on a vampire's fangs would piss off a guy?"

"Yes, most definitely. Do you enjoy provoking fights?"

"No... but... hmm. Maybe. Knowing how to properly insult someone can come in handy."

"As can knowing when to stay quiet."

"So I've been told."

Donella grinned and started the car. As she drove out of the parking lot she looked over at Alexa. "Again you prove you operate well under pressure. You definitely can think on your feet."

"Thanks."

"My friends seemed to like you."

"I like them too. I loved that they tried to teach me new things."

"There's a lot for you to learn. I thought we would also be teaching you about vampires but I think maybe you have most of that figured out?"

Alexa tilted her head. "Maybe? But I would prefer you assume I know nothing and tell me the obvious stuff anyways. Like not calling my new teeth 'fangs'."

"How recently did they come in?"

"Back in August."

"You really are on a crash course trying to catch up!"

"It's been overwhelming, that's for sure. What I've needed is a chance to come up for air and that seems to be happening. Well, until we ran into those guys in the alley."

"Yeah, that was unsettling, to say the least, but I'm glad you're finding what you need."

"Between living with Valerie and working at the firm I've found a nice rhythm, you know routine, and that brings a certain quiet. Not that it's been quiet - I'm definitely getting hit with a crash course, that's a good description, but it feels like it's happening in a safe environment. Does that make sense?"

Donella nodded.

"So Sarah and Valerie are helping add to my new grimoire – mostly recipes. I do find it weird for as much cooking Valerie does that she doesn't have a garden of some sort."

"Really?"

"It's just that everyone I've known to be a decent cook grew their own herbs if even it's just a window container."

"Do you have an interest in herbology?"

Alexa wrinkled her forehead. "Are you saying herbs are a witch thing?"

"No, not at all, but also yes."

Alexa laughed. "I get it. It's hard when I think of my mom. I don't know where the line is between sixty's flower child and witch. She's always trying new recipes and a lot of vegetarian stuff using what she's growing in the backyard. And ohmigod the dandelions. Our backyard is filled with them and it pisses off the people next door. She'll spend the day plucking the flowers and has jars and jars of dried stuff."

Donella laughed. "And you never thought that was odd?"

"Oh I definitely thought it was odd, but I wrote it off as part of her flower child, save the planet, be all-natural, granola-loving self. And to be honest with the way I never got sick I just assumed the gallons of homemade tea she concocted actually worked."

"I'm quite sure your mom's tea can cure any malady on the planet."

"But she's not allowed to practice witchcraft."

"Making tea is not witchcraft, at least not until a spell is cast over it. Tea is made by all sorts of people, including vampires. But why is your mother not allowed to practice witchcraft? You said something about that before, but I just don't understand it. How can anyone block that?"

"There's a lot I haven't been told, but what I've been able to surmise is her mother, my *dear* grandmother," Alexa said with an eye roll, "was horrified by my arrival. She insisted that I be raised as a human. I assume part of that deal was my mom couldn't practice witchcraft so as to provide a fully normal human home. I've learned some things about my grandmother that all of this may be bigger than protecting her reputation. That if she can't harness my energy then no one can use it including me."

"You surely come from a long line of strong witches."

Alexa squirmed recalling the interactions around her grandmother. "I get the impression she may not be as strong as she would like to be. Is it possible my grandfather is the stronger witch?"

"Oh. Yes, of course."

"I really don't know," Alexa said shrugging her shoulder. "Like I said, there's a whole lot I haven't been told. You mentioned someone casting a spell on me to mask my vampire side. Well, the one person who makes sense is my grandmother, but who knows? It's just a guess."

Alexa looked out the window as they passed a grocery store with only a couple of cars in the lot. The restaurant next door had more cars with a few people walking around. She replayed the evening in her head.

"I gotta be honest," Alexa said. "I thought you would open up more when you were around your friends, but you're just a quiet person, aren't you?"

"Is that a problem?"

"No. I mean I wasn't expecting you to get up and dance on the tables. In fact, *that* would have shocked me. But no, it's just interesting to see the group dynamics and how people interplay."

"I think it's interesting too. I don't want to be a performer, I much prefer being the audience. Watching people is very entertaining. Funny thing is, most people assume I'd be happier to spend my weekends camped out at a library or stay home, but I enjoy going out – how else can watch people?" Donella chuckled at herself.

Alexa laughed as well. "Good point."

Chapter Twenty-Nine

Sitting on the floor next to the coffee table, Alexa took another sip of wine while she waited for Sarah to select a jigsaw puzzle from the closet. Valerie emerged from the kitchen with a large bowl of popcorn and sat opposite Alexa.

"Got it," Sarah yelled from inside the closet.

"I have no idea how she squeezes in there," Valerie said.

Alexa grinned and plucked a couple of kernels from the bowl. "Oh! This is caramel corn!"

"Homemade."

Alexa stared at Valerie. "You made this?"

Sarah arrived at the coffee table carrying a puzzle box. "She does it in the microwave. It's really simple, I've made it a couple of times."

"And got your fingerprints all over my recipe card."

"You have the recipe memorized."

Alexa waved her hands. "Wait a minute. How is making caramel corn *easy*?"

Valerie shrugged. "It's something I picked up at one of those home parties a few years ago. The consultant made this concoction in the microwave with brown sugar, corn syrup, butter, and baking soda. Then she…"

"Baking soda?" Alexa asked in disbelief.

"Yes. It makes the mixture frothy and I guess it adds the right amount of saltiness to balance the sweetness. Anyways you put popped popcorn into a paper grocery bag and pour the brown sugar mixture on top of it all, shake it up, roll up the bag, and shove it in the microwave for a few minutes. Then spread it out on wax paper to set up a little bit and this is what you get."

Alexa took another bite. "This is from the microwave?"

Valerie nodded.

"That's amazing."

Valerie picked up the puzzle box. "I don't remember this one."

"This is from the set of puzzles I got at an estate sale last spring," Sarah said.

"Are all of the pieces here?" Alexa asked.

Sarah looked at Valerie and then at Alexa. She shrugged. "I don't know."

"Let's find out!" Alexa said.

Sarah opened the box and poured the pieces onto the coffee table. "You told us about vampires last night, but not about how things went while you were at the club."

Alexa picked several border pieces from the pile and placed them in a line along the edge of the coffee table. "I really liked Donella's friends. I was surprised how quiet she was, she never really let loose."

"Even around her friends?" Valerie asked.

Alexa shook her head. "She's every bit the person we see at work."

"Are her friends quiet too?"

"No. They're boisterous and a lot of fun. They tried to teach me how to see auras – that I have to squint my eyes." Alexa squinted at Valerie and shook her head. "I don't see anything."

"Squinting is a start. Try it out in the sunlight."

"No," Sarah said. "It's better on a cloudy day like today. We should go out and try when we need a break."

"But you can see auras without squinting?" Alexa asked.

Sarah nodded. "Once you realize you've been looking at them all along you'll want to slap yourself upside the head. So how did you like the club?"

Alexa shrugged. "I would be okay never going back. There were a whole lot of people and I couldn't tamp down the flood of visions. Then add on the loud music and all of the movement... I was glad we didn't spend any time near the dance floor except entering and leaving. I'm still exhausted from it, so it's good we're not doing anything crazy today. A puzzle is the perfect pace for me today."

"But you're up for having a proper Thanksgiving meal tonight?" Sarah asked.

Alexa grinned. "I wouldn't miss it for the world."

"I can't believe you've never had one," Sarah said.

"Honestly it never felt like I was missing out on anything. I've had all of the standard foods and Lord knows we've had plenty of turkey over the last two weeks!"

"But that was in chili! This is different!"

"Sarah, I know it's different. I really do appreciate that we are going to have a proper sit-down Norman-Rockwell-style meal. It is special and I think it's great."

"Of course going to a restaurant means no cleanup," Valerie said.

"It also meant no leftovers the next day," Alexa said. "Now *that* is something I did get regularly by hanging out at my friends' houses. They took pity on my hotel dinners and made sure to save a plate for me. I have to admit, though, the hotel's cranberry relish was much better than what my friends saved for me."

"Out of the can?" Valerie asked.

"Tess's family only did the can – her dad insisted cranberries should be rippled like the can! Brie's family had a relish with oranges and walnuts mixed in. The one at the hotel didn't have nuts but it did have apples and it kind of mellowed out the whole thing."

"Oh! I might have to try that," Valerie said.

"Did your family go to a restaurant for Christmas as well?" Sarah asked.

"No, my mom insisted we stay home. She would bake a ham with mashed potatoes and really great rolls. It was quiet until my grandparents stopped by and then we would end the evening with a phone call to my dad's parents."

"Did your mom ever call it Yule?"

Alexa shook her head. "Nope, just plain ol' Christmas like you see on TV."

Sarah looked to Valerie. "Oh, we have to make sure she has a proper Yule!"

After Alexa's stomach rumbled she checked if Sarah heard.

Sarah smirked. "The smell in here is killing me."

"It's past my lunchtime. I might start gnawing on the couch," Alexa said.

"I wish she would let us help."

Alexa pulled back and looked at Sarah like she was crazy. "And get smacked for being in the way? I'd rather get in trouble for eating the couch."

"You're rather obsessed with eating furniture. Were you a dog in a past life?"

"SARAH!" Valerie yelled from the kitchen.

Sarah jumped up. "Maybe she's ready for me to pour the wine."

"I hope so."

Sarah scurried off and Alexa stayed in the living room as instructed earlier. She was not allowed to help in any way, not even allowed to peek at the table. The bowl from the caramel corn sat empty. The puzzle lay incomplete, plenty of pieces begging for assembly, but no, Alexa wanted to eat. She heard Sarah moving around the dining table, dishes clinking, and the swoosh of the kitchen door. Food was soon.

When at last Alexa approached the table she gasped. "How do you guys produce such beautiful tables?" Apples and small gourds surrounded pillar candles clustered in groups of three lining the table. Platters and bowls of food seemed hidden between pumpkins, ears of corn, and red leaves. Acorns scattered around the decorations caught Alexa's eye – she had been asked to collect these nuts when walking around the neighborhood a week earlier because Sarah had a decoration project at the bookstore.

Valerie pushed open louvered shutters separating the dining room from the kitchen. Alexa startled – she had never seen them open. Valerie leaned over the sink and pointed at Sarah. "That is *all* Sarah's creation! She makes everyone think I do this, but no. I make the food and she sets the table. When it comes time for Yule she will have decked out this place into a winter wonderland."

"What about Samhain? I saw you decorating," Alexa said.

"I'm just the muscle. She decides where everything goes."

Alexa looked at Sarah. "It's absolutely beautiful. You should do this professionally."

"Nah," Sarah said shaking her head. "I've helped enough designers just looking for coffee table books and I want nothing to do with that world. I'm perfectly content making this my playground."

"Well, it's stunning," Alexa said.

Walking through the kitchen door Valerie said, "She has to know the entire menu and picks out the coordinating plates and bowls just so she knows where to place each item." She extended a hand to the table. "Shall we be seated?"

As Valerie recited the blessing Alexa watched a candle flicker. "Blessed be," she said in unison with Sarah and Valerie.

"Do you put out this big spread for every occasion?" Alexa asked.

Sarah nodded.

Valerie stood up with carving utensils in her hands. "Sometimes she does it just because it's Saturday." She cut into the turkey carcass, placing a slice on each of their plates.

Alexa scooped mashed potatoes onto her plate and passed the bowl to Sarah. "This is magic, Sarah. I don't know if it's a type of witchcraft, but it should be. This is stunning."

Sarah blushed.

"I agree," Valerie said. "It might actually be part of her chaos magic."

With furrowed forehead, Sarah glared at Valerie. "How is that possible?"

"You took random items and arranged something beautiful."

"Humans do this all of the time," Sarah said.

"Aren't humans the embodiment of chaos?"

Chapter Thirty

The telephone on Alexa's desk rang, startling her. She picked up the receiver. "Hello?"

"Lexie, when you have a moment please stop by my office," Donella said. "I'll be here until two."

Alexa completed her entries before securing the computer and heading to Donella's office. She stopped and returned to her desk to grab a pen and pad of paper – she had no idea why she was summoned, although she assumed to discuss the nightclub and meeting Donella's friends. However, if the request was work-related, pen and paper seemed a good idea.

Donella's face lit up when Alexa arrived in her doorway. "Come in! Oh, and close the door."

Alexa closed the door and sat in one of the beige chairs facing Donella's desk.

"Pen and paper," Donella said nodding to the items in Alexa's hand. "It's a nice touch to keep up professional appearances."

"Well to be honest I wasn't sure if you needed something work-related or wanted to catch up after last week."

"No I don't need anything - your reports have been up to par. I just wanted to let you know that my friends adore you."

"Aw, that's really sweet! I liked them too."

Donella waved a hand in the air. "Dennis had questions about you. He's baffled why you were raised as a human. He thinks there's more to your family lineage like someone is hiding something."

Alexa leaned forward with wide eyes. "Like what?" She knew exactly what her family was hiding – her, the unmentionable child that should never have been allowed to live.

"Well, he thinks maybe your father was connected to a family in power. But he's also baffled why you only carry a witch scent. I told him there's a spell involved."

"Right. Like I said, it's probably my grandmother, but who knows? Why can't I just have a normal, functional family?"

Donella waved a dismissive hand and shook her head. "Based on the stories that have come through my door, I'm convinced 'functional' is just a myth."

Alexa chuckled.

"We can't pick our family but we can pick our friends. And on that note, I just wanted to tell you that if you're up to going out again, you are more than welcome to come along. Dennis and Maurice have been working with a guy who is interested in creating a hybrid coven. It sounds like a great way for you to learn more about being a hybrid. The girls are really interested, we're just waiting for more information about dates and times."

"Are you kidding? That sounds incredible!"

"So you're interested?"

"Absolutely!"

"I don't know when that will come together, but I'll definitely let you know. We were, however, thinking about getting together for Yule, but honestly, with everyone's schedules it won't be until after the first of the year."

"Well, that sounds interesting too!"

"Good. I assume Valerie is putting together her own Yule plans."

"Of course, and it sounds like it will be over the top. She's excited to introduce me to all of this stuff."

"I'm sure she is. I like Valerie and I don't mind you discussing all this personal stuff with her, but…"

"Don't worry, nothing will be said around the office."

"Thank you. It's rare for me to mix my professional and personal lives."

"I've never been in a managerial role before so it never crossed my mind, but I know how office gossip spreads like wildfire. At my last job, everyone seemed so invested in my relationships and when one was sort of progressing I really didn't want to dish it out to anyone, even my closest friends. I'm learning the less said, the better."

Donella nodded. "Yes. We spend so many hours with these people that some feel entitled to all of the minutia of our lives, moreover that they are allowed to have any opinion in those matters. Like I said, the number of family issues that come through this door is crazy. The only thing that tops it are squabbles between coworkers – people all up in everyone's business and then they get their feelings hurt. There are days I swear I would be happier if I had followed my childhood dream of being a crossing guard."

Alexa burst out laughing. "Crossing guard?"

"Oh yes! The uniform, and badge, and those little white gloves, and carrying that little stop sign? That was everything. And getting cars to stop?" Donella shook her head. "Mmmm the power! You know I begged my mother for a set of white gloves?"

"I shouldn't laugh. I wanted a princess crown."

"Who doesn't want a princess crown? I would ditch the uniform cap in a heartbeat if I could have a princess crown! While holding the stop sign in the crosswalk, of course."

"Okay, now that's a picture that will stick in my mind forever."

Chapter Thirty-One

Sarah stopped on the sidewalk and sighed as she looked up. "This is very pretty but it's not like Charlestown."

Alexa noted the tinsel decorations alternating between red bells and green wreaths on the light posts down the street.

Valerie looped her arm in Sarah's. "Trust me, you'll be happy soon enough."

Alexa looked at Valerie and then down a few blocks where several groups of people headed in the same direction. She wondered what Valerie and all of those people knew. As they neared the corner Alexa sensed a large crowd and smelled popcorn and cinnamon. She took a deep breath and prepared to quell the coming visions that being near crowds always brought. At the corner, she found the street blocked allowing only pedestrian traffic for a vendor fair. Tents and booths, all lit with twinkling Christmas lights, lined both sides of the street.

Sarah squealed, "A street fair! Valerie! I do love this!"

With a knowing smile, Valerie pulled Sarah around the blockades.

Alexa followed, walking past the first booth where Valerie and Sarah stopped to look at paintings. Instead, she stepped inside the next booth with wreaths. The balsam scents brought a delightful distraction from the many humans passing by.

Valerie stepped behind her. "Oh, these are nice!"

"I was just admiring the scent."

"Back when I was in law school I couldn't afford a live tree so I would buy live garland and tack it to my wall."

"If you were in an apartment I can't imagine the landlord was too happy about that."

Valerie waved a hand. "Nothing toothpaste and a can of white paint couldn't fix."

"Toothpaste?"

"It's a weak but cheap substitute for spackle."

Alexa laughed. "Law students violating contracts!"

"One does not become a lawyer because of strict adherence to rules. No, lawyers find the loopholes and exceptions so as to sidestep the rules."

"So they cheat."

"No. They win because the rules did not cover every possibility."

Alexa laughed again. "Which is why contracts are so damn tedious to read!"

"Exactly," Valerie said with a grin.

"It's why she reads the rules to any game we ever play," Sarah said.

Alexa spun around surprised Sarah had joined them. Her lavender and honey scent eluded Alexa's nose with the wreaths and other odors in the air.

"You don't read the rules?" Alexa asked.

"I don't need to, Valerie always does. Do you?"

"Always. How on earth do you know how to play the game?"

"Maybe you should have gone to law school," Valerie said.

"Ooh, potpourri!" Sarah said as she walked toward the next booth.

Cinnamon, lavender, and citrus assaulted Alexa. She turned to Valerie. "She could be standing right in front of me and I wouldn't know it with all of these scents."

"She does smell nice," Valerie said.

"Is she drawn to lavender in general?"

Valerie nodded her head. "Are you drawn to roses?"

"Of course, but mostly because it reminds me of my mom. This is completely her scent." Alexa pointed to herself.

"And that is why I'm so drawn to apricot."

Alexa's eyes lit up. "Oh! That's exactly the scent I couldn't identify. Basil is so strong on you and then I would almost guess moss, but I could never nail down what the sweet undertones were. Apricot! Of course!" She laughed at the discovery. "Do you like the color as well?"

Valerie set down the Santa mug she had been holding. "Actually... I'm drawn to it quite a bit." She seemed surprised at the discovery.

Sarah flitted away while Alexa bought a small bag of cinnamon potpourri. When she turned around Sarah re-entered the booth. "You have to come look at these ornaments! They're absolutely adorable!"

Sarah led the way chatting about a list of friends who needed gifts. Alexa stayed at the end of a table watching Valerie and Sarah pick up and discuss the hand-painted glass balls. She thought about her friends in Brentwood - what would they think of this fair? Tess and Lindsey would hang back, like Valerie, talking about anything but shopping. Jessica and Brie would be more like Sarah, dashing from stall to stall, ending the night with several bags hanging off their arms. Chloe would be one of the vendors with the handmade crafts. Alexa could picture Meg standing with her, excited to be out with friends, absorbing the experience. She turned to watch the crowd, people walking in different directions, children pulling their parents; the air filled with joy, cinnamon, and popcorn. Alexa grinned - yes her friends would enjoy this scene very much.

A young man, possibly a high-schooler, strode down the middle of the street as if he were on a mission. Alexa looked back to the intersection where the vendor booths began and then she looked at the opposite end of the street where the teen seemed to be headed. She looked back to the intersection and noticed a man in a blue Chicago Cubs jacket walk to the corner and lean on a building. He made eye contact with Alexa and she quickly turned around to the booth with Sarah and Valerie, but not before taking another look for the teen walking through the crowd.

Carrying a bag filled with four ornaments Sarah moved on to the next booth. The pom-pom snowmen and Santas didn't keep their attention for very long before moving to another booth. As they progressed one booth at a time, Alexa scoped out both ends of the street watching the man in the Cubs jacket at one end and looking for the teenager at the other. By the time Sarah pulled her and Valerie into a booth with carved wooden statues, Alexa saw the teen march back through the crowd with the same determination as he had earlier. She tried to look at a three-foot tall solid wood Christmas tree while keeping an eye on the young man's movements, however, she was too far inside the booth to see if he met up with the guy in the jacket. By the time Alexa managed to casually drift away from the statue the teen and the man in the jacket were walking in opposite directions from the intersection.

Alexa strolled along a table with various bundles of cookies – they all looked delicious. She turned to Valerie and asked, "Are cookies a vital part of Yule?"

"They're not *vital* but definitely can be incorporated."

"Especially if they're homemade?"

Valerie laughed. "Yes, Lexie, we can make cookies. What type do you like?"

Sarah spun around. "I hope ginger snaps are on the menu!"

Alexa nodded. "Ginger snaps are good – chocolate chip, peanut butter, molasses, the chocolate ones rolled in powdered sugar... oh, and thumbprint cookies!"

"With apricot jam?" Valerie asked.

Alexa tilted her head and smiled. "As long as we can have some with raspberry preserves."

Valerie handed a five-dollar bill to the vendor and picked up a small bag of cookies. She pulled out two cookies, handing them to Alexa and Sarah. "I hope a pumpkin sandwich cookie will hold you two over."

Alexa looked at Sarah and asked, "Does she know giving us sugar is only going to make us worse?"

Sarah giggled.

Alexa pointed down the street. "I'm pretty sure hot cocoa is not too far away. I definitely smell coffee, but I think there's also chocolate in the air."

"You're a horrible influence," Valerie said. "Hot cocoa sounds wonderful. I'm saving my cookie until I have my cocoa."

"I like that plan," Alexa said.

"Me too!" Sarah said.

They walked past four booths following Alexa's nose to the end of the block. They found the source of coffee, hot cocoa, and the popcorn – St. Sebastian's Ladies Auxiliary. A bright red popcorn machine billowed steam from the top, emitting its delicious scent through the air. Several tables and chairs filled the street in front of the Ladies' Auxiliary stand.

Alexa offered to get the cocoa while Valerie and Sarah grabbed a table. She handed her cookie over to Valerie and stood her turn in line. A quick review of the menu showed they also offered cookies as well as hot dogs. She groaned at the thought of hot dogs and hot cocoa as she waited behind a woman ordering four bags of popcorn.

She turned and looked at her surroundings. The fair stretched several blocks with this stand denoting the end. Beyond the Ladies' Auxiliary sat four police barricades blocking the intersection. The street continued down a canyon of old buildings, none more than four stories tall. Several people had parked in that direction so foot traffic continued beyond the barricades.

Atop one of the buildings, Alexa saw a gargoyle, however his head flinched just a tiny bit. She realized that wasn't a gargoyle, but a vampire hunched over the edge watching the people below. She couldn't catch his scent but knew he was a guard, she assumed a royal guard, possibly a ranger, or maybe a sentinel. Eric had told her Brentwood vampires were Carinthian, an area in Austria. Did Radcliff fall under Carinthian rule or some other kingdom? Were they called kingdoms? Did she care? No, but she did care about Eric. Was he safe? Was he being trained to be a guard? Did they allow hunters to be part of the guard?

The woman in front of her walked away with her bags of popcorn forcing Alexa to return her attention to the Ladies' Auxiliary table.

"I'll take three hot cocoas."

"Whip cream?"

Alexa smiled. "Of course!"

She handed the woman five dollars and told her to keep the change. As she walked to the table Alexa glanced casually down the empty street. The gargoyle remained at his post, stiff and quiet. She knew jumping off a building that height wasn't a problem for vampires, although four stories was higher than any she had ever tried. She remembered the day Eric met her at the library and she detected vampires on the roof. How did they get there? She didn't recall a ladder anywhere. Did they use an interior access or was there some ability to scale the side of buildings? How high was too high to scale and moreover too high to jump down? She smiled at the memory of Eric's surprise the night she jumped off the roof of the art building.

She arrived at the table as Sarah and Valerie discussed gifts for their bosses.

"Will we have enough time to visit the rest of the booths?" Sarah asked.

"We made good time with the first row," Valerie said. "I don't see why we can't get through the rest before they close. We just have to make sure not to dally in the boring booths."

"None of them are boring!" Sarah said.

"None of us are interested in looking at toilet paper cozies or Kleenex covers," Valerie said.

Sarah rolled her eyes. "That was only one booth."

"Yes, I know, but we've managed to breeze through some of the others the same way. We just need to keep that momentum."

Alexa held her cup close to her mouth catching a hearty whiff of chocolate.

Valerie looked at her. "You're not waiting for that to cool off, are you? You know you can drink that whole cup without scalding your mouth?"

Alexa looked at her and then down at the murky chocolate with melting whipped cream.

"Put your finger in it," Valerie said. "All the way to the bottom."

Alexa looked to the side wondering if anyone was listening. She dipped her finger into the steaming liquid – hot, but not unbearable. She found it toasty. With a raised eyebrow she took a timid sip – so very, very hot. She took a bigger swig without any pain. "Huh!" A puff of steam rolled out of her mouth. She giggled and pressed her fingers to her lips and they were hot. "How is that possible?"

Valerie leaned forward and said quietly, "You're a pyromancer – heat and fire don't affect you. Sarah can barely hold her cup it's so hot."

Alexa looked at Sarah and how her hands hovered very close without touching the cup. Valerie raised her cup like a glass of wine then took a drink. She smiled as she wiped the whipped cream off her lip.

Beyond Valerie, a man walked around the corner of the building and rushed down the sidewalk behind the booths. Sarah lamented her inability to withstand the heat and Alexa grinned, pretending to take in the architecture behind Valerie.

"I wonder how old these buildings are?" Alexa asked as she craned her head looking from end to end of the street. "Old downtown districts tell so much about their history." She couldn't see the rooftops but suspected vampires walked patrol watching the crowd below.

"Do you enjoy studying history?" Valerie asked.

"You know, in high school, my answer would have been an adamant no." Alexa took another drink of cocoa, still surprised her mouth and throat weren't on fire. She pointed to her cup. "Have I always been able to do this?"

Valerie laughed. "Yes, I'm sure you have. You were just conditioned to sip slowly, but I bet you've always drank it hotter than all of your friends."

"This is so weird." Alexa tried to spot the man who had walked behind the booths but from her seat, she couldn't see anything but the crowd of shoppers. She picked up the cookie Valerie had saved for her and took a bite. "Oh my God! This is wonderful!"

Sarah took a bite of her cookie and her eyes widened in agreement.

"Do I dare dip it?" Alexa asked.

"I've been wondering if the chocolate will compliment the pumpkin or not," Valerie said.

Alexa tipped a corner into the cocoa and took a small bite. She scrunched her face. "It's a weird consistency, very mushy."

"That's to be expected since it's soft as cake," Valerie said.

"I don't know that the cocoa works here. It's just wet. The spices of the cookie are much stronger," Alexa said.

"Well, thank you for being our guinea pig," Valerie said.

"The cocoa works well to wash it down, though," Sarah said.

As they finished their cookies Alexa continued to scan for vampires, but only a few vampire shoppers in the crowd flagged her attention. Taking their cups to a large trashcan next to the Ladies Auxiliary menu board, Alexa peered down the empty street. The gargoyle remained, but no other activity except people moving between the cars and the fair.

Sarah walked out of a booth with yet another bag looped on her arm. Valerie leaned toward Alexa and said, "We should have gotten here earlier – she's energized and ready to hit all of the stores."

"No. This was perfect," Alexa said. "I can't keep her pace."

Valerie laughed following Sarah into the next booth.

"Valerie! Look at these mittens!"

Alexa stepped into the booth to see Sarah dangling a pair of red mittens in front of her huge smile. "Who are they for?" Alexa asked.

"Heather, your guys' receptionist."

Alexa nodded in approval. "Oh my God, she would love those!"

Valerie lifted one into her hand and turned to Alexa. "Do you really think so?"

"Oh definitely! She hates the cold and she looks terrific in red. Sarah, you have a knack for finding the perfect gift!"

"Guess I'm buying them," Valerie said.

Valerie paid for the mittens while Sarah sifted through other colors. Alexa stepped out of the booth to wait for them to move on to the next stall where she saw mason jars filled with various mixes. She knew Sarah would find at least a couple of the jars to be the perfect gift for people on what Alexa suspected to be a growing list of recipients.

The teen rushed by again. This time Alexa caught his scent – definitely ranger. She watched him reach the end of the street but people blocked her view as to where he landed. She looked along the roofline and spotted dust blowing as though something up there moved.

Her attention darted to her thigh where a child collided with her. She smiled at the boy and then up at his apologizing mother. "It's okay," Alexa said.

Sarah sidled up to Alexa. "We got a pair for Jeff too!"

"Where's Valerie?" Alexa asked looking behind Sarah.

Sarah leaned her head to the side indicating a different booth. Valerie emerged carrying a slender box with a handle.

"What did you get?"

Valerie balanced the package like a pizza box to reveal blue and clear stained glass with several snowflakes.

Alexa gasped. "That's gorgeous!"

"I did not intend to spend that much money here, but I love this piece."

"I told her we should hang it in the front window," Sarah said.

"Oh wow," Alexa said. "That will look pretty there especially when the sun hits it," Alexa said.

Valerie grinned in agreement. "We can use a strand of clear lights to string around the whole window."

"That's a good idea," Sarah said.

Alexa whipped her head to search the opposite side of the fair. She smelled a dead body... moving. Someone was transporting a dead person just beyond the row of booths.

"What's wrong?" Valerie asked.

"Um, there's some activity happening on the periphery of the fair."

"Are we safe?" Valerie whispered.

"Yeah, the crowd is still a good size for a buffer."

"But we should make our way to the car?"

"There's no rush, but when we see someone walking in that direction we should follow them."

Valerie nodded and followed Sarah into a booth with cinnamon-covered nuts. They emerged with yet more bags.

Alexa smiled and shook her head. "Sarah, you're hopeless when it comes to shopping." She pointed to Valerie. "And *you*! You enable this behavior!"

Valerie laughed.

Sarah grinned without an ounce of guilt. "Who can pass up cinnamon almonds?"

Valerie held up her bag. "And chocolate-covered ones?" She extended another bag to Alexa. "Here's some for you."

"I didn't even know they had chocolate in there!"

"The cinnamon is pretty overpowering," Sarah said. "It would be easy to miss. I guess we're done for the night."

"What about the rest of the booths?"

Valerie leaned in. "I saw a man on top of the building over there."

With a soft voice, Alexa said, "They've been there the entire time."

Valerie stood back in surprise. "Really?"

"On all of the buildings. I'm pretty sure they're a guard of some sort, which is good. They're protecting the crowd."

"Can you be sure?"

"No, but they don't seem to be a threat."

"Just the same," Valerie said. "Let's get out of here."

They followed a human couple walking down the sidewalk in the direction of Valerie's car.

"So what type of stores did we miss back there?" Alexa asked.

"There are a couple of antique stores and one with a big selection of vintage clothing," Valerie said.

"Rupert's Books," Sarah said. "I've sent customers there quite a few times especially when they're looking for something out of print."

"Oh and Gifford's Appliances. That's where I got a replacement for the stove when the heating element went out."

"These all sound like large stores."

Sarah nodded. "They are. I like them, but they're not as quaint as the little shops in Charlestown and none of them carry loose tea."

The human couple turned right at the corner. With Valerie's car in sight halfway down the next block, the women continued straight. Crossing the intersection Alexa looked left to find three vampires standing at the back of a pickup truck. A fourth vampire stood on the ground with a dolly holding a refrigerator box, the conveyance of the dead body Alexa detected at the fair.

"I guess vampires run the appliance store?"

"Yes, how did you know?" Valerie turned to look at Alexa and then in the direction she was staring. "Why on earth are they loading a refrigerator all the way down here?"

Alexa shrugged. "Why on earth are they loading anything at this time of night?"

Valerie tipped her head in agreement.

Alexa stepped up her pace to speed Valerie and Sarah across the intersection before they attracted attention of the vampires. "I mean the street was too crowded to get a truck down there regardless of how late they conduct business."

Valerie stepped onto the sidewalk and looked in the direction where the human couple walked. Alexa followed Valerie's gaze to see more people walking to cars. Headlights nearly blinded her as a car approached the intersection. She turned her head toward the vampires in time to watch them wrangle the box where the contents seemed to shift. She wanted to laugh but returned her focus to reaching the car.

Two vehicles passed and in an unspoken mission, the women crossed the street toward the car. Valerie unlocked the driver's door while Alexa walked with Sarah around to the passenger side. Alexa took all of the bags and slid into the backseat while Sarah got into the front. The ignition started and Valerie drove toward the intersection giving Alexa another glimpse of the vampires loading an unwieldy box onto the pickup.

"Those guys must not work for the appliance store," Valerie said turning the car away from the vampires. "It isn't that hard to move a refrigerator."

"That's not a refrigerator in the box," Alexa said.

"What else would it be?" Valerie asked using the rearview mirror to look at Alexa.

"You don't want the answer to that."

"Well, now I do. How on earth would you know what they have packed in a tall box made for a refrigerator other than a refrigerator?"

"Because I smelled a dead body and the way they were wrestling the box, the body must have slumped or something."

Sarah turned around in her seat to stare at Alexa. "You smelled a dead body?"

Alexa nodded.

"Who killed the person?"

"I assume somebody those guys work for." Alexa looked over her shoulder but couldn't see anything but buildings. She looked back at Sarah. "It was a vampire in the box if that makes you feel any better."

Valerie looked in the mirror again. "Bloodhounds would die for a nose like that."

"I missed the chocolate at the nut booth."

"Well there were a lot of scents bouncing around tonight," Valerie said as she turned onto the next street. "How you could detect anything with popcorn and cinnamon in the air is beyond me."

"Don't forget the humans," Alexa with a grin.

"Humans don't bother me," Sarah said. "I sometimes forget

they have a scent at all."

"It's nice to finally have an identifier for that odor. I mean it was always just air as far as I was concerned, but then my ability to smell got stronger when my teeth came in and I'm noticing all sorts of things. I thought I had a strong sense of smell before but now... well, 'bloodhound' might be a good description."

Valerie chuckled. "But you're upset you missed the chocolate?"

"Well, yeah. That's a pretty basic scent even humans can pick up."

"The cinnamon mixture was being made there fresh, so no, humans wouldn't have picked it up either. I certainly didn't."

"And the chocolates were packaged up," Sarah said.

"Lexie, don't beat yourself up too much over that," Valerie said. "Despite the cinnamon and humans and all of the other scents floating through the air, you managed to detect a dead body inside a cardboard box across the street. I'm certain your bloodhound status remains intact. Now what I am interested in is why you weren't concerned about vampires up on the roof?"

Sarah gasped and stared at Valerie. "There were vampires on the roof?"

"There's always vampires on roofs," Alexa said.

"Why?" Valerie and Sarah asked in unison. They looked at each other, then back at Alexa. Valerie quickly returned her attention to the front, but Sarah remained in her twisted pose.

"I don't know *why* exactly, but Lord knows I've spent plenty of time climbing up on roofs myself."

"Why?" Sarah asked again.

"To jump down."

"What? Why?"

Alexa laughed and shrugged. "I don't know, it's just fun to do. There's a building at the college I went to that was pretty easy to get on the roof and at one end it was a good two stories tall and I would jump off of it."

"In front of people?" Valerie asked.

"No. I learned a long time ago jumping off of things was weird, but I'd sneak up there at night when I needed to get away and challenge myself."

Sarah looked confused. "Two stories?"

"When I was a little girl I would jump out of trees all of the time. My friends called me Tarzan. I didn't let them know I was also jumping off the house – the tree in our backyard was basically a bridge. My mom was terrified the first time she caught me doing it and then when she told my dad he just laughed. *That* was a huge argument. Looking back I think he was a little proud, to be honest - his little witch daughter finally displaying a vampire trait."

"So all vampires like jumping off buildings?" Sarah asked.

"I don't know about *all*, but Eric said he and his friends jumped off buildings a lot and I even took him to my college where we both jumped off the roof."

"You said the men on the buildings downtown were guards. Were they up there for pleasure or for work?" Valerie asked.

"I have no idea, but it's an easy way to monitor what's going on, like making sure no one interferes with escorting a dead body through a crowd."

"Why didn't they just back the truck up to the store?" Sarah asked.

"Or wait 'til later?" Valerie asked.

"Probably because of the crowd."

Valerie nodded. "That makes sense. The fair provided human cover so as not to draw attention to moving an appliance, even if it was a little after hours. 7 pm is far more acceptable than 2 am."

"Yep," Alexa said. "I'm sure some dingdong parked smack dab in the middle of their loading dock."

"What do they *do* with dead bodies?" Sarah asked.

"I don't know," Alexa said. "Dispose of them? My mom said something about a crematorium. I don't know if that's universal or just where I'm from but I have seen the aftermath of a cleanup crew arrive and eradicate all traces. And in that instance, they had to deal with human witnesses so they shot off guns out in the woods, then got the news to report a wild animal sighting. I'm sure people are still talking about the big cat possibly roaming around the edges of town."

"Crematoriums are typically operated by witches," Valerie said. "Pyromancers, to be specific."

Alexa asked, "Would vampires willingly work with a witch that way?"

Valerie laughed as if the statement were obvious. "I don't know if the vampires understand what they're doing. Maybe they're happy to have a discreet connection that likely doesn't ask a lot of questions or charge a lot for disposal services."

"I'm missing something here. What does the witch get out of the deal?"

"Energy," Valerie said. "Remember feeling the energy of the fire? Each person has energy and vampires are walking powder kegs of energy. *You* emit tons of energy. When a person dies that energy has to go somewhere. Some of it carries with the soul. I've heard of people sitting next to someone dying, say that they felt the life leave so I've always assumed that was the soul. But there's still energy within the corpse and when the body is burned that energy feeds the fire. A skilled pyromancer can absorb energy from fire."

"What happens when a body is burned without a witch to absorb it?" Alexa asked.

"I know the answer to that!" Sarah said. "Plants absorb it."

Chapter Thirty-Two

Tapping her pencil, debating whether or not to make the call, Alexa finally relented and dialed the number. At the first ring, she contemplated hanging up. On the second she reminded herself how Valerie agreed she should call.

Before the third ring, a man answered. "Coberg Haldor Companies."

"I was given this number by Mr. Coberg if I had anything to report," Alexa said.

"Harald gave you this number?"

"No, um, Diederich."

"And your name?"

She caught herself before saying, Alexa. "Lexie Meyers from Emerson, Murray, McNeil Law Offices."

Listening to the repetitive chimes of the hold music Alexa considered hanging up. What if she was helping bad people do bad things? What if she was interfering with a federal investigation? What if someone innocent would get hurt because of her? She wasn't sure if Diederich was good or bad. He seemed nice but that didn't mean he was trustworthy. She was convinced the guy that came with him to the office was up to no good, especially after her encounter at the nightclub, but she didn't know about Diederich.

Maybe vampires were morally gray?

What did any of this mean about her father? What did this mean about her?

"Miss Myers, thank you for calling." Diederich's familiar voice came through the phone.

"Yes, um." Alexa cleared her throat. "You asked me to call if I saw anything, but I'm at the office right now."

"Sure," he said. "You may speak in vague terms."

"We were at a vendor fair over the weekend. I was told there's an appliance store you might be aware of."

"Yes, well acquainted and also aware of the vendor fair."

Alexa tried to think of a way to tell him she detected another dead body. "Well, I came across the same scent as I did at the creek when we first met."

"At the fair?" he asked, concerned.

"Not in the middle of the street, but on the sidewalk behind the booths."

"Did you see anything or anyone?"

"Let me tell you what I noticed that had nothing to do with the fair. On our way back to the car there were several guys loading a large box, like refrigerator-sized, onto a pickup but seemed to be having some difficulty, which you know, refrigerators shouldn't be that difficult to maneuver especially for who was handling them, if you know what I mean? It... well, it seems like the contents... *shifted.*"

"Yes, that store often, er, repurposes those sort of boxes for such activity," Diederich said. He paused with a sigh. "This is concerning as I am not aware of any transactions that evening."

"Well, and while I was at the fair, the roofline caught my attention."

"You're saying people were on the roofs overlooking the fair?"

"Yes. Several. In fact, while we were getting popcorn I noticed a gargoyle."

Silence.

Diederich cleared his throat. "Thank you, Ms. Myers. This was helpful."

Chapter Thirty-Three

Geese floated along the serene lake occasionally flapping their wings or bobbing their heads. Sarah led Valerie and Alexa around the lake along the walking path toward the woods opposite their condo. They kept a steady pace with a mission to find the perfect log to burn for Yule.

Sarah darted off the paved path for a well-worn trail up a hill through the grass into the trees. Alexa and Valerie dutifully followed behind, each carrying a canvas tote. The dry, crisp air didn't carry the deep woodsy scents as Alexa had hoped. Sure, she smelled trees, earth, and leaves, but they didn't invoke warmth. Only a fireplace somewhere in the distance emitted any such promise.

"Do you smell the smoke?" Alexa asked.

"Mmhmm." Valerie nodded.

"It makes me think of hot cocoa."

Valerie glared at Alexa. "You're going to rot my teeth out."

"Tis the season," Alexa said with a devilish grin.

Valerie laughed. "Only if we add brandy."

Alexa turned with raised eyebrows. "I've never had it with brandy. We always use peppermint schnapps."

"Oh, that sounds good too! Sarah won't drink it, though. She doesn't like peppermint."

"Really? You totally look like a peppermint girl!"

"Nope," Sarah said turning around. "I hate the stuff. I much prefer brandy. Oh, hey, there are some pinecones!" Sarah dashed off the path and Valerie followed.

Alexa watched in horror as her mind flashed to the day Brie and Tess collected pinecones for a party. The similarities between Tess and Valerie as well as Brie and Sarah struck Alexa hard. She gasped for air looking around, seeing large leaves and tiny pinecones scattered on the ground. The parallels between the two moments, both so quiet and benign, worried Alexa. She tried to scan beyond the trail but all she could see were trees.

A touch on her arm shook her. In a confused haze, she saw Valerie talking to her. Sarah's voice came through the fog. "Are you okay?"

Alexa shook her head. "No," she whispered.

Gentle hands guided her to the ground and Valerie squatted next to her. "Put your hands in the dirt to ground yourself and take several deep breaths to clear your head."

Alexa looked around and only saw branches and pine needles. Her chest felt heavy but not from anyone laying on her. Her eyes burned but not with the blood of a man she had killed. When she looked up she saw branches, not blue sky. When she looked next to her she saw Valerie and on the other side Sarah, not the feet of several vampires trying to lift a dead body off her. She felt the cold powder of the dirt in her hands, not the grass where a man tried to rape her. She wasn't there. She was here.

She was here.

With a deep breath, Alexa realized her entire body was shaking. She ran her fingers through the dirt. "I'm not there. I'm here." She nodded. "I'm here."

"Yes, that's right. You're here," Valerie said.

"What did you see?" Concern filled Sarah's voice.

Alexa shook her head. "Pinecones."

Valerie moved from a squat to fully sitting on the ground. She rubbed Alexa's arm again.

"We were collecting pinecones," Alexa whispered

"Like we're doing here?" Valerie asked.

Alexa nodded. "It was just pinecones. We were going to throw away the little ones. I didn't even understand why we were collecting them."

"Do you understand why we're collecting them today?"

"It's earthy, witch stuff. That's what Brie and Tess said. It was for a party their moms were throwing. It was for Mabon, I guess. I didn't understand it but they said it was part of the Wiccan calendar. Yule was in the list they rattled off."

"That's right. We've talked about the Sabbats. You understand them now."

Alexa nodded. "Yeah, but I didn't then. It just sounded like excuses to drink wine and have a party."

Valerie grinned as she shook her head. "There's no wrong way."

They sat silent as a gentle breeze whistled through the trees.

"Will you tell us what happened?" Valerie asked in a soft,

calming voice.

"We were collecting pinecones. There were a bunch of tiny ones like those." Alexa pointed toward the pine tree where small cones littered the ground. She rubbed the canvas of Sara's bag sitting between them. "Bags. We didn't think to bring bags with us. So Brie ran back to the apartment but when she came back my old boyfriend had her by the arm. Did you know I dated humans?"

Sarah shook her head.

With a snort, Alexa shrugged. "I had no idea. I broke up with this guy over a year ago, but he just kept showing up. Unfortunately, he had a vampire with him this time. I have no idea who this guy was but his intentions were very clear he planned to have a witch – any of us would do. But there they stood like the best of friends with this half-baked idea, I guess. Something like if I saw Jack again we could work things out? I don't know. But I needed to get Brie and Tess out of there. I don't even remember what happened to the pinecones. We had to have dropped them. I don't remember. We had our shirts pulled out like bowls; they were full. I don't remember anything hitting my feet. Where did the pinecones go?"

"But your friends got away, right?" Sarah asked.

Alexa nodded. "Yeah. I swirled up a windstorm and told them to run in one direction and I went in the other. I figured Jack would chase them trying to get his leverage back and the vampire would chase me, because, you know, he wanted a witch and I was probably the easier one to catch."

She wiggled her fingers in the dirt. She wasn't there. She was here.

Deep breath.

"It all happened so fast. He caught me and threw me on the ground. I barely remember if there was a fight at all. I just flipped over to face him but he was so focused on trying to get between my legs that he didn't see my fangs… my teeth."

Alexa closed her eyes and took several deep breaths while running her hands back and forth through the dirt. With tears streaming down her face she looked at Valerie. "What are you supposed to do with a dead body on top of you?"

The shaking returned. Deep remorseful sobs vibrated through Alexa's body. Through the blur of tears, she saw trees - tall with branches weaving a leafless canopy beneath a gray December sky. She leaned into Valerie's shoulder, weak from crying.

"Are you okay to walk?" Valerie asked.

Alexa nodded. "I'm sorry I ruined the outing."

"When you arrived here you said you wanted to come up for air. Maybe you've rested enough that you're finally ready to unpack all that has happened since you learned about your identity."

"Maybe," Alexa said with a sniffle.

"You didn't kill him in cold blood," Valerie said. "You were defending yourself and your friends."

Alexa pulled out of Valerie's arms and turned to face her. "Why don't vampires use weapons?"

Valerie shrugged. "I have absolutely no idea. All I can guess is it's some macho thing to out power each other, like some unwritten code."

Alexa ran a hand through her hair, halfway through realizing how filthy her hand was. "What about the Yule log?"

"Don't worry about that, we can find one later."

Chapter Thirty-Four

A door slammed upstairs and Sarah marched down the stairs agitated. "I can't find the candles we bought in Charlestown," she said.

"Do we need them?" Valerie asked looking at the table lined with taper candles.

Sarah pointed at the box on the floor. "I have pillar stands specifically to add balance."

"Did we put them in the sideboard?" Valerie asked.

Knowing the conversation would likely end in slammed doors and tears Alexa left the room as the two continued to search for the missing candles. "I'm going for a walk," she said as she grabbed her coat and wallet.

Small wisps of snow from the previous day dotted lawns but the sidewalks remained dry. Alexa walked past several homes with yard displays celebrating Christmas. The night before, these homes beamed lights flashing and blinking. She knew beyond many of the windows stood lush trees decked out with ornaments and more lights. In a few hours, the neighborhood would again glitter in a joyous light display.

She pressed on with her walk, not a meandering chance for fresh air. Alexa planned to make a phone call and headed toward a nearby convenience store with a pay phone. She left the condominium community and entered a housing tract. Houses nearly thirty years old lined the street, many with older Christmas décor of plastic characters with a single bulb inside. Outdoor lights adorned the rooflines, some with the traditional big bulbs but others had the more modern, small, twinkling lights. She wondered if the homeowners weren't too pleased about the condominium – the increased traffic and taking away the open field behind their homes.

Alexa turned at the corner. Three boys ran down the middle of the street tossing a football back and forth. She nearly tripped on the uneven sidewalk as she passed the boys. She laughed at herself and continued on, knowing her destination to be another block away. A car turned onto the street and Alexa heard the boys scramble toward the sidewalks on either side.

At last, she arrived at the entrance to the neighborhood. A traffic signal, crosswalks, and four lanes of cars zooming by changed the ambiance. Alexa didn't need to cross the street, to her left a 7-Eleven stood just beyond Elaine's Beauty Salon.

Outside the convenience store, she didn't see anyone at the telephone, a silver metal bay with a blue bell etched on the side. She fished out her wallet with nearly a roll worth of quarters she had squirreled away for this call. She hoped seven dollars would be enough; she didn't want to go inside the store to get more change.

She dropped two quarters in the slot and dialed the number. An automated voice instructed depositing fifty cents for a long-distance call, so Alexa slid in two more quarters. Her heart raced as the phone rang.

"Hello?" the voice answered.

"Hi mom," Alexa said.

"Oh, honey, I'm so happy to hear from you! How are you? Are you safe?"

Alexa laughed. "Yes, I'm fine. I just wanted to call and wish you a happy Yule."

She heard her mother gasp. "Happy Yule to you. Oh, how I wish we could celebrate this together."

"I know. I'm sorry."

"No. I'm sorry. Your first Yule should have been many years ago. Your father and I had plenty of opportunities and... well... You did what you felt was necessary and I support you one hundred percent. Alexa, I'm delighted to hear your voice. Are you learning about Yule?"

"Yes, but this is something you and I should be sharing."

"It would be nice, but the fact that you thought of me, right now for this reason fills my heart. So tell me, how are you celebrating? The solstice was two days ago. Did you do anything special then?"

"We decorated a Yule log that we plan to burn tomorrow and then we spent the evening in candlelight just talking."

"Who are you with?"

"Two witches have taken me in. They know my story and don't care I'm a hybrid. They're teaching me so much. One is a pyromancer and taught me how to pull up fire."

"I thought maybe you would have that power."

"Do you have it?"

"Yes, I do. It comes from my dad. Can you picture him with a flame coming out of the tip of his finger?"

Alexa laughed. "Yes, actually I can. Let me guess, he lit your birthday cakes that way?"

"You know him well! He will be excited to hear you've inherited the ability."

"Is dad there?"

"No, he's supposed to be in town tomorrow."

"Are you okay by yourself?"

Her mother chuckled. "Yes, quite okay. It's nice having the house to myself. There's been a lot of changes since you left, nothing I can get into over the phone but you would be surprised."

"You guys haven't separated!"

"No, no, nothing like that. Your father and I are still passionately in love with each other, but things have changed for people around us. I spent Thursday night with Brie and Tess's parents. It was nice to be among witches again."

"Oh my God! That's such good news! I'm so happy for you!"

"We're both worried sick about you."

"I miss you guys."

"Do you plan on coming home?"

"Not yet. I'm surprised I haven't encountered anyone following me."

"He promised me he would not interfere with your travels, but he has tracked several leads. Evidently, you're hard as hell to keep up with."

"Haven't I always been hard to track?"

Her mother laughed. "Oh, the stories I have to tell you about that. You have baffled his team your entire life."

"Team? Wow. I only thought he had Sebastian following me."

"Nooo. Philippe's daughter required an entire team of bodyguards."

"And your daughter?"

"Oh, *my* daughter has been an elusive skink her whole life that proved to be too much for one well-trained vampire to track."

"Well good. Someone has to keep them on their toes."

An automated voice requesting more coins interrupted their conversation.

"You're on a pay phone?"

"How else can I stay elusive?"

"Good job. Listen. He has men stationed close to some of your locations. If an emergency arises, just call, and help will be dispatched immediately."

"Okay."

"I love you with all my heart. Please stay safe. And Alexa, my dear, Happy Yule."

"Happy Yule, mom. I love you." Tears filled Alexa's eyes as she hung up the receiver. She walked to the side of the store and leaned her head against the brick wall as she cried.

A black car pulled into the parking lot. Alexa's heart dropped, thinking one of her father's bodyguards had traced her call. A woman got out of the car and headed into the store.

Alexa looked at the telephone and wondered if she made a mistake calling home. She wiped her tears and headed back to the condo pondering her situation. Did she care if her father knew where to find her? She liked the idea that he promised not to interfere. But would he stick to that promise? However, the idea that he had guards stationed just to rescue her was oddly reassuring. And yet, wasn't the idea of leaving home to get away from her father's flock of vampires? Seriously, what was a group of vampires called? Should she stay in Radcliff or was it time to move on?

She walked past the boys in the street again. They ignored her until the football ricocheted off the hood of the car next to her. She looked at the car, saw no damage, and then up at the boys. Crap, did she just give them the librarian stare of disapproval? With a big grin, she shook her head and continued walking.

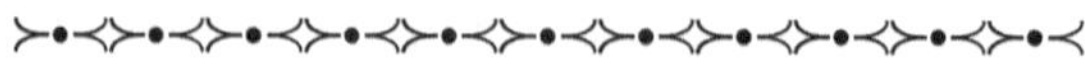

Sarah whisked the front door open before Alexa hit the front steps. "Are you okay?"

"Yeah. I walked up to Seven-Eleven."

"You look like you've been crying." Sarah bustled her through the door with a concerned look. Valerie came toward the door matching Sarah's worried expression.

"A long walk and a cathartic cry," Alexa said. She unzipped her coat and Sarah helped her remove it.

"What's going on?" Valerie asked.

"All of these preparations around Yule made me miss my mom. She should be the one showing me all of this - so I went up to the pay phone to call her. She's sad she doesn't get to be with me on my first Yule but is happy I found people to teach me. I could hear her voice crack when she said she was happy that I thought of her." Tears filled Alexa's eyes yet again.

"I'm sure she was very touched you thought to call. It was a very appropriate Yule gift to give – loving energy," Valerie said.

"It was good to hear her voice."

Sarah looked at her puzzled. "Why didn't you just call from here?"

"So they can't trace the number."

"Oh. Well, you gave us enough time to get everything laid out, but Valerie *lied* to me about the meal."

Alexa looked between Sarah and Valerie, both beaming broad smiles. Sarah took Alexa's hand and pulled her to the dining room. Lit candles lined the middle of the table, including the pillars she needed, surrounded by several large platters piled with food – the very picture of a feast.

Alexa's mouth dropped open. "How did you do this?"

Valerie grinned. "I'm a witch."

"No. I went shopping with you. How did you pull this off?"

Valerie laughed as she handed a goblet of wine to Alexa. "I've been planning this long before you joined our home. When you left earlier I wished you had taken Sarah with you, but it all worked out. This was my gift to Sarah and the look on her face when she came downstairs was worth every moment of planning. She has mentioned wanting a true feast for the longest time. I almost did this for Samhain, but I am *so* glad I waited."

"The turkey legs! I wondered why you bought so many before Thanksgiving!" Alexa ambled around the table taking in all the details. "How did you get so many oranges? We only bought one bag."

"I've been buying them for several weeks. And apples too."

"This is amazing. And a ham?"

"Fortunately it was cold enough to leave groceries in my car last night."

"You're an evil genius. Pies... oh you got the cake I made!" Alexa stood at the end of the table and shook her head in wonder. "Who the hell is going to eat all of this?"

"Well," Valerie said. "You showed up before Sarah and I could discuss this." Valerie looked at Sarah. "I was hoping when we're done eating tonight that we package this up into individual servings..."

"And take it down to Tamm House?" Sarah's eyes widened, bright and hopeful.

Alexa had never visited Tamm House but heard plenty of Sarah's stories of the people who received services there.

Valerie nodded and Sarah rushed around the table to pull her into a hug. Sarah pulled back with tears streaming down her face. "Thank you." They hugged again then fell into a long, deep kiss. Alexa smiled as she refilled her goblet.

Chapter Thirty-Five

Alexa followed Sarah from the garage into the kitchen. The litter scattered across the counters from the previous night when they packaged meal boxes for Tamm House. Exhausted and hungry, Alexa pushed the packaging supplies to one corner and pulled the remaining ham from the refrigerator.

Valerie finally arrived, having driven separately. "Oh good," she said bustling in from the garage. "I'm starving."

"Sarah and I decided this was the easiest thing to throw together. She ran off to the bathroom."

"That's not a bad idea. I'll be back to help in a minute."

By the time Sarah and Valerie returned to the kitchen Alexa had a full lunch laid out and started putting away the remains of the previous night.

"Stop cleaning. You need to relax too," Valerie said.

Sarah burst into the kitchen nearly running into Valerie. "Oh! Let me get drinks. Is pop good for everyone?" She wiggled around Valerie and headed to the refrigerator.

Alexa slumped into her seat at the table. She smiled at the remnants of Sarah's feast. An ornate bowl of oranges decorated with cloves sat between two spent candles. She wondered if the cloves affected the flavor and picked one up. "Are these safe to eat?"

"Sure," Valerie said. "I'd remove the cloves before you peel it, though."

Alexa carefully plucked the spiked pieces of spice from the orange that only days earlier she had decorated.

"Set those to the side. We can add them to the Yule fire," Valerie said, pointing to the cloves.

"Oh that will be an interesting smell," Alexa said.

Valerie nodded. "I've never done it before but it would be a waste to just throw them away. If it turns out the way I think it will, I'm sure we will add cloves every year!"

Alexa lifted her can of Diet Coke. "To new traditions!"

"To new traditions!"

With the peel and cloves removed, Alexa pulled the orange apart and took a tentative bite.

Sarah stared at her. "Well?"

"Um. There's a Christmassy taste. It's not bad, but I think I would rather have it juiced and made into a hot toddy, maybe with a shot of rum."

Valerie looked at Alexa with raised eyebrows. "Oh. That sounds interesting. I was planning on letting these dry to deodorize closets and keep bugs out, but we don't need but just a few."

"Don't we have orange tea?" Sarah asked.

"We might."

Sarah left the table for the kitchen.

"Should I start peeling a couple more oranges?" Alexa asked.

"Sure. Leave four of the prettiest ones, though," Valerie said.

With lunch completed, oranges peeled, tea brewed, and coats donned, Alexa followed Sarah onto the back porch to join Valerie. She held the remains of the branch Sarah dragged home the day after Alexa's panic attack. Now cut down to a reasonable size the log fit neatly inside the fire pit. Branches of pine laid below the log wrapped in a band of braided grasses and a second braid of reeds that once edged the lake.

Alexa smiled at the memory of sawing the branch down to size as Valerie and Sarah held the ends. She cut the branch into sections, the remains piled at the edge of the patio for firewood in the future.

Sarah opened her canvas tote and extracted the pinecones she and Valerie had collected. She spread them evenly over the pine branches around the log and turned to Alexa. "We should add the orange peels too."

Alexa darted inside and returned with her plate. Following Sarah's lead with the pinecones, Alexa walked around the fire pit dropping bits and pieces of orange and cloves around the log. "This is really pretty."

"I agree," Valerie said. "The orange is a perfect accent. Now for the cranberries!" She took a handful from the bag on her chair and sprinkled the berries among the orange peels. "This is the most beautiful one we have ever had!" She turned to Alexa. "Would you like to start the fire?"

"Uh."

"Just focus on one of the pine cones. They're dry and easiest to light. Once you feel the heat, even before a flame flickers, spread the energy to the next pinecone. Spread it slowly, and only to a couple – we don't need a bonfire. There's no rush, we plan to sit out here for a while."

"Okay."

"As we wait for the fire to take hold is when we should consider our intentions." Valerie's voice, soft and soothing, brought reverence to a metal bin holding an adorned log laying on pine branches. "As the flame builds we release our intentions to be carried with the smoke and into the wind. In gratitude to the plants that offered their fruit to our gathering, we promise to stay present until all is spent with their spirit sent into the air and the remaining dust returned to the earth." She sat down and nodded to Alexa.

As instructed, Alexa focused on one pinecone. She recalled the sensation of resurrecting flames from embers and directed the memory of warmth and fire toward the tiny pinecone. Alexa stood for a long time staring at the firepit, the scent of fresh pine in the air. Gradually she felt the warmth inside her grow and heat her entire body. Knowing she had too much power building, Alexa took a deep breath with her eyes closed. At the point she thought she held the right amount of heat she opened her eyes and zeroed in on the pinecone again, this time directing her internal heat toward it. Low and slow, she reminded herself. She directed the same heat toward the next pinecone, then a third and fourth. Alexa detected the smallest amount of heat coming from the first pinecone. She blew a small gust of air over the firepit and a puff of smoke twirled up. After a second gust, a spark popped, and then another.

Alexa sat down without taking her attention off the first pinecone. She knew the heat was there, just waiting to pop into a flame. She felt the burgeoning strength. With a smile, Alexa took delight in her new power. No flame danced to life yet, but she felt it there under the surface. She considered blowing more air over the log and pinecones, but she waited as Valerie had said to not rush the process – there was no need to burn the whole set at once.

Another spark popped and then one from the second pinecone. The second pinecone surprised Alexa. She watched an ember glow from the base of the first pinecone where the flame appeared and receded. No longer sending heat into the firepit Alexa watched as minuscule embers spread between the pinecones. She doubted Sarah could see the transformation, but she knew Valerie was watching.

Finally, a flame danced up the rippled side of the pinecone beckoning more flames to rise.

Sarah squealed. "You did it!"

Alexa looked at Valerie who returned a broad smile. "Your mother would be proud."

Something caught in Alexa's throat as tears filled her eyes. She nodded. Yes, her mother would have been very proud. She did it! She started a fire completely from scratch!

The braided grass darkened as the flames reached the log. A warm-sounding crackle came from the fresh pine needles and the smoky pine scent filled the area.

Alexa picked up her mug of orange tea and spiced rum with a heavy splash of fresh orange tainted with cloves. The first sip didn't warm the gullet as she hoped, but then again, the mug had been sitting in the cold air for some time.

Valerie nodded her head and raised her mug. "What do you think?"

"Not too bad. Actually, I think it could use a light sprinkle of ground cloves."

"I like it," Sarah said.

Alexa nodded in agreement. "The tea was a brilliant idea." She took a second sip – much warmer. She smiled and returned her attention to the fire, pulling a blanket over her lap.

She looked back to Sarah. "The blankets were also a smart idea."

"It's always freezing out here when we do this," Sarah said with a grin. "My grandma would bring big quilts for us when we went to my uncle's house for Yule. There were too many of us to sit around his tiny fireplace so he set up a huge fire out in his field and no matter the weather we would drag chairs out there and grandma's quilts with big thermoses of hot cocoa. The winds were brutal gusting across that open field and almost always we had snow, sometimes up to our knees. We shivered while my dad and him clicked lighters onto balled-up newspaper. I guess we didn't have any pyromancers in my family and had to light it the old-fashioned way."

"But it's not supposed to be a bonfire," Valerie said.

"According to your family," Sarah said with a smile. "I told you our Yule log was always huge, like a whole tree. We always made sure to light it first, and it layed at the bottom with a bunch of other logs leaned together above it like a teepee. It took a while but once it got going we had to move our chairs back. More than once sparks caught something else on fire. All of grandma's quilts had burn holes in them and she would just patch them up for the next time."

"That doesn't sound peaceful at all," Valerie said.

Alexa smiled. "It sounds like a family of chaos witches."

Valerie raised her eyebrows and tipped her head in agreement.

"It's a happy memory!" Sarah countered.

"Of course it is!" Alexa said. "How did you guys decorate the log?"

"Everyone was expected to bring something and attach it before the fire was lit. We didn't set intentions into the wind but said a small thank you while attaching our trinket to the log and we stayed out there until the main log was nothing but coals." She pointed at the firepit. "Ooh look! The orange peels are curling up. And I can smell them!"

Orange, pine, and clove twined in the smoky air. Alexa sipped more tea and grinned. She counted herself lucky to have landed with these two women. She didn't have any intentions to send into the wind, but she did send up her gratitude. Alexa took a deep breath and smiled at this one perfect moment of peace and friendship.

- January 1996 -

Chapter Thirty-Six

Beyond the cubicle wall, Alexa listened to the printer grind out line after line of the report she needed. She tidied her desk and placed folders in a box to return to Lisa in the file room, hoping the report would finish so she could get lunch.

Curious and impatient, Alexa walked around her cubicle wall toward the printer. One of the lawyers, Kyle, darted in front of her and stood staring at the printer churning a continuous feed of paper into a box on the floor. He ran his hand across his mouth and sighed with disgust. He turned, startled seeing Alexa.

She smiled in sympathy. "Sorry," she said. "It's a long report."

He sighed again. "Of course. The one by my office is down and I'm meeting with a client at one."

"I was wanting to go to lunch when it finished, hopefully soon. Do you want me to bring your report to you when it's done?"

"No. Get your lunch – I can't do anything else until I have that in my hands so I'll just keep coming back to check for it." He turned and walked away grumbling about modern technology.

Kyle had just turned the corner when the printer stopped. Alexa pulled the end of her report, carefully tearing along the perforation, but halfway through the printer clicked, ready to start the next job. Alexa hurried before the paper moved and risked her chance to make a clean tear. With the report freed from the printer and the next page inching toward the edge of the table, Alexa grabbed the remainder of her report from the box on the floor. She walked toward Kyle's office as she tore off the perforated edges where the spiked roller had progressed the paper.

"My report is done and the next one is coming through," she said from the doorway. She turned without waiting for a reply and headed to Donella's office.

At Donella's door, she cleared her throat to announce her arrival. "Here's the correction to the fourth quarter billing and a list of refunds."

"Oh good! Come on in." Donella motioned for Alexa to close the door. "Thank you for running these. Jeff is just too busy with year-end to get these for the partners."

Alexa handed the stack of paper to Donella and dropped the edge pieces into the trash next to Donella's desk. "It's not a problem. Let me know what else you need run." She sat down and watched Donella flip through the pages.

Donella looked up and smiled. "I appreciate that. How was Yule?"

"It was really nice. We did something different every day for a week, winding it all up on Christmas with a small gift exchange and then taking box lunches to distribute at a shelter. How as yours?"

Tilting her head with a smile, Donella said, "That was very meaningful – donating food and time to those in need! Very appropriate for Yule! Maurice and I had a private observation for solstice and then on Christmas joined his family. They prefer to adhere to Christian traditions rather than Wiccan. We had a full sit-down meal with all of the trimmings. His sister makes the best prime rib."

"Do you know how long it's been since I've had prime rib? My mouth is watering just thinking about it."

With a small laugh, Donella said, "I imagine full-blooded witches don't eat rare meat on a regular occasion."

"No, they really don't. Valerie is an amazing cook – I should say 'chef'. But she doesn't use beef frequently and only once has she made steak. It was phenomenal but her version of rare was, well, you know, not rare enough."

Donella nodded. "A whole week of Yule? Is that how they normally celebrate?"

"Well they went a little over the top making sure I had the full experience, but yes it's a several-day event for them. I think they combine bits from both of their families. So I learned a lot, but I also had a few breakdowns. At one point I went and called my mom. It was a little rough not having her be the one to introduce me to Yule."

"I'm sorry to hear that. The holidays can be rough especially if you're not with the people you love. Did she update you about what's going on with witches in Brentwood?"

Alexa shook her head worried something major happened. "No. We just talked about Yule and somehow ventured off discussing her birthday parties as a little girl."

"Oh, well it was kind of major. They had a witches' council, which is really odd. Most places don't operate like that, but the council was disbanded. There was a coup where the witches rose up and disbanded the council."

Alexa smiled. "Well good. That damned council made life miserable for hybrids."

"I was shocked you didn't know anything about witchcraft when you came here, but then I saw on your paperwork you're from Brentwood and it all made sense. Hybrids are used to being shunned, but Brentwood has all sorts of restrictions and the things I've heard coming out of there is just insane. So the big news is the head of the council was stripped of her authority and hybrids are starting to practice witchcraft again. Unfortunately, this woman is causing mayhem and is trying to get even with the people who unseated her."

An evil smile spread across Alexa's face. "Yeah, I'm the reason the covens found out she was hunting hybrids for their vampire blood."

"She what?"

"She had people hunting hybrids, attacking them to make it look like vampires did it, and using hybrid blood for spells. The speculation was that she was trying to summon something nasty. I don't know squat about what can be summoned, but my vast experience with cartoons and movies leads me to believe it tends to be evil and is not something the summoner has much control over."

Donella shook her head with a hearty laugh. "You're correct. Summoning dark forces is not for the faint of heart, and no, they're not submissive."

Alexa snorted.

"You'd think someone who managed to rise to power over an entire region of witches would know better," Donella said.

"And yet Beverly let power go to her head."

"Do you *know* this woman?"

Alexa nodded. She delighted at the thought of her grandmother hearing Alexa had mysteriously run away and no one knew where to find her. "Yep. And she knows I'm the one who brought it all to light, so I guess it's really a good idea I left town. Huh, I guess a vampire stalker was the least of my worries."

"What happens if she tracks you down?"

"Dunno. Guess I'll cross that bridge when I get there."

"Well I didn't know the full extent of your story but now I'm glad I helped cover your tracks the way I did."

Alexa tilted her head. "How so?"

"I had a friend in Waukegan run your background check. She even reached out to your friend, Abbey, to verify the story you gave Valerie."

"This was done before I even arrived?"

Donella nodded.

"Ah. I wondered why Valerie agreed to bring a hybrid into her home, even for one night."

"Yes, and when she brought you here looking for work I just faxed your application to my friend. She's the one who called your former employer. Other than being upset you didn't give any notice, they had gleaming things to say about your work. There is a side note to this – my friend is now collaborating with Abbey to help other people on the run. Their biggest hurdle has been establishing employment history with fear of calls being traced so she's offering services to be a point of contact."

"Oh my gosh, that's fantastic."

"It's a needed service," Donella said. "Everyone seems to have a story of an acquaintance who needed to uproot overnight. When things are safer for you, I plan to assist in these efforts. I have enough connections and it's definitely meaningful work."

"Wow! Yes. It's definitely needed. And thank you for keeping my safety in mind, but you know, this puts *you* in harm's way?"

Donella nodded. "When we talked about paths and fate? It really got me thinking. I'm to a point in my life where I'm no longer scrambling. The degree and certifications and getting myself established are all set. Now it's time to do something to help others. I want my path to be one where I've done something meaningful. And yes, I understand the danger, but I would be more upset with myself if I lived a long life without extending a hand out to help others."

Alexa smiled sweetly with an understanding nod while Donella's death scene played out - damp grass pressed to her face, smoke choking her every breath, screams in the fading distance.

"I'm still in the scrambling phase of life, I guess," Alexa said trying not to gasp from the imaginary smoke.

Chapter Thirty-Seven

Alexa got into the passenger seat of Donella's car, excited to meet up with her friends again.

"Is it rude to not invite Valerie along?" Donella asked.

"No, not at all. She's glad I've connected with another hybrid and said the two of you get along but never really struck up a friendship. Besides, this gives her and Sarah a little alone time."

"Do you feel like a third wheel with them?"

"No. It's like we're just three roommates. Every so often there will be a touch or look between them that reminds me 'oh yeah, they're a couple.' I spend a lot of time keeping to myself other than meals and outings, so they have plenty of opportunity for those moments necessary to maintain a relationship."

"Why do you keep to yourself?"

"I've just needed time and space to collect myself, to come up for air. I go for a long walk almost every evening and Sarah has an incredible collection of books I'm plowing through."

"Is it working?"

"I think so. There's something to be said for routines. Even with the disruption of the holidays there's been this... hmmm... warmth and a sense of calm I've been missing for a very long time, like before my teeth came in." Alexa paused and thought. "Maybe since college."

"You're in your mid-twenties, that sounds about right."

"What do you mean?"

Donella shook her head as she brought the car to a stop next to a steep driveway. "It seems everyone goes through some sort of existential crisis in their twenties." She pointed at the house. "Here we are. Now at any time you're ready to bail, just shoot me a quiet whisper and no questions asked, I will make our excuses to leave."

"You don't have to do that for me."

"I know how they get and it's not for everyone."

Before Donella could knock, the front door swung open and Alicia appeared with a broad smile. "Lexie! We're so glad you're here! Hey, Donella!"

Alicia bustled Alexa into the house, taking her coat. "If you don't mind removing your shoes," she said pointing to the pile of footwear next to the entry.

Donella followed behind, handing her coat off and removing her shoes. Alicia disappeared with the coats as the group from the nightclub welcomed Alexa and Donella.

Dennis stepped forward. "Lexie, this is CeCe and her husband Reggie."

Alexa extended a hand and said, "Glad to meet you!"

CeCe accepted her hand. "We've heard a lot about you. Mysterious white girl swaying our quiet Donella to break all of her rules."

"I think she just took pity on me."

"You're quite the rare case. Donella's a hard nut to crack," CeCe said.

Donella moved in next to Dennis. "You all can stop talking about me right now."

"Actually, she's been super sweet," Alexa said. "I know she has firm boundaries about mixing work with pleasure so I definitely feel honored she's introduced me to all of you. I can't explain how excited I am to meet other hybrids."

CeCe tilted her head. "You know, when they said you didn't present as anything but a full blooded witch I had my doubts. How do you do that?"

Alexa shrugged. "Donella and my roommate, Valerie, both say I had a spell cast over me. I've never known my scent to be any different than my mother's so I don't know when that would have happened or by who."

Alicia slid past Donella and rubbed Alexa's arm. "Lexie, come on and sit over here. Do you have a drink of choice?"

Alexa headed to the easy chair as directed. "Oh I don't know. What do you have?"

"A stocked bar. You name the liquor and the mixer and Dennis will get it for you."

"Uh, wow, that's a hard decision. I like vodka or rum with just about any fruit juice, jack and coke is good - just no tequila. That is guaranteed to change the color of your carpet in about an hour."

Alicia laughed and turned to Dennis. He winked at Alexa as he walked around the back of the bar next to the kitchen. He waved a glass as a warning. "I think this rug is ugly, but I sure as hell don't plan on remodeling tomorrow. We will make sure the tequila stays out of your hands!"

A commotion at the front door caught everyone's attention. A man bellowed from the living room, "Dwight is in the house!" Dwight bustled forward carrying two twelve-packs of beer. He set one of the blue boxes on the bar next to Dennis preparing Alexa's drink and then continued into the kitchen with the other box.

Alexa turned in time to catch a silent exchange between CeCe and Crystal of raised eyebrows and rolled eyes.

Crystal saw her looking and leaned forward. "He's available if you're interested."

"Well I'm not, but especially not after I saw you two exchanged knowing looks."

Crystal winked and nodded approval.

Dennis offered Alexa her drink. "He's a nice guy with a big heart."

"I'm not interested," Alexa said.

"She's not into black guys," Dwight yelled from the kitchen.

Alexa leaned around Dennis to make eye contact with Dwight. "I have zero issue with dating black guys. I'm just not dating."

CeCe tipped toward Alexa. "It's because you're a lesbian."

"I *live* with a lesbian, but that does not make *me* a lesbian. I'm just not dating." Alexa took a big swig of her Jack & Coke.

CeCe cocked an eyebrow. "Why?"

Alexa looked around the room. All conversation had stopped and she sat center stage. After a deep sigh she said, "I came to Radcliff to unpack a whole laundry list of issues and one of them is trying to heal my broken heart." She waved a hand to stop. "And before anyone suggests that the way to do that is to start dating – yes at some point I will, but right now I'm not ready. I have such bad commitment issues at the moment I can't even contemplate adopting a dog." She paused and looked at the ceiling. "I honestly don't know what my roommates would think about getting a dog."

Crystal grinned. "Lesbians love dogs."

The room burst into laughter and the small conversations resumed. Donella pulled a kitchen chair next to Alexa. "I told you they were a rough crowd."

"Oh this is nothing. They don't have enough dirt on me to run me through the wringer the way my friends at home do."

Stephanie placed a hand on Donella's shoulder. "Donny-girl is our quiet mouse and enjoys watching the banter but does not appreciate being in the middle of it."

Alexa nodded. "That's what makes a group like this so fun. Some of us enjoy the banter, I definitely dish it out, but we also need the peacekeepers, the ones who play mom that send us to our corners when we get too rambunctious."

"That's Donella to a T!" Stephanie said. "So you have a circle like this?"

"Oh yeah. Complete with nicknames and knowing everyone's scorecard. Of course that's easy since we've all known each other since junior high."

"Scorecard?" Dennis asked.

"Partners and sexual history. Who's the ho and who was the last standing virgin," Alexa pointed at herself.

"You were the last virgin in your group?" Donella asked surprised.

"Remember I was raised human so evidently, I was dating humans. So, uh, kissing didn't really stir anything in me and I couldn't let anything move beyond that. And then I dated a vampire..." she cleared her throat. "Evidently, I'm attracted to vampires."

"Dwight," CeCe yelled, "you don't stand a chance in hell with her. You smell too much like a witch!"

"So does she!"

Alexa weighed her options – should she reveal or not? Go for it. She made eye contact with Dwight and allowed her hybrid scent to come forward as well as her yellow eyes. She flashed a quick grin before making it all disappear.

The room fell silent.

"What the hell was that?" Reggie asked as he leaned around Crystal to look at Alexa.

She shrugged. "When I kissed the vampire my scent changed. So I figured out how to bring that scent forward on demand."

Reggie furrowed his eyebrows. "You can break through a spell?"

"I guess so."

He shook his head. "That's one hell of a curse to put on somebody, but I'm even more impressed you can break through it."

Maurice appeared next to Reggie and tilted his head. "What type of vampire are you?"

Alexa knew but instead shrugged her shoulders. "The guy I dated was a hunter and his best guess was that I'm probably a cross between sentinel and ranger."

"How strong are you?" Dwight asked.

"Stronger than a hunter." She felt her face flush. "I might have held him down."

"A full blooded vampire?"

She nodded.

"You're a strong witch *and* a strong vampire?" Dwight asked. "Oh Calvin is going to want you to introduce you to his coven."

"Is that the dude who showed up at Blaze?" Stephanie asked.

Dwight nodded. "Yeah, I told you all his friend, Nick, is building a hybrid coven."

"Dennis!" CeCe shouted. "Get that bar fired up before Dwight gets his sermon in full gear." She turned to Alexa. "Drink up. You're going to need some heat in your belly for what's about to happen."

Alexa looked between CeCe and Dwight in curiosity.

Donella mumbled, "Whenever you're ready to leave."

"Oh no. I'm dying of curiosity. Is popcorn available for this show?"

Dwight roared with laughter and returned to his perch at the kitchen table, opening a second beer. Crystal moved closer to Stephanie and they chatted quietly with an occasional giggle. Donella twisted to join their conversation.

"Donella didn't warn you about me, did she?" CeCe asked.

"By name? No. She had told me there was a variety of personalities, some quieter, some loud."

"Well loud would definitely be me. I learned long ago if I got something to say, say it."

Alicia handed CeCe a glass and smiled at Alexa. "And she has a lot to say."

"Oh hush! Now tell me about being raised as a human. Who the hell does something like that?"

Alexa shook her head. "Evidently my parents. That's a small

portion of why I left town – nobody would tell me anything."

"How did you find out?"

"My teeth came in."

CeCe snorted. "That would certainly pull the veil back, now wouldn't it?

Alexa nodded. "All I heard from everyone was how surprised they were that I had any vampire traits. Yeah me too, because I didn't know vampires were real. Surprise!"

"Shit."

"But they still didn't offer up any information. They didn't answer any of my questions. I was just told to keep behaving like a human."

"That's some of that Brentwood bullshit," Dennis said as he handed drinks to Donella and Crystal.

"Did you hear about the covens rising up?" Stephanie asked.

Dennis nodded and grabbed more drinks from the bar. "Yeah, they ousted the head of their council."

"Who the hell has a council for witches anyway?" CeCe asked. "That's like herding cats. I can't believe the covens put up with that crap in the first place!"

"What do you mean?" Dwight asked. "The witches allowed that council to form and supported it. It's because of that hybrids were blocked from practicing." He turned to Alexa. "Are you from Brentwood?"

She hesitated in responding, letting a whole room of people know where she was from. Alexa shifted in her seat and finally nodded.

"See?" Dwight said with a boom and his left arm swung wide. "They masked her and raised her to be human. Complete erasure! Had her teeth never come in she would have gone her entire life oblivious. And that is a damn shame because you are a fucking strong witch!"

Alexa offered a weak grin.

Dwight moved to the bar and rested his beer. "I'm telling you this is the model. Brentwood isn't the only place with a council. They establish themselves to mediate problems between individuals or rival covens. It's so innocent, but it always turns political. And there has yet to be a council with any representation for the hybrids. They don't care about our problems and most won't allow us in their covens."

"And now you're going to tell us about all the great things your friends new coven is going to do for us," Alicia said.

"Well, yeah. I tried to bring him with me tonight, but he had other plans. I'm telling ya, you guys will like him."

Donella crossed her arms and said, "That's what you said about Eddie." The room erupted in laughter.

Dwight extended his hands in concession. "Okay, I got that one wrong. But, Nick, he really is a nice guy with a heart of gold. He's putting a lot of effort in gathering hybrids together. We were at Jefferson Park at midnight for the winter solstice with about twenty people. It was everything you would want for a solstice gathering except fire. As we walked back to the cars one of the attendees offered up their farm for Ostara. We're hoping to make it a big event. Can you imagine the energy of a large group? I really hope you guys come check it out."

"Is Eddie going to be there?" Donella asked.

"I haven't spoke to him since Maurice ran him out of the party."

"We'll have to think about it," Maurice said.

Chapter Thirty-Eight

Alexa hung up the phone and turned to Valerie. "That was Donella. Maurice proposed to her last night!"

"Wow! Well, that explains why she was out of the office today."

"She doesn't want anyone at the office to know, but knew I would share the news with you."

"Well good for her! You said he was a nice guy?"

"Very nice. He's not quite as reserved as she is, but they make a good team."

Sarah walked into the living room. "Who's a good team?"

"Donella got engaged last night," Alexa said.

"Oh my gosh, a Valentine's proposal!" Sarah said, pressing her hands to her chest. "Did he do it right? Get down on one knee?"

"I don't know that he got down on a knee. They were at Tennyson's Steakhouse, which evidently they do every year so nothing seemed out of the ordinary, and then at dessert, he pulled out the ring. She said she nearly fainted."

"Ooh!" Sarah said with a huge smile.

"I have to admit I see her in a different light since you've been hanging out with her," Valerie said.

"Honestly, she's not at all the person I thought she was," Alexa said.

"I'll say it again. I am so glad you have been able to connect with another hybrid, but I'm still floored that person is Donella."

"Me too."

"Are her friends going to throw an engagement party?" Sarah asked.

"Knowing them, probably."

Sarah tilted her head and scowled. "Is there some turmoil with the friends?"

"No. They all get along great."

Sarah stared at Alexa for a moment and scrunched her forehead more. "You're uneasy about them."

"No. I like them a lot."

Sarah shook her head. "There's something around them that worries you."

Alexa rocked back and met Sarah's stare. She glanced over to

Valerie and back to Sarah. "Uh, yeah. But I don't want to talk about it."

"Why?" Sarah asked as she crossed her arms.

Alexa stared at Sarah defiant not to discuss the matter, but Sarah held her ground. Alexa knew Sarah could coax a response. She contemplated what to say or how much to reveal. "Okay. It has to do with my premonitions. As I've told you before, everything I see has to do with death." She ran through the visions and plucked which ones to address. "So in Donella's circle, I know somebody is going to die soon. I know it's soon because of how loud and rapid that vision loops when I'm near the person. It struck me at the nightclub and again at the party. I've had nightmares that feel suspiciously like elements I witness when I'm near the person. I'm not sure about the nightmares, they're are a different animal, so I could be off base with that."

She sat thinking about the visions trying to figure out what else to say. "I have a friend who I know will be in an awful accident in the next couple of years. She's the only person I know, or well, connected to closely..." Alexa flung her hands out as she grappled with what to say.

"Someone else you know is going to die soon and you don't know how to deal with it," Valerie interpreted.

"Yes. Exactly. And the same with Donella's friends. I like them a lot, but I don't know if I can hold it together for something that's going to happen real soon." She exhaled a long breath. "I can't prevent anything, I learned that a *long* time ago. It doesn't seem smart to warn someone. All I can do is stand there and watch."

Valerie nodded. "I've heard of psychics wrestling this problem and I believe the advice was to be in the moment, to focus on the activity at hand."

"What does that mean?"

Valerie asked, "What would your reaction be if you didn't know any of this?"

"Well that's basically what I've been trying to do – just act like I don't know anything," Alexa said.

"But?" Valerie asked with raised eyebrows.

"What if the person dies right there in front of me? I can't ignore it," Alexa said.

"I think you're allowed to have a natural reaction to it. If that means doing CPR or pulling someone else away or screaming or bursting into tears, that all seems natural," Valerie said.

"Is doing CPR okay? I'm not allowed to interfere with death," Alexa said.

"Are you not allowed to interfere with death, or not allowed to prevent the incident?" Valerie asked.

The women fell silent as Alexa thought about the death she tried to prevent while on a school field trip. Alexa stopped the woman from stepping into the road as a taxi rumbled toward her only to be hit by bus moments later. As she recalled the actions of that day she realized she hadn't reacted to anything, but instead used her knowledge to prevent.

"There's something else to consider," Valerie said. "If you knowingly remove yourself from an event just to avoid witnessing one person die, what happens in your absence? What if you're meant to be there to save someone else?"

Alexa looked away. Her gaze roamed the room searching for solutions hidden on the walls. She sighed. "I don't know."

Chapter Thirty-Nine

Alexa opted to drive herself to Donella's engagement party instead of riding with Alicia and Dennis. With a gift bag looped on her wrist, she rang the doorbell at CeCe and Reggie's house.

A car door slammed nearby and she turned to see a man walking to the passenger side. Alexa watched as he opened the door and Stephanie unfolded herself from the passenger seat.

The front door swung open so Alexa turned back around to find Reggie greeting her with a big smile. "Lexie!" he said loud enough for the people inside to hear.

"Hi!" she said. "It looks like Stephanie is here too. Did she bring a date?"

"Well, well, well," Reggie said, craning his head around the doorjamb. He snapped his attention to Alexa. "Come on in. No reason to stand in the cold." He stepped aside.

"It's not that bad out here. Not like it was a couple weeks ago," Alexa said.

He sighed. "These bones are not meant for that type of cold."

Alexa laughed. "You're a football coach! Isn't your job to be outside?" She stepped inside as Reggie lingered in the doorway for Stephanie and her date to make their way to the front porch. She slid her shoes off and pushed them next to the others.

He shivered. "I love my job, but I do not like the weather. Over ninety and under forty makes me cranky."

Stephanie crossed the threshold, dropping a kiss on Reggie's cheek. "Are you rattling off your laundry list of things that make you cranky? Lexie! How ya doin', honey?" She pulled Alexa into a hug and turned to the man following her. "Mike, this is Reggie, CeCe's husband. And this is one of our new friends, Lexie."

Mike shook hands with Reggie as he entered the house and nodded to Lexie. After they removed their shoes, Stephanie bustled him further inside and around a corner. Reggie motioned for Alexa to follow as he traced Stephanie's path.

Stephanie stopped at the couch and pointed at the coats draped over the back. "The coat rack! We would use the coat closet but CeCe has it filled with her own array of outerwear. Not a hanger to be found."

Alexa laughed and thanked Reggie for assisting her with her coat. She followed Stephanie and Mike to the kitchen for greetings and introductions. Alexa added her bag to the other gifts sitting on a small side table.

CeCe pulled her into a hug. "You made it!"

"I did! This is a beautiful house."

"I'll give you a tour later. First, grab a plate, there's plenty of food on the counter and more is still in the oven." CeCe flashed a smile and moved toward Stephanie.

Alexa walked over to Donella. "Is your sister on her way?"

"She should be here any time."

Maurice stepped closer and Alexa gave him a hug.

"Congratulations!" she said. "I'm so excited for you two."

Maurice cocked his head. "Am I reading something here?"

"I get hit with visions when I'm near people and I'm getting bombarded right now. I forgot to set my filter when I stepped into the room."

"No, there's something awry with our engagement."

Crap. She scrambled to clear her mind. With a fake smile and zero enthusiasm, she said, "Oh! You're an empath. Fantastic." Alexa felt exposed and didn't know how to dance around what she knew was coming – more questions. Resigned, she decided to share a small glimpse. "Well, okay. There's nothing wrong with your engagement or the happiness you two bring each other."

"But?"

"Please do not ask me what I see. Nothing good ever comes from talking about it. "

"Why?"

"People want to prevent or manipulate their future, which is far more disastrous. What I see isn't a full picture and raises far more questions instead of gaining any insight."

"So something bad is going to happen?" he asked with a raised eyebrow.

Alexa took a deep breath and exhaled. "Uh, there's a rough patch ahead of you, but… you will find a way… to move through it together. Huh. Yeah, that's a good way to put it."

"That doesn't give any clarity."

"No. And from what I do see there are no details to answer

your questions."

"You know more than you're saying."

"Of course I do, but if I told you what I saw you won't like it and will ask me why it's happening or how you got there. To which I truly do not know the answers."

"But it's not good."

"No. My visions are never good."

"So it's really bad."

"Um, life-changing."

Donella rubbed Alexa's arm. "But we end up together?"

Alexa grinned and nodded her head. "Yes. Your destinies are tied together."

Maurice shrugged. "Eh. That was as useful as going to a carnival fortune teller."

The doorbell rang and Reggie passed his drink to Maurice so he could answer the door.

Donella moved toward the front door and shouted over her shoulder, "At least she didn't charge you for the reading."

Maurice sniffed the air. "Ah. Her sister is here!"

Alexa wanted to ask about Darcy since Donella seemed excited about her sister coming, but never talked about her much. Instead, Alicia slid next to Maurice and grinned at Alexa. "You do readings?"

"No. Absolutely not," Alexa said.

"Oh come on, you did one for Maurice."

"Because he read my emotions not matching my words and what I told him was very uninformative."

Maurice leaned toward Alicia and said, "I'm reading she's very agitated by this request and is contemplating leaving the party."

Surprised, Alicia's eyes widened. "Don't do that! Please stay. I would much rather have you here than listen to a half-baked summary of, well, whatever it is you see. I'm so sorry. Please stay."

Alexa smiled. "I'll stay. But, please, I won't ever do readings."

"No problem. We will make sure no one ever asks you."

"Thank you."

Stephanie rested her chin on Alicia's shoulder. "What's this about readings?"

Alicia spun around to face Stephanie. "Lexie is psychic but doing readings it's very upsetting for her so we are not going to ask her."

Crystal joined the group with a wine glass in her hand.

"Psychic? That's a big gift," Stephanie said. "I have an aunt who sees things but she says it's not like you see in the movies. She only gets snippets that don't piece together."

"Holy crap that's exactly what mine is like. It feels very useless."

Wagging a finger, Crystal said, "No, it's not useless, it's just not evident. When the time comes you'll know what to do with that power."

"I've had a moment and it turned out awful," Alexa said.

"Were you trying to interfere with something happening?" Crystal asked.

"Yeah."

Crystal shook her head. "Psychic powers are to guide you, forewarn you of what will be on the path, but not for you to avoid the path."

"How do you know that?" Alexa asked.

"I dated a psychic. He would tell me bits and pieces about the struggle of having that power. Like Stephanie's aunt, he didn't see everything, just bits and pieces. He said many were meaningless, they flooded the field, but when the time came he knew exactly which ones were guiding him."

"Did he know you were going to break up?" Maurice asked.

"I asked him that sometime afterward. He said he knew we weren't meant to be together forever, but that wasn't a reason for him to avoid the experience. He was really sweet about it and said he had learned a lot from me."

Donella brought Darcy to the huddle and introduced Alexa before ushering her toward the table loaded with food. Alexa noted several differences – scents, coloring, smiles. She assumed they were half-sisters. Donella hovered over Darcy in a protective, older sister manner. Darcy's laugh carried through the house and she didn't shy away from any conversation or topic, a near opposite of Donella.

"Not you too!" CeCe yelled.

Everyone in the house turned to see Darcy and Dennis across the counter from each other, frozen mid-debate, necks craned, glaring at CeCe.

"Y'all," CeCe said from the opposite end of the counter. "Our little Darcy thinks we should go to Nick's party next month."

Darcy stood up and faced the group. "Dwight is a damn idiot. He couldn't sell a rosary to the Pope. I'm telling you, Nick has worked really hard to secure a great place with a huge field and a house with indoor plumbing. He's got a committee working on the menu."

"Have you seen the place?" Stephanie asked.

"Yes. It's gorgeous with lots of room. The plan is to raise money to maintain the property so hybrids have a safe place to learn and develop our skills."

"How much is the entry fee?" Dennis asked.

"It's free. The Equinox party is completely free but donations will be accepted. There are plans for future events that will be fundraisers, but first, we have to find our base and get as many people as possible interested."

Two more couples entered the house and the doorbell rang again.

Stephanie turned to face Alexa, Crystal, and Maurice. "Yeah, that's not at all the vibe Dwight gave off."

Crystal snorted. "I really thought he was talking about a cult. I can picture Nick being tall and mysterious in long dark robes, smelling like incense."

"Yeah. Long hair and always has his hands peacefully cupped," Stephanie said as she interlocked her hands together.

Alexa looked beyond Crystal where the new arrivals circled around Donella. She nodded to Maurice. "You need to get over there and save her. She does *not* look comfortable."

Maurice tipped his head with a grateful grin as he departed.

"I told CeCe not to invite so many people," Crystal said.

"She does not understand how to do anything small," Stephanie said.

Two men arrived with Reggie following behind giving directions to get a drink and load up a plate. As they walked past one caught Alexa's eye and smiled. She returned a small grin but quickly returned her attention to Crystal and Stephanie reminiscing about previous parties.

Crystal and Stephanie migrated to the food table. Alexa followed and loaded a small plate with finger foods. She helped herself to a glass of wine with a splash of white soda.

"Whoa, big drinker!" a woman said.

Alexa laughed. "Normally I would go for the whole bottle but since I plan on driving home later I figured I should keep it light." She slid back to a wall and watched the crowd ebb and flow. She was surprised at how many deaths had fire present. Alexa had suspected since the last party that Nick's gathering in March would be the point of demise for many in Donella's group. Now with Darcy's sales pitch, Alexa was convinced that would be the fateful day. As she tried to shake off the death visions the sense of smoke lingered. She wondered what type of fire would impact so many people. Again she tried to suppress the visions and focus on the joviality of the moment. Her bladder called so she parked her wineglass near the kitchen sink and searched for the bathroom that had been pointed out when she first arrived.

Upon exiting the bathroom Alexa almost tripped over a stray pair of shoes. She recovered but as she rounded the corner into the living room she nearly collided with a tall man, the one who had smiled at her earlier.

She pointed over her shoulder. "Be careful. A shoe back there tried to kill me." She laughed at her joke and stepped away.

"I'm Doug," the man said before she turned away.

"Lexie," she said and continued to depart.

"Whoa, what's the hurry?"

"I'm done in the bathroom and would like to get back to the party."

"Aw come on. Let's chat a little."

"No thank you," Alexa said. She turned away but he grabbed her arm. Alexa spun around and faced him glowering, ready to fight. "Get your hands off me."

"Chill out. We're just having a good time."

Alexa grabbed his shirt and pushed him to the wall. "I said I don't want to talk to you. Leave me alone." She pushed him harder to the wall and released him. She stepped back but never took her eyes off him.

At first, Doug appeared bewildered but a stupid smirk

crossed his face further enraging Alexa. She stood firm, assessing, waiting. Alexa knew this idiot would charge at her in a matter of seconds, but instead, two men plowed into him from the side, knocking him to the floor.

Reggie pulled Doug upright and turned him so they were face to face. "You fool," Reggie spat. "She's tracking you and is less than two seconds away from ripping you to pieces."

"Naw man, you hear her purring like a kitten?"

"Mother fucker, that's a lioness ready to serve dinner. Get the fuck out of my house." Reggie tossed Doug to the door where Dennis stood.

"Lexie," Maurice said quietly from the side. "Come away from them."

Alexa continued to stare down Doug as he was pushed through the doorway. Reggie pulled a coat from behind Alexa and tossed it onto the front porch. Dennis slammed the door shut. Doug pounded on the door, screaming something about shoes. Reggie plucked through the shoes and Alexa felt a tug on her arm. She snapped her head to the side and Maurice released her arm, hands up showing no ill intent.

"Come back in here where you feel safe," he said in soothing tones.

She looked over her shoulder to see Dennis open the door and Reggie hike a shoe like a field pass. Alexa turned back to Maurice and heard the second shoe make a similar exit. The door slammed closed again and the locks secured.

Reggie came up next to Alexa. "Lexie, I don't know how you restrained yourself. That is some expert-level stuff, but thank you for not turning my home into a blood bath."

"You okay?" Maurice asked.

Alexa shook her head upset she had revealed her vampire side yet again. She ran her tongue along the roof of her mouth ensuring her teeth remained hidden. "It's time for me to leave."

"Well stick around for a bit to settle down and we will make sure Doug has left before we escort you to your car," Maurice said.

"You'd do that for me?"

"Yeah, of course. We like you a hell of a lot more than we've ever liked him."

Reggie and Maurice escorted Alexa back into the party where she was greeted with a wall of blank stares.

"What type of vampire are you?" CeCe asked.

Alexa shook her head. She didn't want to talk about it and dammit she couldn't stop the tears from bubbling up.

CeCe huffed. "Here I thought you were a full witch with a little dabble of vampire. But damn girl, I think you're more vampire with a touch of witch. Whoever put this masking spell on you had some potent energy to cover up." CeCe caught Alexa's expression and clasped her face. "Oh, honey, that don't mean a thing. Reggie's wrong, you know. A big splash of blood on that wall would be the perfect accent, especially if it's Doug's blood. That bastard has hit on every single woman here and you were the first one to put the fear of God in him. Did you smell how terrified he was? Woo, I could have had a Sunday dinner with that as gravy! Aw girl, a splash of that sorry-ass bastard on my wall would be a tribute, a warning – don't mess with my girls." She shook her head, "Nah we don't want that type around, but we sure as hell want you here."

Alexa mustered a smile.

"Now you gotta tell me something," CeCe said. "You've got three men on you and they're fairly recent. They didn't have a chance in hell with you did they?"

Crap, crap, crap! Alexa did not want to talk about this. "I really prefer..."

"No, no," CeCe interrupted. "You were in full attack mode in my house, ready to kill. What's the story with these guys?"

Alexa stared at CeCe. Her deep brown eyes held no malice, but she expected the truth. Alexa wanted to dart out into the night and drive as far away as possible. She inhaled deeply, searching for the sign to dash away. No sign arrived. With a slow exhale she relented. "The first two attacked me. And no they did not survive. A special cleanup crew was necessary for the second one."

CeCe raised an eyebrow and tilted her head. "So you do know how to paint a wall with blood. Good girl. And the third?"

Alexa brought her gaze even with CeCe's. She lifted her chin and with a small twitch in the corner of her mouth, she said, "I rode him the way a man likes to be ridden." An evil smile spread across her face as CeCe's eyes widened.

CeCe leaned her head back and roared with laughter. She bent forward, her whole body shaking with amusement.

Chapter Forty

Alexa walked into the condo hoping Valerie and Sarah had already retired for the night, leaving the lights on for her. Instead, they sat curled into a knot at one end of the sofa watching TV.

"You're home early," Valerie said.

"What's wrong?" Sarah asked.

Alexa secured the door and removed her coat. She opened her mouth a few times to speak and finally just said it. "I almost killed a man tonight."

"What?" Sarah and Valerie asked at the same time.

"I restrained myself, but I was pretty damn close to ripping him apart. Right there, in CeCe and Reggie's house on their beautiful white carpet."

"What did he do?" Valerie asked.

"He was hitting on me and just wouldn't take no for an answer, but the guys intervened and threw him out of the house. I mean like literally tossed him out the front door." Alexa sighed. "I just don't like exposing my vampire side even if it's to prove I'm a hybrid. But this guy had me almost to the point of revealing my fangs... I mean my teeth. Did you know we're not supposed to call them fangs? But anyways, it was just a rough night."

"Why don't you like revealing your vampire side?" Sarah asked.

"Well, mostly because my vampire scent reveals too much of my identity – it matches my father's scent. I don't think anyone at the party is connected to him, although it's possible. But more likely someone will note the uniqueness of it and somehow word gets around there's a hybrid with this scent in town. My cover's blown and I either have to find another town or go home."

Sarah stared at her for a moment and scowled. "But you're upset about something else too."

"Yeah." Alexa kicked off her shoes and walked to one of the matching chairs on either side of the window and sat down, curled up hugging her knees. "Something really bad is going to happen at this Ostara Equinox event. So many people at the party tonight have such similar deaths. If it's not from fire, it's vampire bites in the vicinity of a fire. So much fear and panic and a lot of darkness."

"You don't want to go," Valerie said.

"No, not at all," Alexa said. "I know better than to warn anyone else to not attend, but shit, it's going to be bad."

"I need to ask you something and please know I absolutely will not do anything with this information except to act on it accordingly when the time is right," Valerie said. "Is Donella one of the people who die that night?"

Alexa stared at Valerie for a long time before nodding.

"When you see these deaths, are other people dying? Is there a crowd?" Valerie asked.

Scowling as she plucked through her memories of the different deaths she saw at the party, Alexa said, "It's hard. I spend so much time trying not to see or hear those visions..." She thought about Donella's death since she had seen it so many times. "Oh, Maurice," she said popping her head up, running his death through her mind. When he asked about his future with Donella, Alexa saw a man approach him and he felt a hard punch to the side of his head. In the background, however, were people running. She wrinkled her nose in memory of the scents Maurice would smell. Death. Alexa shook her head and refocused on the living room. "Yeah. There's a lot of death. It... it... I think it just becomes mayhem. Yeah, I'd say a lot of people die."

"Are vampires involved?" Valerie asked.

Alexa nodded. "Yeah, strong ones." Her sense of foreboding increased.

Valerie tilted her head as she processed the information. "What did you say about a cleanup crew?"

"What do you mean?"

"You said something about vampires using a crematorium when they have bodies to get rid of – are they disposing of all evidence?"

"Wow. That sounded like a TV lawyer," Alexa said.

Sarah giggled as she nodded in agreement.

"Um, yeah," Alexa said. "From what I've seen they erase all traces."

"Do you think the fires in your vision are part of their body disposal, or are people dying in proximity of existing fires?" Valerie asked.

With a slow shrug, Alexa shook her head. "Cremation is a

cleanup, like after the fight. These people are dying in fires. Knowing my own urges to fight I can't see how pushing someone into a fire is in any way satisfying. The urge is to fight to the death. That's what I wanted to do tonight. I was *pissed* that Reggie and Dennis interfered. I wanted to finish that fight right there, to the end. I was going to kill him. Nah, fire and guns, that's not good enough. I wanted to rip him to pieces with my teeth."

"Some time ago you asked why vampires don't fight with guns," Valerie said, tilting her head. "I think you found the answer."

"Huh. Yeah, I guess so."

Rubbing her head, Valerie looked at the floor. "Fire, people running, being killed… That's going to attract a lot of attention. Just a large gathering in general turns heads, but when you add in fire trucks and the general commotion of the night? People are going to ask questions." She exhaled long and loud. "We need to have a plan to get you out of town."

"Isn't that fucking with fate or whatever?" Alexa asked.

"Well ideally you wouldn't attend in the first place," Valerie said.

Alexa blinked at her. "You said I needed to be there."

"No. I said you need to do whatever would be your inclination if you didn't have the visions. Without knowing about the fire and all of the deaths, would you go to this observation for Ostara?"

"Yeah, in a heartbeat. It sounds like something I'd be really into."

"Okay," Valerie said. "So you have to be there, but for your safety when it's all over, you need to leave town. So let's make a plan."

"What? Why?"

Valerie leveled a look. "You're going to survive this event. This isn't how you die, correct? So in your best interests, you cannot face the inquest that will follow. Because there will be fallout. Survivors are going to be interviewed. Friends and family will be asked about all of the details leading into the event. You can't be here for any of that. It jeopardizes your identity and from what I know about vampires, they like easy scapegoats, and who better than a witch that survived a fire-infused event? I don't know who your family is, Lexie, but if they're as well connected as you fear they are, this could result in a vampire war. Let's be proactive and have a plan for when you leave the party."

"What if..."

"There are a lot of what-ifs. But let's start by having a plan to get you out of town the next day," Valerie said. "If we have to deviate from the plan, that's fine, but it gives us something to focus on in the meantime. I'll probably think of a few B, C, and D plans along the way because there are a lot of ways this event could spin out of control."

"You'll be leaving us?" Sarah asked.

"She did say that by summer she thought she would be moving on," Valerie said. "This is earlier than any of us anticipated."

"We can't involve Abbey," Alexa said. "Donella has connected with her and they're helping other hybrids escape bad situations."

Bobbing her head, Valerie acknowledged the problem. "Okay, then we contact her after we have you out of town." She sat quiet for a moment. "Why don't you get some sleep and give me time to think about this? You've had a rough night."

"Yeah, that probably means you should prepare for a growling vampire tonight," Alexa said.

"We're used to your nightmares," Valerie said. "We'll be fine. Try to rest."

Alexa descended the stairs in search of coffee. Her night of violent dreams left her groggier than usual. She walked into the kitchen passing Valerie and Sarah at the table. She returned with a toasted bagel and a full cup of hot coffee. Alexa took her normal seat across from Sarah who pushed the container of cream cheese in her direction.

"Sarah and I were talking about taking a trip in a couple of weeks," Valerie said.

In the middle of spreading the cream cheese on her bagel, Alexa snapped her head to look at Valerie. "What?"

"As your escape out of town. I know you haven't earned any vacation time, but I'm sure if you talk to Donella something can be arranged. I mean you have saved the firm a lot of money cleaning up Greg's mess."

"Uh, okay. Where are you thinking of going?"

Valerie's face lit up. "New Orleans. It's something we've wanted to do for a long time."

"Oh." Alexa dragged the knife across the cream cheese, loading a glob, then looked at Valerie. "Why?"

"I know you're not going to be up for a vacation but maybe it will give you the space to transition to your next stop. I figure we would call Abbey once we got there," Valerie said.

Alexa looked at the glob of cream cheese she just deposited onto the bagel then back up at Valerie. "But it's not Mardi Gras. What else is there to do there?"

Sarah leaned forward. "It's a great place for witches. They have apothecaries tucked in little corners all over the city and you could find other psychics or pyromancers. But you would also love the old buildings. I hear the French Quarter is just steeped in gorgeous architecture."

"Yeah, it sounds interesting." Alexa wished she could be a little more enthusiastic. The idea of visiting someplace new like New Orleans would typically have her mind spinning will all sorts of possibilities. "Isn't that in the middle of the week? Like a Tuesday?"

Sarah pushed away from the table. "Let me grab a calendar," she said as she went into the kitchen. She returned waving the calendar in the air, the pages fanning back and forth. "It's a Wednesday!"

"We're talking about gathering on a Tuesday night," Alexa said.

"That must mean the equinox is happening early in the morning," Valerie said. "We'll have to find out the exact time, but you're going to be really tired."

Alexa shrugged. "We're talking about flying, right?"

"Driving would take all day – at least twelve hours. Flying makes much more sense," Valerie said. "I'll see if we can schedule a flight in the afternoon and that will give you a chance to catch up on your sleep."

"No," Alexa said. "Earlier would be better. It's much easier for me to just stay awake than try to nap. I'll catch up on my rest once we get there and you two can go have a lovely dinner without me."

Valerie cast a stern look at Alexa.

"The first night in a new town should be something special and you two could use some couple time," Alexa said. "I'm going to need several hours of continuous sleep that will definitely involve a lot of growling and gnashing teeth which neither one of you want to be around. When I wake up I know how to find a vending machine."

"Or order room service," Valerie said. "Okay, well that seems settled. I'll reach out to a travel agent on Monday and see what we can arrange. I guess the next question is how long do we want to stay there?"

The three women looked back and forth at each other. "Well," Sarah said. "If we get there on Wednesday that's sort of a lost day. That gives us at least Thursday, Friday, and Saturday. If we come home on Sunday then we'll be back to work on Monday."

"I would plan to have Monday off as well," Valerie said. "Someone once told me to always schedule an extra day of vacation for when we get home. That gives you time to transition."

"Well, I wouldn't be able to do that," Alexa said. "I think asking for three days off is sufficient." She realized that she wouldn't be returning with Valerie and Sarah. The details of her time away from work were pointless.

Alexa looked up to see Valerie watching her process the arrangements. Valerie offered a small grin of acknowledgment. "You're probably right," she said.

Sarah's expression teetered between excitement and dismay. She huffed a heavy sigh. "I don't want you to leave. I think I'll cry the entire time we're in New Orleans."

"Sarah! We cannot focus on Lexie leaving. We have to convince ourselves this is just a normal vacation and be happy about it." Valerie turned to Alexa. "That means you too. You have to be excited about the Ostara gathering as well as going to New Orleans."

"Isn't it weird we would be leaving the very next morning after a big event?" Alexa asked.

"True. We need to have a reason why we're going in the middle of the week," Valerie said, resting her on her fingertips. "I have an Aunt Angelique, she's my father's oldest sister. Now, in reality, she lives in Tampa but she's been to New Orleans several times. I remember her saying there was a cute little community on the other side of the big lake down there. So let's just say she lives in that community and we're going to go visit her."

"You'll have to know the name of the community and probably double-check that it's still cute or charming or whatever it is that enchants elderly aunts," Alexa said.

Valerie chuckled. "There's something adorable about your morning grumpiness."

Sarah giggled and nodded in agreement.

"You can't tell a grumpy person they're adorable," Alexa said.

Valerie pointed to the coffee cup. "Your coffee has kicked in and you're forming complete sentences and using logic."

Alexa stared at her.

"Keep drinking, and yes, I will find out the name and do a little digging to see what's so charming," Valerie said with a smile.

"And what are our jobs?" Alexa asked.

"Make arrangements at work for time off," Valerie said. "And be excited about it. None of us have been there so this is supposed to be a real treat."

Leaning back in her chair, Alexa looked at Sarah. "I don't want to go."

Sarah launched out of her chair and ran around the table to Alexa, pulling her into a tight hug. Alexa bent into Sarah's embrace with tears streaming down her face.

Chapter Forty-One

On Monday morning as soon as Alexa arrived in the office and dropped her lunch off in the break room she headed to Donella's office.

"Do you have a minute?" Alexa asked from the doorway.

Per usual, Donella appeared to have been at her desk for several hours with a tall pile of file folders at one end of her desk and a box of more files sitting in one of the chairs.

"Yes, come on in."

Alexa closed the door and took a seat next to the box of files. "I want to apologize for causing a scene at your party."

Donella shook her head. "Please do not apologize. Doug has never been welcome at our parties. He comes as a tag along with Dwight and Leo. I'm more upset that you needed to leave."

"To be honest I was already a little drained with all of the people there."

"We really were not fair to you by asking you to do readings."

"No. Maurice was an absolute gem about it and Crystal and Stephanie became my guard dogs and made sure to be a buffer for me."

Alexa shrugged and smiled. "I adore them. No, my problem is being in a medium-sized group like that, especially as strangers cluster in. I have no way to filter the visions into white noise. When we were at Blaze there were so many people that everyone's just become a blob."

"Are you saying you have visions every time you're near someone?"

"Oh yeah, on top of the ones I have about myself. It's just a constant loop."

"I have so many questions"

Alexa smiled. "I do too. They're very not informative but according to Crystal and Stephanie and Valerie I'm not allowed to interfere, but if there is an action I'm supposed to take it will make itself evident when the time is right."

"That doesn't subdue my curiosity one bit!" Donella said with a laugh.

Alexa shifted her posture. "I had a second reason to talk to you this morning. Valerie would like to take Sarah and me on a trip to New Orleans, but I haven't been here long enough for vacation time. I was hoping to schedule a few days off even if it was unpaid leave."

"You don't want to be paid?" Donella asked with raised eyebrows.

"It's only three days. It's not going to break the bank."

"Honestly, three days is the max you can take off without a doctor's note. Talk to Jeff about it, but from my standpoint, it's an allowable amount of time especially since you've not taken off any time since you started."

"Okay. Thanks."

"When are you thinking of going?"

"Well. They wanted to be in New Orleans for Ostara, but I said I wanted to go to the hybrid gathering. Valerie feels like if we got to town within twenty-four hours it would still count."

"That's true. There's a forty-eight-hour window around any of these phases. Do you think you'll be up for travel? I've already scheduled myself off work for the next day. With the equinox at two A. M. and likely another hour before the first people disperse, I can't imagine getting home until four or five in the morning. If you're drained by a small gathering of friends then the toll of a big gathering like this could really do a number on you." Donella paused and cocked her head. "I assume you're flying. That's a lot of close proximity with strangers in an airplane who will drain your energy on top of what you'll experience from the gathering."

"Oh crap. I didn't even think about that."

"I'm not saying don't go, but this doesn't sound like a very relaxing vacation."

"No, you're right. I already factored in that I would be exhausted from the night before and would likely sleep most of the day." Alexa sighed. "I didn't even think about the flight. Yeah, they're going to be transporting a zombie to the hotel room. Hopefully, I snap out of it by the next morning. I really want to visit the apothecaries."

"You won't participate in their Ostara observation?" Donella asked.

"I'd like to, but I'll already have done one. This will give them time to go off and do something private."

"Hmm. Well, that may be the beginning of a very auspicious year for them."

"I hope so."

"I hope for your sake you're able to rebound quickly." Donella grinned. "New Orleans is a great experience. When we went it was September - Bourbon Street was mayhem and chaos. I went early in the evening just to say I'd been and that was enough. I can't imagine what Mardi Gras is like."

Alexa leaned forward. "You've been to New Orleans?"

"I have and it's incredible. Lots of history and beautiful buildings, but the nightlife isn't my thing – we just went to nice sit-down restaurants and avoided the whole melee out on the streets. You should, however, seek out a hybrid while you're there. Valerie will be interested in the witch aspects and there's plenty, but it's amazing what the vampires have there too."

"Oh really?"

"One of the best things about that city is that it is not under any vampire jurisdiction. That's not to say there aren't vampire gangs, so you do have to be careful. But there are blood bars and places that offer organ meats that are delicacies. Maurice and I couldn't afford it, but it sounded interesting. Someone told us about meditation salons where you can do an immersive session in a coffin."

"Why would you do that?"

"To be put into a trance and get a full night's sleep - that would be amazing."

Alexa raised one corner of her mouth. "Oh that's right, vampires don't sleep. I guess that trickles down to hybrids too?"

"Do you sleep all night?"

"I do."

"That's interesting." Donella paused as she processed a thought. "I wonder..." She tilted her head and looked at the ceiling then back at Alexa. "I imagine you're a perfect hybrid where witch blood feeds the vampire and vampire energy feeds the witch. You're self-sustaining. That would explain your need for so much sleep. The vampire is so drained that sleep is the only way to restore equilibrium." She rested her chin on a fist. "That is so interesting."

"Perfect hybrid? Is that a thing?"

Donella nodded. "It is. Not that it's common, but there are plenty out there, or at least rumored to be. It's one of those urban myth types of things – somebody knows a guy whose friend dated one. So maybe there are only three on the planet but by association, it sounds like there are more?"

"So it's not like there's a club to join or anything like that?"

"Not that I'm aware of, but then again, I wouldn't qualify."

"Something in my head is screaming that it's not really something I should be bragging about either," Alexa said.

"Well you know me, I think everyone should keep their lives private, but yes I could see how it could put yet another target on your back. Your witch strength is already noticeable; you'd make a great conduit. It's bad enough someone could funnel your witchcraft to boost their own, but if they knew you have a fairly endless source of vampire energy, that could be deadly. So no, I wouldn't suggest making it known."

Chapter Forty-Two

Staring at the computer screen, Alexa read the sentence a third time without focus. The phone rang and she jumped. Without looking at the caller ID she picked up the receiver.

"I have questions that should not be discussed over the telephone," a man's voice said. After a second of discerning the soft lilt of an accent she had heard before, Alexa realized Diederich Coberg was on the line.

"Okay," she said.

"There is a bridge across from your office."

"Yes. I've been there."

"How soon can we meet?"

Alexa decided getting lunch might improve her focus. With a quick glance at the clock – 2:15, no wonder she was distracted. "Ten minutes," she said.

"Good," he said and then hung up.

Alexa secured her computer and grabbed her purse. She stopped at the reception desk where Rena sat. "It's a bit late for Heather to be at lunch."

"That's my fault," Rena said. "I was stuck at the courthouse."

"Want me to pick up anything from Donna's?"

"Nah, I ate in the car on my way here," Rena said.

"Okay. Well, I'll be back soon."

Grateful for not being on rotation for Heather's lunch coverage, Alexa pushed through the massive doors expecting to be blinded by the sun. Clouds had rolled in casting a dull light. She pulled her coat tighter and walked across the street, each step crunching like walking on gravel – salt had been dropped by road crews in preparation for more snow.

She cast a wary eye at the roofline of the air conditioner company. Two vampires walked around in workman jumpsuits – a ridiculous ploy, she thought. How many repairs would a reputable AC company need for their own equipment? And yet, these faux repairmen routinely removed access panels, sometimes carrying a piece of machinery to or from the big metal box on the roof. Other times a van or work truck from different utilities would park next to the building with workmen in different uniforms climbing onto the roof or nearby telephone poles. No one in her office ever said anything about the activities as if they didn't notice, but Alexa noticed. If she hadn't known about vampires she would have thought the company was a cover for something illegal.

Knowing her scent caught their attention Alexa brought her gaze back to the path in front of her. She scanned the bridge for more scents but only caught Diederich's. She stiffened and a jolt of fear let loose. What the hell was she doing? Meeting a vampire in a secluded place!

While getting her fear under control she noticed Diederich had moved further away. He must have sensed her fear and gave her space as a gesture of trust. She glanced up at the workmen and scuttled toward the tree-lined path. As she neared the bridge Alexa didn't see or sense Diederich and again wondered if she was doing the right thing. She continued across the bridge and came out to the sidewalk. He stood in front of Donna's Diner across the street.

"I am being watched," he said with a silent vampiric whisper. "Are you able to whisper?"

"Yes," she whispered back. Alexa stood at the curb watching traffic whiz past and decided to turn toward the intersection to use the crossing lights.

"Are you aware of a hybrid gathering on the nineteenth?" he asked.

She stopped walking and turned to face Diederich, who had moved to a bench in front of the diner. "Yes," she said, wondering how he found out.

"Do you plan to attend?"

Her heart sank. She stared at him as foreboding filled her every cell. Nothing good could come of vampires knowing about the gathering. "Yes."

"What are the planned festivities?"

"I'm not sure." Alexa looked down the street - a steady stream of cars approached. "I was told to bring items to celebrate Ostara, the spring equinox. This is to be a coven gathering and it sounds like a lot of people are attending."

"Have you met the organizers? Do you know their mission?"

She shook her head. "No, just mutual acquaintances. There's a lot of talk about wanting equal footing or at least representation among the witches' covens."

"What happens at coven gatherings?"

Alexa's laughter caught the attention of a woman waiting at the crosswalk. Alexa dipped her head, pressing her fingers to her forehead as she cleared her throat. She resumed her silent conversation with the vampire across the street. "I've only attended one. It was this past Halloween and I don't think it was normal - a spirit spoke to us. But from what I've been told, it's mostly drinking and hanging out with friends with a little witchcraft thrown in for good measure."

"That sounds as if it were a party, not a legislative forum."

"And yet that is how and where decisions are made, where they discuss how to deal with vampires and humans and of course, hybrids."

Three people stepped into the crosswalk and Alexa jolted her attention in their direction. Traffic had stopped so she took the opportunity to cross the street. Stopping near the entrance to Donna's Diner Alexa held Diederich's gaze. She placed her hand to her nose as if she were about to sneeze, only to cover her mouth as she whispered. "I'm disturbed that vampires know about the event. I've had a bad feeling about the gathering and this makes me even less enthused."

Diederich raised his hand to swipe his nose, also covering his mouth as he spoke. "Why would you attend?"

"Because if I didn't see the future and if I didn't get these vibes, and if I never spoke to a vampire telling me he knows about the event, I would be super excited about going to this thing. It's an opportunity to meet other hybrids and learn more about all this stuff that was hidden from me. I want to be around people like myself." She sniffled back the tears. "But I do know the future and now all I can hope is to find a way to protect my friends without violating the rules of prophecy."

He nodded and pressed a fist to his mouth as if he was contemplating a problem. "I fear this could be a ploy to overthrow my father's leadership."

With a turn and a glance down the opposite end of the street, Alexa pretended to search for someone as if she was supposed to meet up with them. "I've not heard any discussion about vampires among my friends. The only frustration has been with witches. This is supposed to be a happy gathering – making new friends and celebrating the promise of spring."

"And yet your visions say otherwise."

Alexa swung around to face him, grabbing the door to the diner. As she pulled the door open she caught the scent of another vampire. Across the street, a vampire emerged from the pathway to the bridge. Alexa looked between Diederich and the man. She returned her attention to Diederich, his death scene played out – he lay on the floor numb, knowing he was dying. A woman ran toward him, tears streaming down her face as she screamed out in agony. He saw her as the young woman who captured his heart despite the age of her face and hair. She dropped to her knees beside him, throwing her body onto his, but he never felt the weight. The last sound he heard was the woman crying out his name.

With a wry grin, Alexa looked again at the man across the street and then back to Diederich. She turned into the diner and whispered, "Yes, my visions say otherwise."

Chapter Forty-Three

Alexa watched the suitcase as if a beast lived inside waiting to consume her. She tried to tamp her emotions, but that damn suitcase symbolized an end – more ends than she wanted to face.

She felt safe here, and the future felt decidedly unsafe. Alexa knew the moment she carried this suitcase out of the condo her residence here came to an end. She liked life here, claiming this small afterthought of a bedroom as her tiny domain. She liked her friends and she liked her job. She did not like what her visions foretold and she very dearly wanted to stop time to prevent it all from happening.

The suitcase loomed, waiting for Alexa to decide what pieces of clothing to pack for only five days without giving the impression she was leaving forever. Her room was to appear as though she intended to return – no empty closet or bare nightstand or stripped bed. The suitcase would be leaving with her and she felt like a thief even though Valerie wouldn't bat an eye at replacing the missing piece from Sarah's collection.

Alexa didn't want to face Sarah's tears. Alexa didn't want to face her own tears. This trip was going to suck in so many ways and she hated that it was going to happen in such a cool place. While Alexa's parents had traveled some when she was an infant, arriving in Radcliff was the first time she knowingly traveled away from Brentwood. The only vacations she remembered were family weekends in a local hotel and visiting nearby sites.

And here she was preparing to visit New Orleans of all places! Even Donella was excited for her to comb through an old city filled with magic and vampire lore and ghost tours and all of the vibrant energy of a town that never sleeps. And yet, Alexa knew she would not be able to muster the enthusiasm necessary to enjoy such a unique community. She worried about her ability to function as she carried the emotional toll of the Ostara gathering.

She brought her focus back to filling the damn suitcase. She didn't know what to expect for the weather on the Gulf Coast in late March. Alexa hoped jeans and t-shirts were sufficient. Maybe a sweatshirt? Oh, and she needed something nice in case they went to a swanky restaurant. Surely Valerie would want to sample the local cuisine?

Ah, switching her focus onto Valerie and Sarah's excitement for a new destination alleviated some of her panic. How cool it would be to watch Sarah take in new streets filled with shops? Ooh, Alexa could make a game out of counting how many different shopping bags Sarah accumulated! Valerie spoke of looking for apothecaries, but surely New Orleans had spice shops and culinary stores. What challenge could Alexa look for in Valerie's experience?

Yes, redirecting her thoughts onto her friends' excitement helped distract her from the weight of the hours looming ahead. Maybe she could focus on her own desire to see what the town had in store. She had only heard about Mardi Gras with topless women, beads, and excessive drinking. What Valerie shared about the abundance of witchcraft and associated supplies, and then adding in Donella's information about vampire experiences all sounded very intriguing.

Alexa took a deep breath as she visualized cobblestone streets, wrought iron balconies, and ancient cemeteries. She wondered what sea air smelled like and if that scent carried into New Orleans. Vacation. She was going on a real vacation to a place she knew very little about and unsure what she would see or do – an idea that felt both exciting and scary. Alexa reminded herself of that same feeling six months earlier when she left home. The terror of the unknown did not outweigh the certainty of moving forward.

With another deep breath, Alexa made peace with her resolve to keep moving forward. Packing that suitcase was a necessary part of moving forward and she began pulling the essential pieces needed for her much anticipated, yet dreaded vacation.

Chapter Forty-Four

The drive out of town seemed to take forever. Alexa hoped each car she came upon would lead the way but then they turned left when she knew she needed to eventually turn right. The directions said three miles past the Eldon Dairy, but Alexa worried she already passed the dairy, driving through random farmland far beyond her destination.

A giant black and white cutout of a cow illuminated by three lights loomed in the distance. Surely that was the dairy. Alexa slowed the car to make sure she caught the name and then dropped her attention to the odometer to precisely measure three miles. She panicked when the third mile ticked, but then she spotted a tiny street sign for County Road 3950.

Alexa made the turn, relieved to still be on asphalt. She wished she had made this journey in daylight a few days earlier just to have her bearings. Fence posts, mailboxes, and trees appeared suddenly and without any reasonable pattern. A set of headlights approached in her rearview mirror and seemed to move quickly. The blinding lights rode behind her for only a short while before rumbling past. Alexa hoped she could follow, but the car blazed ahead too fast and made a sharp left turn. Another car appeared in her mirror in the distance but never advanced like the speeder.

The fields seemed less tended the further down the road she went and the trees increased in number to the point she felt she had entered a forest. When she turned on Hagel Road the trees knitted into a canopy making a dark night even darker. Alexa felt a small surge of relief when headlights reflected off trees behind her – at least she wasn't alone on this road.

With another turn after a line of mismatched mailboxes on a long board, Alexa knew her destination should soon appear. True to the directions, the dirt driveway bumped and twisted. She worried about the branches scraping the sides of Valerie's car.

When at last she drove through an open gate into a clearing filled with other cars, Alexa relaxed. She had worried about arriving at some random farmer's house late at night and being greeted with a shotgun.

Alexa secured the car and walked toward the illuminated

house in the distance. She found the large number of vehicles present surprising despite knowing the goal of attracting as many hybrids as possible. Evidently, the word got out. Two more cars arrived as she walked through the makeshift parking lot.

As she walked, Alexa picked up faint scents of vampires. At first, she disregarded them as hybrids, but she started to notice they didn't match the trail of scents leading to the house. She also noted many of the vampire scents to be rangers. She groaned at the thought of Diederich's men monitoring the party and wondered if the hybrids could detect the vampires in the distance.

Before Alexa reached the door, a tall blonde in a long shawl emerged. "Welcome!" she said with her arms extended.

Alexa grinned at the woman but the woman's expression changed.

"This event is for hybrids only."

"Trust me, I'm very much a hybrid. My teeth came in at the end of summer last year," Alexa said.

With a long, skeptical look up and down Alexa's form, the woman lifted her chin. "Ah. Yes, I was told about you. Well, I hope you brought your moon water and crystals."

"I did! And a fresh egg." Alexa said raising one of Sarah's tote bags.

"Hmm. There's not a lot of space inside, so grab a drink and go through the backdoor to join the bonfires."

Alexa bypassed the temporary bar in the living room, lured by the delicious aromas of something bread-based baking nearby. She noted three people in the hallway waiting for the bathroom, or so she assumed. In the kitchen, two women tended the oven, the source of the warm bread making Alexa's mouth water. She smiled at the women as she made her exit back into the chilly night air.

The door hadn't even closed behind her when the foreboding chill of death surrounded Alexa. So many people would die in this yard. Alexa shivered as she pushed her mind to the present, observing the physical realm.

The backyard sloped into a valley retaining most of the noise of the crowd - the parking lot did not reveal nearly this many people. Alexa wondered how she would find Donella and her friends.

Small campfires dotted the yard and down the hill. In the middle lay a wooden stage with no one on it. Alexa glared at the structure as the hair stood on her neck. She fought the urge to turn around and leave. No, she needed to find Donella.

Five people came through the backdoor and Alexa stepped to the side. They toddled their way down the hill with disposable cups in hand.

"Did you come alone?"

Alexa turned to find an older woman with a welcoming smile looking at her.

"Um, no. I think my friends are already here. I just don't know where to begin."

"You don't like crowds," the woman said without question.

"No, not really."

"Come, I'll walk with you." The woman stepped off the porch and Alexa sensed the expectation to follow. "I'm Fawn," the woman said.

"Hi! I'm Lexie," she said catching up with Fawn.

"Have you met Nick?"

"No, but I've heard about him."

"I'll make sure to introduce you if we find him. He's flitting around here trying to meet everyone while also making sure everything is in place." Fawn's gown fluttered behind her even with a heavy coat restraining most of the outfit. Bracelets jingled as she waved her hands while speaking. Alexa thought of a hippy, but not one of the teenagers from the sixties like her mom, someone much older, more of her grandmother's age. Alexa wanted to giggle thinking of her grandma meeting this jingle-jangle, free spirit. Eh, Grandma would hate her for being a hybrid long before scorning her attire.

Alexa stopped in her tracks causing Fawn to turn around. Alexa twisted as she took in the crowd. "I've never been around so many hybrids at one time," she said in awe.

"It's amazing, isn't it? Can you feel the energy?"

Yes. Buoyancy and joy floated through the air. Unfortunately, the general happiness didn't lift her. The death scenes flowed in despite her earlier effort. She turned to Fawn with a big, forced grin.

"There's definitely a lot of positive energy here. It's hard not to feel it."

"You need to *absorb* it. Let it creep into your bones. Even a dark witch needs a little joy to balance her chakras."

Alexa laughed and shook her head. "I don't know how to balance my chakras."

Fawn turned to fully face Alexa and looked her up and down. "Who has been training you, child?"

Before Alexa could explain her complete lack of witch upbringing she felt an electric jolt in her neck with a flash of the woman's death. Alexa didn't know where the warning came from but she understood not to speak about her inexperience. Alexa shivered and plastered a broad smile. "I was raised in a very traditional home."

Fawn sighed. "Traditional witches have so much to learn from new age methods. You should come to my studio sometime. It's two blocks from St. Sebastian – Fawn's Yoga."

"Okay. I'll make sure to look you up."

"Sasha!" Fawn yelled as she waved into the crowd. A slightly younger woman turned around and waved back. She hitched up her flowing skirts, revealing brown hiking boots, and made her way toward Fawn and Alexa. "Sasha, look at this darling girl!"

"A full-blooded witch?" Sasha asked.

"Well, actually my dad was a hybrid."

Sasha's scowl faded into a broad smile. Her nose flared as she assessed Alexa's scent. "Well, I can't tell you're a hybrid, but that's probably from those vampires on you."

"Yeah, they kinda muddy my rosy presence."

"Oh no," Sasha said shaking her head. "Your rose perfume is a breath of fresh air. I also catch clover and raspberry."

Alexa smiled. "You have a bloodhound nose." She tried not to flare her nostrils as she assessed Sasha's scents – apple and fern for her witch side, but ranger for her vampire side. Alexa still didn't understand how to determine witches' strengths but she knew ranger made this woman stronger than most hybrids – not stronger than Alexa, but enough to cause concern if one challenged the other.

Sasha continued to read Alexa as her eyes roamed up and

down. "We were told a hybrid presenting as a full-blooded witch would join us tonight. I hope you enjoy your time here. Something says you're going to have an incredible experience during our celebration."

Alexa tipped her head and smiled in return, not believing a single word the woman said.

Sasha and Fawn exchanged a quick nod and possibly something nonverbal and then Sasha walked toward another group.

"Well that was very welcoming," Alexa said with fake exuberance. "I hope my friends are meeting new people too."

"I'm sure they are."

"Dwight!" Alexa yelled to the blur dashing through the crowd.

Dwight turned three times before he spotted Alexa. He ran up to her and Fawn. "Hey, Lexie! We were wondering if you got lost. Hi, Fawn."

"Oh! Lexie is part of *your* 9group?"

"Yeah," Dwight said out of breath, and turned to Alexa. "Hey, can you wait here for a sec?" He ran back into the crowd.

Alexa and Fawn watched as Dwight disappeared. To break the silence Alexa chuckled. "He sure does have a lot of energy."

"That he does."

Dwight burst out of the crowd, running. "Alright! Fawn, thanks for taking care of our girl. C'mon, Lexie, let's get you to the group." He stopped and looked at her. "Didn't you get a drink?"

"Nah, I'm fine. Let's go."

He shrugged and led the way into the crowd. Dwight walked fast and while Alexa found his pace a bit excessive around so many people, she also appreciated that her focus stayed on her feet and keeping up with Dwight, instead of trying to block death visions.

"I found her!" Dwight announced.

Alexa arrived out of breath.

"Dwight Masterson, did you make her run the entire way?" Stephanie asked as she cast a chastising look at him.

"I'm fine," Alexa said. The friends gathered around and pulled her closer to the fire.

"Here, warm up," Crystal said.

"Did you get a drink?" Dennis asked.

"Did you have a problem finding the farm?" Donella asked.

Then they held a dizzying round of introductions to other friends. She lost count but it seemed everyone loaded their cars with coworkers and family members to attend this event.

One by one, Alexa nodded to new people and answered questions until small conversations broke off in different directions. She spotted where others had laid their bags with supplies so she slipped away and gently dropped her bag in the mix.

Dwight rushed over to Alexa, handing her a plastic cup. "We're going to hold communion so don't drink it all unless you have extra in your bag or something."

"Communion? Like church communion?"

"Of course. Where do you think they got it?" Dwight didn't wait for Alexa's response before he darted back up the hill.

"You look overwhelmed," Crystal said.

"Is he on something?" Alexa asked looking up the hill where Dwight disappeared.

"Dwight? No, he's just hyperactive. There's something about being in a crowd that energizes him. I don't get it," she said shaking her head. "I always feel drained by crowds."

"Do you feel drained now?" Alexa asked.

"I did when I arrived, but hanging out here on the periphery near a fire has helped a lot."

Alexa cocked her head. "Does fire help?"

"For some people it does. It just depends on how you receive energy. I bet with your smoky aura, fire is a dominant element for you."

"I don't know, I've never really paid attention." Alexa stepped closer to the fire, glad for the warmth. She looked around the hillside where people gathered around multiple fires – she tried to count the fires but several sat out of sight. The forethought to construct so many fires on a cold, winter night with such a large crowd was brilliant. Looking down at her group's fire Alexa didn't feel any surge of energy, just coziness and the delicious smell of burning wood.

A gong sounded in the distance, and then again, and yet again. The gong became louder each time. Dwight ran up the hill carrying the gong on a rope, striking it every few steps. The crowd had fallen silent long before Dwight reached the platform, everyone focused on the dark figure standing above where Dwight stopped. Alexa assumed the figure to be Nick.

Someone further down the hill shouted "microphone". Others joined in until a chant filled the air. Nick bent down to Dwight and after a small exchange, Dwight ran to the DJ on the side. Alexa didn't realize a DJ was present. She had heard music in the background but only thought someone was playing a radio. With some shuffling a microphone ended up in Nick's hand and the crowd erupted in applause.

Nick thanked the crowd again and introduced his team, which included Dwight, Fawn, Sasha, and several other people. He then spoke about the inspiration for the gathering and plans for future events. Alexa listened as she watched the crowd; they were growing restless, ready to party. The event crew dispersed into the crowd carrying baskets, Dwight running down the hill with his.

Alexa turned to her group and said, "I'm exhausted just watching him run."

CeCe faced Alexa. "You and me both."

"You'd think he'll sleep for a week straight," Dennis said, "but he will be at work on time in the morning."

"He actually took tomorrow off," said a man Alexa had met during introductions, but couldn't recall his name.

"What does he do?" asked a woman whose name Alexa also forgot.

"Trashman," Dennis said followed by several nods of understanding.

"Good pay and all you can eat!" Reggie said. The women groaned and the men laughed.

One of the ladies with a basket approached the group. "We will be doing communion with hot crossed buns," she explained. "Due to the size of our gathering, we ask you to share one bun among several people." She handed two buns to Alicia and moved on to the next group.

The crowd returned to socializing as they waited for the bread distribution to end. Alexa stepped back to the tree with everyone's bags. She looked out to the woods beyond the clearing. A soft hand on her shoulder startled Alexa. When she turned around Crystal and

Donella stood there with concerned looks on their faces.

"You seem very detached tonight," Donella said.

"It's a lot of people and a lot to process."

Donella nodded and offered a sympathetic grin. "Why do you keep looking off into the distance?"

Alexa snapped her attention back to Donella. "Um... I think there are vampires out there."

"Of course there are," Donella said. "They're always watching us and there's no way a gathering this large didn't get leaked to the guard."

Amazed no one was stunned that vampires might be watching, Alexa looked out to the field and then at Donella. "The guard?" She didn't mean to sound ignorant of vampire guards – she was surprised how casually Donella mentioned them. Alexa continued with feigned ignorance as Donella and Crystal explained the royal family ruling over Radcliff and surrounding areas.

"So there are different kingdoms?" Alexa asked.

"That's correct," Donella said.

"So how many different kingdoms are there?" Alexa asked finally happy to find someone to explain vampire royalty.

Donella looked at Crystal, and Crystal scrunched her face as she shrugged her shoulders. "A lot," Crystal said.

"So they set the rules and we just have to do what they say?" Alexa asked.

Crystal shrugged. "We're hybrids. They don't care about us unless we get too witchy like we're doing tonight. So as long as we're not riling up the humans or flashing our teeth, they're just going to sit in the trees and jerk off or whatever keeps their little selves happy."

"So they're not going to come down here and bother us?"

"Nah. They're just making sure nothing gets out of hand. Now if you met one of them on the street they might hassle you for being a hybrid and pull some stupid power play..." Crystal paused and looked sideways at Alexa. "Well, *you* would catch their attention for being a witch and that's a whole different problem. But me and Donny? They would try to scare us and hassle us. But with the guys, maybe provoke a fight, you know, just to prove their superiority."

"The crap they pulled in the alley after we left Blaze," Donella said.

"What?" Crystal screeched.

Alexa stood quietly, watching Donella describe the encounter. Evidently, she hadn't told anyone about the vampires or how Alexa stood up to them. Slowly other members of the group came closer causing Donella to stop and repeat. Alexa wanted to fade into the darkness as questioning eyes rested on her.

"You threatened to kill a vampire?" Stephanie asked in disbelief.

"Well it wasn't a hollow threat when she had Doug backed against the wall, now was it?" Dennis asked.

"We don't need to talk about that out here," Donella said.

"Sorry, Lexie," Dennis said.

"You know Doug's here," Darcy said. Alexa looked at Donella's sister - no, she didn't even think about Doug coming to the event. Of course, he was present - he was friends with Dwight who worked hard to recruit people to attend.

Alexa looked toward the crowds, wondering where he was hiding. She shook her head. "No. I can't stay here. If that man is anywhere near me I *will* kill him and then the vampires will show up and I just... nope, I'm outta here." She turned to find her bag.

A hand rested on her shoulder. "Lexie, we will protect you," Reggie said.

She turned to face him. "It's not me who needs to be protected. I've killed before and he's easy prey. So I'm leaving before *I* cause a scene. Besides, I have a trip I'm leaving for in a few hours. It's all the way around just better if I go now."

Alexa picked up her bag, said her farewells, and left the party.

Chapter Forty-Five

Choosing to walk around the side of the house instead of going through, Alexa hoped to avoid any questions about her departure. Instead, she came across a man leaning against the front corner of the house smoking a cigarette.

"Leaving so soon?" he asked.

"I was going to grab some mittens out of my car."

He looked down at her bag and back up at her with his head cocked in disbelief. "Did somebody tell you about the prize you were going to win tonight?"

"There are prizes?"

"Mmm, yeah. Big ones. And I believe you were number 307 to walk through the door tonight – the grand prize winner."

"How the hell would you know who out here was number 307?"

"Well, Fawn said it was the girl that smelled like a full-blown witch bathing in roses."

"Huh. Well. I guess they should pick 308. I really don't like being the center of attention." Alexa smiled and stepped around the man.

"Now that's not fair, we have no idea who that is," the guy said following her.

Alexa looked over her shoulder and said, "sorry. I'm not sticking around." When she looked forward two men stepped out from the corner of the house. Her stomach sank. She swung her bag with three pink crystals, an egg tucked in an otherwise empty egg carton, and a mason jar of water she and Sarah had set out under a full moon only weeks earlier. She aimed the bag in the general direction of the closest man in front of her but he leaned back and the second man caught the bag while staring at her, never blinking.

Disoriented and unable to focus – Alexa assumed she had just awakened from a nightmare. With a sigh, she moved to roll over. Panic fluttered through her, something had her restrained. She couldn't move her arms or legs and when her eyes adjusted, Alexa discovered fabric wrapped around her head. No, it was carpet. She was rolled up in a dirty, stinky rug!

Rolling side-to-side Alexa tried to break free. Her fear ran full force. Between the restraint of the rug and her inability to get a full intake of air, she was convinced she was about to die. She wanted to scream but snot choked her. As she coughed and sputtered something hit her leg. Laughing ensued on the other side of the carpet as she was lifted off the ground.

"Shame I can't take a bite," a man said as she tilted upward. The movement brought in a gust of fresh air that Alexa couldn't inhale fast enough.

"Shit. She's shakin'," another man said with amusement in his voice.

Alexa's body was slammed against something hard.

The first man laughed. "Damn that fear smells goo-ooh-ooh-ood!"

"I wouldn't mind getting a good lick of that witch," the second man said.

Alexa recognized the second man. He was the one smoking at the side of the house. She stiffened and listened as they rustled around her - she suspected she was up against a tree. Something cinched around her thighs. The men's movements sounded and felt like they were tying rope around her and then they repeated the movements around her arms.

The smoker stood mere inches from her. She listened to his heavy breathing and smelled the cigarette stench ooze off of his person. He ran a hand down her side and Alexa's fear flipped to anger. She jerked her head back and stared in his direction. She wished her eyes could bore holes through the disgusting rug.

A singular desire to kill that man brought her clarity on how to escape.

Alexa continued to stare in the direction where the man last stood. She summoned her powers to bring heat to that exact spot where she stared. Blocking out the noise and commotion around her, Alexa kept her focus staring forward and summoning heat. A tiny ember sparked, but quickly faded as she panicked thinking she might suffocate herself with smoke.

"Die from smoke," she told herself, "or die at the hands of these assholes."

"What?" the first man yelled at her.

Alexa resumed her focus and summoning. The ember reappeared.

"What did you say, witch?" the man said, this time much closer to her. Alexa remained focused on the ember and did not respond. A solid thump hit her lower right leg – the bastard kicked her! The pain jettisoned more energy to the small spark burning a circle. Alexa looked up following the tiny line of smoke. She could barely see the branches above her but noticed illumination from nearby fires. How far away were those fires?

She returned her focus to the burning circle, hoping to burn into the next layer. She felt the heat while the smoke burned her eyes, but Alexa didn't find the sensation bothersome. Casting her attention to the area beyond her carpet tomb, Alexa wondered if she could detect other fires and lure them closer. If she could burn the tree supporting her, the carpet would surely burn quicker than the tiny bit in front of her eyeball. But if that was possible how would she contain the flames and not injure other people?

Did she care?

No.

A quick memory arose about Valerie emphasizing the importance of payment for magic. Alexa tipped her head upward and whispered, "Dear tree, thank you for your support. I beg you to allow me to burn your wood to free me from this binding." She blew air upward, pushing a line of smoke up to the limbs. A chill ran through her body and she closed her eyes. "Thank You."

Sensations of warmth surrounded Alexa as she sought out the small campfires nearby. One fire directly behind the tree seemed to be the closest. As she stared forward watching the burning circle expand and char into the next layer of carpet, Alexa focused on the tingle in her back. She inhaled and exhaled in slow measures building a sensation of a magnet, trying to draw the flames toward her.

Watching the circle glow, she inhaled, exhaled, pulled the campfire closer:

Watch the circle, inhale, exhale, pull the fire,

Watch the circle, inhale, exhale, pull the fire.

Screams jarred Alexa's internal mantra. Pissed that she would have to reset her focus from scratch, she took another deep breath but realized some screams were about a fire. Did her attempt to move the campfire work?

An incredible amount of noise arose. Alexa wondered if it was new or if she had been so absorbed in building the fire she hadn't noticed the commotion. She heard people running in different directions, glass crashing, and a lot of screaming. The music came to an abrupt stop after what might have been the table falling over. Loud motors revved - motorcycles? Vampires. Alexa definitely smelled vampires nearby.

A man rushed past Alexa yelling a woman's name.

Alexa looked up to find the light reflecting off the branches had grown brighter. She thought she heard crackling nearby. Casting her attention behind her the warmth seemed closer. Having mastered the sensation of pulling, she tried again and this time physically felt warmth on her backside.

Unsure if she was about to scald her entire body, Alexa shook her head to the side with a now-or-never shrug, and pulled the fire even closer. The crackling became intense and she felt the flames surround her.

Someone yelled for a hose. Someone else barked commands to remove her from the tree.

Alexa looked up at the branches and saw the tips of flames just above her head. "Thank you, tree. I hope your seeds spread far and wide."

Something tugged on the rug and Alexa in her carpet cage fell sideways. Pain rippled the length of her body, but before she could catch any air, she was dragged away from the warmth of the burning tree. Someone hit the rug in several places, probably swatting at the flames. She felt tugging on the rope around her legs and suddenly felt the release. The same tugging started on the rope around her arms. She heard the back-and-forth ripping of a knife against the rope. She was rolled and finally released from the rug. Alexa flipped to her back and took a deep breath of clear air... and coughed. She opened her eyes to find four vampires standing around her.

Diederich loomed above her with an extended hand to help her up.

She gasped for air and coughed heavily. "They tried to burn

a witch," she said with a graveled voice. Alexa sat up and coughed several more times. Running her arm across her face she looked over to the tree, fully engulfed. She accepted Diederich's assistance and coughed again.

"Talina! Where is Talina?" A man yelled running up the hill toward the burning tree. He stopped short of the tree, looking between it and the group around Alexa.

Diederich yelled to him in a language unfamiliar to Alexa. Panic took over the man as he looked around the yard. He turned in circles, looking in every direction. Alexa recognized him from Blaze and finally connected the similarity of his and Diederich's scents, brothers.

Alexa had no idea who Talina was – she assumed a vampire, but when did vampires arrive at the party? The smell of death became stronger as more bodies fell to the ground amid the fighting. She looked in the direction of her friends' fire but couldn't see past the smoke and running bodies. When did the motorcycles arrive? So many were present – some parked, some laid in the grass.

Diederich's brother rushed toward them. The two men spoke in their language, both gesturing toward the house.

At the house several hybrids stood holding hands, creating a chain around the building. Diederich and his brother kept looking at the house as they spoke. Other vampires watched the house but kept their distance. Diederich's brother stated something in a commanding voice and several vampires rushed toward the hybrids. The vampires bounced backward as if they hit a wall, several landing on their bottoms.

Alexa stepped forward, still coughing from the smoke. If she was a pyromancer impervious to fire why the hell was she so unable to handle smoke? She tried again to look for her friends but the guy who had kicked her while rolled up in the carpet ran past her with a vampire chasing him. She watched as he ran toward the house and the ring of hybrids. At the very last moment as he reached their perimeter the hybrids broke the line allowing him as well as the vampire chasing him to run inside the house. The hybrids quickly came back together to form their invisible wall.

"They just allowed that vampire to go in there," Alexa said. Before either Diederich or his brother could argue otherwise she shook her head. "Nobody made a move to close the circle until both men made it through. Moreover, there's no fighting going on inside."

The men turned and stared at the house and then looked back at Alexa.

"They're working together," Alexa said. "And the hybrid? He was one of the guys who tied me to that tree." She tipped her head toward the fire and coughed again.

"My wife is in there," the brother said.

"Why would she go in there?" Alexa asked.

"She was kidnapped and brought here," he said. "She's pregnant and I think they want the baby."

Alexa wrinkled her forehead. "What? Why?" She shook her head. "Wait, no, don't tell me."

"You're a witch, you understand these things," he said.

"No, I don't understand. I'm horrible at being a witch – I came here to learn."

Diederich offered a half smile. "No one here believes you're a hybrid. They think you're a full-blooded witch and I imagine the reason you were tied to a tree is part of what's going on in the house."

Alexa looked at him blankly.

"A blood sacrifice," he said.

"Nobody is getting my blood," she said and coughed.

"If they knew what type of hybrid you are they wouldn't need Talina."

Alexa glared at him and then looked at the ring of hybrids. "I know how to break the line." She cleared her throat, trying not to cough again. "Tell your men to prepare to rush forward but wait until somebody drops hands. Warn them it's going to get windy."

While Diederich and his brother made nonverbal commands, Alexa stared at the line where the two men ran through. She brought small puffs of wind from behind her but that stirred an already raging fire. Small embers fell around her. Alexa changed her focus and instead pulled air from the field to move sideways toward the house to avoid drawing in the fire.

She had hoped to cause a break in the line at the back porch, but instead, the line broke on the side of the house where she had directed the wind. Fortunately, the vampires saw the breach and ran forward, tossing men and women into the yard. Diederich and his brother ran toward the house.

Alexa felt her job was done and turned to find Donella. A scent wafted down from the house and Alexa spun around to find the man attached to it. Although vampires had already made their way into the house, hybrids scrambled to reform their line. But there he was, Doug, the asshole she wanted to kill at Donella's engagement party. Next to him, holding hands to recreate the circle around the house stood the Smoker, the guy who rolled her into the smelly carpet.

Everything clicked into place. She hadn't thought much about people knowing a full-blooded witch would be present, just that one of her friends alerted the greeters when they arrived. But the weird reception from Fawn and Sasha, the attack at the side of the house, being tied to a tree? Diederich was right - Alexa was supposed to be part of a ceremony and not one slapped together last minute. No, they knew Alexa would be present and even prepared for a way to restrain her – the carpet. She didn't know how they lured Talina to the gathering, but this was planned for some time.

Watching Doug and the Smoker join hands with other hybrids Alexa sent another blast of air toward the house as she ran forward. She kept her focus on Doug with her anger building. He fell to the ground with several others and she heard glass shatter. Alexa pulled up short realizing her anger fed into the winds and blew out the windows.

Doug made eye contact with her and scrambled to the back door. Alexa caught his collar and yanked him backward.

"WHAT THE HELL DID YOU TELL THEM?" Alexa screamed.

He waved his hands and shook his head with fear oozing out of him.

"Did you tell them I would be here?" she demanded.

"No, no, I swear..."

"You're a lying sack of shit."

Doug flailed, unable to get his footing. Alexa leaned him back further with the zipper pressed to his neck stopping his airflow. He gasped and his face turned white. Alexa craned her mouth open and took a lot of pleasure watching Doug's expression when she revealed her teeth. He tried to scream but he fell silent as she sank her teeth into his jugular and pulled forward puncturing his windpipe.

Alexa saw his death scene play out as he fell to the ground still alive – he watched people run away screaming and then everything went black. As she pressed a hand to her mouth to wipe away the blood, Alexa saw the Smoker run into the house. She marched up the stairs and pushed a woman to the side, knocking her to the ground.

Inside shuffling and screams as hybrids fought against stronger vampires. She kept her sights on the Smoker, already in the grip of a vampire, struggling to get away. Alexa grasped the back of the Smoker's coat, locking eyes with the vampire holding him.

"He's mine," Alexa said with a snarl and pulled the Smoker backward out of the vampire's grasp. The Smoker's body cracked and his legs went limp, but Alexa maintained her grip and supported his body. His death scene played out with numbness in his feet as he stared at the ceiling. Alexa smelled his death as he fell listless in her arms.

Confused she looked up at the vampire who stared back in disbelief.

"You're a fuckin' hybrid and you broke his back with one hand?"

Alexa looked back at the Smoker, his eyes still and his head awkwardly hanging to the side. Did she break a man's back? Fear jolted through her and she dropped the body. The vampire chuckled, but his expression changed to a leer.

Two men fighting slammed into the vampire, knocking him into another man. Alexa took a deep breath to subdue her fear and retracted her teeth. The smell of death flooded her nostrils along with more visions. Something was burning and the air filled with the scent of pot, sage, and cedar. She turned toward the front door and saw a plume of smoke waving back and forth. Through the fighting and yelling, she heard the hum of a chant. As bodies moved back and forth Alexa spotted a tall man waving a stick in the living room where she had entered hours earlier. Her nose detected several hybrids in that direction and she suspected they were holding hands in a protection circle.

Pushing two men fighting to the side, Alexa walked toward the smoke. As she expected several hybrids held hands while sitting in a circle. Nick stood inside the circle waving a bundle of smoking herbs in the air as he chanted over the body of a vampire woman laying on the coffee table with her bare stomach exposed. Fawn stood at the woman's feet and Alexa sensed Sasha nearby, likely in the circle.

Diederich barked commands to the vampires who ushered people out the backdoor while his brother stood in a corner near the circle. The brother's fear ran unchecked and the scent nearly overpowered what wafted off the smoking stick in Nick's hand.

The stick.

Alexa fixated on the plume of smoke. Nick yelped, dropped the stick, and stumbled back. As he fell, he broke the circle. Diederich's brother launched forward, yelling Diederich's name.

Nick was on his hands and knees attempting to get back on his feet when Alexa grabbed the back of his cloak. She pulled him out of the living room and into the space where she had broken the Smoker's back. Nick grasped Alexa's ankle, but she kicked him with her other foot. He didn't let go and she felt her leg getting warm.

Flames erupted from the floorboards next to her restrained foot. Then a flame shot up next to her other foot. He slammed his free hand between her feet and a flame ignited, sparking toward her groin. Resisting the urge to jump back, Alexa kicked Nick's shoulder and felt something snap. She suspected she broke his collarbone. He grunted but didn't let go of her ankle nor did the fires simmer.

Refusing to release the cloak Alexa tightened her grip as Nick squirmed to get his knees under him. She pushed him down and heard his head thump the ground. Another flame popped up. Alexa knew if he got to his feet, height would play to his advantage. She also smelled in his hybrid scent a combination of ranger and noble meaning his strength possibly matched hers. A pyromancer of equal strength but with a height advantage and maybe proper fighting techniques meant Alexa needed to keep him on the floor. She pressed harder and his free hand attempted to clamp onto her other foot. Alexa stomped down, unsure how close she got. She stomped again, this time hitting something. And she stomped again while pressing him to the floor. As she bent, Alexa rammed her knee into the top of his head.

Pain surged up her leg and she worried she may have damaged her kneecap. She toppled forward, landing on Nick's back with her face just above his ass. He released her ankle and lay still for a moment. Alexa, reeling in pain, didn't wait to see if she knocked him out - she couldn't afford for him to stand up. She pushed back, clamping his head between her knees and jolting another shock of pain up her body, right to her eyeball. Craning her mouth open, Alexa dropped her teeth and plunged into the soft tissue just below the ribcage, hoping not to get a mouthful of intestinal muck.

Blood and urine oozed into Alexa's mouth. She tried to spit it out as she ripped toward the ribcage. The body below her shook and squirmed. She withdrew her teeth and vomited onto Nick's body.

Someone grabbed her by the armpits and hoisted her into the air. With her feet dangling, Alexa was rushed toward the open front door and tossed forward. She landed with a heavy thump on a questionable lawn.

Alexa lifted up and shook her head. Wiping the dust off her mouth, she assessed if any bones broke in the fall and seemed to be okay. She flipped over and winced, but through her squinted eyes she saw the house on fire. A lump lay in the doorway. Dwight.

Jumping to her feet, Alexa ran limping toward the house. She reached Dwight and pulled him to the porch but screams inside caught her attention. Diederich and his brother huddled in a corner away from the flames, trying to make their way to the door. Beyond them, the kitchen fully engulfed three vampires while four hybrids wailed in pain.

The scent of Dwight's death struck Alexa. She looked down at his lifeless form and sniffled back her grief. She rushed into the house toward Diederich with extended hands pushing the flames to either side, creating a path.

"RUN!" She yelled.

Diederich hurried forward while helping his brother carry Talina. Alexa stepped aside as they ran out the door.

She turned to help the people stranded in the kitchen but she couldn't see anyone and their cries had fallen quiet. Moving closer she saw two people with flames consuming their clothing. If anyone were still alive they wouldn't survive much longer. Then she spotted Nick. He continued to move but still facedown. She knew fire wouldn't kill him but he had a lethal stream of blood flowing from his back. His death scene included a searing pain in his lower back and staring at floorboards and smoke.

With no one to save, Alexa ran out of the house, stopping to pull Dwight's body to the yard. She flipped him to his back and pulled his arms across his chest. Dropping a kiss on his forehead, Alexa pictured Dwight standing in Alicia's kitchen holding a beer with a big shit-eating grin. She hoped that would be her lasting memory of him.

At the corner of the house sat a white box truck seemingly parked in a rush with the doors open. The name on the side of the truck caught her eye – Gifford's Appliance and Service. She stopped and stared at the name, recalling the Christmas fair and the dead body in a box. Walking past the back of the truck she noted Talina's scent in the gaping cavern without so much as a bed or even blankets to transport her to this field of death. Chills shuttled through her as she noticed a couple of boxes. Looking over to the men circled around Talina, Alexa figured they were aware of the truck. As she walked past the driver's side, Alexa caught a familiar scent of a vampire whom she couldn't name. Her mission, however, wasn't to confront more vampires but to find the rest of her friends.

Chapter Forty-Six

Behind the house, most of the fighting had subsided. Bodies laid scattered on the ground as a few vampires skirmished with each other. Alexa sidestepped the bodies and avoided the fights as she made her way down the hill. Smoke from the smoldering campfires blocked her view like a thick fog. Several times she coughed, annoyed she could stand inside an active fire without even her clothes getting singed, but smoke choked her.

"Why is the witch here?"

Alexa didn't wait to figure out from whom or where the question came, the tone and intent sounded harmful. She turned and ran toward the burning house. Sensing several vampires behind her Alexa pushed herself to run faster only to discover the back porch collapsed. She worried about how much longer the roof would stand and if the house was the best way to escape the vampires. Instead, she ran around the side of the house, running directly through flames hoping to slow her pursuers. She kept running until she reached the clutch of vampires circled around Talina.

Five vampires in leather jackets turned around, poised to fight. Alexa stopped short, questioning her instincts to flee toward these men.

"Get behind us," one yelled.

Before Alexa could take a step they moved forward toward the vampires chasing her. More vampires emerged from the parking lot rushing to join the fight.

Diederich grabbed Alexa's wrist. "Please stand over Talina and protect her." He and his brother stepped away from Talina to join their men.

Alexa sat down next to the woman lying on the ground. The listless body covered in blankets took a slow breath in her involuntary slumber. The baby in her womb had no soul, no life force Alexa could sense and she knew the baby would die, likely from the evening's trauma. Talina however, would live. Alexa saw her death many years in the future, fighting with a man who had just bitten her neck. Alexa viewed the man's face clearly and had the feeling she should remember him. She stepped through the vision of Talina's death several times to fully imprint the man's face.

A scent caught Alexa's attention. A vampire ran toward her appearing to be concerned about Talina.

"The princess!" he wailed as he fell to his knees. "Is she going to be okay? What about the baby?"

Alexa whispered to Diederich, "You need to get back over here now. We're in danger."

Diederich pulled his brother and two more vampires from the fight as Alexa tried to look sympathetic to the man running his hand over Talina's face.

"It's been a rough night," Alexa said.

"Elmar!" the brother shouted.

The vampire hovering over Talina wrapped a hand around her neck. Alexa reached out and grabbed his neck and squeezed. He locked eyes with Alexa but confusion crossed his face as he lifted off the ground. Diederich and his brother had each taken an arm to pull him away. The two escorts, Alexa assumed were bodyguards, stood at Talina's feet watching Elmar's fate.

"His scent is in the driver's seat of that truck over there," Alexa said, nodding to the big white truck.

"She's lying," Elmar screamed. "Who takes the word of a witch?"

The brother lifted a chin and one of the guards ran to the driver's side of the truck. Alexa didn't twist around to watch the confirmation but kept her gaze firmly affixed on Elmar. She never did trust him.

"She started the fires!" Elmar protested as he squirmed under tightening grips.

The brother released his hold to grab Elmar's hair then dropped his teeth. Alexa watched, almost with fascination, as teeth struck Elmar's jugular and ripped into the muscles of his neck below the ear. Blood poured down his body but he continued to breathe. Once released, Elmar collapsed to his knees and clasped his injured neck. Before he could retract his hand he wobbled forward, crashing face-first into the gravel – exactly as Alexa had seen in her previous encounters with him.

In a single motion, the brother retracted his teeth and shoved his right hand into a pants pocket. He extracted a black cloth with which he wiped his face, erasing all visual traces of blood. The scent remained, fresh and meaty. Too late, Alexa realized she had flared her nostrils in front of an audience of vampires.

The brothers held a quick, silent conversation of vampire whispers. Diederich turned to the vampires and said, "Give us space for a private conversation with the witch."

A vampire stepped forward and pulled Elmar by the feet. Alexa watched Elmar's head bounce along the rough terrain until another vampire grabbed his arms. His body was unceremoniously tossed toward the raging house fire.

When Alexa returned her attention back to the brothers, they had squatted on the ground.

"Who are you?" the brother asked.

"And don't say, Lexann Meyers. You do not match any profiles with that name," Diederich said.

"I can't tell you," Alexa said.

"You owe us answers," the brother said. "I just killed one of our closest advisors for a string of incidents tied to you."

"I only said his scent was in the truck."

"You told Diederich you didn't trust Elmar during his visit to your law office. You accused one of Elmar's friends of inappropriate advances at Blaze. You indicated his scent was present in the truck, and when we approached a few moments ago Elmar's hand was on Talina's neck. At all other times, this man has been a faithful employee, a trusted confidant, and a good friend. And yet, when you are near he becomes a criminal."

Alexa shrugged. "Then dig deeper. I don't know what to tell you, just that the man gave me weird vibes since the moment I first met him."

Diederich tilted his head. "You were correct about Elmar. After we first met at your office I kept a closer record of his activities. When you told me of the gargoyle at the Christmas vendor fair I was honestly dismayed. There was no possibility for you to know Elmar had an obsession with using guards as gargoyles during night patrols. Neither Harald nor I received a report about any activities that particular night, nor had we sanctioned the kill you noted, also a disappointing loss. As a result we placed a man on his team who, fortunately alerted us of tonight's gathering." He nodded. "We are grateful for your intervention, but we do need to know where you are from."

Alexa shook her head. "I refuse to say."

The brother scowled as his anger built. "Why?"

"I don't know who *you l*are."

"I am the Prince Harald of Solje. Who are you?"

"Glad to meet you but that doesn't tell me if I can trust you or how you're connected or not connected to the people I know. What I do know is saying my name or where I'm from could put me and the people I love in great danger."

"Why are you here?"

Alexa sighed. "I needed to get away from home and just… collect myself."

Harald shook his head, his face flat with frustration.

Taking a deep breath Alexa struggled to think of how to explain herself. "As I told Diederich, I was raised as a human. I didn't know any of this existed so when I found out, it was just a lot to absorb and I needed time to come to terms with all of it."

"You were hidden," Harald said with a dismissive shrug.

"Yeah, I was hidden. I was hidden for *twenty-five* years with not a fucking peep that I had any sort of powers. I didn't even know I was a witch. And then one day my teeth came in and all anyone could tell me was to keep behaving like a human. There's no explanation, no introductions, nothing! The only person giving me any information is a guy I met at work." She pointed at her shoulder. "The one who tagged me, who I consensually slept with and have zero regrets, but evidently that's a big no-no. That was the first time in my life I was informed that my future husband would be selected for me. I guess I screwed that up, didn't I? Evidently, there's a whole side of my family I've never met holding titles I don't quite understand. I won't even get into the witch side of my family because they've been keeping secrets too. Grandma evidently wants my blood, probably for some ceremony similar to what they were going to try here tonight. So no, I don't want to talk about my hometown, my bloodlines or anything that helps you identify me, partially because I don't want to deal with any of those people."

Harald pressed a knuckle to his lips and Diederich cleared

his throat.

Squinting his eyes, Harald asked, "You ran away from home?"

"It sounds juvenile, but yes."

"And you have the strength to break a man's back with one hand..." Harald shook his head. "Is your family aware of your strength? And your fully-formed teeth?"

Unsure where the line of questioning was headed, Alexa sat quiet. She wondered where Harald was when she broke the Smoker's back.

"You are an anomaly, that is for certain," Harald said. "I have my guesses where you belong, but I will respect your desire to remain anonymous for the time being." He sighed and shook his head. "You need to go home. You do not belong here, nor can I protect you... and before you say anything I am aware you can protect yourself quite well, but that also makes you a danger to my people."

"As I said, we appreciate your assistance," Diederich said. "However, you cannot remain here."

"That's fine. I don't want to stick around – I'll be gone before noon. But I am worried about my friends here. I would like to find them and say goodbye... and make sure they get home safely." Alexa looked toward the burning house and sighed. "I believe several have died, but the ones who survived..."

Diederich shook his head. "Leave them to believe you died tonight. This will be easier for you to cover your tracks. Now, what do you mean you will be gone by noon?"

"I told you the other day I had a bad feeling about this gathering. After discussing it with Valerie we decided my stay here needed to come to an end. So in the morning, we're going on vacation, if you can call it that, but that's what we're telling our coworkers. After I leave town I'll connect with another witch and be out of your hair for good." She looked toward the house and spotted Dwight lying on his back, arms crossed on his chest. Alexa shook her head as tears rolled down her cheeks. "I can't stay here."

Chapter Forty-Seven

Fear and death filled the smoky air. The burning house became a convenient dumping ground for bodies, some not yet dead. Burning flesh added to the sickening miasma of the evening… actually morning. Had the equinox arrived yet? Alexa didn't know.

Commotion arose beyond the fire. Shouts and thudding feet rounded the house. Four vampires in leather jackets rushed forward escorting a black man carrying a body. Reggie! Alexa looked among the people running in her direction saying something about needing a witch. She spotted CeCe running to keep pace with the men.

As Reggie knelt in front of Alexa she heard his escorts explain to Diederich and Harald how this hybrid assisted them in fighting other hybrids.

"Lexie, you gotta save her," Reggie begged. He laid Donella's limp form on the ground.

CeCe dropped next to Reggie. "She fought hard, girl. She was coming to save you but some big ol' ox knocked her to the ground and she hit her head."

"Is Maurice dead?" Alexa's voice felt detached, soft, and floating in the air. She wondered if she even spoke aloud.

"Yeah. The ox took him out," CeCe said.

"She's dying." Alexa stroked her cheek knowing at that moment all Donella smelled was grassy ground and smoke. Buzzing rang in Donella's ears drowning out other sounds. "Go be with him," Alexa said with another stroke, knowing she wasn't heard. "Your destinies are tied. Be with the one you love." Tears flowed down Alexa's face so she could barely see Donella as she faded into death.

Alexa looked up at CeCe staring at her.

"You're supposed to save her," CeCe said with her lower lip quivering.

Shaking her head Alexa said, "No. It was her time to go. She walks with Maurice, that's where she belongs. I saw that a long time ago."

CeCe looked down at her friend on the ground and back up to Alexa. "That was your vision? That's what you saw at their engagement party?" CeCe's face twisted, almost to anger. "Their *engagement party*?"

Clasping CeCe's shoulder, Reggie bent his head.

Alexa nodded. "Yeah. That's why I got so upset about the reading. How the hell do you tell someone they're not going to make it to their wedding? She was so happy." Alexa shivered. "I wasn't lying when I said they'd go through it together."

CeCe glared at Alexa. "But you could have told *us*! We could have…"

"No. My visions don't work that way. We don't get to change the outcome. I tried that once and it was gruesome and the person still died."

"They didn't even get married!" CeCe bellowed.

Reggie stared at Donella, tears streaming down his face.

"It's just a ceremony. They didn't need to prove their love to anyone," Alexa said.

CeCe fell across Donella sobbing. Reggie stroked her back. Alexa made eye contact with him. "I'm sorry. I know Maurice was a good friend to you."

He nodded.

"I saw others in our group died, but not everyone," Alexa said.

"Darcy got separated from us shortly after you left. Alicia and Stephanie are dead. Crystal ran off and Dennis went to look for her. I don't know where Dwight is."

"He's over there," Alexa said pointing across the lawn. "He was trying to save me from the burning house. The smoke got him." She closed her eyes and wiped the tears away. "He was a good guy."

Reggie kept a hand on CeCe's back as he stared at Dwight's body.

Alexa said, "But Crystal and Dennis are still alive."

Reggie snapped his attention back to Alexa. "Where are they?"

"I don't know, but they survive this."

"We have to find them!"

A silver sedan approached from the driveway stopping near the cluster of vampires surrounding Diederich and Harald. Other vampires approached from behind the house and the surrounding fields. They formed a perimeter and Alexa began to surmise the position of the princes – sons or possibly grandsons of their king.

She wondered if Harald was heir to the throne.

Alexa didn't have a firm understanding of vampire royalty. She watched with curiosity as all of the vampires in this gathering deferred to Harald as their leader and in his absence, Diederich. The loyalty was obvious – every single man present, at least on the inside of the circle they formed, was prepared to die for Harald and Diederich.

Harald lifted his wife off the ground and carried her toward the car. Five men clustered around him and others opened doors. Diederich turned away and started issuing orders.

Despite her fascination with watching the orchestration of orders being meted out, Alexa brought herself back to the problem at hand – how to find Dennis and Crystal. She whispered to Diederich, "We have two friends that ran into the fields and need help finding them."

Diederich continued to direct his men in different directions as if he hadn't received Alexa's request. She turned to see Reggie watching the vampires disassemble and go forth with new orders.

"How did all of this happen?" Reggie asked.

"I don't know," Alexa said. "I was unconscious for a good part of the chaos. What did you see?"

"They started the communion," he said. "It was peaceful. There was positive energy in the air like you could feel it, you know?"

Alexa nodded. "I felt that when I arrived. It was amazing."

"Well, Nick had a big drawn-out ceremony and was chanting. To be honest I think he was speaking in tongues." Reggie shrugged his shoulders. "But that's when the energy changed and it was very dark. Dwight showed up in a panic, looking for you. He said there was going to be a blood sacrifice of a witch and a vampire to strengthen all of our powers. When he heard you had left, he ran off toward the house. We started to follow, but then the vampires flooded in from the fields. Lexie, they weren't looking for whoever was going to be sacrificed. They were out for a killing spree."

Diederich stepped closer, his attention on Reggie.

Reggie dipped a small nod toward Diederich and continued speaking. "The first deaths were at the bottom of the hill. The screams and the smell of death sent a flood of people running in our direction. Then the guard arrived. I guess one of them skidded their motorcycle through a campfire because then that started raging out of control. That's when our group got separated and it was rough. Several of the guard joined the vampires coming up the hill."

"I started that fire," Alexa said.

"You did what?" Reggie asked.

"I was tied up against a tree and, well, I'm a pyromancer."

"Reg, look at her aura," CeCe said, still cradling Donella. "She has a smoke ring."

"I do not believe I wish to know what any of this means," Diederich said. "But, we did have a breach among members of the guard." He turned to Alexa. "We have contained the situation well enough to assist in finding your friends and any other survivors."

Perplexed, Reggie looked between Diederich and Alexa. "How did he know?"

"Lexie whispered your request while I was working with my men," Diederich said. "What is your name?"

Reggie stood up and bowed his head again. "Reginald Hayes and this is my wife, Cecelia."

CeCe offered a nod. She let go of Donella and stood up, nodding again. "Your highness."

Reggie pulled CeCe to his side.

"I apologize for the loss of your friend," Diederich said.

"She worked with Valerie and me," Alexa said.

"That is unfortunate," Diederich said. "A sudden loss of a good employee is difficult. Two is catastrophic."

"Two?" Reggie asked. "What do you mean?"

"Despite her assistance, Lexie is not allowed to remain here," Diederich said, then turned to face her. "This is unfortunate – you saved our lives by guiding us out of the fire. If it had not been for your assistance Princess Talina would be dead." He paused with a concerned look. "She *will* survive tonight?"

Alexa offered a soft smile. "Yes. She will live for many years and she and your brother will have a full house of children."

Relief swept his face and he nodded to Alexa. "That is very good news. You are a good witch, Lexie. Thank you for saving our kingdom."

"Then why can't she stay?" Reggie asked.

"That is a private matter," Diederich said, "and for her safety, we shall not discuss it any further. Before you arrived we agreed that her friends should believe she died in the fire and I will trust that you will carry that story *for her safety.*"

Reggie stared at Diederich and then darted his attention to Alexa and scowled. "What the hell did you *do*?"

"It's something to do with my past and some bullshit about politics. So yeah, I have to leave." She turned and looked at Diederich. "I assume you're not going to let me help find Dennis and Crystal?"

"No. I have arranged for trusted guards to assist in the search and I will personally escort you to your apartment and follow you to the airport."

Chapter Forty-Eight

Surprised to see Sarah standing at the front door, Alexa had hoped to slide inside quietly and get some sleep. She didn't remember the drive from the farmhouse, only that she struggled to stay awake in the backseat of Valerie's car as Diederich and one of his men drove her home.

"Why are there vampires in Valerie's car?" Sarah asked.

Valerie rushed to the door and Alexa turned around to watch Diederich and his driver get into the car that followed them to the condo.

Alexa handed the car keys to Valerie. "They'll be sitting there until we leave later on and will follow us to the airport to make sure I leave town. I am officially no longer welcome here."

Sarah pulled her into a hug and Alexa burst into huge gasping sobs.

The smell of coffee filled the air. Alexa opened her eyes realizing she must have fallen asleep. She sat up finding herself on the couch wrapped in an afghan. Sarah launched out of her chair to sit next to Alexa.

"Are you okay?" Sarah asked.

"Not really," Alexa said, her voice hoarse.

"Do you want some coffee or maybe juice?"

"No. What time is it?"

"A little after five," Valerie said.

"A. M.?"

Valerie offered a sympathetic grin. "Yes, A M. We have plenty of time to get to the airport. Do you want to tell us about what happened?"

Shaking her head as she sat up, Alexa shrugged. "Evidently the organizers wanted a blood sacrifice and I walked right into their hands. They also had Diederich's sister-in-law. She was pregnant."

"Oh my God," Valerie said in horror.

"They never got any blood from either of us. The whole thing was just chaos. At one point I was rolled up in an old rug and tied against a tree. I had to use fire, I couldn't escape but it caught Diederich's attention enough to free me. Once things settled down CeCe and Reggie brought Donella to me thinking I could save her life, which of course I can't. She died there in front of us. Donella and her sister never knew the other died." Alexa shrugged. "It's probably better that way. I can't imagine what their mother is going through. I'm sure CeCe has called her by now. Maurice died too."

Valerie sat shaking her head. "That's a lot of death," she whispered. She shook her head a few more times then scowled. "Why aren't you allowed to stay here?"

"Diederich knew from the first second I ran into him in the creek that I was a hybrid"

"What creek?" Sarah asked.

"My first day here," Alexa said. "When you and I went out for a jog and there was a dead body under the bridge."

"*That* is Diederich? The one you've been reporting to about vampire activity?"

"Yeah. Evidently, he's a prince."

"Really?" Valerie asked with raised eyebrows.

"I suspected as much based on his scent but I don't know how the royal titles work or any of that stuff. Just that they exist," Alexa said. "He knew from the beginning what type of vampire I am but as a hybrid, especially as one who presents fully as a witch, it's possible I wasn't aware of my vampire side or that part of my family."

"But when Diederich came to our office the second time," Valerie said, "he confirmed you knew your family."

Alexa nodded.

Valerie sighed. "That explains his reaction. I remember he said you needed to be with your family."

"Yeah. After tonight... last night, whatever. My vampire side came out," Alexa said. "Word is going to get out about the hybrid everyone thought was a full-blooded witch has the abilities of a full-blooded vampire and that makes my presence here a problem for the vampires. So yeah, it's time for me to leave." Tears rolled down Alexa's face. "It's a good thing we made these arrangements, otherwise... I don't know. They'd probably drive me out of town without so much as a good-bye to you guys."

Valerie scrambled out of her chair to the couch and with Sarah, they held Alexa as she cried.

Alexa sniffled and tipped her head to Sarah's. "I hate the idea of leaving!"

Nestled with her head against the window, Alexa watched the patchwork of farmland pass below. Her body begged for sleep but her mind raced. Angry she couldn't savor the joy of her first airplane ride, Alexa blocked out all of the details. She didn't remember anything after leaving the parking garage. She suspected she fell asleep prior to boarding the plane and probably only woke up enough to blindly follow Sarah – she remembers Sarah walking in front of her.

Alexa twisted in her seat and watched Sarah take a sip of a clear bubbly liquid from a small clear cup.

"Would you like something to drink?" Sarah asked.

Alexa shook her head.

"Are you okay?"

Alexa shook her head. She hated that she wasn't returning with Valerie and Sarah. She liked them so much. No, she loved them. They had become her family. Alexa liked the soft routines they had formed, an odd synchronized dance of each person filling a space, an ebb and flow of daily life.

Not wanting to think about leaving them yet, Alexa wanted to focus on the next few days together. But was that disrespectful to the memories of the friends who had just died? Was it wrong of her to be dashing off for a vacation mere hours after their tragic deaths?

All of this felt wrong.

And yet this was what had to happen. Alexa recalled the day she left Brentwood realizing a chapter of her life had closed and felt hopeful about the future, ready to start a new chapter.

Now she saw another chapter coming to a close. She knew another flurry of transfers and sleepless nights on random couches lay in her immediate future, but she didn't hold any of the enthusiasm she had six months earlier. In September Alexa felt in control of her life, taking ownership of her decisions, no matter how hair-brained they seemed to the rest of the world.

She questioned if she was still in control. She wondered if

staying on the run was her best option. What if she didn't find good roommates? What if the vampires there were less accommodating? How long would her family allow her to stay in hiding?

As a new chapter lay looming, Alexa failed to feel any excitement. Her time with Valerie and Sarah had been the soft landing she desperately needed. Yes, she had actually come up for air and finally felt more comfortable in her skin. Losing a whole circle of new friends, however, added to the nightmare essence of her life.

Alexa laid her head back, staring at the knobs and buttons on the ceiling above her seat. She hadn't paid attention to the attendant at the beginning of the flight – something about equipment would drop down in an emergency. Alexa didn't see where anything could drop down – did the whole compartment open up?

She was on an airplane! For the first time! She was actually in the air! Alexa leaned her head to the side and watched more farmland whisk by. She was up in the sky, in an airplane, going on vacation. Even though this trip was just a ploy to get her out of town, it was also supposed to be fun. And yet, all she wanted to do was curl up in a ball and forget everything.

No, she wanted to wake up.

She just wanted to wake up

Acknowledgement

There are not enough words to express my gratitude for the assistance and encouragement I've received in my writing and publishing journey. The most hands-on people have been my sister Glennda and my daughter Amanda. They are my behind-the-scenes team shouldering editing, marketing, accounting and other duties as needed. They have picked up the pieces as technology failed me (or I failed to update my technology?) and gently kept me on track.

There are my circles of friends who were surprised I was writing and those who've known all along. Donna (yes, I named a diner after her) who was my writing buddy back in junior high, and with our cohort Judi (the waitress at my fictional Donna's Diner) are an endless source of laughs, stories, and loving support. They are who I modeled Alexa's childhood friends after – it is indeed possible to have more than one best friend.

I never expected the rest of my family to be so vested in what I write. Even my grandchildren ask questions, but at the moment they are much too young to read this series. Fortunately, saying it's about vampires and witches seems sufficient. My brothers and their children received their own copies of Blood Of Discovery and one in particular has read it several times (and likely knows the story better than I do) as they impatiently wait for this release.

>•<>•<>•<>•<>•<>•<>•<>•<>•<>•<

I would be remiss to not tell you about my mother because she is the first person to let anyone and everyone know that *her* daughter is a published author. She makes sure to have a few copies in her car and a bookmark always on hand. I know not everyone has a parent proud-as-punch of their accomplishments, and that truly is a shame. It really is the best feeling in the world.

Thank you to everyone for the love and support. None of this would be possible if not for you, the reader. Thank you for being here.

Cautious Readers

Not all books are for all readers; and with that in mind I have listed below possible concerns that may lead you to *not* read Blood Of Escape or the Blood Of Discovery series. An updated list can be found at maggievalleypublishing.com

First and foremost, this series is written about adult characters with adult situations using adult language. While teens will read this series and likely enjoy the content, they are not my target audience and parents should be aware of the graphic nature of these stories.

Alcohol	Gore	Panic Attack
Assault	Hallucinations	Profanity
Blood	Kidnapping	Pregnancy
Death	Miscarriage	Pregnancy Trauma
Decapitation	Murder	Sexual Harassment
Fire	Nightmares	Smoking
Fights	Occult	Violence

>•◇•◇•◇•◇•◇•◇•◇•◇•◇•◇•<